NOTHING BUT A RAKE

The Ashton Park Series
Book Three

Abigail Bridges

© Copyright 2022 by Abigail Bridges
Text by Abigail Bridges

Dragonblade Publishing, Inc. is an imprint of Kathryn Le Veque Novels, Inc.
P.O. Box 23
Moreno Valley, CA 92556
ceo@dragonbladepublishing.com

Produced in the United States of America

First Edition July 2022
Trade Paperback Edition

Reproduction of any kind except where it pertains to short quotes in relation to advertising or promotion is strictly prohibited.

All Rights Reserved.

The characters and events portrayed in this book are fictitious. Any similarity to real persons, living or dead, is purely coincidental and not intended by the author.

ARE YOU SIGNED UP FOR DRAGONBLADE'S BLOG?

You'll get the latest news and information on exclusive giveaways, exclusive excerpts, coming releases, sales, free books, cover reveals and more.

Check out our complete list of authors, too!

No spam, no junk. That's a promise!

Sign Up Here

www.dragonbladepublishing.com

Dearest Reader;

Thank you for your support of a small press. At Dragonblade Publishing, we strive to bring you the highest quality Historical Romance from some of the best authors in the business. Without your support, there is no 'us', so we sincerely hope you adore these stories and find some new favorite authors along the way.

Happy Reading!

CEO, Dragonblade Publishing

Additional Dragonblade books by Author Abigail Bridges

The Ashton Park Series
To Stop a Scoundrel (Book 1)
A Rogue Like You (Book 2)
Nothing But a Rake (Book 3)

Dedication

To Kimberly Cantrell Haynes Titlebaum
Tolkien and Kimbrell brought us together. Friendship kept
us going.

And to my writing tribe
Jamie, Bonnie, Jack, and all my encouragers. You have made this
journey possible.

CHAPTER ONE

Saturday, 16 July 1825
London
Half-past noon

L ORD MICHAEL GABRIEL Matthias Ashton, third son of the Duke of Kennet, stared at the glass of champagne as if it were an asp, his eyes wide, as small beads of sweat formed in the dark curls at his temples. Even the aromatic scent of the savory beef on his plate did not draw his eyes away. He had known his brother's wedding breakfast would be a challenge, but he had not expected it to be this difficult. Sitting just at the far edge of his place setting, the sparkling liquid beckoned like a long-ignored temptress.

Not ignored long enough, apparently. He had not indulged in strong drink in three months, but the need remained, that unending desire to escape the pain in his heart, to drown the restlessness in his spirit. The relentless hunger became a burning coal in his gut. *Just one sip. It would be cool on your tongue. Soothe the fire in your stomach. Refreshing. Courage to get through this blasted day. One taste . . .*

Michael forced his gaze away from the glass and toward the happy couple—his older brother Thomas, heir to the duchy, and his new wife, Rose—their heads together in a congenial intimacy as they settled at the head table, an enormous brandy-soaked and frosted cake in front of them. This was their day, a celebration of their love, of the joining of two powerful families. The joyous crowd of almost seventy people surged and flowed in clusters around the room, like starlings in murmuration.

Michael brushed away the twinge of jealously that stung his heart. He had surrendered the idea of such happiness in his life more than four years ago, when his own *beloved* Eleanor had taken his money and left him standing by a crossroads in Gretna Green. But he had never quite been able to drown the agony in his heart, the unending craving for something he could never quite define, no matter how much ale he had assigned to the task. A great deal of ale, in truth, since that day. Ale, grog, rum, brandy, wine, anything that would dull the pain and douse the restlessness for a few hours.

He had also indulged in enough women that the memories of Eleanor should have been blotted away. Yet neither strong drink nor numerous wenches had done so. Still, Michael had disappeared into them, and the pubs of London, for those four years, returning only when his father had yanked him back into Society—and the family—in April.

One small sip . . .

A movement caught his eye, and he turned toward his plate to see a small, gloved hand clutch the champagne glass and return it to the tray of a passing footman. His mother, whose dark eyes with their intense scrutiny made him want to squirm as if he were four years old again.

"Someone," she murmured, "did not receive my instructions about your service."

"It's a complicated event." Michael glanced at Rose's mother, whose frantic movements around the room gave all the servants reasons to avoid her. "And you are not the hostess."

That scrutiny continued, and Michael fought the urge to look anywhere else in the room but at his mother's face. It was not an unexpected response. Of her four children, only the second son of the family, Robert, could return that stare with equal confidence and assurance. The others—Thomas, Michael, and their sister Beth—would wither within seconds. The woman stood less than five feet tall, as petite and elegant as a fairy, but with the emotional strength of a dragon.

"What do you want from me, Mother?"

"Reassurance that you will not flounder in this first outing into Society. Confidence that your sobriety continues, and that you will be able to accompany your sister to the remainder of this season's events."

He swallowed hard. "That is a great deal of responsibility to place on one breakfast."

Emalyn Ashton, Duchess of Kennet, scowled, but the intensity of her glare lessened, and she let out a long breath. "Robert has already left. In a few moments, your father and I will be doing likewise. I have another headache. I have already requested that the Marquess of Aldermaston and his mother escort Beth home. You have done your duty here. You have stood up for your brother and witnessed the marriage. Would you prefer to join us?"

Home. Ashton House. Where he could change clothes and retreat to the stables. Perhaps go for a ride. His work with the Kennet horses had been the only times in the last three months when he had not been tempted to retreat into a keg of ale.

Michael nodded.

So did she. "Meet your father in front of the house. He is having the carriage brought around. You have another outing later in the week. Perhaps that one will be easier."

He was on his feet immediately. "Thank you, Mother."

"Hmph." The duchess walked away, strolling toward the bridal couple, two fingers pressed against the side of her head.

Michael watched her, a new emotion stirring within him, pushing all the others aside, a nagging feeling of uncertainty and dread. His mother's headache had gone on for several days, unusual for a fierce woman who could take control of an entire ballroom of people with a few well-chosen words. She never flinched, especially not out in Society. Something worrisome plagued her.

He would speak with his father. Michael's world had already been upended once this year when his family had yanked him from the depths of his hiding places, as if they had pulled a mole from its hole. After four years underground, Michael still felt odd in his own family home, as if he were still blinking in the sunlight, but he had found some balance. He was not convinced, however, he could survive another upheaval.

Saturday, 16 July 1825
Beckcott Abbey, Berkshire
Near the River Kennet
Quarter of five in the afternoon

"HAR! HAR!"

Lady Clara Durham's deep guttural call echoed across the field and tree line near the edge of the Earl of Beckcott's property. She had taught Maid Marian to recognize and respond to the sound when the peregrine had been little more than a fledgling. At the signal, her gamekeeper released the dog—currently on point—and the setter dove into the bushes near the trees. Grouse exploded into the air, the thunder of their wings sending a surge of excitement through Clara, who straightened in her saddle, watching the drama play out, her eyes turned to the sky, anticipation surging through her like a rising fire.

Mere seconds passed as the falcon tucked her wings and dropped in a full teardrop stoop toward the climbing flock of grouse. Clara's chest seemed to swell with the thrill of watching her beloved companion streak toward the ground almost too fast to see. The attack, swift and deadly, ended as the falcon struck one of the birds with a force that snapped the neck of the grouse and sent a flurry of feathers into the air as they both landed in a thick patch of grass browned by the heat of the summer sun.

Almost invisible in the clutch of sward, Marian perched atop her kill, looking around, an instinctive search for other predators as well as her handler. Clara, her red hair flying around her shoulders, squealed with glee and dropped from her horse, her boots thudding on the ground as she ran toward Marian. She slowed her approach as the falcon let out a stark cry, then Clara rained praises on her and bent, holding out her right hand, which was encased in a thick leather glove. Marian arched her neck, pleased as punch, and gave a quick hop, landing on Clara's glove with a quick beat of wings to find her balance.

A smothering, dry wind surrounded the hunting party with sharp gusts, billowing Clara's long curls around her as she drew her arm in and stroked Marian's head with a feather she kept tucked in a band on the glove. "Precious joy," she whispered. "You are a queen." The bird preened a bit, then settled as Clara slipped a leather hood back over the peregrine's head and secured it.

"Please, your ladyship. May we go back now? It is almost time for the dressing gong."

Clara looked up at her maid, whose unsteady seat on the sweet pony Clara had persuaded her to mount for the hunt reminded her that maids did not ride, and Radcliff seemed particularly unsuited to the out-of-doors on the best of days. Her disheveled blonde hair poked wildly from beneath her simple cap, and her ruddy cheeks seemed to blaze in a face distraught with discomfort.

"I'm going to lose another one, am I not, Marian?" Clara murmured to the peregrine, who merely twisted her head at the words.

Radcliff was maid number four in less than five years. Being a lady's maid to the daughter of an earl was a prime position for a servant, but all of Clara's seemed to rapidly find even better positions.

Clara looked from Radcliff to the gamekeeper, who paused, removed his cap, and mopped his forehead with a handkerchief. Sutland, unlike Radcliff, had been with the Beckcott earls his entire life, having grown up in the stables with his father, still one of their best grooms. "It *is* miserably hot, my lady." He nodded at the setter, one of Clara's favorites. "Even Moses seems to be desperate for a bit of water." Sutland shrugged, then headed over to pick up the grouse and add it to the game bag slung over the saddle of his horse.

Clara glanced at the setter, whose tongue, indeed, lolled out the side of his mouth as he panted.

Lost in the thrill of the hunt, Clara had not felt the heat. Now she became all too aware of how the sun beat down, even this late in the afternoon. Since the beginning of the month, it had been one of the hottest Julys any of them could remember, and the drought on the surrounding estates had been a frequent topic at the dinner parties as the summer had progressed. If it did not rain soon, the harvest would be sparse—as would the income of the tenants and their host estates. It was even hotter in London, which was one reason Clara had been able to persuade her parents to spend a few weeks in the country, even in the middle of the social season. But they would soon return, heat or no.

"Of course, we should." She twisted, peering at the tree line. "Before we do, shall we rest a moment under the trees? There's a stream that flows along that line. The horses and dogs can drink, and we can cool a bit." She headed for the closest copse of yew and oak trees, immediately feeling a break from the heat as she took shelter beneath their broad limbs.

The others joined her, although Radcliff still looked disgruntled. "It is cooler, my lady, but I dare not get down. If I do, I'll never get on this beast again. And we do not have time for me to walk back."

Clara grinned and stroked the nose of the gentle pony as she looked up at her maid. "I know you do not enjoy these outings. I only wish I could convince my parents that I do not need a chaperone here on our own property. Sutland is more than honorable, and he would skin the boys alive if they so much as touched me." Clara glanced at the others in her small group—Sutland and two stable boys who had come along to wrangle the four dogs they had brought. "It's not as if we are expecting raiders from the Highlands."

Radcliff shook her head. "You know it's the appearance of the thing, my lady. If any of the neighboring residents—"

"It's just silly. Who would see?" She pointed to the other side of the tree line. "The closest house is Ashton Park, and Kennet and his clan are almost never there." Clara remembered the four Ashton children well—from when they *were* children. In age, she fell between the two youngest—Lady Elizabeth and Lord Michael—and had shared the children's activities with them at house parties. She had seen Lady Elizabeth at events earlier this season, but she had not seen the boys in years and doubted she would know any of them on sight. The Kennet clan were seldom in residence at Ashton Park except during the Christmas season—months away.

Marian shifted on her hand, and Clara stroked the peregrine's back with the feather. "I should not let it upset me so. Marian feels it. But it is quite frustrating when all I want to do is let her fly and ride beneath her as fast as I can."

"And if you got hurt?" Sutland moved up beside Clara and handed Radcliff a cup of water as her pony dropped his head toward the stream to drink. "Riding aside is not the safest way to go galloping across the land."

Clara scowled. "That too."

"I'm sure the countess only wants what is best for you, my lady."

Shrugging, Clara turned toward the stream. Sutland was right—her mother did care for Clara. If only what her parents considered "best" did not make Clara wish to find a cave and hide away. Parties. Soirees. Yet one more season in London. As if the *ton* would forget her disastrous spill the year before. First ball.

First dance. And Clara had tripped over her own feet and fallen face-first onto a table loaded with glasses and lemonade. The host had to stop the orchestra and clear the dance floor until the servants could clean away all the shards of glass. Her whole family had been asked to leave, and it had taken the countess the entire season to make amends.

Clara found a low branch and urged Marian to step over onto it. "I have to admire my mother's ambition, Marian, but I will always be known as the lady who went swimming in the lemonade. And that wasn't even the first disaster, only the latest." She did seem to have such a fall every year since her debut four years ago, but none quite so devastating. Pulling off her gloves, Clara knelt by the stream and plunged both hands into the water. Immediately she felt cooler, and she withdrew them, patting her face, her eyes closed.

She could still hear the laughter. The derisive comments about her size, her clumsiness, the unfashionable red hair that fought every style, her lack of grace in satin slippers and lack of skill on the dance floor. The comments had gone on and on until she left, only to recur at every event. Whispers behind hands that felt like relentless torture. She tried not to care what those people thought, but the humiliation stung and went on stinging no matter how she tried to ignore it.

An entire year of grueling lessons in dance and comportment had followed, more intense than anything leading up to her debut, but with little success. Clara still bore more resemblance to a deer on ice than a graceful lady of the Beau Monde out on the market for a husband. The few events she had attended this season had been equally uncomfortable, although no great fall had happened—yet. Now the earl had started mumbling about "arranging something," to "end the girl's pain," and that sent sheets of dread down Clara's back each time she recalled the overheard words. Her father's kindness toward his youngest daughter warred with his impatience for her future to be settled.

No wonder she preferred her hunting dogs, her kitten Pockets, her horse Aethelred, and her precious Marian.

Clara let out a long sigh and stood up. Wishful thoughts were a waste of time, as her mother often said. She brushed off her skirt, pulled on her gloves, and gathered Marian for the ride home. Time to stuff her hopes for happiness back into the closet.

CHAPTER TWO

Monday, 1 August 1825
Ashton House Stables, London
Half-past two in the afternoon

MICHAEL MOVED FROM one stall to the next, checking on each of the Kennet horses, a habit he had developed not long after returning home. Although the animals were well-cared for by the grooms of the estate, Michael's affection for the beasts had been a lifelong draw to the stables, his pockets full of apples, carrots, and lumps of sugar. As a child, he had learned to ride early, constantly begging for more time with the horses. The grooms had indulged him then—and now—even teaching him to ride bareback, to the horror of his mother. Now he supposed they all saw that his time with the animals kept him from sinking back to the bottom of a rum cask, especially after the last two weeks. Here was his escape from chaos, his place of peace.

The Kennet household had been in a frenzy since the day of his brother's wedding. That night, his mother had collapsed with a hemorrhagic apoplexy, from which she still struggled to recover. Thomas and Rose had canceled their honeymoon trip in order take over the day-to-day management of the estate, and— for some unknown reason—seemed to be at each other's throats. His brother Robert's life had imploded, and he had landed in

Newgate prison as a result, thrusting the entire family into scandal. The charges had been dismissed, but he'd been badly beaten. Like their mother, Robert had retreated to his bedchamber to heal.

And Michael had, once again, become the invisible child. As the third son—and not the beloved daughter Beth or the troublemaking Robert—Michael's childhood had been one of solitude and isolation as he demanded less attention from either his parents or tutors. Now, with the focus on his mother's illness, his injured and disgraced brother, and the chaos surrounding the newlyweds, Michael's presence at Ashton House had been as prominent as the wallpaper. The stables had become his solace.

Until this morning, when his mother had informed him that it now fell to him to salvage what was left of his sister's debut season. The next ball was Wednesday, giving him a mere two days to gather himself together enough to escort Beth. An engagement for his sister to the Marquess of Aldermaston loomed. Despite the turmoil within the household, propriety must be maintained. Michael had fled to the stables to fight a growing sense of trepidation and a lingering desire for ale.

The matched team of four blacks always had been his first stop, each receiving a stroke along the nose, a scratch behind the ears, and a snack. Next, the two matched grays that pulled the smaller carriages and the curricle. Robert's, Beth's, and Thomas's personal horses got equal treatment, of course, but his final stop—and the most treats—were saved for Copper, his bay. His beauty. He murmured nonsense noises as the horse pressed against the door of the stall and draped his head over Michael's shoulder. Michael stroked the long, arched neck, then dug into a pocket for a carrot.

"Are you ready for a ride later?" As much as he despised putting in an appearance in Hyde Park, it would help for Beth to be seen out, and it might even help his own reputation somewhat. He had heard the gossip about why his two brothers had made inroads back into Society, yet he had not. Rumors that swirled with speculation that he had ailments ranging from gout to the pox. None of which he had. So at four this afternoon, they would ride out together.

"I promise you a good stiff run tomorrow. We will go out early." As Copper munched an apple, Michael heard a rustling in the empty stall behind him, turning just as Rufus, a large orange tabby, leaped onto the top of the stable door, a ball of white fluff in his mouth. "Mousing again, Rufus?"

The cat looked up at him, let out a low growl, and disappeared back down behind the door, fluff and all. That's when he heard a furious squeal and hiss.

That was not a mouse.

Michael's curiosity spiked. The cat was a long-time mouser in the stables, and often ate his prey or presented them as a gift to one stable boy or another. He did not hide them. Michael opened the stall door to find the tabby pressed into a corner. Just under the cat's rear foot, the white fluff squirmed. Michael approached the cat slowly, squatting and brushing away some of the hay until his breath caught.

Behind the orange tabby, one of the prettiest—and tiniest—kittens Michael had ever seen pushed away from Rufus and backed into the wall, bright blue eyes wide with fear. A pristine white coat was broken only by black markings on the ear tips and the very end of the tail. "What do we have here?"

Rufus gave another low growl that ended in a hiss, then moved in front of the kitten.

"Do not worry, mate. I do not intend to take your friend. Where did he come from?"

A piercing shriek rent the air, followed by a harsh and alarmed, "My lady!"

Michael stood and left the stall, latching it behind him. As he headed for the stable door, a boy slid into it, his face frantic. "My lord, you need to come now!" Then he vanished.

Breaking into a run, Michael followed him out and into the alley behind the stables, skidding to a halt at the sight before him.

A young woman lay face down in one of the alley's mud puddles, struggling to push up. Hovering over her, a maid tugged at one of the woman's arms, fussing, and occasionally snagging one of the long red locks streaming from the woman's head. Two stable boys stood by, eyes wide, clearly at a loss at what to do.

After one significant tug, the one on the ground pushed the maid back. "Leave off, Radcliff! You are making it worse!"

"Dear God in heaven, my lady! You must get up! People will see!"

Michael moved closer. "May I help?"

The maid shrieked again, stumbling backwards, one hand covering her mouth.

The lady on the ground tried to push up again, but the heel of her hand slipped on the mud, and she floundered again. "Oh, bloody hell!"

Michael looked at the stable boys. "Bring two blankets," he said to one. To the other, "Fetch Lady Newbury. Now!"

He squatted next to the woman. "Stop struggling. The mud is too slick."

The woman glared at him. "Mud! The countryside is parched in this heat, and London has mud!"

Michael raked a hand over his mouth to fight a smile. "It's from where the boys washed out the stalls."

"Lovely. Mud *and* muck. My mother will kill me. This dress may not be new or expensive, but it *is* one of the few I have."

Michael's eyebrows arched. Ladies did not discuss the financial aspects of their wardrobe, especially not with strangers.

"My lady—" the maid began.

"Just hush, Radcliff."

The lady pushed back mud-streaked strands of her hair, which was a glorious mane, the red of a sailor's favorite sunset. Michael watched it flow down her back to her ample waist, as she pushed up one more time.

"Our savior is obviously here—"

He should not have, but he did anyway. Michael reached out

and grasped her bicep. The strength he felt beneath the sleeve of her gown surprised him. This was no delicate debutante maneuvering for attention. "Just wait," he said softly.

She hesitated, glancing at his grip on her arm, then peered up at him with eyes the color of emeralds. "Who *are* you?"

The stable boy pressed a blanket at him. Michael took it and spread it on the mud in front of the woman. "I'm Michael. Grab my arm and pull yourself onto the blanket. I'll be able to help you up from there without your slipping."

She did, pulling herself and her soaked gown forward with the same strength he had felt in her arm. He looked around at the maid. "Help with her skirts."

The younger woman leaped into action, and together they lifted the lady back to her feet. Michael took the second blanket and wrapped it around her shoulders. She paused to wipe some of the mud from her face, then took a long, deep breath and seemed to gather her dignity. "Thank you, sir, for your aid."

"Lady Clara!"

They all turned to see Rose standing at the corner of the stable. The alarm in her eyes counterweighed a stern set to her mouth as she looked from one person to another.

The lady muttered a low curse, then made a quick curtsy. "Lady Newbury." Behind her, the maid did the same—a curtsy, but without the curse.

Rose stepped closer. "What the devil is going on?"

"I tripped."

Rose put her hand over her mouth. "Oh, Clara. Not again."

Clara straightened her shoulders, and Michael watched as a bit of pride came back into her face. "It seems to be a rather unfortunate habit of mine, my lady."

"But what are you doing in our alley? Your house is on the other side of the square."

Twin spots of red appeared on Clara's cheeks, and Michael realized it was the first sign that Clara—whoever she was—felt the least bit of embarrassment about all of this. Most of the ladies he had met would have been mortified into silence by now.

"I was looking for something, my lady."

"Looking for—"

"Her cat!" The two words seemed to burst from the young maid, and they all looked at her.

"A cat?" Michael asked, an uncomfortable suspicion growing in his gut. "What kind of cat?"

"A kitten, to be precise." Clara tugged the blanket tighter around her shoulders. "Pockets. That's her name. Because she rides in my pocket all the time." She patted the side of her muslin skirt. "I always ask my modiste to put pockets in my skirts because a reticule is nice but often never enough." Her eyes brightened, and her gaze grew distant. "You never know what you will find when you are riding or walking across the fields." She bounced up on her toes, excitement lighting her face. "I find some of the most amazing things. That's how I found Pockets. I mean, Maid Marian almost found her, which would have been most unfortunate—"

"Maid Marian." Michael had thought he was following her words until that moment.

Clara seemed to return to earth then, her eyes dulling a bit as she glanced at him, then back to Rose. "My peregrine. But Moses—he's a dog, a setter we hunt with—got to her—Pockets, that is—first. Wee thing. Must have gotten lost from her mother. But so adorable. I had to keep her. I probably should have left her in the country, but she sleeps on my pillow, and I really wanted to—we were out for a walk around the square and she just jumped out of my pocket and ran. We tried to follow her, but she ran too fast. I thought I saw her come down this alley—and that's when I tripped, and this gentleman came—"

Her words cut off and her eyes shot wide as she looked from Rose to Michael. "Oh. Michael." Her hand went to her mouth. "Oh! You are *Lord* Michael Ashton!"

The maid let out a tiny squeak, and she curtsied again.

Clara looked at Rose again. "What have I done?"

Rose shook her head and shot a warning glance at Michael. She held out her hand and gestured for Clara and the maid to follow her. "Nothing yet. Come, let us get you cleaned up before you venture back out into the square." Rose glared at Michael and the two stable boys. "And no one here will *ever* mention this to anyone. Understood?"

"Yes, milady!" The two stable boys nodded at her, then fled.

Michael watched the three women head around the stable, following them from a distance as they entered through the servant's door, chatting as if they were old friends. Rose kept murmuring quiet reassurances to Clara, who seemed to volley between irritation about what had happened and embarrassment that she was imposing on Rose's good nature.

As the door closed behind them, Michael leaned against the wall of the stable, mentally cataloging the details of the past fifteen minutes. He had learned to do such intellectual organizing over the past three months. It had helped direct him as he tried to keep the goal his father had laid before all three of his sons: return to Society and find wives. It had helped him make sense of his world.

Not that the lady he had just met made a lot of sense in *any-one's* world. She was *Lady* Clara. Rose knew her, and she seemed a bit older than a recent debutante; she must have made her debut a few years ago. Yet her hair was unbound, a mane of curls so thick and wild it begged to be clutched in some man's hands. Green eyes that flashed in both defiance and pride, dulling in embarrassment. A plush, round figure that reminded him more of the buxom wenches he had loved bedding over the past four years than the wraithlike debutantes who looked as if they would be lifted away by a stiff breeze. A body made for a man's comfort yet a lady who chased with abandon after a lost kitten. Who had a peregrine falcon named Maid Marian and a dog named Moses—who *hunted*. With a house, like theirs, near Berkeley Square. Who was embarrassed because she had not recognized him as a lord, but not because she had found herself wallowing in mud—that had simply made her angry.

Mud she could cope with, but an offended aristocrat knocked her off-kilter. *Who* is *this woman?*

Not that Michael was particularly offended, and he felt confident Rose would reassure Lady Clara of that. No . . . offense was not at all what he felt.

Intrigue might be a better word—and a stirring deep inside, in a part of him Michael had long thought dead. It was as if a woman who represented the best of both sides of his world had suddenly dropped into his life. He wanted to know more.

But that would have to wait. Michael straightened and headed back toward the stalls. For now, he needed to convince Rufus that a certain kitten probably had a much better home waiting for her.

⬎⟫⟫⟨⟨⬍

CLARA FELT BOTH guilty and relieved that Rose's maid Sarah had taken charge of Radcliff, urging her toward the servants' quarters for a wash and clean dress. The girl's unending fussing had been silenced when Rose's bedchamber door closed behind them. Rose pulled the blanket away from Clara and dumped it in a heap in the middle of the floor. The overwhelming stench of mud mixed with muck hit her again, and both women flinched.

"My apologies, Lady Newbury. I am so sorry. I should never have let you bring me up here. You have too many burdens already." Clara's guilt surged again as she realized how exhausted Rose looked. Even the simple hairstyle Sarah had arranged for Rose's reddish-blonde hair looked deflated. All the *ton* knew what mayhem had settled on the Kennet family since Thomas and Rose's wedding. Now Clara had added to that.

Rose, however, merely waved a hand. "Do not talk nonsense. And I'm still just Rose to my friends. I could not bear the idea of you walking across the square looking like that. And I certainly could not undress you in the game larder."

"Both would probably serve me right. I'm sure Radcliff would think so. I am afraid I have given her far too much leeway in how she speaks to me."

"She is . . . new, is she not?" Rose asked, surveying the caked mess of Clara's gown.

"Yes. I cannot seem to keep an adequate lady's maid."

"Perhaps if you did not make them ride horses on your hunts."

Clara felt heat sting her cheeks. "You have heard?"

"We have to get you out of this. There is no way to clean it while it is still on you. Hold your hair up." As Clara did so, Rose went on as she loosened the laces at the back of Clara's bodice. "Of course, I have heard. The servants tell me everything, especially what is going on in other households. I'm going to unlace you."

"If my parents would only let me ride without a chaperone."

"If wishes were horses, beggars would ride. Maids as well."

Clara sighed. "I will never be able to return this kindness."

Rose pushed the bodice forward, and Clara pulled her arms from the sleeves. The brown muslin day gown fluttered to the floor, and Clara stepped out of it. As Rose kicked it over next to the blanket, she smiled. "Actually, I already owe you. And I am about to put you in one of my most detestable day gowns. You would do me a great favor to not return it. Ever."

Clara scowled. "It will never fit."

"Oh yes, it will. It may be a bit long, but you are not that much larger than I am, and if it does not come together in the back, I'll slip a scarf beneath the laces to cover the gap. You are a bit more ample in the bodice—

"More than ample, according to my mother."

"Mothers worry too much about their daughters' size. We cannot all be slight as lampposts. But never mind that. We will tuck a fichu around your shoulders. It will service during the short walk to your house." Rose disappeared into her dressing room.

Clara raised her voice a bit. "Why do you say you owe me?"

Rose returned carrying a gown in a shade of chartreuse that made even Clara's eyebrows arch. At the expression on her face, Rose let out a burst of laughter. "My mother had two of these made. I have managed to divest myself of one. Now you will be taking the last one off my hands."

Clara was aghast. "Why in the world would a countess pick such a color for her daughter?"

Rose smirked. "She believed it would make me invisible next to my sister Cecily on our daily walks. We soon realized it had the opposite effect."

Clara had to smile. "It will certainly make my walk across Berkeley Square . . . intriguing."

Rose pointed to a stool near her dressing table. "Another reason we need to complete your cleansing. Let me see if I can brush some of the mud out of those curls."

Staring at her, Clara slowly shook her head. "You are a marchioness. You cannot brush my hair as if you were a maid."

Closing her eyes for a long moment, Rose let her shoulders drop. "I have been . . . *that* . . . for only two weeks. And I brushed my sisters' hair for years because I enjoyed it." She opened her eyes. "To be frank, this is the most fun I have had in weeks."

Clara hesitated, doubting those last words. Rose's husband, Thomas, was one of the three Kennet sons, widely rumored to be outrageously handsome, their height as well as their dark hair and skin drawing the eye of every lady in their vicinity. *I should have recognized Michael Ashton.*

But it had been so long since she had seen any of them. In her memory, Michael existed as a gangly boy who preferred horses to pretend swordfights, and galloping wildly across the fields to the sedate classrooms of their studies. He had been scrawny and wild, laughing as he rode, hanging back only when surrounded by a passel of other children at house parties. That long-legged boy bore little resemblance to the intense man who had helped her out of the mud, who had known the solution immediately, whose deep brown eyes took in every detail all at once. And he was definitely no longer gangly.

"He is handsome, is he not?"

Startled, Clara jerked from her reverie. "My lady?"

Rose's grin broadened. "Michael."

Clara felt her cheeks heat. "I should have recognized him."

"Nonsense. He has not been in Society for more than four years. He has changed."

Changed for the better. The heat spread down Clara's neck and chest. She cleared her throat and eased down on the stool, facing the mirror on the dressing table as Rose reached for a brush. "Why did you say that you owe me?"

Rose's smile remained gentle as she closed one hand around a clump of mud-drenched hair and began working the brush through the curls at the end of it. "Two reasons. One is that I appreciate how kind you were to my sister Cecily this season. Although she has found a good position with Lord Philby, it has been a tumultuous year for all of us, including her. I know you stood by her after the incidents at the Blackmore Ball."

Clara flinched, but not from the brushing. Rose had been attacked at the Blackmore Ball, and Cecily had been left behind with Lord Philby—soon to be her betrothed—as the rest of the family had departed. "It was nothing."

"It was not nothing. You were kind when others only thought of being tainted by scandal."

Clara shrugged. "I have obviously felt that sting myself."

Rose paused in the brushing and looked at Clara in the mirror. "About that . . . I have some information. From my network."

Meeting Rose's eyes with her own, Clara stilled, an odd feeling of worry settling on her, as if the humiliation her mother had worked so hard to overcome was about make a second appearance in their lives. Over the decade of her spinsterhood, Lady Rose Timmons had put together an extensive web of informants who had helped her protect young ladies vulnerable to the machinations of degenerate rakes and scoundrels. She had prevented any number of debutantes from ruination as a result. "What is there to be known about me tripping over my own feet and landing face first in a bowl of lemonade? Everyone knows how clumsy I am."

"True. Which is why no one suspected it was not *your* feet that were your undoing. It was someone else's."

Clara blinked. "What?"

Rose continued brushing Clara's hair. "Lord Richard Hadleyton. You turned him down for a dance earlier in the evening."

"Of course. He is one of the most inappropriate men I have ever met. And I knew about his debts"—Clara paused—"through you."

"He took his revenge for what he saw as your humiliation of him. Do you remember him standing near the table?"

"Yes. There was a group of young—" Clara stopped, heat filling her face again, for an entirely different reason. "He—"

Changing positions, Rose attended to a different section of Clara's hair. "Do not worry, my dear. I have put the word out to a few close friends. Lord Richard is presently courting a young lady whose father is beyond reproach. I suspect he will not take kindly to the information. I only wish I had known sooner."

Clara looked down at her hands. She tried to feel some sense of satisfaction about what Rose had said but could not. "Are you sure it is worth the effort after all this time?"

Still brushing, Rose did not look up. "Sometimes, Lady Clara, you are too kind for your own good."

"You should tell my mother. She thinks I'm an undisciplined hellion bent on destruction."

"A prerogative of the mother of a marriageable daughter. Why do you not wear your hair up?"

Clara snorted a laugh. "No one believes me. I begin every day with my hair filled with pins and combs in a coif as tight as a banker's fist. By noon, it looks like this, even if I spend the hours at needlepoint or the pianoforte. Or reading in a corner, still except for a cup of tea. All I have to do is move an inch, and it begins to fly apart."

Rose bounced the long curls in her hands, then ran her fingers through the strands. "I will put it in one braid today, but I have a suggestion that a new lady's maid may not have considered. Separate it into three strands. Tie each close to your head with a ribbon, with a long tail of ribbon hanging down." Rose demonstrated what she meant, then began to braid Clara's hair, tying the thick plait at the end. "Then divide the strands in two and plait using the ribbon as the third in the braid. Tie each on the end, then braid the three plaits together. Curl the braid around your head and secure with combs and pins. It's a bit of extra work but could tame it a bit. And will reduce your urge to cut it all off."

Twisting on the stool, Clara stared at her. "How did you know?"

"I have yet to meet the woman who did not want to do that at one time or another."

"I had no idea."

"Men and mothers, my friend. They make us think our hair is the essence of our womanhood, no matter how frustrating it gets to keep it brushed and untangled. I assure you, it is not. As can be seen with some of the newer, shorter hair styles."

"My mother thinks they are scandalous."

"And I would be willing to bet your mother has never brushed mud out of these curls."

Clara laughed. "My mother touch a hairbrush? Never!"

Rose chuckled. A knock on the door got their attention, and she called out, "Enter!"

Sarah came in, an amused look on her face. She whispered in her mistress' ear, and Rose coughed a laugh. "Have him meet us in the entrance hall. Bring Radcliff as well." As Sarah left, Rose motioned for Clara to stand. "Let us have a look at you." Clara turned for inspection and Rose nodded. "You'll do for the walk home. But indulge in a long hot bath when you get there." Rose grinned. "And burn that dress. Now come with me."

Clara followed Rose down the broad central staircase of Ashton House, pausing as they reached the entrance hall and she saw Lord Michael Ashton waiting for them, his hands behind his back. Her chest tightened as he smiled up at her, his dark eyes bright with a touch of affection. She dropped into a curtsy almost involuntarily. "My lord. Again I apologize for my clumsy—" Her words cut off as he slowly brought his hands forward.

Cupped in the palm of one sat a tiny white kitten, black tips on its ears and tail.

Clara screeched and bounded forward off the steps. "Pockets!" She tripped on the hem on the chartreuse dress and stumbled, but both Michael and Rose reached out to steady her. Michael's free hand closed on her elbow, and the heat of his grip sent an unexpected wave of . . . something . . .through her. Her gaze held his for a mere second, then she reached for the kitten. "Pockets," she murmured again, gathering the soft fluff up near her face.

Pockets mewed, a precious sound, and pressed her front paws against Clara's cheek. A sweet if sketchy purring emerged from the small body.

Clara looked up at Michael, who towered over her. "Thank you, my lord. Thank you. Where did you find her?"

His eyes seemed to brighten even more. He still held her elbow, but his grip loosened, turning tender. His thumb slipped back and forth over her bicep, and Clara's breath caught as he spoke, his voice soft and deep.

"In a stall. One of our stable cats had adopted her. He did not want me to take her."

Rose grinned. "Rufus?"

Michael nodded. The action shook loose a black curl, which drooped over his forehead. "We will have to be careful. Despite the fact that there is so little resemblance, he seems to think she is his child."

Rose glared at him. "Michael!"

He stepped away, releasing Clara's arm, color shading his dark cheeks. "My apologies, Lady Clara, if I have been inappropriate."

"My lord, you picked me up out of the mud. You rescued my kitten." Clara kissed Pockets on the forehead, then looked at Michael again. "I owe you more apologies than you will ever owe me."

He stepped toward her again, lowering his head. "Never, my lady."

A clatter in the hallway beyond the staircase caused all three of them to look as Sarah led Radcliff toward the entrance hall. Cleansed of the mud and resulting embarrassment, Radcliff had returned to her normal fussy state. "I cannot go out the front door! It is not done!"

Clara moved toward the maids. "Radcliff, you are acting as my chaperone. It is fine. In terms of protocol, your accompanying me out the front is better than my slinking out the back with you. Settle down."

The maid huffed but crossed her arms and fell silent.

"Good start," Rose muttered under her breath. "She may be trainable yet."

"I would suggest keeping a tight leash on both, although I would not be averse to finding Rufus tending to a certain kitten again." Michael's *sotto voce* words still left Clara feeling as if he had stroked her arm once more.

"Michael!" Rose seemed even more startled than before.

Is he flirting with me? Clara looked up at Michael. His eyes still held that light of affection in them, but Clara had never been certain where men were concerned. The entire species befuddled her. "I—" She swallowed any other words.

Rose once again came to her salvation. She urged Clara away from Michael and toward the door. "Ignore my brother-in-law. He is still finding his way back into proper Society. I can only imagine how he will behave at the Aldermaston Ball on Wednesday."

Clara glanced over her shoulder at Michael, who watched the two women, curiosity on his face. "He will be at the ball?"

Rose nodded. "Escorting his sister. The marquess is courting Beth, so it is vital that she be there."

"Of course." Clara stepped through the door, curling Pockets inside her elbow as she gripped the rail. "Thank you, Lady Newbury." Rose nodded but watched as she and Radcliff safely maneuvered down the steps and onto the pavement. Clara glanced back once but saw that the door was already closed.

Then she spotted Michael in one of the windows. He remained in that spot until they had rounded the edge of the square and turned toward home.

Wednesday night. She would see him again Wednesday night. Perhaps by then, she would have deciphered what was going on.

But, somehow, she doubted it.

CHAPTER THREE

Wednesday, 3 August 1825
Aldermaston Ball, Percy House
Nine in the evening

MICHAEL FELT AS if he were drowning in lemonade. He had promised his mother he would pick up a cup of the lukewarm swill every time he had the urge to reach for something more potent, and so far, he had. But he had been at the Aldermaston Ball exactly two hours, and he had already downed six cups.

And he had yet to locate Lady Clara Durham. He had scoured the terrace, the hallways near the retiring suites, and the edges of the ballroom. Michael had even circulated by Spinster's Row, although he could not imagine Lady Clara being there. True, she had several seasons behind her—according to Rose—but at two and twenty she was nowhere near spinsterhood.

He had quizzed his sister-in-law repeatedly over the past two days, to the point that Lady Rose had seen him enter the dining room at today's luncheon and had escaped through the servants' door. Tonight, as his valet helped him ready for the ball, he had turned those questions on the startled young man. Booth had only been his valet for three months, but they had seldom seen each other. Even then, their conversations had been limited to topcoat repairs and cravats. Michael had rarely been out in public, and he did not need a valet to dress him for the stables. But that was beginning to change. Much to his chagrin, returning to Society had been about far more than remembering dance steps.

"What do the servants say about the Durhams?" Michael had asked Booth, pointing at the house across the square. "Any impressions of the Earl of Beckcott and his family?"

Booth stared at him, then cleared his throat and stiffened his spine. "Sir. I'm not sure what you mean, sir."

Michael checked his cravat in his dressing mirror. He and Booth had agreed on relatively simple attire for this first evening out—a black-and-white kit with a gray waistcoat. "Fine deal on the cravat, Booth. Thank you."

"You're welcome, sir. My job."

"So no *on dit* about the earl?"

"I—I do not spend much time with the lower servants, my lord. Perhaps you should ask one of the maids."

Michael turned his back as Booth helped him into his skirted topcoat and checked the flared fabric and single row of gold buttons for flaws. "I appreciate the suggestion, Booth, but I doubt Mrs. Hodges would take kindly to me waylaying one of her maids in order to gossip." Mrs. Hodges, their housekeeper, had been with the family for thirty-five years and kept a watch on the women under her care with a diligence that would make a goshawk envious.

"I'm sure that's true, my lord."

Michael turned to face him. "Then perhaps you could—"

Booth's face reddened to the hue of a polished ruby, and his mouth gaped, although no word came out.

"Ah, perhaps not."

A poke at his side broke through his reverie, and he almost spilled his latest cup of lemonade.

"Woolgathering already, brother? It is not even ten."

Michael smiled down at his sister, whose beauty and dowry had been the talk of the season—until their brother Robert had brought scandal down on their whole house. To attend this ball, Beth and her modiste had spared neither expense nor frill with the gown, which made her seem to glimmer in the candlelight of the massive chandeliers overhead.

The primary color of the satin silk gown, royal blue, reflected her eyes and emphasized her pale, clear complexion and light golden hair. The neckline, wide and trimmed with silver ribbons, brought many a man's eyes her way. The puffed sleeves were cinched around the upper arm, with three companion ribbons tied into intricate bows at the wrists and forearm. The shoulder puff was royal blue with white ruffles, while the lower white sleeve was detailed with blue ribbons and a white ruffle at the wrist. Her bodice was a solid royal blue and gathered at the waist by a silver sash. The floor length skirt of the dress was royal blue and had a wide band around the hem of cross-hatched light blue material.

She wore sapphire blue earrings, along with a sapphire and diamond bracelet that he recognized as an heirloom set from their mother's family. Her head was crowned with a pale blue turban with silver stripes and trim, adorned with white feathers near her neckline. When Michael had suggested she use the feathers to "tickle the Marquess's fancy," she presented him with a scowl that could melt metal.

Beth floated in a cloud of blue and silver, and heads turned when she passed. But the words muttered behind their hands had not always been kind. Trailing in her wake, he had heard more than a few murmurings about their brother and pending downfall of the House of Kennet.

"I'm looking for someone. Why are you here instead of danc-ing with your marquess?"

Her brows furrowed. "I—we have had one dance. It would be improper to dance with him again so soon." She glanced around, as if waiting for something. Or avoiding someone.

"Elizabeth, what is wrong?"

She gestured toward a corner of the room. "May we talk over

there?"

Concern for her grew in his gut. "Of course." He set the cup on the beverage table and offered her his arm. She took it and he led her toward the corner. "Now tell me what is wrong."

Beth held up her arm and nodded at the dance card. "It is empty. I have had one dance with Ludlow, but no one else has even asked."

Michael fingered the card. Indeed, all the lines but two—claimed by the marquess—were blank. "Perhaps they know they have no opportunity with you."

Her scowl deepened. "That has never been a problem before. Before"—she paused and looked around again—"all that with Robert, my card was always full."

"We knew his behavior would have an effect on all of us—"

"I did not think it would be this awful."

Michael tried to respect the concerns of a debutante in her first season, but he could not quite see how—

"It's as if I'm ruined."

Ah. "Have you received a"—his brain fought for the phrase—"a cut direct?"

Beth shook her head. "No. But it is coming. I can feel it. Whenever I approach any of my friends, they are polite but move away quickly. I believe they are just waiting for one of the *ton's* dragons to do it."

"Do you wish to leave?"

She glanced at her dance card again. "I cannot. Not until after the second dance. And it is too early."

"Should I dance with you?"

Beth looked down again and her shoulders shook. For a moment, he thought she had begun to cry, but when she looked up, her eyes gleamed with mirth. "I'm sorry, Michael, but I've been your partner for the last two days. I value my feet more than that."

"You little rotter."

She hid her open laugh behind her hand. "Brother, I love

you." She slipped her hand around his elbow. "Have you asked anyone to dance?"

"I—" He grimaced. "No."

"See, even you realize your feet are a danger to ladies' slippers." She looked around. "Besides, I don't think Lady Clara has arrived yet."

He gaped at her. "How did you—"

Beth squeezed his arm. "Naïvétè does not become you. All the servants are talking about the endless questions you have been asking since Monday, and Rose has begun to mumble ominous threats about your curiosity. If you want to know so much about the lady, why not ask her yourself?"

"I would, if I could see her again. I thought she would be here tonight."

"Why not court her?"

Michael stared at her. "I do not think—" He stopped. "I would like to know more first."

Beth pulled away from him. "Let me see if she's hiding in the ladies' retiring suite. She does that sometimes when a crowd overwhelms her."

He glanced around at the press of people on and around the ballroom floor. The entire area felt compressed with people and their chatter. "I can understand."

Beth patted his arm. "I will return in a moment."

Michael watched her go, a knot of anxiety forming in his gut at the thought of seeing Lady Clara again. He had not had a reaction to a woman like this in more than four years, not since Eleanor Carlson had enchanted and abandoned him. Wariness seemed to entwine into every other emotion of the evening, along with dread and more than a touch of fear. The last time he had been at a ball, the last time he had danced—prior to his lessons with his sister—had been on Ellie's arm.

For the past four years, however, he had met women only in a variety of pubs and gaming hells, his tastes running to buxom, gregarious, and plump wenches who sold their bed for the night.

He relished their warmth, their comfort—and above all—their honesty. Even when they tried to deceive him or win money from him, they both knew what they were about. The ones who had robbed him the morning after had not destroyed him as much as the sweet-faced Ellie, who had promised eternal love and a lifelong marriage only to bolt when she finally realized he was destined for a vicarage and not a life at Ashton Park.

Michael returned to the beverage table and picked up another cup of lemonade—the burning in his gut a deep craving for something stronger—but he set it down again. If he took even one more sip of that swill, he would likely cast up his accounts before he made it out of the ballroom. Instead he wandered closer to one of the potted trees festooned with paper lanterns that populated the edges of the dance floor. The Duchess of Aldermaston had chosen an Eastern Asian theme for the evening, with decorations based on popular knowledge and assumptions about China and Japan covering every surface.

Dodging one of the lower-hanging lanterns, Michael turned his attention to the dancers, to the complicated—at least to him—steps of a Scotch reel. The adept dancers pranced through the routine, their faces glowing with the effort. The young debutantes mostly looked thrilled to be on the floor with their partners, the men less so. What an odd ritual, Michael thought, this series of balls and soirees with the idea of finding a spouse. Like birds on the hunt for a mate, the men preened and sought out the women most likely to produce healthy children and a substantial dowry. Love was not part of the game, as Society's "Marriage Mart" was far more about legacy and dynasty than affection. Essentially the women went to the highest bidder.

His stomach churned, and he squelched a belch.

"Ashton."

Michael turned, surprised to see Ludlow Barstable, the Marquess of Aldermaston, at his elbow. "Aldermaston." He gestured toward the dancers. "Your mother has presented an outstanding evening of entertainment."

Aldermaston's mouth twitched. "Society chitchat does not become you."

"I admit I am woefully out of practice."

"I understand Lady Elizabeth is aiding you in this endeavor."

"She is, although I'm afraid she has not made much progress."

"This is why you are not dancing?"

"That, and the fact that I doubt any of these lovely women would accept an invitation from me. At least not tonight."

"Ah. Your brother."

"Robert's—um—difficulties do seem to have affected our reception tonight."

Aldermaston fell silent, and his eyes narrowed as he scanned the room. Michael understood, disappointment for his sister sinking in. "So, Aldermaston. Not just tonight."

The look in the marquess' eyes turned sharp for a moment, then sorrowful. "I'm afraid so. I will speak with Kennet tomorrow about our arrangement."

"You have not told Lady Elizabeth?"

Aldermaston shook his head. "I intend to after our next dance. I'm telling you so that you will be prepared to take her home."

"So there is no hope if you wait—"

"I'm afraid not. My father is being . . . absolute about this— what the devil?" Aldermaston's gaze shot over Michael's shoulder.

Michael turned to see Beth and Lady Clara Durham nearing the foot of the steps leading down into the ballroom. His breath caught at the sight of Lady Clara, who was stunning— resplendent—in a white silk gown trimmed with emerald-green satin. The tapered skirt flared at the base, anchored by a wide, heavy border of embroidered ivy vines. The tabbed bodice, with a V-point over her breasts, had a faux front-lacing of green ribbon. Her sleeves echoed the hem with the look of slashed sleeves through which emerald silk peeked. Her hair, which had been wrestled into intertwining braids woven with matching satin ribbons, was festooned with daisies. A simple gold necklace with an emerald pendant matched her earrings. White satin gloves and slippers completed her attire. She looked young and angelic, and Michael's heart pounded at the sight of her.

But his chest tightened when he realized what had alarmed Aldermaston. A cluster of young people had stopped them near the last step, blocking the ladies' path, and Michael realized the conversation had turned ugly. Aldermaston headed toward the group, and Michael followed, their long strides covering the room in a few seconds. An unexpected rage surged up through him, the need to protect Lady Clara almost consuming him.

They closed in just as one of the young men pretended to stumble, dumping a full cup of lemonade down the front of Lady Clara's white dress. Aghast, she staggered to one side and bumped into Beth, who tried to steady her. The young man, however, was having none of it, and pushed Clara's shoulder, causing her to lose her balance on the step and fall forward.

Michael caught her by the arms, almost lifting her off the ground as he set her aright. She stared up at him, those brilliant green eyes edged with tears.

"Are you all right?" he asked softly.

She nodded and mouthed, *Thank you.*

He turned on the young man, advancing toward the group.

The man smirked, his face a mask of disdain. "Clumsy oaf!" he called toward Lady Clara. "She should not be allowed anywhere near a ballroom." But his eyes widened as Michael stepped in and grabbed the man's cravat in one hand, twisting it and lifting the man up on his toes.

"Ashton!" The man wheezed.

Michael towered over the slighter man and clutched the man's bicep with his other hand. As he tightened his grip on the cravat, he felt the man's toes leave the floor. He put his face close and hissed, "You are a bully and a cad who just insulted a lady of the *ton*. You will be lucky if no one calls you out on this."

"Ashton." Aldermaston put a hand on Michael's forearm. "Enough. The boy is a fool."

Michael released his grip in a way that made the boy drop and stumble trying to regain his balance. He caught himself and snarled. "You're nothing but a rake who should have stayed in the gutter where you belong."

Aldermaston leaned toward him. "And you owe Campion's Emporium several thousand pounds, boy. I should be careful who I insulted."

The boy paled suddenly and stared at Michael. "I didn't mean—"

Aldermaston made a cutting gesture. "Just go, son, before the duchess asks you to leave." He turned to the group of friends. "All of you. And if you are wise, you will stay away from that cad."

Michael glanced at Aldermaston, who shrugged. "Richard Hadleyton. He makes a habit of this, and he has been particularly cruel to Lady Clara in the past. I have wanted to be rid of him for years, but my mother keeps insisting on inviting him. His father is a minor baronet, and she is all about keeping the peace whenever necessary."

"Thank you."

"Well, I didn't want you to call him out in the middle of our ballroom."

"I was close."

"I know. But we did not need any more of a scene." He gestured around them, and Michael turned.

So many heads were looking their way that it felt as if the entire room was watching. Michael let out a long sigh. "My mother is going to kill me."

"I suspect she will have to wait." Another gesture, this one toward the stairs.

Beth and Lady Clara were gone.

CLARA HELD BOTH hands over her face, her arms and legs still trembling from the encounter, tears leaking down her cheeks. "Why does he hate me so?"

Beth sat next to Clara on a settee in the anteroom of the ladies' retiring suite, stroking her arm. "As my brother said, Hadleyton is a bully and a cad who seeks out victims. He has done this for some time." Beth paused. "Did Rose tell you—"

"That he tripped me last year? Yes." Clara dropped her hands into her lap and glanced down at the Aldermaston maid who was desperately trying to clean the lemonade from Clara's skirt. "You have done all you can. It could not be removed from the other dress either."

The woman had managed to draw out much of the stain, but it was clear the dress was ruined. She shook her head as she peered up at Clara. "I'm sorry, my lady."

Clara pursed her lips, then nodded. "Thank you for attempting it." She watched as the woman stood and returned to her duties as the room's attendant. Then she wiped her tears and sat a bit straighter. The humiliation, the shame she felt made her head hurt, but she had to find a way to get to her mother and retreat as gracefully as she could from the ball. The hope that this season could be different from the last ones evaporated.

She turned to Beth. "I appreciate your kindness, Lady Elizabeth. But I must find my mother. My dress and my evening are ruined, but I cannot hide in here all night."

"Do you wish for me to locate her? Bring her in here?"

Clara shook her head. "No. It is not the first time I have crossed a room in shame, and it will not be the last, as long as my mother insists I attend these monstrosities."

"Lady Clara—"

Clara clutched Beth's hand. "No pity, my friend. I do not mean to whine, but it is simply clear that I am more suited to the fields and fens than fetes and frolics. I wish my parents recognized that. It would make life much easier on all of us." She smiled in spite of herself. "My father has already picked at least one duke and two earl's sons as possibilities for marriage. Part of me wants to tell him to move ahead with his plan." She sighed. "And the other part wants to flee to Scotland, never to be seen again."

"If you do, take me with you."

Startled, Clara studied Beth. "You have a marquess on your arm."

Beth pressed her lips together.

"Do you not?"

Her friend shook her head. "I suspect he is about to end our arrangement. He has not said anything, but he was quite . . . chilly . . . during our first dance."

Clara gasped. "Because of your brother?"

"It will affect all of us, I'm afraid."

Squeezing her hand, Clara murmured. "I am sorry. It should not be that way. Your brother's actions are his own. But that is the way of the Beau Monde, I think."

Beth gave her a quick hug. "If only they were all as enlightened as you."

Clara stood. "Well, as your new sister-in-law told me on Monday, 'If wishes were horses, maids would ride.'"

Beth clamped her hand over her mouth to stifle a laugh, her eyes gleaming. "That does sound like our Rose."

Clara slipped her hand around Beth's arm. "Come, let us scandalous women find our way to my mother, whom I am sure is already in a state of mortification."

But as Beth opened the door and they stepped out into the hall, they found the Marquess of Aldermaston and Lord Michael Ashton waiting for them just outside. Beth and Clara jerked to a halt, staring as the two men bowed.

"Ladies," Aldermaston said.

Beth looked from one to the other. "Why are the two of you lurking in this hallway?"

Michael gave a light snort. "We are most definitely not lurking. We have been busy, and we are now waiting"—he gestured to the two of them—"for you."

"The question remains as to why," Beth said. Her gaze lingered on Aldermaston, and Clara felt her heart break a little for her friend. The marquess looked staid and kind, but no affection shone in his face.

Aldermaston focused on Clara. "At Lord Michael's suggestion, I have arranged for your mother and your carriage to meet you at the side entrance." He pointed down the hallway—away from the ballroom. "We will both escort you there, so that any untoward comments will be squelched before they can appear."

Clara's eyes snapped to Lord Michael. "You suggested it?"

His deep brown eyes lit with amusement as he reached for her hand, their brightness glowing against his dark skin. "I have been known to have a creative idea on occasion."

Beth pushed his hand down and Aldermaston cleared his throat. "Settle down, Ashton. No need to curry any more scandal tonight."

Michael stepped away, but his gaze never left Clara's face. She stared back at him, unable to look away from the warmth there. Her stomach clenched, and she realized her breath had drawn up short.

The marquess went on. "Oh, and Hadleyton and his party have been asked to leave. The duchess saw all that happened and was wholly appalled. She sends her apologies to you. Anyone who lays blame on you for this evening's ruction will find themselves responding to her."

Clara finally forced her gaze from Michael to the marquess. "I thank you, my lord."

Aldermaston stepped back and held out his arm toward the end of the hall. "This way."

Michael immediately stepped into the gap and offered his arm to Clara. "My lady?"

Clara glanced at Beth, who gave a slight shrug. "He's mostly harmless in public." Her eyes bright with glee, she lifted a corner of her upper lip as she said to Michael, "Do not make me a liar."

His eyebrows arched. "I would not dare, sister mine. The

consequences are unthinkable."

Aldermaston cleared his throat, leaning a bit closer to Clara. "Before you ask, yes, they are always like this."

"Then I would consider them most fortunate, my lord. My siblings would not find humor in any of this."

"Indeed. A fortunate family indeed." He held out his arm to Beth, who took it more gingerly than Clara expected, and Clara knew her friend's suspicions were well-founded.

Clara reached for Michael's elbow, and his other hand closed over hers. His arms felt strong, the muscles pulling a little snug on the fabric of his coat, and even through his glove his hand was warm and firm, as if he were afraid she would pull away. He stood almost a foot taller than she did, and he bent slightly as he whispered. "I only wanted to help."

"And you have." She peered up at him as they walked toward a door at the end of the hall. "Is it true, what I've heard the servants saying? That you have been asking questions about me?"

The skin over his cheekbones darkened. "Yes."

"Why?"

"Because I find you a remarkable and intriguing woman."

"Because I lost a kitten and fell into your mud?"

He grinned, and the color spread down his neck. "No, although I admit it got my attention. Do you truly hunt with a falcon?"

Clara found it fascinating that his blush was not the bright red of her own, that his dark skin shaded a hue that was between a light brown and maroon. She stared at him, and he met her gaze.

His eyebrows arched. "My lady?"

Clara stumbled over the hem of her gown. "Oh!"

Michael caught her as her hand shot out and thumped Beth in the back. The other couple turned, as Michael steadied her. She knew her own blush had to be a ravening scarlet.

"My apologies, Lady Elizabeth." She tried to straighten her gown.

Beth glared at Michael a moment but addressed Clara. "I'm

sure the maid's attempts to clean your skirt stretched it some-what." To Michael she whispered, "Behave!"

His wide eyes were the picture of all innocence. "I did noth-ing, I swear."

"Hm." His sister faced forward again.

Michael winked at Clara and put a finger to his lips.

She nodded, trying hard not to snicker. *No more talking.*

They continued their journey through the door and down two flights of stairs. Another short hallway led them out beneath a *porte cochère*, where the Durham family carriage waited. A footman standing nearby spotted Lady Clara and opened the door.

She released Michael's arm and stepped toward the carriage, then paused and turned back to the three of them. "I am forever in your debt, gentlemen. Your kindness is beyond measure. As is yours, Lady Elizabeth."

The two men bowed. "Our pleasure," Aldermaston said. He moved as if to help her into the carriage, but Michael stepped between them, again offering his arm. She grasped it lightly, but his strength was enough to boost her into the carriage. Her mother scowled at both of them, then gestured to the footman to shut the door.

The scolding she expected began the moment the carriage pulled away from the *porte cochère*.

"Can you not attend one single event without causing a sce-ne?"

"Mother, I promise it was not my doing. Hadleyton—"

Her mother interrupted with a wave. "Oh, I know all about Hadleyton. The duchess was livid with him and absolutely filled my ears with apologies and explanations. The duchess! Apologiz-ing to me! That in itself is scandal enough!"

"But if she—"

"If you had not tripped last year, he—"

"He tripped me."

Her mother stopped. "What did you say?"

Clara let out a long sigh, a deep weariness filling her. "Lady Rose found out that Lord Richard intentionally tripped me last year because I had turned him down for a dance. The fact that I would dare refuse him set him on this idea to make me look like a fool. Repeatedly, I'm afraid."

Her mother stared at her. "He . . . how could he? You are a lady!"

"Not in his eyes, apparently. And after tonight, I am assured he will make every event a nightmare for me."

The countess's lips pressed together. "Because of what Lord Michael Ashton did to him."

"Lord Michael was only trying to defend his sister and me."

"By lifting the son of a baronet clear off the floor by his cravat."

"He is rather strong."

Her mother's fan slapped Clara's arm. "You should not be considering Lord Michael's strength. Or anything else about him."

"Why not? He's handsome. And the son of a duke. And I think he enjoys my company, which is more than I can say about any of the other men you and Father have pushed me into meeting."

"He's nothing but a rake. Son of a duke or not, he will have no inheritance. He will be lucky if he ends up a vicar."

"And he came to my aid when none of the men you have thrust in my direction were anywhere in sight. Were any of them even there tonight?"

"They are busy men."

"I'm sure. And when they do look at me, they look as if I have bag of money around my waist and a haunch of bacon on my neck. Can you not see I'd rather have a vicarage with someone who suits me, who likes me, than a lifetime with someone who just wants to spawn a bushel of babies on me?"

"Clara!"

"Mother! Stop it!"

"How dare—"

Clara put both hands over her face, growling in her throat. "Please, Mother! I'm sorry!" She dropped her hands back into her lap. "But you know I am miserable attending all these Society events, and these men Father brings home are all distracted and distant. I am just part of their business and estate plans. I do not matter to them at all, except for my name and Father's title. They don't want a wife—all they want is a dowry and a womb."

"It is your duty—"

"I know my duty!" Clara's voice echoed off the walls the carriage, making her mother wince. She softened her voice, trying to tamp down her frustration. "And I will do it. Because I have to, not because I want to. Because I have no choice. But do not for a moment think I will be happy about it. Or silent."

"So you intend to make everyone around you miserable as well."

"I will do my best to be congenial, Mother. As Nanny once told me, 'You can get used to walking with a pebble in your shoe if you do it long enough.'" Her mother looked away from her, her jaw grinding. Clara closed her eyes for a moment. "Why do you and Father not simply send me away somewhere no one knows me?"

Her mother stared at her, the lines in her face deep and hard. "So you would prefer to abandon us. Abandon your family, your society for a life in some rural backwater?"

"As opposed to you abandoning me to a life of misery married to some monster?"

"You do not know they would be—"

"Of course not. But my brother has given Father an heir. My sister is about to do the same. Why must I follow the same path?"

"Because it is what is done. We are trying to introduce you to men like your brother. Kind but who need an heir. It is not only your path that's involved. Your duty is not just to us but to a larger society."

"Brood mare to the elite."

The slap was unexpected, and Clara yelped, lurching away from her mother, whose rage overflowed.

"Enough! Enough of this vulgar talk! You are a lady of the *ton*, and you will follow a lady's path and do your duty, or you will find that the misery of an arranged marriage is the least of your concerns. If this is how you feel, then we will no longer foist prospects on you. You will marry the man we choose for you, and you will speak no more of this!"

The countess twisted away from Clara, turning her back.

Clara sank back against the velvet squabs, her cheek burning, and her eyes filling with tears. *So this,* she thought, *is what a cut direct looks like. From my own mother.*

CHAPTER FOUR

Wednesday, 3 August 1825
Aldermaston Ball, Percy House
Ten in the evening

MICHAEL STEPPED OFF the pavement to watch the Beckcott carriage disappear down the curving drive, his curiosity about Lady Clara Durham more intense than before, creating an unexpected longing in his chest. He hoped her mother's angry expression did not foretell things to come, and he worried he had caused the lady despair in his attempts to shield her from the likes of Hadleyton. His abrupt need to protect her puzzled him even more. He had never felt such an intense desire to protect anyone outside his own family—not even Eleanor Carlson.

So many questions!

As the vehicle disappeared, he turned back to find both Beth and Aldermaston watching him, eyebrows arched. They looked like such a matched set with their fair hair and skin—and Aldermaston's evening kit was almost precisely the same blue palette of Beth's dress, although his hair a shade more ginger than hers—that Michael would have laughed . . . if not for the knowledge of what was to come later in the evening.

"Is something amiss?" he asked.

"Other than your complete lack of subtlety?" Beth crossed her arms. "No, nothing at all."

He scowled at her. "Subtlety is overrated."

"Not," she said, with a matching scowl, "amongst gentlemen of the *ton*. Must I remind you that you recently lifted another gentleman off the floor *by his cravat*? You are showing your arse."

Aldermaston let out a bark of laughter that made even the footmen near the door break their stolid expressions. When brother and sister turned to him, he held his arms wide. "The Kennet clan in the wild is something of a marvel of nature."

Beth glared at Michael. "A marvel of murder, more like it, if my brothers do not learn to control themselves."

Grinning, Michael brushed her cheek with one finger. "You love us, little sister."

"Which is the only thing that keeps you alive most days, brother."

He stepped toward the entrance, and the footmen opened both doors. "We should get you back to the ballroom. Or you'll miss your last dance."

They entered the short hallway, but Beth stopped, looking down at the floor a moment. The two men did as well, waiting until she looked up, first at Michael, then at Aldermaston. She moved closer to the marquess, her eyes moist. "Because it will be the last dance, will it not? While you are more subtle than my brother, this evening you have been, perhaps, less so."

The silence in the hallway suddenly felt heavy across Michael's shoulders. He moved quietly away from the couple, halfway toward the stairs. He could no longer hear the words, but he saw the tenderness in Aldermaston's face as he spoke. As the marquess took Beth's hand, Michael realized his sister's body trembled. Her lips quivered as she nodded. Aldermaston then kissed her hand and exited out the side door again.

Michael's heart broke for Beth as he watched her take several deep breaths and try to steady herself. He had been there, had felt that burning ache when someone had walked away. He wanted to go to her but knew she needed a moment.

Finally, Beth turned and approached Michael, her face solemn and still, although tears slid down her cheeks and her voice was choked. "He is going to send for our carriage, then re-enter the ball through the front. He will speak to Papa tomorrow."

"Speaking of subtle," Michael murmured.

Beth slapped his chest with the flat of her hand, then used it to cover her mouth as she gave a half-laugh, half-sob. "You are a monster."

"Without a doubt."

She studied his eyes. "You knew."

Michael cleared his throat. "I was . . . forewarned."

"In case I created a scene?"

Michael shook his head slowly and reached for her hand. "No, Lady Elizabeth. He has more respect for you than that. He did not want you to be alone or have to explain to your rather reckless brother what had happened." His mouth twisted. "I also think he did not want me to punch him in the face."

Beth leaned against him, her voice still low and gravelly. "Rotter."

He put his arm around her. "Well, you and he both know I might have done so."

She looked up at him. "Did you not have a top hat?"

"I doubt it will be the first top hat abandoned at a ball."

"It is a good top hat."

"Top hats. They come. They go."

"Michael?"

"Yes?"

"Thank you."

He stepped away from her and offered her his arm. She took it and they strolled back toward the side door. "You know, when you were born, I told Mother that I would much rather have had a pony. She assured me that someday I would change my mind about that."

She squeezed his arm. "And have you?"

"Not yet." She punched his chest, and he laughed. "You are

not persuading me."

He escorted her outside just as their carriage pulled up. A footman opened the door, and Michael helped her inside. As he settled, he reached for her hand again. "You know we will get you through this."

Beth nodded. "The power of the Kennet clan, right?"

"Without a doubt. The Ashtons can withstand any storm."

"If only," she muttered, "we were not quite so adept at causing them."

"Life, my dear sister, is nothing if not exciting."

Wednesday, 3 August 1825
Beckcott Hall
Eleven in the evening

THE COUNTESS EXITED the carriage without looking back at Clara, who gave her mother time to stalk into the house before she stepped down. The servants all cautiously kept their faces averted and their expressions still as stones. Even the footman waited patiently for her to emerge, offering his arm as she finally did so. She moved just as slowly up the stairs, with hopes that Honora Durham would have escaped to her own rooms by the time Clara got to the third floor where the family bedchambers were.

Without a fire in her grate—the summer was too hot, even at night, for a fire—Clara maneuvered by the silver light of the moon and the streetlamps outside. Her suite of rooms—her bedchamber, dressing room, and a retiring room—also held a small nook she had set up for reading and writing. Her slippers padded on the thick emerald-colored carpet, which matched both the silk wallpaper, with its swirls of vines in a lighter hue, and the curtains and bed covers, most of which were cotton for the summer.

She lit two lamps on her mantel, smiling as a soft mew

sounded from her pillow, and the white cat with the black tips stretched, blinking in the new light. Clara paused to stroke the soft body. "Sweet Pockets." The kitten wrapped her paws around Clara's fingers as she set up an irregular and unbelievably loud purr for such a tiny body. "Miss me?"

Pocket nipped her thumb, and Clara laughed under her breath. She extracted her hand and reached for the bell pull near the fireplace. She then lit the lamp by her bedside and one on her dressing table.

Radcliff arrived quickly, breathless, her eyes wide.

"My lady, we did not expect you back so soon. I hope you had a good—" The girl stopped as Clara stepped closer, her gaze slowly sinking to the gown's skirt. "Oh, my lady!"

"It's lemonade."

"Again?"

"Unfortunately. Ruining two gowns in one week is unexpected, even for me." She turned her back. "Please."

Radcliff rushed to her and began unlacing her bodice. "Ah. On that account."

Clara sighed as the first bindings loosened. "Yes?"

"It seems that the scullery maids at Ashton House have some kind of compound they use on, um, the particular combination of mud and muck you fell in. Apparently, since Lord Michael's return to the house, they have had to deal with a number of such stains on his clothes. Since your day gown was muslin and brown, they were able to remove the muck from it, with no lingering marks."

"That's . . . remarkable."

"I know! I've asked for the recipe for the compound, given how often you traipse about hunting, and they said they would include it with the dress. They soaked the dress for a day, then scrubbed it. It's in their drying room now, and they will box and send a note over as soon as it's ready."

"Did you take care of the dress Lady Rose sent me home in?"

Radcliff paused as she finished loosening the laces on Clara's stays. "Well . . ."

Clara looked over her shoulder. "Yes?"

"Since there's a compound that removes those stains, and you have always given me some of your older day gowns . . ."

"Do not tell me you like that awful color."

"A gown is a gown, my lady."

Clara winced from a prick of guilt. "Of course it is. If you want the gown and can clean it, you are welcome to it." She arched her shoulders as the stays came free. "Do my gowns fit you?"

Radcliff disappeared into Clara's dressing room and returned with a night rail made of light blue cotton. "With a bit of tucking and a border at the bottom. And they give me practice on making repairs and removing unexpected stains."

Clara laughed. "The gift of working for a lady whose grace in satin slippers is somewhat lacking."

Radcliff's cheeks pinked. "I meant no disrespect, my lady."

"None taken. Although I suspect my acquisition of new gowns and new stains is about to become severely limited."

Radcliff helped slip the night rail over Clara's head. Clara reached for the satin ribbon at the neck then settled on the stool in front of her dressing table. Radcliff began the process of unweaving the intricate braids circling Clara's head. "How so, my lady?"

The process of taking down the hairstyle was as painful as it had been going up, and Clara grimaced as a pin scraped her scalp. "I had a bit of a row with my mother tonight. Taken with what happened with the lemonade, I suspect my days of attending balls will become limited."

"But what about your need for a hus—" Radcliff broke off. "My apologies. Not my place, my lady."

Clara observed the young maid in the mirror. Yes, she was outspoken and scolding, but she had learned a great deal about being a lady's maid in the past few months, and Clara was, after all, a bit to blame for not reining in her words. "I suspect, Radcliff, that horse is quite out of the barn where you and I are concerned. I *would* ask you try to curtail your outspoken nature when we are in public."

"Of course, my lady."

"As to the other matter, my mother and father will pick someone for me to marry, and if the gentleman agrees, my father will make the contract arrangements."

"You will have no choice in the matter?"

"I am afraid that my having any choice in this was an illusion at best. Even if I found a gentleman to my liking, my father would still have the final say. Ladies of the *ton* are not free to marry whomever they choose. It is not the way things are done."

"'Tis a pity then, that such a handsome gent is interested, if he is not on the list."

Clara stilled, watching Radcliff in the mirror. "Whatever do you mean?"

The young maid shrugged a shoulder as she extracted another ribbon and began to unwind another braid. "Lord Michael's questions about you over the past two days have been rather enthusiastic."

Michael Ashton's dark and handsome face flitted through Clara's mind. His abrupt interest in her had been both confusing and startling, but the memory of his strength, and his virtual assault on Richard Hadleyton, left her feeling . . . warm. In the mirror, her cheeks brightened with red blotches, and Radcliff smiled as she reached for a hairbrush.

And an idea blossomed in Clara's mind. She cleared her throat. "Radcliff, when you're ready to go to Ashton House to pick up my dress, please let me know. I will have a note to send with you."

Radcliff's grin broadened as she ran the hairbrush through the long, wild curls at the back of Clara's head. "Of course, my lady."

CHAPTER FIVE

Thursday, 4 August 1825
Ashton House, London
Quarter-past nine in the morning

BREAKFAST HAD BEEN a haphazard affair since his mother's collapse, so Michael expected to be dining alone at this hour. No one in the Kennet clan—apart from his new sister-in-law Rose—emerged from beneath the covers early even on the best of days. Now, in the weeks following his mother's illness, the family tended to wander about in a chaotic miasma that would make Emalyn Ashton insane once she regained her faculties and control of the house.

Michael desperately wanted that to happen, and not only because he wanted his mother well again. Despite how he had chaffed under her rules and strict schedule when he had first returned in April, he had come to depend on it, especially during his struggle to break free of the alcohol that had consumed him for so long. A regular routine helped. Yet, to be honest, Michael also relished the relative quiet of the recent mornings. Even without Emalyn's structure, Ashton House tended to operate in what Beth called "a high bustle." With twenty bedchambers and a staff of thirty-five, constant movement was relatively normal. Most of the upper servants moved back and forth between

Ashton House and the family seat of Ashton Park if the entire family changed residences, but Ashton Park also had its own resident staff of fifty to keep it running. How his parents kept control of it all was beyond him, and Michael was beginning to understand the duress Thomas and Rose were under, now that they had stepped up to help.

Yet another reason he normally appreciated being the third son. No one relied on him for anything. Of course, this was also why he was often the invisible son as well.

Michael examined the chafing dishes on the sideboard to find a goodly stock of fried gammon, eggs, and kedgeree, as well as cold dishes with jams, pastries, fruit, and toast. He spooned up a bit of all of it as a footman poured coffee. He settled and began to feast when a rather coarse voice sounded from the door.

"You look as if you are preparing for a day of hard labor."

Michael glanced up at his brother Robert and hid a grimace behind a sip of coffee, although apparently not very well.

"I look that bad, do I?" Robert gestured for the footman to pour coffee in a cup near one of the place settings, then began filling a plate.

Michael set down the cup. "Not as bad as when I picked you up outside court."

Robert, who had been attempting to rescue a kidnapped boy, had been caught up in a raid by the Bow Street Runners. He had been badly beaten, then left in Newgate Prison overnight. By the time he had been released the next day, a deep infection had set up in a cut on his face. His left eye socket had been cracked. Michael had met Robert after his release and escorted him home. The doctors had done what they could, but Robert's face would be permanently scarred and the left side somewhat malformed.

"No doubt. Even now the mirrors tell me I appear to have been stitched together by Mrs. Shelley's misbegotten doctor."

Michael gave a quick shrug. "Not quite that bad, although I suspect you'll terrify the dogs."

"Your encouragement knows no bounds."

"And if I gave you any less, you would think you were dying."

Robert slathered butter on a piece of toast. "True." He took a bite, then gestured at his brother with it. "I hear you had quite the adventure last night. Coming to the rescue and all that."

"I—" Michael's eyes narrowed, an odd bit of suspicion stirring in his gut. "How and what did you hear?"

Robert grinned, a crooked affair that made his wound tighten. "My valet is apparently not as averse to gossip as yours. And I fully intend to quiz Beth about it, so do feel free to state your account of events first."

Michael stared down at his plate. "Do not be hard on Beth."

Robert stilled for a second, then put down the toast and sipped his coffee. "So he did it last night, the bastard?"

"Yes."

"Hm. That explains why there is a message for Father on the foyer salver this morning."

Michael peered at his brother. "Do you know everyone's business in this house?"

A shrug. Another bite of toast. "Usually. As would you if you spent time outside those stables and away from the horses."

"I am fond of the horses."

"I would not state that too openly, brother. It could be easily misconstrued."

"And I could easily make the right side of your face match the left."

"Ah, yes, but then you would have to put up with me even longer than expected."

Michael resumed his breakfast. "So this is a temporary reprieve?"

"It is. I am still officially disinherited due to an ongoing scandal, no longer a son of the Kennet duke." Robert also continued eating. "As soon as I am able, I will return to my rented rooms and the fine establishment of Campion's Gentlemen's Emporium. Then it's off to Kent." Bill Campion's establishment—a gambling hell and brothel Robert had recently inherited—was the source of his current scandal and recent disinheritance from the Ashton family.

Michael's brows furrowed. This was news. "Why Kent?"

Robert gestured to the footman for more coffee. "Part of what I inherited from Bill was an estate in Maidstone and a boy's school. It has been suggested"—Robert paused to clear his throat as the coffee was poured—"by a friend that the two could be combined. I'm going to make a survey of the estate and see what needs to be done."

Michael leaned back in his chair and studied his brother for a moment. Robert was not normally so reticent. "What's her name?"

Robert looked placid, sipping his coffee almost as if he had not heard Michael, who merely waited. "Who?"

"Your, um, 'friend.' Is this the woman I saw outside the court? The one who told me to remind you that you are never alone? That, um, 'friend'?" Michael speared a piece of gammon on his fork and lifted it, studying the sliver of meat as if it were the most interesting piece of gammon ever fried. "Because I know that my brother who prefers gambling hells to stables is not about to turn into a country gentleman without a little feminine encouragement."

Robert's face did not change. "Funny that you should mention stables—"

"Oh, please do not tell me you are already talking horses at the crack of dawn." Beth sauntered into the breakfast room and dropped into a chair next to Robert. While her dress and hair were impeccable—Beth had one of the finest lady's maids in London—her face remained sallow and drawn, her eyes red-rimmed, and Michael's heart hurt as he watched her fiddle with the silverware next to Robert's plate. As the footman stepped forward with the coffee, she waved him off. "Is there tea?" she asked, her voice both kind and weak.

"Of course, my lady." The footman set the coffee on the

sideboard and disappeared through a servant's door at the back of the room.

Robert straightened, examining his sister, and gently retrieved his silverware from her fingers. "I do not see why this should distress you. Horses are a fine topic for any meal."

She dropped her hands into her lap and her shoulders drooped as her gaze turned distant. "So is sewing, or embroidery, or whatever else it is women are supposed to do, but you do not see us clattering on about it endlessly."

As Michael exchanged a look with his brother, another voice joined the fray.

"What is it we are clattering on endlessly about?" Rose entered through the servant's door, carrying a small tea service on a tray, which she set next to Beth.

Beth scowled at her. "Why are you bringing my tea?"

"Because I felt like it." Rose sat in the chair next to Beth, turning slightly sideways to watch her sister-in-law. "I honestly did not expect to see you this morning."

Beth's eyes glistened but her scowl deepened. "I do not see why not. I am disgraced, not dead. And I still wake up hungry."

Robert's face tightened. "Beth—"

She reached out and gripped his arm. "Do *not* pity me. We knew it was coming. And for God's sake, stop blaming yourself."

"But it is my doing."

"And if Aldermaston cannot withstand a bit of a family scandal, then we were not as well suited as I thought."

When everyone remained silent, Beth looked at each of them in turn. "Is it not true? This family courts scandal on a regular basis. It was a scandal when our parents married, and they obviously set the standard—and survived it to become paragons of Society. Rose and Thomas created quite the stir, and"—she focused on Robert—"while you have certainly raised the bar, you are far from the only one. Now I have been overthrown by a duke's son, which makes me nigh on to untouchable for at least the rest of the season if not forever." She turned her gaze on

Michael. "And your behavior last night will occupy the gossip sheets for at least two days."

All eyes shifted to Michael, who tried to appear as innocent as he could. "I am sure I do not—"

"Michael?" Rose's quiet voice had a bit of a growl to it. "Did this have anything to do with Lady Clara?"

Robert perked, straightening sharply. "What is this? Who, pray tell, is Lady Clara?"

"Lady Clara Durham," Beth explained. Michael noted some of the bitterness left her voice as she found a new topic. "The daughter of the Earl of Beckcott. They have a house on the other side of Berkley Square—"

"And our neighbors in Berkshire. I remember."

Beth nodded. "I believe she is in her, what"—she looked at Rose—"third season now?"

"Fourth."

"And she is not yet married?" Robert asked.

Beth shook her head. "She is a bit odd—"

"I beg your pardon." Michael felt that odd sense of protectiveness flaring again. "She most certainly is not odd. She is attractive and kind and remarkably intriguing."

The room went silent as the three of them stared at him. Quite slowly, Robert grinned. "Tell us more, brother."

Michael felt his face heat.

"She is somewhat clumsy," Beth said.

"She is not—"

"And she hunts," Rose interjected. "With a falcon. A peregrine."

Robert's eyebrows arched. "Which means she rides? As in horses?"

"She even makes her maid ride," Rose continued, "so that she can accompany Lady Clara as a chaperone on her hunts."

Beth tried to look aghast, but it was a poor effort. "Her maid? On a horse? Heaven forfend. And now we are back to horses."

Michael glared at her. "I hope you have no aspirations to the stage, sister. You are quite horrid at pretending."

Robert leaned closer to Beth. "So tell me more about our brother's scandalous behavior."

Beth matched him, lean for lean, her voice a stage whisper that bounced about the room. "An extremely boorish young man named Richard Hadleyton—"

"I know the cad," Robert interrupted. "He owes Campion's several thousand pounds. A rolling debt that's been going on for at least three years."

"Which I informed Lady Clara of last season," Rose said. "She rejected him, and he took great umbrage."

"I bet he did." Robert glanced at Michael but urged Beth to go on. "So?"

"So Lady Clara and I were coming down the steps to the ballroom floor, and this boor absolutely doused her with lemonade."

"It was a cup," Michael grumbled. While he appreciated his sister's change in mood, he did not like the way this was going.

"The rotter. And?"

"And Michael rushed to her side and picked the man up by his cravat. Lifted him clean off the floor. Absolute madness!"

"Scandal! What happened next?"

Michael turned his scowl on his brother. "Will you stop?"

"I am far too eager to know more. You seemed to have emerged from hiding with a rather abundant flare."

"I was not—"

Beth went on. "Lady Clara was so mortified, I took her to the ladies' retiring room to regain her breath."

"It's a wonder she did not develop the vapors." Robert appeared breathless and put a hand on his chest.

"I was wrong. The two of you should really take to the boards with this act."

Rose giggled, hiding her mouth behind her hand.

Beth leaned back in her chair, and sadness seemed to settle over her again. "Truthfully, Michael was quite the hero last night.

For Lady Clara *and* me." Her eyes glistened again, and she grabbed a serviette and wiped them with quick swabs.

Rose reached for her hand. "Beth—"

Beth sighed. "I do not know why I'm tearing up so. It was not a great love match, but I thought we were well suited and everything was settled. I just wanted everything settled."

"Beth, I am truly sorry—"

Beth flopped her serviette at Robert. "Stop. I would choose you over an old marquess any day of the week and twice on Sunday." She looked at Michael. "And thank you. You made the evening much more bearable. I know you did not want to go"— she gave a wry smile—"but you seemed to find the evening a little more to your liking once you got to destroy Hadleyton in defense of your lady."

Michael shook his head. "She is hardly my lady."

"And she may soon be betrothed." Rose's calm voice rendered another silence to the room.

Michael felt as if a cricket bat had landed across his middle. "Whatever do you mean?"

"The prominence of Lady Clara's family and the size of her dowry has brought many prospective suitors to her door. Many have made it clear they find her rather odd and dowdy—"

"What?" The heat returned to Michael's face.

"—and that their interest is primarily in her money and position. And her father's vote in Parliament."

"Speaking of boorish," Robert muttered.

Rose went on. "Needless to say, she has rejected most and only tolerated a few. Her parents have lost patience. The *on dit* among the servants is that she and her mother had a major row last night, and the results are that Lady Clara will be betrothed to the first suitable candidate, whether or not she agrees."

Michael and Beth stared at Rose, while Robert fiddled with the remains of his breakfast. Michael knew his sister-in-law's gossip network among the servants was legendary, but he didn't realize it was quite so efficient. "You heard all this today?

Already?"

She nodded. "I was in Mrs. Hodges's parlor working on today's schedule when I overheard the scullery maids. Because of the incident on Monday, they have been in touch with Lady Clara's maid."

Robert peered at Rose. "What incident?"

"It was nothing," Michael muttered.

Rose smiled at him, then Robert. "Michael, being Lady Clara's hero again." As she detailed the events of Monday, Robert leaned back in his chair and Beth grinned broadly. Michael got up and helped himself to more coffee, which had gone cold in the pot.

"You found her kitten?" Robert asked.

Michael waved it away. "I am no one's hero. Total coincidence."

"No such thing," his brother said.

"You are if you had to battle Rufus to retrieve it," Beth said. "No wonder Lady Clara looked at you as if you had recently hung the sun and moon in the sky."

There was that heat in his face again. "I'm sure she did not." Michael took a sip of the coffee, grimaced, and set the cup aside. "May we talk about something else?"

"As long as it's not horses," Beth said. She looked around at one of the footmen. "May I please have more tea? And bring my brothers hot coffee before they scowl themselves into a permanent frown of disappointment?"

As the footman exited, Robert tilted his head, examining Michael. "Are you telling me you have fallen for a woman because she tripped into a mud puddle?"

"I have not—"

Beth touched Robert on the shoulder. "You should have seen him last night, watching her carriage drive away. Stepped out in the middle of the drive. A puppy gazing after a ball that has gone over the fence."

Michael stiffened. "I beg your pardon."

"All I can say is that it is about time you turned your attention to something besides the horses," Beth said.

"Ah," Robert said. "Speaking of horses—"

"I was not," Beth hissed.

"Perhaps you could call on her father." Rose's calm voice stopped the room.

Michael's gut tightened with a sense of fear. "I do not think"—he shook his head—"I'm not . . . I have nothing to offer her."

Beth stiffened. "The Kennet name is not enough?"

Michael shook his head again, looking down at his plate of cold food. He pushed it away. "I haven't even decided—"

Robert's low voice held a sympathetic tone. "You do not think she would be interested in a vicar or a soldier."

"Most likely not."

"There are other options."

Michael looked up at him. "What do you mean?"

His brother grinned but glanced at Beth. "Well, it does involve horses."

Rose stood, fighting a smile. "I'm going to check on the coffee."

Beth, snarling once at Robert, also rose. "I'll go with you. I also wanted to talk to you about your aunt. The one in Yorkshire."

Rose headed for the door, glancing over her shoulder. "Aunt Sophie? Whatever for?"

The two women disappeared through the servants' door, leaving the room oddly silent. After a moment Robert cleared his throat. "Her name is Eloise. Lady Eloise Surrey."

Michael's eyebrows arched. "The Earl of Pentney's daughter?"

Robert nodded.

"You are in love with her?"

Another nod. "Although, like you, I'm not sure I have anything to offer. But if I could turn this estate in Kent into something profitable . . . honorable . . . it might convince her father, who currently despises me."

"As does half the city at this moment."

"Always the encourager."

"So how do you think I can help?"

As Robert talked, Michael found himself more engaged than he had in a long time, and an odd feeling started to grow in the back of his mind, something he had not felt in almost four years.

Hope.

CHAPTER SIX

Thursday, 4 August 1825
Beckcott Hall, London
Half-past ten in the morning

CLARA SEALED THE last of three notes and handed them to the waiting Radcliff, then leaned back as the maid gave a quick curtsy and rushed out of the bedchamber. Radcliff seemed to rush everywhere, and Clara would have ordinarily cautioned her about showing more decorum in the house, but today she appreciated the maid's sense of urgency.

Two of her letters would go downstairs to the box in the kitchen, where all usual outgoing mail awaited the messenger who gathered them twice a day. The third would go with Radcliff when she went to pick up the cleaned and dried day gown left behind at Ashton House. A message to be privately delivered, if possible. A risk, but what happened after that would tell Clara a great deal about how she would proceed next.

She had taken an early breakfast tray in her room, knowing her mother would do the same, and Clara had no stomach this morning to face her father. She did send a message down, asking if she could meet with him later that day. Then she had settled at her escritoire and penned the first two notes quickly—one to the Duchess of Aldermaston, offering her apologies for the misunderstanding that had happened at the ball, and an anonymous one to her favorite scandal sheet, offering her explanation of the event. Clara often wrote to a scandal sheet or two after such an event, as she knew many other ladies did, as seeing their versions of the tiny dramas that happened in the corners of ballrooms around the city gave them a rather vicarious thrill. The scandal sheets thrived on these accounts, and even if sent anonymously, everyone seemed to know who was who.

A polite game within a polite society, although sometimes the results could be disastrous. Clara knew too well if only Hadleyton's version was known, Lord Michael would pay the consequences, as might she. The full story needed to be told. Conflicting stories always added to the drama and the spread of the *on dit* about any event.

The final note took more care and focus. She was about to step over a line in initiating contact with an unmarried gentleman, and if it did not go as she hoped, the costs for her could also be somewhat unfortunate. She included his formal address, then began carefully.

Lord Michael,

I hope you will forgive this rather forward breech of propriety, but I felt the question you asked me last night should not go unanswered.

Yes, I truly hunt with a falcon. I realize this is unusual behavior for a lady, thus your doubts about my statement about Maid Marian on Monday. But it is not unusual for me. As my mother frequently points out, my behavior varies from the "usual" for a lady far too much for her comfort.

Mr. Sutland, our gamekeeper, comes from a family long employed by the earls of Beckcott, and his father is one of our grooms at Beckcott Abbey. His mother, however, descended from a family of falconers, and is to this day recognized as one of the best in all of England. I frequented her mews as a child, and she introduced me to the sport. She also helped me capture and train my own peregrine several years ago. Named, of course, for the lovely maiden of the Robin Hood legends. I hunt with her as often as I can, much to the chagrin of both Mr. Sutland and Radcliff, who my parents insist accompany me as a chaperone into the fields. A ludicrous proposition, as Mr. Sutland is beyond reproach, and it makes Radcliff most unhappy. But I can be rather stubborn about going out with Maid Marian in a regular fashion. She needs the exercise, and it relieves me of my mother's rather excruciating oversight.

I also want to thank you for your kindness in coming to my aid on Monday, as well as with the rather despicable Mr. Hadleyton. He has seen me as his nemesis for some time, I'm afraid, and thinks it a proper goal to humiliate me whenever possible. That he experienced a bit of his own at your hands gave me a great deal of joy, despite the embarrassment of it. Please be assured that my mortification was due to Mr. Hadleyton's actions and not your own.

If you have other inquiries you would like to express to me, please know that I receive callers—at least for now—at two in the afternoon most days. If no one calls by three, occasionally Radcliff and I will take a short sojourn in the park. In such a crowded arena, my mother trusts that not even I can create too much chaos. I try not to see this sentiment as a challenge, but it becomes more difficult the longer we are in the City.

Finally, I would appreciate a return of the favor—an answer to a question of my own. According to rumor, you have been back at Ashton House since April. How is it we are only now seeing you at Society events?

Until both our curiosities are sated, I remain,
Yours truly,
Lady Clara Durham

The words of her note hovered in her mind as she organized the rest of her correspondence. There were three invitations from friends, asking her to tea on a variety of afternoons, and several letter from acquaintances she had met in previous seasons, who were now married and settling into their own homes and estates.

She would need to show the invitations to her mother and gain permission to go, since she would need her parents' approval to secure the transportation. Their city grooms had strict orders from her father not to obey requests from Lady Clara about any vehicle, especially the curricle, not after an unfortunate incident in the park earlier this year.

While it was most definitely not Clara's fault that her horses were startled by a pack of wayward squirrels, she had been going, perhaps, a bit too fast. It had cost her yet another maid, and Clara had spent a great deal of time acquiring Radcliff. Apparently, word among the servants traveled quickly.

A knock on her door broke her reverie. "Enter!"

A young maid, a tweenie by the look of her, opened the door a mere crack. "My lady?"

Clara stood and motioned her to come in, which the maid did not. She did open the door a bit farther. "My lady, I was sent to let you know your father would like to see you."

"Thank yo—"

The door shut, and Clara heard the rapid patter of the young girl's footsteps heading down the hall. "Am I that terrifying?" she asked the closed door.

Apparently.

Clara checked her appearance in her looking glass. The hair, of course, had started to creep free of its bondage, but she was otherwise appropriately attired in a dark green day gown of muslin and cotton. Day boots instead of slippers, to cut down on the risk of tripping.

She turned to Pockets, who had made a nest in a shawl at the foot of the bed. "Want to go out for a bit? Chase a few butterflies in the garden?"

Pockets stretched all four legs, then began to knead the shawl. Clara snatched her up, untangling the tiny kitten claws. "Oh, no, you do not want to do that. That is one of my best shawls." She tucked the little cat into the pocket of her gown and headed down the servants' staircase at the rear of the house. In the basement, she passed the kitchen, giving Cook a pleasant wave and greeting, then exited into the side yard. She skirted the remnants of the morning's deliveries—empty crates, discarded burlap sacks, and a variety of bottles—and made her way into the house's back garden through a side gate.

Clara sat on a wooden and wrought-iron bench near one of the paths that led a circuitous route through the plethora of rose bushes and hollyhocks. She inhaled deeply, closing her eyes, relishing in the fresh scents of the flowers and blooming shrubs. Trees shaded several areas, and an Italian-style pond shimmered near the greenhouse that provided vegetables, spices, and flowers for the household year-round. The Beckcott Hall garden was smaller than that of similar houses, but Clara knew their gardeners had tried to compensate by crowding as much foliage as possible into the limited space.

She eased Pockets out into the sun, once again extracting kitten claws from fabric. She pressed the warm cat against her cheek and was rewarded with that juddering and rapid purr typical of young cats. Grinning, Clara set the kitten on the ground and watched as Pockets disappeared underneath a thick patch of sage, which was part of Cook's summer herb garden.

"Well, at least you will smell pleasant." After one previous outside excursion, Pockets had returned bearing the distinct odor of a horse's stall, which had netted her a quick exit from Clara's bedchamber and a bath—both unwelcome, as far as Pockets was concerned. An experience repeated after disappearing into the Kennet stable this week.

Pockets did not care for water. And she had a surprisingly loud voice for such a miniscule creature.

"Don't think you'll have my comfortable pillow for a bed if you return with the aroma of horse." A flash of white told her Pockets had found new game and would be occupied for a while.

Clara stood and brushed off the back of her dress. She entered the house via the garden door, which led through a small conservatory and out into a rotunda, from which several rooms and hallways extended. To her right, an arched doorway led into the home's entrance hall, which also gave access to the grand staircase leading up to the second-floor ballroom. To her left lay the library, her father's study, and a hallway to the breakfast room, her mother's boudoir, and two receiving rooms.

She knocked on the door of her father's study and waited for his welcome. She took a deep breath and entered, easing the door closed behind her. She stopped, watching as he finished a bit of correspondence, folded the letter, and set it aside. He peered at her over the top of his spectacles as he replaced his quill in its mount.

Jerome Durham, the eighth earl of Beckcott, had once had a regal bearing, and Clara well remembered his strong, straight body in the saddle at many a hunt. A big man, her father had once been almost sixteen stone, standing well over six feet tall. His powerful bass voice carried weight in Parliament and caused more than a few servants to quake. His had been a respected and admired presence in Society.

All of which changed two years ago after a disastrous fall from his stallion and a long bout of pneumonia afterward, from which they had not thought him to survive. He did, but with a substantial loss of weight and ongoing ill-health. His breathing remained labored; his voice a rougher version of what it had once been.

Although he was barely fifty, he seemed shrunken to Clara, like a ripened apple left too long in the sun. She took another steadying breath. "Papa."

Durham took off his spectacles. He rubbed the bridge of his nose then leaned back in his chair. "I have determined," he said slowly, his low voice the now familiar sound of wheels on gravel, "that it is impossible for you to leave this house without creating a calamity intended to give your mother a heart attack."

Clara's chest tightened and she stepped closer. "Papa, I did not—" She stopped as she realized a smile tugged at the corner of his mouth, and a gleam appeared in his eyes. She clasped her hands in front of her. "It truly was not my fault."

He nodded. "I know." He gestured at the chair in front of his desk. "Please sit." As she perched on the edge of the chair, tucking her skirts around her feet, he went on. "But your mother still had to resort to her laudanum again last night in order to sleep."

Laudanum. Again. An all-too common occurrence. She swallowed, looking down at her hands. "Papa—"

"And what is this I hear about Lord Michael Ashton?"

Clara's gaze shot up. "Um . . ." *Did he know about the letter?*

"That he came to your aid?"

Ah. "He did, sir. And the Marquess of Aldermaston. Lady Elizabeth Ashton was with me. I suspect it was more for her than—"

"You do know his reputation, do you not?"

"I do. I also know he and his brothers are trying to regain their place in Society and their reputations."

"Not to great effect, I am afraid."

Clara studied her fingernails again. "Not yet, sir. No."

"Not yet. So you have hope for them? He is still nothing but a rake in many eyes. Including mine."

She met his face again. "I have heard much about their efforts. It is not an easy thing they seek to do."

"I am glad you understand that."

A spark of worry nagged at the back of Clara's mind. "Sir?"

"Reputation, once ruined, is not an easy repair. Often the stains remain, like glue on a mended vase."

She stiffened. He was no longer talking about the Ashtons. "Papa—"

"Your mother's concern is not unwarranted. You create chaos wherever you go because of your attitudes and your interests in things a young woman should never find intriguing."

"But I—"

"The clear answer to this is for you to find a place, a husband, and settle before ruination finds you in an irreparable way. You are in your fourth season, and inquiries have stopped coming as often, even with the amount of your dowry and my good name."

That spark became a raging fire. "Papa, please—"

He held up a letter. "I have an inquiry here from the Duke of Wykeham. Christian name Owen Colbourne. I believe you met him not long after we returned to the city."

Clara's eyes narrowed as she racked her memory for a face—*ah, there it was.* "Yes, sir. At the first ball. He's a great deal older. A widower, if I remember."

He put down the letter, the skin around his mouth tightening. "You make him sound ancient. I believe the man is just beyond forty."

"Papa—"

"No." He pressed both hands flat on his desk, any humor leaving his eyes. "Listen to me, Clara."

She stared at him but nodded, her mouth tensing as she held back her words.

"You are our last unmarried child. My health, as you well know, is not what it used to be, and will only continue to decline. When I die, your brother will take over the estate. He will take care of your mother as the dowager countess, but we do not want to burden him with you as well. So we need you settled. You have pushed aside every potential suitor that you did not otherwise offend or terrify."

Terrify? The fire of her worry settled on her shoulders. She grew hot as dread seared through her.

He tapped the letter. "This is a serious inquiry. From a duke. None of your other recent callers have been as well set in life. His wife died two years ago in childbirth with their fourth child. He would like to remarry soon and return to his estate. It would be the countryside you adore, and he will not even expect an heir from you. He will call on you this afternoon. If he thinks you are well suited to him, he will make an offer, and I will accept it. It is a good position for you, the best you will likely receive. If he proposes, you will not be allowed to turn him away. Do you understand?"

Clara stared at him, at the intensity in his face, his words absorbing into her soul. He did not want her brother "burdened" with an unmarried sister. They saw her as nothing but a problem to be rid of. Sold to the highest bidder. A duke.

Understand? God help her, she did. She understood to the

depth of her being.

She stood, swallowing the first lump growing in her throat. "I do understand, Papa." She backed away from the desk, wanting to be out of the room before the first tears came. "I will do as you instruct." Two more steps and she would be at the door. "I will do my best to help you relieve yourself of this unfortunate burden."

"Clara—"

She did not wait for his next words. She pulled the door closed just as those tears slid free, but she managed to hold on to the sobs until she had passed through the rotunda and up the grand staircase to the second floor, then the third. But they had consumed her, blinding her, as she found the door to her bedchamber and locked herself in. She sank down on the bench at the end of her bed and released them, indulging herself in a cry that lasted a good long while, exhausting her strength and clogging her nose and throat.

As they ended, Clara pushed away from the bed and found a handkerchief. She poured water into her washbasin and finished cleaning away the signs of her sorrow. Then she sat down at her escritoire and reached for her journal. She had a lot of thoughts about her impending doom—this disastrous betrothal to a duke who had made so little impression on her that she could barely recall his face—and she knew that she needed to express them in writing before the man arrived on her doorstep. Otherwise, they might just find their way out of her mouth before she could stop them.

And she had been serious about her promise to her father. Since her family obviously saw her as more an incumbrance than a beloved daughter, then she would make sure she did everything possible to relieve them of her presence.

If marrying an unknown duke was the answer, so be it. But Clara suspected there were other options as well, and no time remained to decipher them. She had to discover them now. Whatever it took.

Reputation be damned.

CHAPTER SEVEN

Thursday, 4 August 1825
Ashton House, London
Half-past one in the afternoon

MICHAEL READ THE note one more time as Booth sorted through the starched cravats in Michael's dressing room for one that matched Robert's purple and silver waistcoat. A twinge of nerves twisted his stomach again as he took in the words again.

What a risk she had taken sending it! When one of the hall boys had tapped on his door with the odd request to come to the servants' hall, Michael had been curious enough to go. But, startled to find Radcliff waiting for him, he had accepted the proffered note more out of pure astonishment than curiosity. No one sent him messages now, and few had ever sent them, even during his year of making the rounds of Society balls and soirees. Once he had made his association with Eleanor Carlson clear, they had stopped altogether. And after she had ended their relationship in such a scandalous way, he had vanished into London's underworld—which was not a place that traded in handwritten missives.

He had retreated to his bedchamber to read it—twice— before checking the time and ringing for Booth. Michael had shown the note to Robert, asking for advice on dress and comportment, which had resulted in the borrowed waistcoat. Robert, whose lopsided grin had only added to Michael's nervousness, had encouraged him to relax and avoid stairs and mud puddles.

Advice that did not help one whit.

"Here, sir." Booth emerged from the dressing room with a pale gray cravat. "Allow me."

Michael stood as still as possible as the valet wound the cloth around his neck and deftly tied the requisite knot. At his side, his fingers fidgeted, and he clinched his fists trying to stop them. "You would think I had never called on a lady before," he mumbled, annoyed at his own nervousness.

"You have not done so this season, my lord." Booth stepped back to check his work. "At least as far as I know."

"No. It has been a while."

Booth reached to adjust the cravat a bare fraction. "How long?"

Michael hesitated. "Four years."

Booth's gaze shifted from Michael's garb to his face, his eyebrows arching. "Four . . . *years?*"

"I might be a bit out of practice."

"I would think that to be a distinct probability, my lord. If you do not mind me saying so."

Michael shook his head. "I do not mind. I appreciate honesty in a valet, Booth. It will help prevent me from looking like a fool even more often than I do."

"At least where your wardrobe is concerned, my lord."

Michael smothered a laugh. "So do you approve of this waistcoat? It feels a bit tight."

Booth tugged at the bottom of the waistcoat and checked one of the buttons. "Your brother has a slighter build but not significantly so. But if you wish to wear more than black and white on your outings, you might consider visiting your tailor soon."

"These changes were all so . . . unexpected."

"I had assumed so, my lord."

Michael focused on Booth's face. "You did?"

Booth's mouth jerked, becoming a thin line.

Michael stepped away from him. "All right, Booth. Speak. What are they saying downstairs?"

Booth's cheeks reddened. "My lord, I really do not wish to—"

"Tell me."

Booth stared at the floor a moment. "They say"—he took a deep breath—"the ones who have been with the household for many years. They say your time away changed you."

"And not for the better."

"No, sir."

"Are they specific?"

Another hesitation and a hard swallow. "That you are . . . more distant. Reserved. And that when you first returned, you were quite ill."

"I was drunk, Booth. Not ill. Morose and mean. You did not come on 'til that had passed. I am surprised I did not send some of the maids fleeing for safety."

"They do think you are better now."

"But not back to my old self."

"No, sir."

Michael turned and checked his image in the mirror. Suitable, he thought, if not superior. "I doubt I will ever be that, Booth."

"No, sir."

Time for a different conversation. "When I return from my call on Beckcott Hall, I will be accompanying Lord Robert to Covent Garden. If I have not returned before midnight, I will undress myself. Go on to bed. No use in you losing sleep as well."

"Yes, sir."

Booth scooped up the detritus of Michael's toilette and change of clothes and left silently. Michael continued to stare in the mirror. He *had* changed, in many ways. Less naïve. More worldly. Less trusting. Lady Clara intrigued him, but a nag at the back of his mind reminded him she was still a lady of Society, and possibly prone to the machinations they all seemed to learn at an early age. He sometimes wondered if women were taught by their governesses how to deceive men at the same time their brothers were learning Latin and mathematics.

He tested the fit of the topcoat by rolling his shoulders. Although it had been made for him in the spring, it—like the waistcoat—fit a bit more snugly than he preferred. His work with the horses had been beneficial, physically as well as mentally. And quite possibly socially, if Robert's idea had any merit to it.

His brother's goal felt remarkably ambitious, even for Robert. He wanted to take the boys' school that his mentor and business partner—Bill Campion—had been supporting and move it to the estate in Maidstone that Bill had confiscated from a man deeply in debt to him. The place had been abandoned for years, and the house needed refurbishing and the land and tenancies put in charge of a steward who knew how to turn them around. The money involved would be astronomical, and Michael had no idea where Robert would get it. But he had assured Michael it would be available.

Most of all, Robert wanted Michael to take charge of the stables. The estate no longer owned any livestock, which would require a number of animal purchases, as well as a new staff. Robert wanted the boys to learn to ride, and also to build a breeding herd.

The entire conversation at breakfast had amused but interested Michael. Robert had long been the most Town-oriented of the four children, with no affection for the countryside at all. This new direction could only be laid at the feet of one person: Lady Eloise Surrey.

Robert's fall from grace had been swift and devastating, and it had separated him from the woman he loved. So he immediately sought solutions to the dilemma, determined to prove himself to Lady Eloise's father as well as to the lady herself.

"What we do for women, eh?" he asked the mirror, which

remained silent. He looked down, checking the toes of his boots once again, then pivoted and headed out.

Thursday, 4 August 1825
Beckcott Hall, London
Quarter of two in the afternoon

CLARA JERKED TO a halt just inside one of the downstairs receiving rooms, causing Radcliff to bump into her.

"My lady? Is something wrong?"

Clara inhaled deeply and straightened her shoulders. "Do you hate these afternoons as much as I do? The room always smells like Mother's perfume and all we do is stare at each other."

Radcliff brushed by her and headed to the far window, setting her sewing box on the floor next to the waiting armchair. "Well, I intend to do quite a bit of sewing today, my lady. You have ripped out two more hems this week. And I need to repair the fichu that kitten snagged on Saturday. We really must remember to close the dressing room door."

Clara grimaced and trod to the settee facing the door and not far from Radcliff's chair, her embroidery hoop dangling from her fingers. She dropped it onto the settee along with her gloves and a book she had tucked under one arm. "No one comes. Ever. It is as if I've already been consigned to a solitary country existence. But at least there I would have Maid Marian." Plenty of callers had come round the year of her debut, but far fewer since. This year . . . none so far. Clara often felt like an abandoned pup on the side of a road, watching the glittering carriages rush by. Another reason she despised the city.

"Downstairs they are saying a duke is to stop in today." Radcliff perched on the chair and arranged her skirts.

"Perhaps."

"Would that not be a great honor?"

"I suppose."

"If he does, I do hope he is a gentleman. I am still unsure what I am to do if he is not."

"Perhaps poke him with one of those needles?"

Radcliff's eyes widened. "A duke? They would hang me!"

Clara grinned and settled on the settee. "They would not. And I would speak up for you. But I suspect you would simply need to dash across the hall to my father's study. He will be there all afternoon, the door will be open, and I can almost assure you he will be listening to every word."

Having Radcliff as her chaperone on these afternoon calls had at first seemed odd to Clara, as Radcliff was still considered to be "in training" as a lady's maid. She had not been—as Clara's previous maids had—employed as such and had not come to the position in the usual manner. Agnes Radcliff had been a tweenie at a country estate near the Scottish border and had come to London to take care of an extremely ill aunt, who had since passed. Instead of returning to her previous employer, she decided to stay in London, and had applied for the position on a whim.

Clara and their housekeeper had been interviewing potential maids for weeks, with no results. The housekeeper, annoyed at the constant stream of maids who worked for Clara but resigned abruptly, had hired Radcliff on the spot. As she had explained to Clara, "Sometimes a dark horse wins." Radcliff had since been under the tutelage of the lady's maid who tended to Clara's mother.

Yet Clara was glad it was Radcliff who sat with her instead of her mother, who had done the duty the previous years. Then the afternoons had passed even slower, as the countess saw it as her duty to school Clara endlessly on the proper comportment of young women and the lineage of each visitor. At least Radcliff remained silent most afternoons.

Clara toyed with the embroidery at her side. It would be best if the duke did not see her work on this project—definitely not her best efforts, and needlework had never been one of her greater talents. She preferred to be outside, and even now her heart ached for the open fields of Beckcott Abbey and the weight of Maid Marian on her hand.

"Perhaps we can go for a ride in the park if no one arrives."

Radcliff looked up, her face pinched. "A ride?"

Clara smiled. "I meant in the curricle. I would never ask you to mount a horse in the city."

"Ah, thank goodness." The maid turned her eyes back to the needle at hand.

Jennings, the Durhams' butler, appeared in the door, his face held in the usual solemnity he adopted when making announcements. "Excuse me, my lady, but you have a visitor." He held out a small silver salver with a calling card on it. Clara stood and picked up the card as Jennings spoke just under his breath. "Lord Michael Ashton."

Clara's entire body tensed, and her breath caught as she looked from the card—and that was indeed what it said—to Jennings. The butler waited a moment, then whispered. "My lady?"

Clara found her breath, in one deep gasp, finally letting it out. "Please send him in."

With a crisp nod, Jennings turned and ushered Lord Michael into the room as Clara snagged her gloves up and yanked them on. She then stared up at him, again caught by the pure loveliness of his form—the breadth of his shoulders and the trim line of his waist, the clarity in his dark eyes and the perfect symmetry of his features. The smooth, even brown of his skin seemed to glow in the afternoon sunlight streaming in through the windows. He seemed radiant to her, healthy and lively as he strode across the room and bowed before her.

Although his waistcoat did seem a little snug.

"Lord Michael," she said, her words soft. Almost too late, she lifted her hand, which he caught immediately, kissing the gloved knuckles. Clara continued to stare, suddenly imagining his lithe form astride a horse, galloping across an expansive, green field, his well-muscled legs gripping the horse's girth. Her chest tightened, her lips pursed.

"Sit!" Radcliff hissed.

Clara jerked, the image vaporizing. She slipped her hand from his, then eased back down on the settee. "I apologize, my lord. I did not know if you would come."

Michael's brows furrowed. "Was I not expected to?" He gestured toward the door. "I can leave if you wi—"

"No!" Clara swallowed hard. "No," she said, more quietly, as she motioned to the chair near the end of the settee. "Please sit. I am very glad you came."

He sat on the very edge of the chair, his posture stiff and formal. "Please forgive me. It has been quite a long time since I have called on a lady, especially one as lovely as you."

A small doubt nagged at Clara. "Lovely?"

He smiled. "Of course." Then, examining her, those beautiful brows furrowed again. "Should I not have said so?" He glanced at Radcliff. "Is it improper to praise your beauty?"

Clara clutched her hands together in her lap. "Not at all, my lord. And I am flattered. I appreciate the compliment, although I can assure you the rest of the *ton* does not consider me so."

"Then they are fools."

Radcliff gasped and Clara shot her a stern look. When she turned her gaze back to Michael, his eyes gleamed but his face remained placid, his tone even.

"I have discovered, my lady, that I have been away from Society for so long that my interests and tastes have changed somewhat. My brothers have cautioned me to keep such things to myself, but I find that harder than I used to."

"So the world in which you have been immersed was more outspoken."

"Indeed it was. I have become quite accustomed to speaking my mind, which can lead—as you witnessed last night—to some unfortunate confrontations."

"I suspect, sir, that in the long term, the only one who will consider last night's events as unfortunate will be Lord Richard." Clara paused. "And my mother."

Michael bowed his head for a moment. "Yes, I could see she was less than pleased. I hope she was not too harsh on you."

Radcliff sniffed, and Michael's smile widened as he leaned a little closer to Clara, whispering. "I see Radcliff is as opinionated as ever."

Clara could not help but grin. "So did you believe my answer to your question?"

He leaned back in the chair. "I did, and I admire you the more for it. I would very much like to see you and Maid Marian on the hunt someday. I am sure it is a magnificent sight."

Clara felt her tension lift and she looked up, as if she could see the peregrine on the ceiling. "It is! She is intelligent and devoted, and simply glorious in flight. To see her soar, respond when I call her, hover, then stoop into a dive nearly stops my heart. It's as if I am with her, up there. The wildness of it captures me."

Radcliff cleared her throat, and Clara looked down, realizing Michael's eyes had gone wide—and her hand was in the air, waiting for her falcon to land. She dropped it into her lap. "Apologies, my lord."

"No!" He reached over and snagged her hand, clutching it. "Do not stop. Your passion for her is compelling."

This time Radcliff hissed again. "My lady!"

Clara shivered, the heat of his hand on hers pulling her closer to him. The intensity of his deep brown eyes captivated her. He had not been shocked by her—he had been fascinated.

"Thank you, my lord," she murmured, slowly drawing her hand from his. Again. And she realized that she very much did not want to do so.

But Michael, too, seemed to return to propriety, pushing back in the chair, the light in his eyes dulling a bit.

Clara cleared her throat. "And, you, my lord? Did you give any consideration to the question I asked you?"

"Indeed I did, although I can assure you the answer is far less entertaining than yours." He sat a bit straighter. "When I returned to Ashton House, I was"—he hesitated and looked away for a moment—"less than fit for proper Society. I needed to recover and spend time reacquiring the lessons we learned as boys, but which I had long since forgotten."

She studied him. "Such as?"

He cleared his throat. "Dancing, for one."

"Dancing?" Even as she asked, Clara realized she had not seen him at a ball all season, until last night. "You have forgotten how to dance?"

"I am afraid so. Any skill left unused for four years will become . . . unlearned. My sister has been aiding me in that matter, but my progress has been slow. And now I suspect it will stop altogether."

A tinge of worry tugged at Clara. "Why do you think so?"

"Because Lady Elizabeth has decided to retire to—" He paused again, and a dark blush filled his cheeks. "I—I should not say—"

Clara's eyes widened. Michael may not have retained his Society savvy, but Clara heard the implication in his words all too well. "Are you saying the marquess has rescinded—"

Behind them, Radcliff gasped.

Clara shook her head. "Surely, not because of last night—"

Michael leaned forward, grabbing her hand again. "No! Of course, not. He told me earlier—before all that—" He released her hand abruptly and pressed both of his down on the arms of the chair, gripping them tightly. "It's because of my brother. The marquess had already planned—"

"Ah."

He stared at the floor. "I should not have said anything. It is not to be public knowledge."

"They may not make an announcement," Clara murmured, "but it will be public knowledge and sooner than you may realize." She sighed. "I am so sorry. She must be devastated."

A smile tugged at the corner of his mouth as he focused on her face again. Some of the tension left his fierce hold on the chair. "My sister is more resilient than most people realize. She plays the Society debutante well, but she grew up with three rambunctious brothers. She will find a new path for herself and may have already done so."

"In what way?"

"I am not sure yet. But I can promise you Lady Elizabeth is not one to mope, sigh, and wring her hands."

"So she has your mother's strength."

His eyes gleamed. "You admire my mother?"

She returned the smile. "Very much so. I hear from the servants that her spirit has not been dimmed by her illness."

"So there are rumors wandering about?"

"Of course there are. Nothing happens among the *ton* about which there are no rumors. Gossip is our lifeblood. They say your father will not leave her side, and that she has been able to make herself quite understood, despite the limits on her speech. It sounds as if Lady Elizabeth inherited some of that stubbornness."

"The whole family, it seems, with me as an exception."

Clara scooted closer to the end of the settee and lowered her voice. "You are not a stubborn man?"

"A trait that seems to have escaped me, along with my brothers' glib talent with words."

"So if you had your mind set on a goal, you would not pursue it with all possible efforts?"

Michael stilled, and his lids lowered a bit, as he looked away from her a few moments.

"Ah," she whispered. "You are considering something specific."

He smiled, his voice as soft as hers. "You are as perceptive as you are charming. My brother has brought me a proposal that could reverse all my fortunes, set aside my obstacles. That could, indeed, be something I could invest all my efforts—"

"My lady?"

Startled, Clara's head jerked up.

Jennings stood in the doorway, his face stolid, but his eyebrows peaked in a touch of warning. "The Duke of Wykeham." He stepped to one side as a man strode by him, brandishing a cane and an amiable if vacant smile.

A smile that froze, as did the duke's approach, when Michael Ashton rose to his feet. Wykeham cleared his throat as his cane tapped twice on the floor. The smile vanished. "Ashton."

Michael bowed slightly at the waist, his eyes fixed on the duke's. "Your Grace."

The duke glanced at Clara. "I did not realize there would be other . . . callers."

Michael stepped away from the chair and moved closer to Wykeham. "My visit was a bit impromptu, Your Grace. Lady Clara was not expecting me."

Oh, yes, I was! Clara bit her tongue, realizing the most pleasant encounter she had experienced in months had been interrupted—and ended—by the duke's arrival.

"And I am afraid I have already taken up too much of the lady's time. I was about to leave, if you will pardon me."

No! She started to stand, then heard Radcliff's own throat clearing and low, "Sit!"

Michael turned to her, and he bowed low this time, his fingers touching his brow. "It has been my pleasure, my lady. Perhaps we will see each other again."

Yes, please! She ached to beg him to stay, to not leave her alone with this man, but another voice in her head reflected the eternal lessons of her mother and governess. *Stay calm, Clara. You agreed to this. It is your duty.* "Perhaps, my lord. I thank you for coming."

Michael backed away, nodded to the duke, and left. As he passed Wykeham the comparison between the two men struck Clara in a way that almost took her breath. Michael's dark to the other's fair features, his height and breadth overshadowing the older man, whose sour expression immediately conveyed his displeasure at finding a competitor in the room. Michael's calm and pleasant demeanor to the duke's stiff posture. His composed, handsome face to Wykeham's abruptly pinched cheeks.

The duke's mouth thinned as his lips pressed together and curled downward, and his eyes narrowed as he watched Michael leave. Wykeham's trim frame had neither the strength nor structure of the younger Ashton, although his appearance remained pleasing, despite his age. He had the slender build of many English men, and his steps revealed a rather mincing sway as he approached her, as if his shoes were far too snug. His blond hair, which had been curled, cut, and affixed to his scalp in one of the current styles, receded slightly from his forehead, but his face seemed agreeable enough, except for the scowl creasing it. His attire, however, seemed overly elaborate to Clara, especially for an afternoon visit, with an intricately embroidered waistcoat in blue and silver, an indigo topcoat of brushed silk, blue cravat, and cream-colored buckskin breeches.

Clara's examination of the duke caused her to hesitate long enough that he glanced at the chair Michael had vacated, his eyebrows arched.

"Oh! Yes, Your Grace." She gestured at the chair. "Please." She turned to Jennings, who waited just outside the door. "Jennings, would you please send up tea for His Grace."

Wykeham gave a dismissive wave and addressed the butler. "There is no need for that. This visit will not take long."

Jennings looked at Clara, who shook her head. "Very well. Thank you, Jennings. That will be all."

The butler disappeared from the doorway, but Clara knew he had not gone far. She turned her attention to the duke, who crossed to the chair, smoothing the tails of his topcoat as he sat. He leaned the cane against the chair, then rested his hands on the arms of it, as if he were holding court, his chin down. He studied Clara as he spoke, his voice a smooth tenor, if overly loud for the small room. "Has your father spoken with you about my visit?"

Clara winced at the volume of his words and fought the urge

to flee from the room, to call after Michael, to plead with him not to leave. She was a bit surprised by the intensity of that desire, and she again pushed forward in her mind the words of her parents—*duty, burden.* They wished to be rid of her. She clutched her fingers together in her lap, looking down at them, realizing the duke was about to become the proverbial pebble in her shoe. "He has, Your Grace."

"So you understand my intent?"

"I do, sir."

Wykeham straightened his shoulders and leaned forward approximately one inch, a move so insignificant Clara wondered if he realized he had even made it. She met his eyes again as his lips parted to speak. His eyes widened a bit as he glanced at her hands, and whatever he had been about to say seemed to vanish. He pressed his lips together again, examined her more closely, and when his spoke, his tone had lost some of its formality. "You find this an unpleasant prospect?"

Clara's chin lifted. *If he wanted a challenge . . .* "I cannot say one way or another, Your Grace, as I do not know you. But it seems to me that my desires in this matter are irrelevant. You are in need of a wife. I am in need of a place, sooner rather than later, as my parents wish me to be out of the house as quickly as possible. You are here to see if I will suit you in that role."

Radcliff choked and coughed.

Wykeham leaned back in his chair, his gaze now traveling over her, bonnet to slipper. After a moment of silence, a smile crossed his face, and he nodded. "Your father warned me that you were outspoken."

"I am sure he had other warnings as well. He is not a man who would send another into the lion's den unprepared."

Wykeham's laugh echoed off the walls, as did his words. "My God, woman, you are exactly who I was told you were. Terrifying and delightful."

Clara's eyebrows arched. "And this description brought you to me?"

He leaned forward again. A bit more than an inch this time, but only a bit. "My estate is up near the Scottish border. It is wild and frigid in the winter and pleasant only a few weeks during the summer. But I prefer it to the city. I spend as little time in London as possible, only when Parliament is in session, as it does not suit me. I have little use for frail girls who will want to huddle by the fire with their needlepoint." Another inch forward. "I am only recently out of mourning for a wife who was just that."

"She could not have been very frail if she gave you four children."

A nod. "She did. Three daughters but only one son, all of whom are beginning to show their own wild streaks. They need more feminine guidance than their nurse can provide. I also find I miss a woman's companionship, and I would like another son, if at all possible."

Radcliff made a small hacking sound, as if a hairball had appeared in her throat, and Clara bit her lower lip to keep from laughing.

Wykeham shot a glance at the maid, then gave a dismissive wave with one hand, a twist of the wrist made without lifting his arm from the chair. "I realize it may be improper to speak of such so early in our association—"

"Early indeed, sir."

"But you will find that I am as direct as you are, and I, of course, have the weight of my title behind my words."

"I see."

He leaned back two inches, paused only a second, took a deep breath, then went on, his words bouncing off the walls in harsh waves. "So let us get to the business of it, shall we not?" He reached into his inside coat pocket and placed a folded piece of foolscap on the table. "I have made a list of the events I will be attending over the next two months. The list includes the palettes of each evening's attire. I expect you to attend each event, and to have your modiste draw up gowns in complementary colors. The first event will be the Blackwell ball Friday fortnight, which should give her ample time to prepare the first frock."

Clara stiffened. "Your Grace, I do not—"

He gave that dismissive wave again. "Do not worry about the expense. Once we are married, I will reimburse your father for any expenditure along these lines. We will make our association known obliquely at first. If it continues appropriately, I will make it more apparent that my suit of you is progressing. In addition, I will call on you each Tuesday afternoon at two o'clock for conversation and tea, or a promenade in the park if the association goes well. If after these two months, I continue to find we are well suited, then I will consult with your father about the marriage contracts. I expect our betrothal to last no more than a month after which the banns will be read."

"And if I do not suit?"

"Then I will end the association quietly, as to not embarrass you or your family. If my other prospects do not work, I will retire to my estate and try again next year."

"So you have other prospects under consideration?"

"Three. A wise man never gathers all eggs into one basket."

"I appreciate your confirmation that I am little more than an egg."

His eyes gleamed. "I can see that our winter evenings beside the fire will be delightfully challenging."

For you. She looked down at her hands again, realizing her grip on her skirt had become so tight that the wrinkles might have become permanently imbedded. She fought all the words that surged through her mind, and defaulted to, "Do you have other requirements for our . . . association, Your Grace?"

A forward inch. "I assume it goes without saying that you will refrain from any of the feminine machinations young girls seem to be so prone to in circumstances like these."

Clara's eyes narrowed. "I do not—" *Whatever did he mean?* "Machinations?"

Another wave. "Those weak attempts to manipulate. Saying one thing and doing another. Pretending you will be some place and either going somewhere else or simply not showing up at all."

God forbid I become ill. "I see."

"And you will eschew any hint of scandal, of course. This will include your acquaintance with Lady Elizabeth Ashton and Lady Newbury. I understand you are friends with both."

"We are, but I don't see—"

"Lady Elizabeth has become a pariah."

Clara's eyes shot wide. "I beg your pardon."

"Since the Marquess of Aldermaston has set her aside. It was expected, obviously—"

Clara's hands clutched the fabric in her skirt, twisting it into a knot. "I saw them just last night. They were lovely together. I know she will be devastated, and I do not think we should be discussing such a thing."

Wykeham went on as if he had not heard her. "It must have been after then. Obviously, he could not continue with her after the scandal her brother has thrust them all into. You will avoid her, Lady Newbury, and all the Ashtons."

Clara scoured the room, looking for anything to focus on but the duke's face. The fireplace. The mantel clock. The empty doorway. The sideboard near the door. "Beth," she whispered, her heart aching for her friend. Her fingers tightened, and Clara suddenly wished they were around the duke's neck.

"It is best for both. Now he can pursue someone more suitable—"

"Is there anything else, Your Grace?"

"I assume you dance."

Clara's eyes snapped to his, the change of direction almost as off-putting as what she had just heard. "Dance? Did you say 'dance'?"

"Do not all ladies dance?"

Clara had to find a way to get back in control of her reactions to him. She twisted her left thumb and pressed the nail hard again her right palm. The slight pain drew her attention and cleared the fog about Beth. She straightened. "Most do. Some are more adept than others."

"Dance is a frequent pastime on my estate. Everyone, even the servants, participate. It helps keep our moods light and helps to pass the long winter evenings. I employ a dance master and two musicians, who live on the estate."

"I see."

"I am particularly fond of the Scotch reel."

Wonder how he feels about lemonade. "I will do my best, Your Grace."

He scowled. "You do not dance?"

"I know the steps, sir. I am not particularly adroit at completing them."

"That will change, I'm sure. And the dancing will help with your—" The man faltered then, and red tinged his cheeks.

Clara stilled. "My what?"

He waved again, up and down this time. The red deepened. "Your appearance."

Radcliff definitely had developed a hairball.

Clara understood her maid's reaction. She looked down, biting her lower lip. Michael thought her lovely. This man apparently agreed with the rest of the *ton*.

"Then they are fools."

She sought refuge in those words, slowly raising her gaze to meet the duke's, knowing the rage in her eyes could not make it to her lips. "If I am an embarrassment to you, Your Grace—"

Another wave. "Do not talk nonsense, girl. I already told you I have no interest in a frail wraith. I was merely thinking of Society's expectations. You will be my duchess, the face of my estate and family when we are in Town, until my son comes of age. Although I do not care much for the workings of Society, we must adhere to their protocols, should we not?"

Clara had no words that would not create more trouble. So she merely said, "Your Grace."

And with that he stood, nodding his head once. "I thank you

for seeing me today, Lady Clara. I look forward to furthering our association." Tapping his cane twice on the floor, he turned for the door and strode out. Jennings was at his side immediately, the duke's top hat in hand, and he escorted Wykeham down the hall.

Clara and Radcliff sat in silence a few moments, waiting until they heard the front door close.

Radcliff made a noise that sounded like a teakettle beginning to boil. "Are all dukes so demanding?"

"I do not think so, although I have not met that many. Perhaps it is a trait that comes with the title." Clara shook her head as she slowly peeled her fingers from her skirt. "I rather feel," she murmured, staring down at the wrinkles, "as if I have been squashed by a runaway carriage."

"He *was* rather . . . abrupt."

Clara's head jerked up and she stared at her father, who stood in the doorframe. "Did you hear his words?"

Durham crossed his arms. "I suspect the entire household heard his words."

Clara swallowed. "He is somewhat loud."

"Somewhat?"

Clara finally smiled but held her tongue.

Durham eased down on the settee next to her, grimacing as he braced against the arm on the way to the cushions. He stretched his left leg out, absently massaging the muscle of his thigh, and Clara realized how shadowed and gray his face appeared.

"Are you in pain, Papa?"

He gave her a slight smile. "Almost always, my dear. I try not to dwell on it any longer, but some days it becomes hard to do so."

"I am sorry."

He patted her hand. "And I am sorry if I made you feel as if you are nothing but a burden to this family. That was not my intent, but my discomfort sometimes renders me less than polite."

"Perhaps not polite, but it is the truth. While it was difficult to hear, it was most likely the bluntness I needed in order to understand your position."

"I did not want to hurt you. But it's clear that your mother and I have given you too much leeway."

"You allowed me to hope for a different life."

"Unfortunately, one which is not one available to a lady of your station."

"I see."

Durham hesitated, then withdrew his hand from hers. "In light of that understanding, you cannot see Ashton again."

She stared at him, her lips parted. "But—"

"You heard the duke. It is not just Lady Elizabeth you must avoid. I have already given Jennings instructions not to admit Ashton if he returns."

"But, Papa, he—"

Durham's voice darkened. "There will be no discussion of this, Clara." He pushed up off the settee. "It is settled. You will focus on the duke's suit of you." He nodded at the paper on the table. "Take that to your mother. She will ensure you have the appropriate invitations and escort you to the modiste."

The rage that surged through Clara stiffened her spine and her jaw. She glared at her father, all her words wrapped tightly within.

"Do you understand?"

Clara gave a single nod, snatched up the foolscap, and strode from the room.

CHAPTER EIGHT

Thursday, 4 August 1825
Campion's Gentlemen's Emporium
Covent Garden, London
Half-past eight in the evening

"Y OU WERE THERE less than half an hour. It could not have been that remarkable a visit."

Michael looked up at his brother, unsure if he had heard Robert's words correctly. "I beg your pardon?"

Robert grinned and rested his elbows on the broad cherry desk that was the heart of the Emporium's office. "Have you heard anything I have said in the last ten minutes?"

Ten minutes? Michael shifted in the wingback that sat in front of the desk. "Um, apparently not."

Robert chuckled. "I suspected as much, given you have been staring at the window the entire time, looking at nothing but the beams supporting the gaming floor."

The one window in Robert's office did not have a view of the outside streets but of the largest room of Campion's Gentlemen's Emporium. The office overlooked a gambling hall with more than forty tables of dealers and games, all intended to take money from gamblers of every social status and income, from the poorest apprentice to the richest duke. All were welcome to try their luck. While none of the tables were rigged, games of chance always favored the house. It had made Bill Campion, who had begun the Emporium and its associated businesses more than twenty-five years earlier, a most wealthy man—a wealth and estate that had passed to his protégé Robert Ashton when Bill had died a few weeks ago.

Robert's involvement with the various and sundry businesses—a few of them illegal and most of them scandalous for a nobleman—had threatened to drown the Kennet name in disgrace. But the family was beginning to find a pathway through it, as the duke advised patience and caution. Robert, in the meantime, had focused on expanding his new empire instead of divesting himself of it.

One such effort was the reason Michael now sat in the Emporium's office. After almost an hour of going over plans and ledgers, however, Michael's mind had been jerked back to a receiving room in Mayfair, to a mane of red hair and eyes the color of emeralds, to a mind and heart that could be enraptured by the flight of a falcon. "Sorry, brother. I suppose I was distracted."

Robert held his hands wide. "Far be it from me to criticize a man whose mind is muddled by thoughts of a lady. I have experienced just such a muddle over the past few weeks."

"Lady Eloise Surrey."

"Yes."

"You think you can win her favor?"

"It's more her father's favor that I need to win, but if you had been listening to me, you would know that." Robert's grin twisted, as the left side of his face did not quite cooperate with the right. "And I am proposing to help you win the father of your lady fair as well." He placed his hands flat on the desk. "It is always the fathers we rakes and rogues have to convince, especially if there is a rival in play. You mentioned something about a duke."

Michael nodded. "Wykeham. Weaselly fellow with a loud

voice. He arrived with such a flourish it was obvious I had to leave."

"I know the name but not the man. I've seen his name on our books. Frequently."

Michael's eyebrows arched. "Indeed? He is indebted to the Emporium? He gambles here?"

Robert shrugged. "Most of the peers do, at one time or another. It's one reason the house limit is so high. Why did you think there has been such an uproar about my inheriting Bill's empire?"

"And here I thought it was because it is scandalous for a nobleman to own a brothel."

His brother chuckled. "Hardly. It's far more about the son of a duke now holding all their secrets, all their debts to the Emporium. A businessman, even a wealthy one, can be bullied by a title. I may not be the direct Kennet heir, but they have no leverage to bully me. Thus, they want to bring me down through scandal. The world is changing, as we both know, but the aristocracy still holds the power. Do not forget that we grew up with the Prince Regent attending our family's Christmas balls. Because I assure you the other nobles do not overlook that detail, especially since he became king."

"But even the heir to a duke, much less a third son, cannot compete with such a title."

Robert leaned forward and gestured over the papers and books spread across the desk. "Do not count yourself out just yet, brother. Not when we have such plans in store."

"I did hear your explanation about converting the estate in Maidstone to a boy's school. Do you plan to draw students from the Emporium's staff?" Michael knew that Campion's Emporium had been long known as providing secure and safe employment for young children from the rookeries. Bill and Robert's goal had been to keep them off the streets and away from more dangerous ways of acquiring money. He had seen the boys at work and knew the effect it had on them. He also knew his brother had longed to do more.

"Most likely. I doubt any of the sons of aristocracy would be drawn to it. But it is not my aim to compete with Eton or Harrow." Robert tapped a piece of paper on his desk. "I have already begun a list of the older boys I think would benefit. Some have been working a variety of Campion businesses as apprentices and are remarkably sharp."

"What is your goal for them?"

Robert straightened his shoulders. "Mostly I wish to get them out of the rookeries and into respectable professions. Or service. I can envision a time when some *could* matriculate to Harrow or Eton, perhaps with the idea of becoming a professional. But I would be pleased just that they will learn to read and do more than pick pockets and cut purses."

"So why the horses? With the idea of becoming grooms or stable boys?"

"Or coachmen. But knowing how to ride gives a man a leg up in the world, so to speak."

"But you could teach them to ride. Or hire an instructor. You do not need me for that."

Robert shook his head. "No patience for it, and I barely ride myself. I have not raced an animal in years. I have not even been in a saddle since our last visit to Ashton Park."

Michael grinned. "And only once then."

"It was too bloody hot, thank you very much." Robert pulled another page from a stack of papers. "I also know nothing about the horses themselves." He passed the page to Michael, his words piling over each other as he spoke, picking up speed along the way. "While I could hire all this out, who better to trust than my own brother?"

"Plus you won't have to pay me."

Robert laughed and stood, beginning to pace back and forth behind the desk. "True. But I plan to. As I told you at breakfast, I want to bring you on to help return the stables to what they once were, and I plan to offer you more than the cachet of the position.

I've had it inspected, and the facility is sound and needs little except a bit of cleanup. The *ménage* is in a shambles, and there are two riding trails surrounding the property that need repair, and a park that needs to be examined for any issues that might create harm to the animals.

"Your primary responsibilities will be to hire a head grooms-man as well as the grooms, stable boys, coachmen, and begin to purchase the appropriate animals. I have re-hired the land steward who had managed the property for the previous owners. He had resigned in disgust at the neglect and is excited about the opportunity to bring the estate back around. Mr. Peter Stewart. I think you will find his company somewhat stimulating. When can you begin?"

Michael blinked. "Take a breath, brother. I can't remember when I've seen you so excited."

Robert's crooked grin returned. "This is different from any-thing else I've tried. It's unlike anything I've known. And I truly want it to succeed. And I want you in it with me."

Michael glanced down at the page in his hand. "You are talk-ing about a great deal of money."

"I'm setting aside one-hundred thousand pounds for the horses. As a start."

Michael's mouth gaped. "Do you want thoroughbreds?"

"For the boys? Of course not. We are not going to race them. Yet. But we will have to face the miasma of Tattersall's eventual-ly. But I had in mind several sweet ponies for the younger boys, work horses for them to learn field work—some would work with our tenants—and mares and geldings for the older riders. Twenty or so, total, to start with. Stallions to come later, as I would like to build a breeding stock so that we are not always replacing horses through purchases. Geldings for racing someday, or a stallion if he had the temperament. The visibility of a few wins could increase his value as a stud."

Michael put the page back on the desk. "Are your plans for the rest of the estate this ambitious?"

Robert stopped pacing. "Yes."

"Where are you getting the money?"

"Best you not ask." His brother shrugged one shoulder. "Not yet."

"And all of this with the idea of winning Lady Eloise?"

This time the smile held a slight slyness to it. "Primarily. But also for my boys." Robert stood and went to the window, looking down over the gambling floor.

Michael could hear the thrum of the crowd, the occasional call of a dealer or unhappy gambler. "You have already pulled them off the streets."

"No one deserves that life, that filth. They work hard," Robert murmured. "And I can see how having a regular job and income changes them. It gives them hope." He looked back at Michael. "It's addicting, that providing of hope. You see it once, you want to do it again and again." He pointed at the desk. "Come with me, and you'll see it."

"When are you going next?"

"Tomorrow morning."

Michael hesitated, his mind immediately darting back to that Mayfair receiving room. That glow when Clara spoke of the peregrine, lips pursed so sweetly as she looked up as if watching that falcon soar over her head.

Robert's eyebrows arched. "Were you planning to see her again tomorrow?"

"Is it that obvious?"

"To those who know you. To those of us who have seen you give that look to nothing but a pint of ale for the past four years." Robert returned to the desk and perched one hip on it. "You need to make sure, Michael, that she is not your new rum."

Michael scowled. "What are you talking about?"

"That you are not trading your fascination with spirits for a fascination for a woman. Both are equally deadly."

"That's rubbish."

Robert studied him. "Perhaps. Are you sure she will want to

see you again? A duke has a certain allure to all women."

Michael hesitated, his mind focusing on the look of dismay that had crossed her face for a brief instant as he had risen from his chair to leave. But it had been replaced quickly with a look of welcome for Wykeham, transforming Clara into a proper lady of the *ton* again. "She . . . when he arrived . . ."

"And it is not quite proper to call on a lady two days in a row without making your intentions clear."

"I had planned to talk to her father."

"And say what? That the impoverished third son of a family in disgrace wants to marry his beloved child? 'Sir, I do wish you to set aside the duke with the estate and a mound of pounds to allow me to pull your daughter into titled poverty.' I know I would find that appealing as a father."

Michael stared at his brother, annoyance growing. "Do you always make things so difficult?"

Robert spread his arms wide. "It is what I do best." Robert dropped into the other wingback sitting in front of the desk. "Michael, you have to be able to make your case for her. To illustrate why you would be a better match than a duke. Coming with me, helping me build this could be the opening volley of something much bigger and more expansive in your life."

"And if I don't have time? If she marries him quickly."

"Then you will have another focus in your life to help you get past it. Because if she breaks your heart, I know you will try to wallow in it, just as you did after Miss Carlson bolted."

That stung. "You should work on your persuasive abilities."

"Sometimes honesty is more suited for the situation."

A sharp rap on the office door got their attention, and Robert stood. "Enter."

The door opened and a large man leaned in. "You need to come. There's trouble on the floor."

Michael got to his feet and followed Robert, who headed down the open stairs from the office to the gambling hall with a sense of urgency in his steps. The big man—Michael remembered him from previous visits to the Emporium as Gilley, one of Robert's enforcers—led the way. The low roar of the gambling throng swept over them as they strode across the broad floor toward a table where a tighter cluster of people had begun to push together. The acrid scents of smoke, sweat, and fried foods stung Michael's nose as the three men formed a bit of a plow that pushed aside people as they made headway. Michael could hear shouted accusations of cheating and other assorted name-calling. As they approached, the crowd around the table parted, a human curtain pulling away to reveal the action before them.

Michael stopped, holding back, as he realized the man doing the shouting was the Duke of Wykeham, his bold tenor soaring over everyone's heads. He still wore the indigo, blue, and silver kit from this afternoon, the brushed silk of his topcoat standing out in a crowd of mostly factory workers and lower-level nobility. His attitude also marked him as an outlier. The crowd at Campion's tended toward congenial competition, as anyone who grew too belligerent with the dealers or staff found themselves quickly ousted.

The game, obviously *vingt-et-un*, had fallen still. The other players remained seated, their eyes looking either at their cards or the dealer, their mouths pressed into tight lines. The duke, however, stood, and—spotting the three men—switched his haranguing from the dealer to Robert. "You! Your man is cheating all of us."

Michael watched, curious to see his brother in action again— he had not visited the Emporium since returning to Ashton House in April. He also waited to see if the duke recognized him. Robert slowly looked at each player in turn, ending with the dealer, whose face was calm. He had his hands covering the money in front of him.

"Jimmy."

"Lord Robert."

Formal, and Michael realized the dealer acknowledged the seriousness of having a peer of the realm make such an accusation. Most of the staff referred to his brother as "Robbie," no matter what.

"What seems to be the problem?" Robert's tone was firm but even.

"The problem," announced the duke, "is that the table is rigged." He thrust a finger at the dealer. "He is cheating me and the rest of us."

Robert kept his eyes on Jimmy's face. "What happened?"

Jimmy sat a bit straighter, his gaze not wavering from Robert's. "He always bets too high." He nodded at the man sitting next to the duke. "This gentleman tried to caution him, but he will not listen."

The gentleman in question began to pocket the money in front of him and stack his cards together.

"Because I know how to play this damn game." The words emerged from the duke on a snarl. "I do not need help. I need an honest dealer."

Robert still looked at Jimmy. "How much has he lost?"

"Three-hundred pounds."

A low murmur made its way through the crowd on a wave. Three-hundred pounds was more money than many of these people would see in a decade. Some in a lifetime.

Gilley leaned closer to Robert. "That puts him close to five-thousand owed the house."

The murmur grew louder and more menacing. Michael looked around at faces beginning to cloud with distrust and anger. This was about to turn ugly if not diffused quickly.

Robert nodded once, and his focus shifted abruptly to the duke.

Wykeham stared at him. "What of it?"

"That's the house limit, sir."

Wykeham's chin went up. "Do you know who I am?"

Robert's eyes narrowed. "In Campion's Emporium, we all play on an equal footing. Some simply are in a position to lose more money than others."

Wykeham switched his glare to Michael. "Is this how you challenge a rival? Attempts at public humiliation?"

Robert glanced over his right shoulder at Michael, his slightly twisted grin returning. "This?" He pointed across the table at the duke. "This is the one?"

Michael stepped forward, his own smile grim. "Lord Robert Ashton, may I present the Duke of Wykeham. And, yes, I met His Grace for the first time earlier this afternoon." He bowed slightly. "It is mere providence that brought me here this evening, Your Grace. Lord Robert is my brother—"

"Oh, I know well who he is."

"And I had no reason to think a man such as yourself would frequent this establishment. It is a complete surprise to find you here. Especially given the location of our recent acquaintance. And trust me, sir. If I wanted to challenge you in that rivalry, this would not be my battlefield of choice."

Wykeham froze. "Do you intend to challenge me?"

"Careful," Robert muttered.

Michael ignored his brother. "I do not, Your Grace. I believe the lady is perfectly capable of making her own choices."

Wykeham's slow grin was sly, his eyes narrowing. "Actually, sir, you will find that choice has already been made for her, in a far wiser fashion, by her father."

It was a bolt to the heart, blindly sent but hitting home. Every muscle in Michael's body tensed as the desire to launch across the table at Wykeham seized him.

But so did a vise-like grip on his forearm. Michael glanced down at Robert's hand as his brother spoke. "Mr. Gilley, would you please escort Wykeham to the door?"

Wykeham flared. "What about my money? What about his cheating?" He pointed again at Jimmy. "What if I spread the word—"

"You will discover, Your Grace, that the entirety of Mayfair knows the legitimacy and honesty of my dealers, especially this young man, who has run tables here for many years as our lead dealer. However scandalous they consider my involvement in these operations, they all come on a regular basis. You, however, will leave tonight and not return for three months, and only then if you make a substantial payment on your current debt or offer something up equivalent in barter. Until you do, you will find your account frozen, with no additional credit available."

Wykeham glared up at Gilley as the big man moved in behind him, then turned back to Robert. "And tonight?"

"Tonight's losses will be added to your total debit to the Emporium."

"Even though it was achieved by cheating."

"An accusation, sir, is not proof. And if you had proof, we would have seen it by now. The fact that you continue to ineptly lose money is not proof that the table is rigged or the dealer dishonest."

Wykeham's face flushed red. "The only way I lose this amount of money is when someone is cheating."

Robert looked at the other men around the table, who suddenly found their cards of vital interest. He looked back up at Wykeham. "If not the dealer, then who? Which one?"

Wykeham faltered for the first time. "I—I am not sure, but I know—"

Robert held up his hand. "Before you say anything more, remember that you are about to slander men of your own ilk. Men who might very well take issue with such."

Wykeham looked around at the rough dress of the other gamblers and shook his head. "I do not think any—"

"Careful, Wykeham," Michael said. "Not every noble traipses into Covent Garden looking like a peacock. But they do know where the dueling field in Hyde Park lays."

Wykeham paused then and grew quite still. He looked more closely at each face, all of whom met his examination with a stern expression. The duke's eyes widened with recognition of two of them. He swallowed and straightened his topcoat.

"Mr. Gilley," Robert said.

Gilley held out his hand in the direction of the front door, and Wykeham silently made his way there. They watched him leave, and the cluster of folks around the table slowly dispersed. Robert nodded to the remaining players. "Thank you, gentlemen, for your patience. Jimmy, please add a twenty-pound credit to each of their accounts."

"Yes, sir."

Robert finally released Michael's forearm and urged him toward the office. The normal waxing and waning of the noise on the floor washed over them, and Michael found it almost a relief from the silent tension of the previous encounter.

"Does this happen a great deal?" he asked as Robert closed the office door.

Robert dropped into his chair behind the desk, his body sagging in relief. "Thankfully, no. Most evenings I never even go down there." He shrugged. "Not since Bill died and I had to stop being Robbie Green. But now you see what I meant about being bullied by a title. Wykeham is a fool but hardly the first one to attempt pulling rank." He gave Michael a grin. "I thought you were going to launch across the table at him. You were in a high color."

"I did want to."

"Do you believe him?"

"That Lady Clara's father has made the choice permanent?" The thought felt too much to bear. "I hope not."

"Well, if your heart is entangled enough for you to maul a man, you had best find out." Robert straightened in his chair. "Now may we finish this discussion?"

They did, and the next two hours slipped by rapidly. Near midnight, Michael took a hackney back to Ashton House. Robert would follow later, and the next morning they would leave together, taking one of the Kennet carriages to Kent.

Although the hackney dropped him in front of his home, Michael walked to the edge of the property and slipped down the alley to the mews. He had no treats, but his desire to check on the horses, especially Copper, would keep him awake if he did not take the time. The solace and silence of the stables this time of night soothed him in a way hard to explain, even to the others who loved and worked the horses as much as he did.

Michael eased the stable door closed, pausing to inhale the familiar scents of hay, leather, and horse. As his eyes adjusted to the change from streetlamps to shadow, he looked toward a table near the door, where several lanterns waited. Before he could light one, however, he realized a lantern already cast a dim yellow glow down the aisle between the stalls. His eyes narrowed as he spotted the light near Copper's stall, hanging on a wall hook.

What the devil—? He moved slowly in that direction, careful that his boots did not clomp loudly on the stone floor.

That's when he heard the sobs.

Soft, low, almost controlled . . . but not quite. And murmured words, muffled, as if spoken into a thick cloth.

Or fur.

Which is what he saw as he peered cautiously over the top of Copper's stall door. In the far corner, barely illuminated by the one lantern, Lady Clara Durham sat on a pile of hay that had clumped into the corner, her face buried into the fur of Rufus, the big orange stable cat. Rufus, who allowed no one to touch him, was placidly wrapped in Clara's arms. He did not squirm, spit, or buck as he always had in Michael's experience, especially in such proximity to a horse. Like all cats, he diligently avoided the possibility of being stepped on. But Rufus curled against her shoulder, his head against hers, as peaceful as a morning dew. In the voluminous skirts gathered around her legs and in her lap, the white head and wide blue eyes of her kitten peeked out, looking around in apparent confusion.

"I cannot, I cannot, I cannot." Clara repeated the words between gasped sobs. "I will not. They cannot."

While Michael was certain the thoughts were completed in her head, they never made it from her lips before a sob swamped them, her tears streaking the orange cat's fur.

He looked at Copper, who was awake and had moved to the far side of the stall. Lady Clara had taken up refuge in one of the most dangerous spots she could possibly have chosen—behind the hooves of a stallion—but Copper seemed to be as calm about her presence as the big barn cat. Still—

"Clara?" He kept his voice soft, but she still jerked, her head popping up, her eyes wide.

She stared at him, then released the two cats. Rufus seemed to regain all his energy then, leaping from her arms, snagging the white kitten in his jaws, and disappearing over the stall door.

"Pockets!" Clara's voice rasped through her tears as she made a vain reach for the cats.

"Let them go," Michael whispered. "We'll find them later."

Clara wiped her eyes, her face turning an even brighter shade of pink. Her thick mane of red curls billowed around her shoulders, and she brushed several strands away from her face. "Lord Michael." She sniffed and pressed her back into the corner. "I did not think anyone would be around this late."

"You would be correct, most nights. What are you doing here?" He opened the stall door and stepped inside, putting a soothing hand on Copper's neck as he pulled the door closed.

She licked her lips and pressed harder against the wall, using it as a brace as she struggled to her feet. She gave a quick point at the door. "Pockets. When she did not return from the garden after supper, I went looking for her."

"That must have been hours ago."

She glanced down, her fingers fidgeting in her skirts. "I—had a row with my father after supper. I—I did not look for Pockets until late . . . when I realized she was not in my room."

Michael moved closer to her, the urge to comfort her swamping him like a rogue wave. "Over Wykeham?"

She finally met his eyes. Hers were rimmed with red, salt lines streaking each cheek, her nose swollen. This woman had been crying for a good long time. She nodded.

"They want you to marry him."

Another nod. More tears leaked from her eyes, and her entire body trembled. She weaved as if she were about to fall.

Michael could stand it no longer. He reached for her, pulling her into his arms. Clara seemed to collapse against him, the sobs bursting forth anew as she buried her face in his coat. His grip on her tightened as he willed his strength into her. Time seemed to still as he held her, kissed her temple, and stroked her hair. When the wave of grief seemed to ebb a bit, he whispered, "Let me help."

She shook her head, even as she continued to press her face into his chest. "There is nothing you can do." She took a deep breath, her body quivering with the effort. "Nothing anyone can do."

He relaxed his hold on her, stroking her face as she leaned back to peer up at him. "Your father is determined?"

Clara nodded and swallowed hard. "He has—he has banned you from the house. You cannot see me again."

Anger surged through Michael, a hot poker in his gut. The unfairness of it, before he even had a chance to try, seized him, and his throat tightened as he fought it. Not now. This was no time for his own anger. "Clara—"

"I tried to make him see. But he will not. All he can see is that title . . . and a burdensome daughter."

This time the wave of anger shifted. "He thinks you are a burden?" Behind him, Copper shifted at the rough sound of his voice, and Clara flinched. Michael took her face in both hands. "You are not a burden," he whispered. "You are the most extraordinary woman I have ever known."

Her responding smile held a great sadness, and she touched his cheek. "If only you could—"

Michael kissed her. He had not intended to, but holding her, trying to comfort her, wanting to ease her grief had almost consumed him. He wanted to do more, to be closer. His lips pressed against hers, gentle at first, a move that surprised them both. Her eyes widened as they parted for a moment, then closed as he kissed her again, the first butterfly brush of his lips growing firmer, more determined. He tugged at her lower lip, and she whimpered, opening to him. He closed his arms around her again, pressing her tight against his chest as he explored her mouth, their tongues caressing with a fervor he had not expected from her but relished.

As the kiss ended, she leaned against him, and he held her as their breathing eased.

"You deserve better than Wykeham," he whispered. "If not me, then someone who will cherish and desire the woman you are."

She slipped away from him. "And what if I only want you?"

This time, the sensation that consumed him held more fire, more drive than any rage he had felt. "What if—what if I can prove myself? What if I could prove myself to your father?"

Clara shook her head. "I do not know if you can—"

"How long do I have?"

"Two months." These words came without hesitation. "Two months. Wykeham will decide in two months if I am proved worthy of him."

Another rush of anger began to crest. "He wants *you* to prove—"

"Two months is not a long time."

Michael and Clara spun, Michael shoving her behind him. He stared at Robert, who had reached over the stall door to scratch Copper's forehead. Michael glared at him. "What are you doing here?"

Robert grinned. "I went to your bedchamber to ask you a question, only to find that you had never returned. Somehow, I knew you would be with the horses. I did not expect the stall to contain quite a bit more than Copper." He tilted his head. "Lady Clara Durham, I presume?"

Clara stepped from behind Michael, her chin up. "You would presume correctly. And I presume from your appearance, you are

Lord Robert Ashton."

"Ouch." Robert chuckled, his gaze shifting from Clara to Michael. "I can see why you like her."

"Robert—"

"You see, Lady Clara, we have a plan, Lord Michael and I."

She looked up at Michael. "A plan?"

Robert went on. "A plan to make Lord Michael as appealing to the fathers of marriageable daughters as any duke of the realm. Two months is not a long time to achieve this—I had thought six months, perhaps a year—but we will certainly put in our best efforts, starting tomorrow."

Michael winced at the light that sprang into her eyes. A light of hope. "Clara, I do not know—"

"Try," she whispered. "Please."

And in that moment, Michael knew he would not fail. Not unless it killed him. Or unless the duke did.

CHAPTER NINE

Saturday, 6 August 1825
The shop of Madame Adrienne Chenevert, London
Half-past ten in the morning

CLARA WATCHED HER mother fidget as their modiste, Madame Adrienne Chenevert, slowly went through Wykeham's list, a slender finger of her left hand trailing down the edge of the paper, her lips pursed as she made notes on a separate piece of foolscap. The modiste's wild mane of ebony hair seemed to ebb and flow around her face, the thick curls held in place with pins, combs, and feathers. It seemed to be unmoving and undulating at the same time, and Clara found the effect fascinating.

The three women sat around a small table in the front salon of the shop, which smelled of cinnamon and cardamom, a soothing combination, although one that made Clara's nose twitch. The two broad front windows of the shop were covered by burgundy satin curtains, which had been pulled apart about a foot by lace ties, a space that let in a bit of light from the street outside but made peering in difficult. Most of the shop's illumination streamed in from short but wide windows near the high ceiling, giving the shop a bit of a golden glow from the morning sun. Clara had always found the shop to be an efficient, comfortable space. The front salon, with its small counter and several plush sitting areas, was for refreshments and consultation, and a tea service with three cups sat on the table between the women.

Fittings took place in an elegantly decorated room adjacent to the salon, where armchairs gave spots for companions, mothers, and chaperones to watch as the clients were fitted with new frocks. It was separated from the front salon by a narrow door draped with another burgundy satin curtain. Clara could hear at least two threads of conversation from behind the curtain, one of which seemed to be Lady Dorothea Timmons—Lady Newbury's mother—whose shrill voice instructed a seamstress on how to do her job.

Clara knew the shop had to have other areas—a workroom or two and living quarters for the modiste—but she had not seen them. She could not imagine making a living dealing with entitled aristocratic women on a daily basis. Even socializing with them in limited ways made Clara's skin prickle. She looked again at Madame Adrienne with a new appreciation for her patience and forbearance.

The modiste murmured to herself as she continued to review the list and made more notes, occasionally glancing at Clara, her dark eyes taking in every inch of Clara's appearance, from the hair that had begun to squirm loose from its bindings to the scuffed day boots on her feet. And, as not all her words or sounds were encouraging, Clara did not find it surprising that her mother fidgeted. Honora Durham did not handle with aplomb displeasure from anyone, especially someone so far below her station.

Madame Adrienne, however, was one of the finest modistes in the city. It did not do for anyone to displease *her* either.

The trailing finger stopped, and her brows furrowed. "This," she said, her French accent thick and tight this morning. "This is not a good color for Lady Clara." The words were a pronouncement worthy of royalty. She placed her hands flat on both pages and looked up at the countess. "And overall, these are not colors frequent in this season. And this came from a duke, you say?"

Honora stiffened. "Yes. The Duke of Wykeham."

"And this is his tailor's name?"

"Yes."

"Hm. I will talk to him. Perhaps we can complement without, um, shall we say, embarrassment."

"Dear God," Honora muttered.

Madame Adrienne folded the list and returned it to Honora, who tucked it into her reticule. The modiste stood and motioned for Clara to do the same. She circled Clara, looking her up and down, and Clara shivered, despising the feeling of being a horse on the auction block.

Her mother sniffed. "I realize that her figure is—"

The modiste waved a hand. "Her figure is not a problem. I already have her measurements. You did find her earlier gown satisfactory?" She peered at Honora, waiting for a sign. Honora gave a terse nod.

"Although it is now ruined," Clara muttered.

Madame Adrienne drew in a deep breath. "I have heard. Odious man, Hadleyton. Even his own tailor—" She broke off with a wave of her hand. "If you will send the gown over, I will repair it. At no cost." She aimed the last three words at Honora, then went on. "No, if we are to please the duke, we must find a way to make"—she pointed to her notes, with more than a touch of disdain in her voice—"*those* flatter instead of distract. This duke, he is blond?"

"Yes," Clara said. "And a bit of a peacock."

"Clara!" Her mother's eyes flew wide. "You should not—"

Another wave from the modiste. "All is well, your ladyship. We are like—how do you say—a father, pére. Priest! We keep all secrets." She paused and placed her hands on Clara's shoulders, as if measuring their width. "And he is fair. In his face? Eyes?"

Clara nodded. "Almost sallow. His eyes are pale blue. He's from the north. Not as far as Scotland but quite close. I do not think he sees much sun."

"So he is a gentleman with a gentleman's pursuits."

"I'm not convinced he has a gentleman's tastes."

"Clara!"

Madame Adrienne chuckled. "He has not taken into account your brilliant hair and eyes if he wishes you to wear these colors. And he seems to have missed the shift from pale to bright over the past few seasons."

"She cannot outshine him!" Honora fidgeted again, an action that took over her entire body this time.

Another wave. "Do not concern yourself with this, your ladyship. We never wish to outshine the peacocks among us until the day of the wedding." She addressed Clara. "Then your beauty will soar."

Clara looked down, feeling the words to be a kindness. "You do not have to flatter me, Madame Adrienne. I know I am not lovely."

Madame Adrienne stilled, her head tilted to one side. "Who has told you this?"

"She has a mirror." Honora's lips formed a tight pout.

Clara winced, watching her mother over Madame Adrienne's shoulder. The scowl on the modiste's face deepened, and she stepped between Honora and Clara, her voice dropping in both tone and volume. "You should not listen to them, my lady. I dress all ranks of the aristocracy. There is more to beauty than appearance. And yours glows from within. If your duke does not see this, shame on him."

Without waiting for a response, Madame Adrienne pivoted and addressed Honora. "And you want all of these? Twelve gowns in the next two months?"

The disbelief in her voice was understandable, and Clara almost smiled. She had been allowed one new ball gown a season for the past three years. The remainder of their clothing budget had gone to her younger sisters, with their debuts. They had both found husbands in their first seasons, but Clara's clothing allowance had not changed. Clara and Radcliff had retooled gowns from her previous seasons in order to keep some variety— and now her newest gown had a lemonade stain across the front.

"Yes." Honora sniffed, as if the question was beneath her.

The modiste pressed her hands together. "Excellent. I will send over the first sketches for you Monday, with the goal of having the first gown ready the day before the event at the head of that list. The others will follow in short order after that. I will send those dates Monday as well. Once you approve the sketches, we will talk costs and payments. Acceptable?"

Honora stood. "Perfectly."

Madame Adrienne spun again, facing Clara, and grabbed both her hands. "We will make you shine, Lady Clara. The most beautiful on every occasion."

Clara could not help but grin. "Then you will be the magician all my friends say you are."

The modiste's smile lit the room. "I am honored you trust me with this most vital of tasks."

"Hmph." Honora stood and smoothed her skirts. "And you smell the cost of twelve gowns."

Madame Adrienne's smile broadened, and she curtsied to Honora. "Of course, my lady. It is, after all, my business. And I am most appreciative of yours. I would be less than forthright to pretend otherwise."

"Hmph." Honora marched toward the door. "Come, Clara."

Clara gathered her reticule from the chair and followed her mother but turned back to Madame Adrienne as she reached the now open door. "Thank you."

Madame Adrienne clasped her hands in front her, abruptly a demure and calm presence. "You are most welcome, Lady Clara."

Clara took the three steps from the shop up to the street, where the Beckcott carriage awaited their return. She dodged two small puddles of rain, left over from the previous day's storm, which had raged over the country, leaving much damage but a brief respite from the heat. The liveried footman stood near the open door, and her mother had already settled on the cushions inside.

She motioned for Clara to hurry. "Do not dawdle, girl. We

have more stops to make."

"Merely trying to avoid any other puddles."

Honora sniffed. "What does that mean?"

Clara shook her head and settled back against the squabs with a sigh. "What other stops?"

Honora glared at her. "Do you really think you can attend events with a duke without looking like a duchess?" She shifted, spreading her skirts around her legs, then knocked on the carriage's roof.

Clara braced herself as the carriage jerked into motion. "Whatever are you talking about?"

Honora gestured up and down at Clara. "All of it. Jewelry, slippers, hair."

"Hair?"

"Yes. My maid has commandeered Radcliff for some lessons on hair styling. We have appointments at the jeweler's and cobbler's this morning, then we will stop at Gunter's. I sent a note to the jeweler this morning that we will be interested in at least three suites, which can be used with several gowns. I sent him the duke's colors—"

"How can we pay for all this when I have been allowed only one gown a season?"

Honora's lips pursed so tightly Clara wondered if it hurt. "We do not discuss such things. That is for the gentlemen to decide. Your father gave me the permission—"

"Is this all based on the duke paying for it after the wedding?"

Honora glared at her.

"Mother—"

"You will not concern yourself—"

"And what if there's no wedding?"

Honora's eyes widened, although her mouth remained a thin line. "That is not an option."

Clara sagged against the seat. "In other words, we cannot afford this and if the duke does not find me worthy, Papa will be in debt up to his eyeballs."

"He finds you worthy. You should not—" Honora stopped and stiffened, as if gathering herself together. "He will—he *will* find you worthy."

Clara tried to ignore the despair that clutched at her throat. "He already does, doesn't he? It's already decided."

"He finds you engaging, although I cannot fathom why. But nothing is certain until the marriage contracts are signed."

"If he already knows, then why all this show? Why not just have the banns read and whisk me off to the far north?"

Honora's face reddened. "Because he is a proper gentleman, and he will do things as they should be done. So shall you."

"So he's going to peacock about town for two months, make a lot of noise in Parliament, *then* whisk me off to the far north."

"You will keep this lack of respect to yourself when you are in his company."

"Papa once told me that respect is to be earned."

"*Not* if you are a duke. Certain positions are granted respect due to what they are. You would have learned that by now if you did not spend so much time with animals and servants."

"I prefer their company."

"Which is why you have the manners of a barn cat."

"Yes, I believe Papa pointed this out just last night."

In truth, her father's words the night before had been far more vulgar and harsh. As an obvious result of his increasing frustration with Clara's resistance, Jerome Durham's temper had blasted out of control. In response to her strident pleas for more time and more options, he had lashed out, deriding her for her manners, her behavior, her disobedience, and her defiance. Oh, and her position as a burden on the family. He had even raised his hand to slap her, withholding the blow at the last minute as a fit of coughing overwhelmed him, leaving him wheezing and searching for a handkerchief.

Clara had fled to her bedchamber in tears, only to discover her kitten's absence. She had followed Radcliff's instructions about how to traverse the alleyways between the two grand houses in order to take refuge in the Kennet stables, knowing Pockets would have returned to her friend. The encounter with Michael Ashton had been startling, reminding Clara that her reaction to the man had not been isolated—and that the attraction was mutual. His kiss had all but seared her soul.

But it had also eased her mind and engaged her heart with a new emotion: hope.

None of which she could share with the Countess of Beckcott.

"Your father wants you in a good position, one with security as well as status."

"He also wants me out of his care. I am, as he so politely phrased it, a burden on the family."

"Would you prefer he hid the truth of your situation from you? You cannot expect your brother to keep you eternally supplied with clothes and food when he will have his own family to see to."

"You speak as if Papa is already dead." Clara stiffened, a horrific thought seizing her. "Mother?"

Honora turned to look out the window of the carriage.

"Mother, what are you hiding from me?"

Her mother remained silent as the carriage slowed, drawing to a halt.

"Mother?"

The footman opened the door, and her mother prepared to get out. "We will speak of this later." Holding on to the footman's arm, Honora stepped down and out of sight.

Clara gathered her skirts, once again feeling as if her life had been jerked from her hands and set upon an unstoppable path.

"Michael," she whispered as she pushed out of the carriage. "Please hurry."

Tuesday, 9 August 1825
The former Broxley Estate, Maidstone, Kent
Half-past eleven in the morning

"THIS IS WHAT you referred to as needing 'a bit of a cleanup'?"

As if prompted by Michael's words, a clay tile slipped free from the gabled roof of the main stable, clattered across the other tiles and crashed to the stone pavement a mere fifteen feet from where he and Robert stood. He turned to glare at his brother, reaching into his topcoat pocket for a handkerchief to press over his mouth and nose.

Robert did the same. "It helps somewhat if you breathe through your mouth."

"Somewhat."

Robert shrugged one shoulder. "Apparently they released the stable boys a few days before selling the last of the livestock."

"Smells more like a few months."

"It's not that bad."

"Apparently that blow to your head blocked your sense of smell."

Behind them, their own carriage, from which they had recently alighted, waited, the team of four blacks moving restlessly as their coachmen stood patiently. Their valets, along with the two footmen who had accompanied them, had unloaded their possessions and disappeared into the house. The sound of hammer on stone drew Michael's attention, and he looked over his shoulder at the main house, where scaffolding had been erected on two sides, and workers were prying free cracked and crumbling stucco from the neoclassical façade of the mansion. "Is the roof sounder on the house, or do we need to tell Booth and Fletcher to move our trunks to an inn?"

Robert growled. "That roof is fine. The house is in better shape, and I have already replaced the staff. Many of them worked here before and know the house intimately. So you will be well taken care of. *This* roof is fine as well." He gestured at the stable building.

"Not for long, if it keeps shedding tiles."

"It's not—"

"Lord Robert!"

A man rounded the corner of the main stable, his dark brown cotton suit and loping stride pegging him as the land steward. Reddish brown hair poked from beneath a woolen hat, which he doffed quickly, touching his forehead at the same time as he approached the brothers. He bowed slightly at the waist as he halted in front of them. "I was not expecting you back so soon."

"Mr. Stewart, I simply could not stay away." Robert gestured at Michael. "This is my brother, Lord Michael Ashton. He is here to help with the stables. Lord Michael, Mr. Peter Stewart, who worked this estate for more than twenty years before Broxley tried to destroy it."

Another bow, this one in Michael's direction. "And my father before me. Lord Michael." Peter Stewart, shorter than the brothers by several inches, had a wiry build, probably gained from walking frequent and lengthy rounds of the surrounding countryside. "The house was maintained the longest, for the comfort of the owners. But, as you can see, the neglect to the stables has been substantial."

Michael lowered the handkerchief from his face. "There certainly seems to be plenty to do."

Stewart's mouth twisted. "I should not speak—"

Robert waved a hand. "Speak freely, Mr. Stewart. You will be under no judgment from us. We both despised Broxley, peer or not. What he and his kin did here is reprehensible. And my brother is quite free with his opinion, even when it is unwarranted or unrequested, a habit not even our mother has been able to dissuade him from. Too many altercations in London's finest pubs, I am afraid."

Michael glanced at Robert but addressed Stewart. "I do not have my brother's gift for blather, I will admit. But he is right that we must be straightforward with each other if we plan to return the stables here to their original glory. What do you believe is our first step?"

Stewart looked from Michael to Robert, flinching a bit as his gaze rested on Robert's injuries. He cleared his throat. "Lord Robert and I have discussed hiring the staff first. As you can tell, quite a bit of cleanup is needed before any stock is brought in."

"And did you have anyone in mind?"

Stewart glanced at Robert again, who nodded his encouragement. "I have, my lord. The head groom, who worked here for many years, has a new position at another estate nearby, but he is not entirely happy there. I believe he would return. There are several boys, good boys, in the local village who would be ripe for apprenticeships as groomsmen."

Michael paused to survey the stables again. Located more than fifty yards from the main house, with an overgrown garden between them, the stables were laid out in a long rectangle, with the main two-story stone building at one end. Along each side and the far end, one-story wooden buildings, although with matching gabled roofs, looked to be additional stalls and storage. The open area in the middle held pens for livestock along one of the buildings, with the remaining open area meant for staging and training. According to Robert, beyond the far building were several other *ménages* for training and exercise, along with an extensive park and trails. The open countryside beyond had once been the scene of massive hunts.

He glanced again at the four blacks. "Mr. Stewart, since my brother has been here before, am I safe in assuming there are stalls and rooms for our team and coachmen ready?"

"Yes, my lord, for the team." He nodded toward the main building. "The rooms for the staff are on the second floor . . . but need a bit of work."

"The coachmen have been staying in the house," Robert muttered. When Michael's eyebrows arched, he explained. "With the other servants. I still need to hire several footmen. They stay in those rooms."

"I suppose flexibility is key in a situation like this."

A brief smile crossed Stewart's face. "Indeed, my lord. And you will get used to the smell."

Michael grinned. "I will take your word on that. But let us get those boys in here as soon as possible. And I'd like to get your groom here quickly."

"I will send him a message right away."

The groom arrived late that afternoon, along with four boys from the village. After brief conversations with Michael and Mr. Stewart, they were put to work immediately. The next three days became a clamor of activity as shovels clanged against stone. A wagon and team borrowed from one of the tenants began hauling massive amounts of manure and other waste away from the stables, and two of the boys began raking the dirt in the stable yard and clearing out the pens. Robert retreated to the mansion to finish establishing his office and hold meetings with an architect.

Word spread quickly that the Broxley estate's new owners were hiring more staff, and three footmen and two more grooms appeared the next day looking for work. Michael immediately put the grooms under the charge of the now head groom of the estate, a burly, rough-voiced man named Whitby Little, who had a firm but gentle demeanor with both the boys and the horses.

And, much to Booth's dismay, on day two Michael cast off his coat and cravat, rolled up his sleeves, and grabbed a shovel. He loaned handkerchiefs to all the men and boys as they shoveled, raked, and hauled. He doused his own in cologne, as he never did get used to the smell. But by the dawn of the fourth day, as the borrowed wagon returned with loads of fresh hay, the area began to take on the more familiar smell of a well-tended stable. Robert put two of the workers from the house onto the stable roof, two more to painting the peeling sides of the wooden buildings, and the signs of neglect eased. Although several more weeks of work lay ahead of them, Michael knew they had hired a competent group who could handle the changes, and he began marking the days with a bit more hope, his eyes firmly on that two-month deadline Wykeham had set as he made detailed plans.

But as Michael and Little began an inventory of the remaining items in the stables, they discovered that most of the tack had been sold, and any blankets, grain, or barrels still on site had rotted. Disgusted, Michael kicked over a barrel that had been shoved to the back of a storage room. It cracked wide, releasing a flood of blackish water that reeked of the dead rats floating in the deluge. He and Little backed away from it, and Michael reached for his handkerchief again.

"The surprises never end do they, Little?"

"Apparently not, my lord." The man's face was stoic, but dismay clouded his eyes.

Michael turned to face him. "Little?"

"Yes, sir?" He looked up at Michael.

"Tell me again how long you worked here."

"Twenty-two years, my lord, before I left last winter. Like Peter—Mr. Stewart—my father was here, brought me on when I was just a lad."

"So you remember its heyday."

Little's eyes brightened. "Oh, yes, sir. A dozen or more thoroughly bred horses for the hunts and races, matched teams for the carriages, ponies for the children. The earl—the old earl—had house parties that went on for weeks. Nobles showed up with their horses, and we got to care for some of the finest in the country. Beautiful animals from the best lines." The man's enthusiasm shone in his face and voice.

"You understand my brother's vision for the estate?"

A vigorous nod. "Yes, my lord. I know it won't be what it was, but the idea of all those boys . . ."

"I believe he will also want to host house parties for donors, investors. He has quite an extensive set of plans."

"Yes, sir."

"So we have a lot to do to help him."

Little paused, studying Michael. "*We* do?"

Michael grinned slowly. "I never intended to do this alone, Little. I am a decent judge of horses. I can tell balance, topline, whether a horse is downhill. And I will, of course, be in charge of the purchases—"

"Of course, my lord."

"But I need someone by my side who knows the ways of a horse far better than I do, who can tell a well-trained thoroughbred from a nag, who can tell the difference between a well-trained but spirited horse from a calm but inexperienced gelding who will buck his rider at the first opportunity. Who *knows* rather than assuming anything from mere appearances."

Little's eyebrows arched. "Sir?"

"I want you to organize your staff, choose an associate who can oversee this cleanup while you're gone."

"Gone?"

"I want you to accompany me on our buying trips—and we need to start right away."

"My lord—"

"I have a goal, Little. I have to make our major purchases in the next two months." He gestured widely. "And I cannot delay much longer on this stage."

The man paused, looking away, watching the last of the dark water flow out of the room and down the central hall of the building. "My lord, I do not have garb to attend such—"

"I will take care of that once we are back in London."

Little's mouth gaped. "London?"

"Of course, I want to start with some purchases in the neighboring estates. The lesser horses for the boys. Small, gentle, but well-trained. You will not need a new wardrobe for that. But I do intend for us to end up at Tattersall's. I plan to make a rather distinct impression. We will be buying several of the best, including a thoroughly bred stallion for my brother and geldings or mares for ladies."

Little crossed his arms. "I was told your brother did not ride."

Michael grinned. "My brother is a better horseman than he

allows himself to be. He despises hot weather, so this past summer plagued him. And one of our Ashton Park stallions tossed him arse over teakettle a few weeks ago, and he has resisted getting back on any horse, even his usual mount. But if he is going to run this school and have the boys ride, he has to get his arse back in a saddle, and soon. We will find him the right steed."

Little looked around. They stood in one of the side stables, where the cleanup of the stalls had not yet been completed. "How many are we talking about?"

"Twenty, including the ones at Tattersall's."

The groom's gaze traveled over the empty stalls. "Let me talk to my boys. When did you want to make the first trip?"

"Tomorrow. Make sure you take a bath."

Little grinned. "I will, my lord. Where are we headed?"

Michael clapped the man on the shoulder. "To the closest estate most rife with gossip, Little."

CHAPTER TEN

Friday, 19 August 1825
The shop of Madame Adrienne Chenevert, London
Half-past nine in the morning

T HE NEW HAIRSTYLE—WHICH consisted primarily of some sort of odd paste and a plethora of ribbons wound around numerous strands braided into loops and secured with combs and pins—hurt. With every move of her head, something tugged or pulled, and the sensation of locks of hair struggling to escape from their bonds made Clara's scalp itch. Or maybe it was that paste, which smelled of stale lavender. All of it added to the misery that started in her new and overly tight slippers and worked its way up through the constricted fit of the new gown.

The first ball under Wykeham's auspices would commence in a few hours, and Clara's dread grew with each moment. According to his list, his kit for the evening included a skirted frock coat in pale yellow silk and a canary yellow waistcoat with bronze-colored embroidery. A single row of bronze buttons closed the coat, which had matching silk velvet cuffs and lapels.

A color combination that made even Clara wince.

But Madame Adrienne had lived up to her promise, constructing Clara's new frock from a deep coppery silk that would cause the duke's bronze accents to shine when they stood next to each other. The color also seemed to tone down the fire in her hair, allowing the blonde highlights to appear more prominently. And although the gown had the low waistline, tight bodice, and puffed *en gigot* sleeves of the current style, Madame Adrienne had kept the sleeves even trimmer and the waist slightly lower, sitting just above Clara's hips. Ignoring the trend of accent colors, Madame Adrienne had instead focused on thick embroidered vines in the same copper color on the cuffs and hem. The overall effect made her look taller and thinner than she truly was.

The snug fit, however, meant her stays had to be laced tighter, and Clara resisted the urge to cough as long as she could. Stays were meant to support comfortably, not make the wearer feel as if a boa constrictor had surrounded her. But without the extra pull, the laces on the new gown would not close.

Too much. A cough finally burst out of her, and she covered her mouth, apologizing from behind her palm.

Madame Adrienne, circling the fitting platform, paused. "Perhaps I should loosen—"

"No." Observing from a chair a few feet away, Honora Durham stiffened. "No. The duke requested a slimmer profile. As I told you, the duke approved all your designs and their colors, but requested a tighter fit on all of them. She will learn to take more shallow breaths like the rest of us."

"Thus the increasing need for swooning chaises in the retiring suites," Madame Adrienne muttered.

This time the sound from Clara was more of a snort.

"Are we quite finished?"

Madame Adrienne turned to the countess. "*Mais oui,* your ladyship. I will make these last tucks myself and deliver the gown within the hour." She raised her gaze to Clara's hair. "I will include several matching ribbons your maid can use in your hair as well." She ran a hand down the back of the gown and fluffed out the narrow train. "And the image will be complete. Your duke will not be disappointed."

Clara doubted the truth in that statement but dared not speak her mind. The last two Tuesdays had brought encounters with Wykeham that had been as brief and harsh as the first one, focusing on the designs of the new gowns, the dancing master he had sent to Beckcott Hall—who now took up much of Clara's afternoons—and news from his border estate. The duke had not asked her a single question, nor had she offered up much but the occasional sarcastic remark, which made him laugh, sometimes as if he were indulging a disobedient child. Overall, he spoke, she listened.

Clara stepped off the platform and retreated to a changing room, where Radcliff waited with uncharacteristic patience—and silence—to help her. In fact, Radcliff had grown increasingly wordless whenever they were out with Honora, and Clara wondered if her mother's maid had said anything to the girl.

They did not partake in the usual post-modiste visit to Gunter's Tea Room. Instead they returned to Beckcott Hall, where Honora ordered her daughter to skip luncheon in order to rest for the evening to come. The gown arrived just before tea, which Clara took in her room, and Radcliff managed to sneak two scones and a bit of clotted cream on to the tray. Delighted, Clara gave her maid a quick hug, embarrassing them both, but breaking the somber mood.

As Radcliff began reworking her hair with the new ribbons, Clara released a long sigh. "Mother is correct in one way."

Radcliff did not respond.

"I do seem to act as if I am marching off to an execution."

Her maid's eyes gleamed. "A reasonable response, in my eyes."

Clara smiled. "I suppose I should be thanking my heavenly stars, instead. The duke is considered quite a catch."

"No fisherman I know keeps every fish he reels in, my lady. Especially the ones who are not quite the catch they appear to be."

"You are a wicked influence, Radcliff."

"So I have been told."

As I thought! Clara's eyes met Radcliff's in the mirror. "Who has scolded you thus?"

The young girl shrugged.

"My mother's maid."

Another shrug. "She is my superior."

Clara glowered. "I know we have had our problems, but I prefer us to work those out between us. You may want to keep silent in my mother's presence, but not in mine. If I do not like what you say, I will tell you so."

"She tells me there are rules—"

"And you will learn them. But there are rules and there is what goes on between a lady and her maid. That side is private. Between them. Follow the rules where the house is concerned. Where I am concerned, you should listen only to me."

Radcliff slowly smiled. "She thinks you are too full of yourself."

"Ha! So I am. Which is none of her concern. Agreed?"

"Yes, my lady."

Clara stood. "Now, help me with this blasted gown."

The box rested on the bench at the foot of Clara's bed, and Radcliff lifted the lid, then frowned. She plucked a small piece of foolscap from within the box. "There is a note."

Clara took it, smiled, then read it to Radcliff. "If your mama needs a fitting before the ball, keep the dress as-is. After, look for the yellow threads on each side. A quick snip-snip and an inch will give. Still slim. More air. She will never know." She laughed as Radcliff pulled the gown from the box, spread it across the bed, and found the bright yellow threads basted into each side. A quick clip from Radcliff's scissors, and the threads slipped out of the fabric, revealing the more secure side seams in the bodice.

The gown still fit quite snuggly, but without the feeling of breathless restriction. The box also contained a light silk pelisse in cream and gold—intended to complement all of the duke's outfits for the season, cream silk gloves, and two copper-colored feathers for Clara's hair. The slippers remained a size too small, and her scalp still ached, but the overall effect was almost as magical as the modiste had promised.

As Clara descended the main stairs to the entrance, both her parents waited in the foyer, and her mother actually gave a quick smile before looking away to tug on her gloves. The earl, however, beamed, holding out a hand to assist her on the last few steps.

"You look magnificent, my child."

Your burdensome child. "Thank you, Papa. Madame Adrienne is quite the magician."

"Not at all. You are lovely."

Clara stared at him a moment, then looked away, unsure of what to say. Her father had always been kind, but never complimentary. "I—" She tried to take a deep breath but only managed a short cough. "I appreciate you saying so."

Honora spun on her heels. "Let us go, girl. We are later than usual." She marched out the front door and down the steps to the waiting carriage.

"Good luck," her father whispered as he released her hand.

The carriage ride was both mercifully short and silent, with Honora spending almost the entire trip staring out a window into the dark. She broke the silence only long enough to remind Clara of the importance of pleasing the duke. They arrived at the entrance of the Blackwell mansion just as a light sprinkle began to fall, which Clara knew would be the primary topic of conversation for the first hour. It was the first rain London had seen since the aberrant storm two weeks earlier, renewing hopes the summer drought had come to an end. Men would hope it would continue, watering parched country estates, while women would complain about what it would do to their hair. Her head still throbbed, but Clara realized she should probably be grateful for the new style, given the intent to impress a fussy duke.

Said duke waited for her, approaching just after she and Honora were announced. His face beamed as his gaze traveled over her, feathers to hem, and he gleefully took her hand when she offered it, his lips grazing the gloved knuckles. "Just as I anticipated, Lady Clara. We make for a matched pair."

She smiled as sweetly as she could manage. "Like a pair of matched bays for the ducal carriage."

"Clara!"

But the duke laughed, pulling her closer and tucking her arm into his as he escorted mother and daughter to a spot near the head of the dance floor. "Exactly so. Do you not think that a duke and duchess should lead their estate together, much as the crown fronts the ship of state?"

"I am not sure the king would relish being compared to a wooden figurehead."

"Oh, dear God," Honora muttered. But Wykeham's low chuckle seemed to pacify Clara's mother, who murmured something about ratafia and excused herself with a curtsy to the duke.

Wykeham paused and released Clara's arm. "I do look forward to evenings in your company," he said, *sotto voce*, as the orchestra began to tune their instruments. "But we should not spend too much of this night together."

Clara stepped away from him. "Other eggs to tend?"

He gave a single nod. "And other business. Men do more at these things than entertain the ladies."

"I have no doubts about that."

Wykeham held out his hand, and Clara lifted her arm, letting her dance card dangle before him. He pressed it into the palm of his hand and used the pencil attached with a narrow ribbon to add his scribbled name to two of the dances. He bowed as she curtsied, then turned away and disappeared into the crowd.

She peered at the card. He had claimed a cotillion and a quadrille. Safe. They would barely touch, much less converse, but she suddenly wondered who he would choose for the Scotch reel, his favorite dance. It would be telling, she thought, and definitely reveal which lady of the *ton* held the duke's eye as well. Business, he had said. He would be conducting "other business" at tonight's ball. Since Clara knew he saw their potential marriage as "business," she knew that if she paid attention, she would learn much more about the duke than he might expect.

She wandered through the expanding crowd, greeting several friends, most of whom complimented her on her new gown or hair style. Smiles broadened and she heard words like "lovely" and "beautiful." Two of her female friends pointed out how "elegant" she looked in the new style, although they stumbled over the word. She knew what they meant: thinner.

And more than ever, she wanted to hide. Her head hurt, her ribs ached, and her toes felt squashed. Clara moved farther away from the dancers, who had finished the first reel and were lining up for the next dance. She slipped in next to a potted fern on a tall pedestal. Since every move caused her pain in one place or another—and her mother had given her strict instructions about dancing with other men—Clara decided to play observer for most of the evening, staying away from both courtiers and tables of refreshment. With luck, Hadleyton and his friends would be missing from the limited invitation list.

As events of the season went, the Blackwell ball was a small-ish affair, one that Lord and Lady Blackwell held more out of obligation than enthusiasm. A former ambassador, Lord Blackwell had been a privy acquaintance of King George III, and his son a close associate of the Prince Regent, now George IV. Both royals had developed the rather unfortunate habit of showing up at Blackwell events unannounced, entourage in tow. The result was that the Blackwells felt obligated to host at least one ball each season, and since their home had only a moderately sized ballroom, they limited any event to two hundred guests— making it one of the most desired invitations of the season, despite a smaller orchestra and simpler decorations. Clara's fern, in its Grecian-themed pot with a few spotty orange ribbons, was one of the more elaborate displays of the evening.

Half-hidden behind the fronds, Clara watched as Wykeham circulated through several clusters of men, a peacock in full preen—wide smile, shoulders pressed back, ever-present cane at his side. The cane seemed more affectation than necessity at first, then, as he approached the terrace doors at the rear of the ballroom, he stumbled, catching himself with it. He limped once, twice, then paused and seemed to catch his breath, a bit of concern on his face as he looked around.

But no one seemed to be watching, except Clara.

He turned then and saw her, their eyes meeting across the expanse of the ballroom. He hesitated, then one side of his mouth curled up, he bowed slightly toward her, and he pivoted, disappearing out the terrace doors.

Why should I be surprised that a duke has secrets?

Those long winter nights felt more and more like an inevitable but interminable nightmare.

The crowd surged around Clara, ebbing and flowing as the fern acted as a rock in a stream, guiding them away from her. Few noticed the red-headed lady shadowed by the tall plant, and she watched the next two dances, comparing herself with the waiflike debutantes, then the older sisters who mingled, some obviously desperate for a dance. Their gowns sparkled with jewels and beading, their hair pleasantly coiffed with flowers, pins, padded combs, or stylish caps. For the first time, Clara almost felt as if she fit in, and she smoothed her skirt with one hand.

Amazing what money could do.

But in the back of her head, she could hear the frantic anger in her father's voice during their last row, the increasing frequency of his coughing bouts, and her mother's stern warning just before they exited the carriage tonight: "The duke is your last chance. Do not foul this."

They were hiding something from her, which was making them desperate. Whatever it was had caused this change in their attitudes toward her, and she fought the dread that lingered over the possibilities.

Clara sighed, which made her ribs ache, and tried to focus

again on the duke and her competing eggs.

"Why are you hiding?"

Clara yelped, jerking away from the fern and turning toward the baritone voice that had sounded in her ear.

Michael Ashton grinned. "It took me forever to spot you behind this plant. You blend right into it."

Clara looked around quickly, searching for her mother. Honora was nowhere in sight.

Michael also scanned the room. "For whom are we searching?"

"My moth—what are you doing here?" She lowered her voice. "I thought you were in Kent."

His smile widened. "I have been. But back now. I'm in the process of stirring up some business."

Business again. She was beginning to despise the very word. "How did you"—she dropped her voice to a whisper—"get an invitation? I thought they were hard to come by."

He bent toward her, matching her tone. "My brother may be disgraced, but my father is still a duke. And Blackwell cares less about Society's vagaries than you might think." He reached out and touched her dance card, fingering it almost affectionately. "You still have not answered the question. You should be dancing. Why are you hiding?"

"I—" Clara hesitated again, scouring the area around them. The clusters of nobles moved about, yet still no one seemed to pay them any mind.

Michael looked from the card to her, his dark eyes bright with glee. As usual, his evening kit was black on white, and his white waistcoat, entwined with black embroidered swirls, hugged his trim form. The handsome joy in his face urged her on, and she tried again. "New slippers. They—I am not used to them. Tripping again is a true risk."

He tilted his head to one side, his gaze focusing on her feet. "Why do you have new—" His brows furrowed and his expression tightened as his eyes traveled from her hem up to her bodice, pausing slightly at her waist, then her décolletage, finally to her face. "You look—" He swallowed.

Clara closed her eyes waiting for another lie cloaked in a compliment. *What would he come up with? Beautiful? Lovely?* She let out a sigh. *Thin?*

"Trussed."

Her eyes flew open. "I beg your pardon? *Trussed?*"

Michael pointed at the bodice. "Can you even breathe in that?"

Clara was not entirely sure whether to be insulted or relieved. She tried insulted first. "Lord Michael, I'll have you know that one of the finest modistes—"

"Has she never fitted you before?"

No. Insulted was not working. "Of course, she has. She made my only gown for this season, the one you saw at the Aldermaston ball."

"Which was lovely and fit you far more adequately." He paused, his eyes narrowing. "What do you mean that was your only gown for this season? What, pray tell, is this monstrosity?"

Monstrosity? "Lord Michael, you should not . . . it's just—"

He leaned closer, his mouth now a faint line. "Was this the duke's idea?"

She should be relieved, but Clara also felt more mortified. This was getting out of hand, and someone could easily hear his fresh talk to her. "You should not be talking to a lady like this."

"Ah, so, yes. He's the one who wanted you wrapped as if all your ribs were broken. To turn you into something you are not."

"Lord Michael, really—" But Clara looked at him closer as his cheeks darkened and his eyes widened, the glee turning to something darker. Anger.

Why is he angry?

He turned toward the dance floor, his gaze running along the outside walls.

"He is outside." With her voice low, she touched his arm. "Lord Michael. Please. I agreed to this."

Michael lowered his head a moment, then peered back at her. "You are in pain. I see it in your eyes."

"All women deal with some sort of pain in the name of beauty."

He winced. "Which is pure rubbish. He has no respect for your—" He glanced at her décolletage again, and his breath stalled. He scrubbed his mouth with one hand, looking around the room again. "He wants you on display. To show Society you are worthy of being his duchess." His head jerked toward the terrace doors. "I will kill him," he muttered.

Clara clutched his forearm, her chest tightening in desperation, her voice a low hiss. "Michael! You must stop! Please."

He looked back at her, drawing a ragged breath.

Her grip tightened. "You must listen. Wykeham is not Hadleyton. You cannot pick him up by his cravat and thrust him into the wall."

"In truth, I could," he whispered. "But so could a strong wind."

The image almost made Clara smile. "He would call you out. He's a duke. And you absolutely cannot—can*not*—thrust your family into more scandal."

He took a deep breath, and he seemed to relax a bit as his expression turned tender. "It would be worth it. You would be worth it."

She focused on his face, words escaping her again. *"You would be worth it."* She whispered his name.

Slowly he straightened, a smile creasing his face as he took a step away from her. "Perhaps," he whispered, "we should dance."

Clara shook her head. "I'm not supposed to—"

"I doubt your mother would stop us in the middle of a ball."

This time she did smile. "You know this is a risky proposition."

"The duke will call me out for dancing with you?"

The smile turned into a grin. "No. New dress. New slippers. I could very well trip us both onto a table of lemonade."

"I am not very good either. Perhaps between the two of us, we can manage one dance." Michael reached down and took her hand, tucking it into the crook of his elbow. "But if you fall, I will catch you. I will always catch you."

Clara's throat tightened, and whatever resistance she had crumbled. She glanced quickly at her dance card, and her words turned hoarse. "It is a Lancers Quadrille."

Michael's opposite hand covered hers. "Do you know it?"

"Barely."

"We will survive."

This time, she did laugh, allowing him to lead her onto the floor as the orchestra tuned again and settled for the start. They took their place in a square with three other couples. The ranking member of the group, and thus first gentleman of the dance, was a duke from the Lake District and his wife Sarah, a lady Clara had known for several years. She smiled at them although her husband looked somewhat askance at Michael.

"Ashton."

Michael bowed from the waist. "Embleton."

The duke glanced at Clara but spoke to Michael. "Behaving yourself?"

"Above reproach, Your Grace."

"Hm."

The second and third couples took their spots, with Michael and Clara taking position as fourth couple, which would give them a few moments to get their bearings. The music, a spritely tune led by the violins, lifted into the air, the partners bowed to each other, and the first lady stepped off, reaching for the hand of the second gentleman opposite her.

Her slippers pinched, but Clara found herself moving through the steps with more ease than she had expected. The bouncy steps, in-and-out and circles, the star shape left her a bit breathless but exhilarated. Each "return to partner" meant a tight grip from Michael's hand and a gleam in his eye as he focused on her face. He was a better dancer than he had led her to believe, his steps light and sure.

But as the dance ended, Clara saw the duke—who had seemed to favor his left arm during the dance—lean over and whisper something to Michael, whose face brightened with a smile. He gave the duke a sharp nod, and she saw his lips form the words "Monday" and "thank you" as he reached for her again. But her delight began to wane as he escorted her from the floor, dissipating entirely as her mother met them at the edge.

Honora glared at Michael but turned a quiet wrath on Clara, her words so low that even Clara barely heard them. But her expression left nothing to the imagination. "I spoke to you about this."

"Mother, I—"

"Release him."

Clara looked up at Michael, whose face had turned placid, immobile. "Michael—"

He slipped his arm away, took her hand, and kissed the tips of her fingers as he bowed to both of them. "Thank you, Lady Clara, for the dance. Lady Durham." He stepped backward and turned, disappearing into a cluster of gentlemen, most of whom greeted him with pleasant nods.

Honora gripped Clara's forearm with an unexpected force, leaning forward to whisper, "I told you to stay away from him!"

Clara jerked away. "Am I to disrespect the son of a duke on the ballroom floor?"

"You could have declined the dance. You have certainly done it before."

The reference to Hadleyton felt like slap. "And you know how that turned out."

"Wykeham is watching you."

"He has been on the terrace for the past three dances, Mother. He's conducting business and taking stock of the other women he is courting. He could not care less about me dancing with another man."

"He certainly will care about you dancing with Michael Ashton. He told you to stay away from him." Honora paused and some of the color drained from her cheeks. "What other women?"

"You know he warned me to stay away from Lord Michael but not that he is courting more than one woman? It was all part of the same conversation."

Honora stared at her daughter. "What other women?"

"I was trying to find out when Lord Michael asked me to dance. That is why I know the duke is still on the terrace." She lifted her dance card and turned it toward her mother. "Wykeham claimed his two dances—"

"It would be improper for him to claim more."

"So I planned to see who else he danced twice with. I did not expect Lord Michael to be here, much less ask me to dance. No one else has, for which I am grateful."

Honora frowned. "Why are you grateful?"

"Because these slippers are pure misery."

"Small feet are more attractive."

"Small shoes on large feet are agony. I will not do this again."

"You will if he asks it of you."

Clara slowly shook her head. "No. If having small feet is a requirement of marriage to him, then we had better end this now."

All the color left Honora's face, but her eyes narrowed, turning dark, and her fists clenched at her side. "You had best be grateful we are in public. Your insolence will not be tolerated."

"Why, my dear, how fortunate to find the two of you together!" Wykeham's sing-song voice came from over Clara's shoulder. Neither woman had seen him approach.

Honora transformed in an instant, a wide smile splitting her face as she curtsied to the duke. "Your Grace. It is a pleasure to see you again."

Clara turned and mirrored the curtsy. "Your Grace."

Wykeham reached for her hand, kissing the back of it lightly. "My dear, I believe our cotillion is coming up shortly."

Clara did her best to look demure, lowering her eyes. "Yes, Your Grace."

"But as it is yet a dance away"—he turned to Honora—"I hoped Lady Durham would honor me with a trip around the floor."

Her mother's eyebrows shot up and her cheeks reddened. "Me, Your Grace?"

"Yes, indeed. This is the Scotch reel, my favorite dance." He winked at Clara even as he spoke to her mother. "You will be the perfect partner."

Honora actually stuttered. "I—why, it has been years, but I—yes, Your Grace. I would be honored."

His responding smile made Clara's skin prickle. He held out his arm, and Honora took it. She put a hand to her cheek, clearly flustered, as he led her in among the other dancers, who parted around them. One of the highest-ranking nobles in the room was about to dance, and they all waited to see where he would stand. Around the edges, heads turned, and tongues wagged, carefully hidden behind fans and hands.

Wykeham smiled at Clara over her mother's shoulder, a sly, wicked expression that told her exactly what he was doing. Her mother had been on his side in this campaign before. Now she would be relentless. And the rest of the dancers would immediately recognize his intent toward Clara. An eligible duke did not randomly dance with a married countess unless something else was afoot. He had indeed seen her dancing with Michael Ashton, and his response was to lay a clearer, broader claim.

Business, my arse, Clara thought. *He's playing politics, even with my own mother.*

Without looking, she could feel people in the room shifting to look from the dancers to her. And Clara knew, without a doubt, that that interminable nightmare had already begun.

CHAPTER ELEVEN

Friday, 19 August 1825
The Blackwell ball
Half-past ten in the evening

MICHAEL WATCHED, HIS anger tamped down to an ember's burn, as Clara's face moved through a half-dozen tight expressions in response to her mother's harsh words. Although he could not hear Honora's voice, the fury in her eyes shone like flinted sparks. He saw Wykeham saunter through the mass of people, his simpering steps precisely lined up so neither woman could see him approach. The sly smile on the man's face made Michael's gut roil, and he fought the urge to swoop Clara up and take her far away from this place and those people.

And exactly where would you go in the wake of such an action? Scotland? The south seas? India?

Michael growled under his breath. The voice of reason in his head sounded a lot like Robert, but he knew it was his own good sense breaking through the anger, the intense desire to protect Clara.

"Ashton?"

"Yes?" Michael pivoted around and froze as he spotted Matthew Rydell, the Duke of Embleton, who had been on the dance floor as their first couple. He bowed his head. "Apologies, Your

Grace."

Embleton smiled. "I'm not sure what scheme you and your brother—"

"I assure you it is no scheme, my lord. We are not—"

Embleton held up a hand, and Michael stopped. "Whatever your goals, the progress you have made in the last sennight has been remarkable. Everyone is talking." He stepped a bit closer. "Making your first purchases from the estate in Kent was brilliant. You solidified a good relationship with a neighbor, and the gossip spread like wildfire. I knew you were coming to visit me even before you sent the request."

A tinge of worry hit the back of Michael's mind. "But you will still bring the two geldings and the black stallion to Tattersall's Monday?"

A curt nod. "Of course. I have to admit, I was curious about why you wanted to do the sale there instead of privately, and why do it now. An auction could drive up the price, and the geldings are not yet ready for the track. But it did not take long for me to decipher that you want the price and your interest public."

"I think it will also benefit your stables to see the quality of your stock."

"You do not strike me as being that altruistic."

Michael grinned. "No. But it cannot hurt my position for the other traders to see that you have some of the finest thoroughly bred horses in all of England. To see I recognize that and how I bid."

"So we will be washing each other's backs, so to speak."

"Indeed."

Embleton glanced at the dance floor, and Michael followed his gaze. He stiffened as he realized Wykeham had led Honora Durham out for a dance, and the duke cut a gaze at him. "Does all of this have anything to do with your lovely dance partner?"

Michael's teeth ground. "Possibly."

"Hm." Embleton leaned a little closer. "Do not take Wykeham for granted."

Michael looked at him. "Sir?"

Embleton, a veteran of the Napoleonic wars who reminded Michael of his father, both in age and wisdom, looked out over the dance floor again. "He appears to be a simpering pink, but it is a façade. He is far wilier than that, and his goal is always about gaining more power. His machinations in Parliament are legendary. If he is determined to marry Lady Clara—and according to all rumors, he is—he will not take competition gracefully. He wants Durham's favor in Parliament. He is also an experienced duelist, and despite current protocol, is still prone to take umbrage at the least slight." The marquess stepped back. "Now. I must find my wife, Lord Michael. Good luck to you, and I will see you Monday."

Michael bowed. "Your Grace."

As Embleton weaved his way through the crush, Michael looked back at the dancers. The tune ended and Wykeham escorted Lady Durham back to the edge and claimed Clara for a dance. Although her mother appeared flushed and joyous, Clara looked as if she were marching to the gallows, her eyes down. Wykeham spoke to her, but Clara barely nodded a response.

The cotillion began and Michael watched the duke bounce in step beside Clara. With a start, Michael realized that the color of her gown matched the accents on Wykeham's topcoat and waistcoat, and he knew he had been correct—the gown that so painfully re-formed her had been the duke's idea. *Rufus marks his territory with more subtlety.* A petty thought, but Michael didn't care. Yet he would not ignore Embleton's words either: *"Do not take Wykeham for granted . . . his goal is always about gaining more power."* The man might not be subtle, but he was devious. It would not do to become the man's enemy. A different tack would be needed.

As the cotillion ended, the duke returned Clara to her mother, then searched the floor until his eyes met Michael's, a move Michael had waited for. When the man smirked, Michael bowed from the waist, then mouthed the words, *She's yours.*

The smirk became a grin. *Of course.*

Another bow. Then Michael pivoted and headed for the front of the mansion. He needed air and a lot of it. Instead of waiting for his carriage, he strode toward the line of parked vehicles near the back of the house. He found the Kennet carriage completely blocked in. He released the coachman to return to Ashton House whenever he could find a way out, then Michael walked back to Berkeley Square, his long legs making quick work of it. The earlier rain had left the air, if not entirely fresh, somewhat cooler and cleaner than in the recent summer drought. He took long, deep breaths, which helped clear his head. But still lost in his thoughts, he was not quite prepared to return home. The nagging restlessness Michael had felt since a child had returned in full force, pulling at his spirit, making him want—something—he was never sure what. A deep yearning for something . . . *more.*

He made a second circle around the square, then aimed his steps farther afield, relishing the sounds of the night—wheels on cobblestone, the occasional call of one voice or another, tinny echoes of a pianoforte from this house or that, the varied chirps and whistles of a nightingale.

A memory hit Michael with lightning clarity, and his steps slowed. Home from school for the Christmas holiday, he had sneaked his pony out of the stables and set off for a wild gallop across the fields. It had been cold, the midnight air slicing through his clothes and chilling him to his very marrow. But he barely felt it, the exhilaration far more consuming as he pushed the pony harder and faster than he had ever been allowed to by his father or the grooms. The darkness of the countryside had turned the stars to diamonds, the Milky Way—*Caer Gwydion*, according to the Welsh—a bright fire in the sky. When he finally halted his mount at the top of a steep hill, he stared up at the display before him. In that moment, the unfathomable restlessness had lifted, and Michael had felt a happiness he had seldom known before or since. A moment he had never shared with anyone, not even

Eleanor. He had wanted to, but the time to share such a thing needed to be special—and that had never come to him since that night.

It had cemented his love of horses, although he realized now it had been a pure miracle that they had not both been killed. Horses, he knew now, had been his life all along; he had simply refused to acknowledge it in the wake of all that had happened to him. Horses—and the brilliant fire of the midnight sky.

This has to work.

Michael stopped, looking up, but in London few stars were visible, even in this part of town. Even on relatively fog-free nights a haze hung over the city, obscuring all but the brightest points of light. Still, the memory left him feeling emboldened. He needed advice, most likely from his father, who would have insights on business, horses, members of Parliament, power—and women.

Tonight, Michael had recognized the danger Wykeham represented, and not just to his courtship of Clara Durham. His attempts to build his reputation as a horseman—a businessman who dealt wisely with horses, the way the Tattersall family did— were on sketchy ground. A noble with the power of the Duke of Wykeham could blow to flinders any of Michael's efforts.

Thus, Michael's apparent surrender of Clara Durham to the "greater" man. Public versus private. To all observers, Clara would be the duke's to win or lose. But Michael had seen the look in her eyes as he had partnered her in the quadrille, a light as bright as any star as she gazed at him. He had also watched that beautiful gleam fade into an impassive expression, dull and placid, as her mother had harangued her and the duke had taken over the evening.

He would do anything it took, whatever it took, to return that spark. He *would* find a way.

Saturday, 20 August 1825
Beckcott Hall
Half-past midnight

EVERYTHING ACHED. HER head. Her feet. Her ribs. Even Clara's fingers seemed to throb, most likely the result of clenching her fists at her side to keep from screaming. But it was finally over, thank God, and she sank back against the cushions of the carriage in pure relief. Even Honora seemed exhausted, limp against the carriage door, her eyes closed. But she was not asleep.

"You almost ruined the evening, you realize. Dancing with that man."

Clara's patience had evaporated. "He is a lord. His father is a duke. His family is nobility."

"A family steeped in scandal."

"Which will pass. I do not think it wise for either of us to insult the Duke of Kennet's son. Like it or not, Kennet wields more power than Wykeham."

Her mother opened one eye. "But you were not dancing with Kennet, were you? Just his *third* son. Who will inherit *nothing*. It is merely a matter of time before he joins the military or the church. Or takes up some godforsaken profession."

"God forfend."

Honora opened the other eye. "You enjoyed dancing with the duke. I could tell."

"I enjoyed dancing, yes."

Her mother closed her eyes again. "Clara, it is well after midnight. I am far too fatigued to continue this."

Good.

"We will talk this afternoon. Despite your displeasure with the duke and your obvious infatuation with Michael Ashton, this is a good course for you. A proper position and a secure future."

I thought you were tired.

"Eventually you will understand that happiness is a myth born of fairy tales and nursery rhymes."

Clara studied her mother. "Have you never been happy?"

Honora remained silent several minutes. "Sunday afternoon, we will have tea with the dowager duchess."

Clara blinked. "Wykeham's mother?"

"Yes. She is in Town to host a soiree at their townhome. She wants to meet you."

The numbness in Clara's toes seemed to spread upward. "I—"

Honora waved a hand. "This afternoon. We will speak this afternoon."

Clara held her tongue in the face of a useless situation, and an odd grief settled over her, a sense of helplessness. She had known—had always known *intellectually*—that as a lady of the *ton*, she had no real control over her life. Yet some semblance of hope that she could find a path—a husband—that would suit her had been entrenched in her heart. A hope now wrenched free and tossed onto the fire, for a hidden reason she could not understand. Tears clustered at the corners of her eyes and her nose stung, but she swallowed hard and dabbed away the tears.

They arrived home, silently entered Beckcott Hall, and trudged up the stairs. But Clara paused at her bedchamber door, waiting until her mother's door had closed. She pushed her own door open, slipping inside as the first tears leaked from her eyes. She needed to get out, to get away, to find a place of solace where she could collect her thoughts.

But first she had to get out of these blasted shoes.

Clara lifted one foot, then the other, chucking the awful slippers to the far side of her bed. She grabbed her favorite day boots from the dressing room, sighing in relief as she tucked her feet inside the soft, well-worn leather. Her sorrow eked into rage as she headed for the servants' stairs, padding as quietly as possible on the treads, the train of the dress and her pelisse trailing after her. Illuminated only by a lamp near the bottom, the stairs felt familiar and warm, as Clara often took this route to the gardens with Pockets tucked in her skirt. But the kitten was not the solace she sought tonight. She needed more—more weight, more fur, more muscle. She eased out the back entrance and used the distant glow from the streetlamps of Berkeley Square's primary avenues to wend her way through the alleys to the mews of Ashton House. She lifted the latch on the stable door as quietly as she could, then lit a waiting lantern near the door. She closed the door and lifted the light, whispering softly, "Rufus?"

Silence.

She took a few more steps, noting the horses in the darkened stalls along the way. The four blacks she had seen pulling the Kennet ducal carriage seemed to be asleep, taking no note of her passage. Likewise the two matched grays that had pulled their landau in the park.

"Rufus?"

A faint meow echoed from one of the far stalls. Copper's. Michael's favorite mount and the big barn cat seemed to be old friends. As she headed that way, she realized the big cat perched confidently on top of the narrow stall door. He looked at her, meowed again, and she ran the last few steps. Hanging the lantern on a nearby hook, she scooped Rufus into her arms.

The cat had to weigh almost twenty pounds, one of the largest she had ever seen, solid and warm in her arms. He hissed once, as if to remind her he was not, in fact, a timid house cat, then his innards rumbled with a loud purr. She stroked him, and he curled around her shoulder and neck as if he were made for this.

A shuffling sounded in the stall, and Copper hung his head over the door with a welcoming nod.

"Thank you," she whispered to the horse, shifting Rufus to hold him with one arm and stroking Copper's nose with the other, leaning into the horse's strong neck. Sandwiched between cat and horse, Clara sighed, feeling the grief, the despair . . . the tears . . . leech away. "I don't care what they say." She pressed her face against Copper. "This is where I belong."

Another shuffling sound came from within Copper's stall, even though the horse stood absolutely still. Clara looked up to see a top hat rise from behind Copper's back and trace along his rump. Michael Ashton appeared, staring at her, eyebrows arched. "If I had known my cat was such a draw for the ladies, I would have engaged him in my efforts sooner."

Clara's gut tightened and every muscle seemed immovable. "What—what are you doing here?"

"Apparently the same thing you are. Finding comfort with the animals. But may I ask, why not your own stable?"

Clara took a shallow, ragged breath. "I was not allowed to bring Aethelred." She nuzzled the orange fur. "And we don't have Rufus."

"Aethelred?"

"My horse."

Michael stepped closer, his hand idly stroking Copper's back. "You named your horse for a Saxon king?"

"He is quite regal."

"I have no doubt."

Clara gave a slight smile and nuzzled the big cat again.

"The last time you were here, Rufus did seem to bring you a great deal of comfort."

She nodded.

"That he tolerates you in this way is nothing short of a miracle. Good mouser, but he will not let any of us touch him. Takes absolute umbrage at being petted."

Clara swallowed. Michael's low voice seemed to relax her, almost like Rufus's purr. "Perhaps he simply does not like men."

Michael grinned. "As good an explanation as I have heard." The grin faded to a slight smile. "Or perhaps he knows you need him."

She wrapped both arms around the cat, who shifted but purred louder. "I did. I do."

"I apologize if my desire to dance with you created problems."

The soft confession shook every emotion Clara had been fighting, and she trembled, burying her cheek against Rufus again.

The tears sprang into her eyes again, and this time she could not stop them. "But I wanted to. It was the finest moment in the entire evening." She bit her lower lip, but the sob still escaped, sounding far too loud in the quiet stable.

Michael's eyes widened. "Oh, my darling!" He pushed out of the stall, forcing her to move back.

Clara stumbled, losing her grip on Rufus, who pushed off her chest and dove for the ground. Michael caught her shoulders and pulled her hard against him, wrapping his arms around her as his hat toppled to the floor. The hug felt like being enveloped in a hot blanket and she collapsed against him, the tears soaking the black and white cloth covering his chest. He held her, murmuring nonsense against her temple until the deluge eased. She sniffled and looked up at him. "I seem to do this a lot."

He smiled. "Cry into my waistcoat?" When she nodded, he stroked her cheek with one finger, brushing away a tear. "If it gets you into my arms, I cannot despise it too much. I do wish you were not in such pain."

She shrugged, that annoying sense of despair trying to capture her again, even over his words. "It cannot be prevented."

His brows furrowed as he studied her. After a moment, he looked around, as if a herd of stable boys were about to appear. He looked behind her, then eased out of her arms, holding on to one hand. "Perhaps I can help."

Michael opened the stall door across from Copper's and held his arm wide. "Step into my parlor."

Clara blinked, peering into the stall, sadness giving way to curiosity. "In there?"

He nodded. "It is clean, I promise you. This stall and two others were scrubbed just today, with fresh hay put down. We are preparing to bring on more horses Monday."

Curiosity stronger than caution, Clara entered the stall. Michael, scooped up his top hat, stepped in, and closed the door. He balanced the hat upside down on the narrow edge of the door then looked at her. "Slip off your pelisse." She did, watching as he draped it over the door next to his hat. "Now turn around. Face away from me."

Her eyes narrowed. "Michael?"

"I'm going to loosen that blasted dress."

She stepped backward, staring at him, a tinge of fear spiking in her gut. "You cannot! You cannot undress me! Not here."

"I do not intend to undress you—as much as I would like to. I do want to see you take one good deep breath. Why is it so tight anyway?"

She shook her head. "It was supposed to be even tighter—"

"Tighter? Why the devil—"

"The duke is concerned that I am too—" She swallowed. "Too—"

"Too what?"

"Round."

"So I was right. He wants you on display."

Clara winced, and Michael's teeth ground, his cheeks darkening. "Turn around."

Slowly she did, shivering as his fingers found the laces at the back of the gown. "My chemise and stays will show."

"Your pelisse will cover them."

He kept working, and Clara felt the dress give away. Then his hands moved up again and she realized he meant to unlace her stays. "Michael!" She twisted, but he placed both hands on her shoulders, keeping her faced away from him.

He took a deep breath and kissed her temple. "Listen to me," he whispered, then he kissed the lobe of her ear, and a wash of desire flooded her.

"I should not—"

"The duke is a fool, and apparently your mother as well. Some men"—he kissed her temple again—"want more than a wraith in a silk dress. They want more." His lips brushed her shoulder. "More here." His hands slid down her sides. "And here." They came to rest on her hips. "And especially here."

Clara shuddered, his hands like fire, even through her clothes.

"I do not believe—"

"I do not lie. Men discuss such things more than women would like to think. We like to take comfort in a woman's body as well as pleasure. A woman should be more than a dowry and a legacy." One hand caressed her stomach as the other cupped one of her breasts, and her breath caught.

"Michael—"

"And there is great comfort in a woman who comes to a man with more."

"You make me sound like an overstuffed pillow."

Michael snorted a laugh. "You are most definitely not an overstuffed pillow. Unfortunately, I am not a wordsmith. Not a poet. Even if I were, when I am with you, words become a complete jumble in my head. I become desperate to show you more than tell you." The hand on her stomach slipped downward to caress her upper thigh, his fingertips pressing in on the fabric of her skirt.

Clara's breath turned ragged, and she gasped, needing air she could not pull in.

"Another reason you need to be able to breathe freely," he whispered. He returned to her stays. They loosened quickly and she sucked in a deep gasp. He pulled her against him again, and his strength and warmth filled her with the very solace she had longed for.

She stroked his forearm as she took several deep breaths. "Thank you."

"Oh, I am far from finished, Lady Clara."

She twisted to look up at him, her curiosity spiking again. "Whatever do you mean?"

His eyes gleamed as he turned her to face him. "May I take down your hair?"

Her eyes narrowed. "Are you trying to seduce me, sir?"

He shrugged one shoulder, a sly smile twisting his mouth. "Perhaps. Is it working?"

She laughed. "Perhaps. Why my hair?"

"Because it looks uncomfortable."

"It is."

He sombered, shaking his head slowly. "Lady Clara, I have made no secret that I would like to court you." He ran one finger along the edge of her neckline. "That I would like to be close to you. Bed you." His finger trailed up her neck and touched her lips, a move Clara found mesmerizing. "But no one should ever make you this uncomfortable. There should be limits on what you bear for the sake of beauty."

"Women do so all the time."

"I do not care. You should not. You are beautiful as you are."

And for the first time in her life, Clara believed the words. "Thank you."

He urged her to move closer to the door, then reached up and removed the first pins and combs, dropping them, one by one, into his top hat. The hairstyle came down much faster than it went up, and as the tension in her scalp eased, Clara let out a soft whimper. Michael's teeth ground again and his hands moved faster. As the last ribbon slid free and her curls bounced loose around her head and shoulders, he fluffed the curls out, running his hands through them several times before entwining his fingers into the locks, tugging her closer. He focused on her, his eyes darkening. "I love your hair. Soft. Wild. Free. Like you."

The focus of his eyes on her face stilled her, settling a calm in her spirit. As she whispered his name, his lips brushed hers, a feather touch, then he pulled her against his chest again, his arms a comforting warmth around her. She could hear the soft thumps of his heart, feel each rise and fall of his breathing. His voice rumbled deep in his chest as he murmured her name. This was a peace such as she had never known, and in that moment, Clara dearly wished it could last forever.

Although she knew it could not. She should release him. Walk away. But this place, in his arms, against his body, felt like home.

"Clara?" Her name was soft on his lips, and she leaned back

enough to look up at him. He stroked her face. "May I kiss you? Truly kiss you?"

A tinge of confusion touched her mind. Had he not already done so? The last time they had met in this stable, his touch had made her heart sing, her body flush with desire. Had that not been a true kiss?

She also knew she should shake her head. Refuse him. Step back . . .

"Yes."

His smile was slight, gentle. "Hold on to my waist, my darling. Hold on until you cannot. And I will catch you."

CHAPTER TWELVE

Saturday, 20 August 1825
The Ashton House stables
One in the morning

M ICHAEL'S WORLD NARROWED to a single pair of lips, rosy pink and perfect. A natural bow with a delicate arch in the middle, a moue begging to be kissed. Round and full . . . more.

He cupped Clara's face in both his hands, his palms firm against her cheeks as his long fingers brushed her hairline. He tilted her head slightly, his lips making a feather pass over that perfect bow . . . once . . . twice. He paused a moment then pressed his mouth against hers for a few seconds before his lips parted, and he pulled on her lower lip, a slow caress he repeated over and over, each time tugging harder. He repeated this with her upper lip, and his thumbs stroked her cheeks and his fingers slid along her jaw.

When he pressed his tongue against the sweet line of her mouth, urging her to open, a tiny whimper echoed in her throat as she did, and her fingers dug into his waist. His tongue delved into her mouth as if each touch were a new and unproven sensation, and the fire that had kindled in his loins flared, sending a flash of desire up through his chest. He gave a low moan as he hardened, and his fingers pushed farther into her hair, entwining into the curls, holding her tightly, tugging on the thick strands.

He explored her mouth with slow, firm strokes, and Clara began to shiver under his touch, pressing her body harder against him. He became almost painfully rigid, and he ached for her with a longing he had not felt in years. More than his physical need, his very soul wanted to consume her.

Michael gently broke the kiss, and a quiet, mewled, "No," escaped her.

"Patience, my love," and one hand traced the tender line of her face, soft touches that he followed with his mouth, flicking his tongue against her jawline, slipping it down toward her ear, where he seized the lobe between his teeth and tugged.

Clara writhed, melding against him, her back arching, as his whispery kisses moved down her neck, then her shoulder, to the edge of her gown. His fingers pushed it off her shoulder, and he nuzzled the hollow beneath her collarbone. His hand cupped her breast, squeezing it as his thumb found the swelling tip of her nipple. He swirled around it as he tugged her dress away, and she sighed.

Then Michael closed his thumb and forefinger around the taut bud with a sudden pinch. Clara gasped and her knees gave way, her hands falling from his waist as his name burst from her in a hoarse cry as she clawed at his chest. With a grin, he caught her, easing her down onto the fresh hay. He lay beside her, propping on one elbow, and watched her face as he again traced the neckline of her gown with the back of his fingers. Her breath came in quick gasps, causing her breasts to push up against the fabric. Her cheeks glowed, and a light scent of lavender and roses blended with the cleaner scent of the hay. Her eyes were half-lidded as she searched his face.

"Do you wish me to stop?" he asked, one finger skidding lightly over the mounds of her breasts, pausing at the edge of the exposed nipple.

She shook her head slowly. "That was . . . remarkable. And scandalous." She took in a long breath. "I have never felt—" She stopped, resting a hand against his neck.

He chuckled. "I want to make you feel like a queen."

She stilled and continued to study him. "Michael, the duke—"

He cupped her face. "Cannot know."

"But he would withdraw—"

"And he would do whatever he could to destroy both our families. We cannot let that happen. He cannot know as long as . . . not until we know . . ." He looked away, his heart aching against his intellect. He could not accept, not in this moment, that his Clara would go to another man.

She touched his cheek, then pushed a lock of hair behind his ear. "But you are the one I want. No matter what."

Michael looked back at her, then took a strand of her hair between his thumb and forefinger, twisted it, then drew it down over her shoulder, his eyes following the long red curl. He kissed the tip of it. "Clara—"

Her hand pressed harder against him, her fingers clutching his hair. "I do not want him, Michael. I want you. I do not care if he—"

He kissed her, a brief touch. "You must, Clara. His power is not to be trifled with. And there is so much at risk."

Her eyes clouded. "You are afraid of him?"

Michael moved over her, easing his legs between hers, letting his hard shaft press against her. He sighed, his fingers glazing over her neck again. "It is not about fear." He nestled his hips into hers. "It is about our future. Both of ours. I want to best him, yes, to win you. But in the right way—one that will leave you safe and secure." He kissed her, a soft but thorough kiss. She arched against him, an insistent pleading with her body, and Michael's resistance began to tremble.

"Then we will do what is necessary. Out there." Her voice softened. "But what do you want of me now? Here," she whispered. "Truly want. Please tell me."

He gazed down at her, his hesitancy about his need for her, what he truly desired of her, waning. "I want—" his voice broke, his words clogged.

"Tell me."

"I want to claim you—"

Her fingers tightened in his hair, and her other hand squeezed his shoulder.

"I want to make you mine. I want—"

A thud sounded on the stall door, and Michael's top hat hit the ground with a soft thump, scattering combs and pins across the hay-covered floor. Both of them yelped, and Michael was on his feet in a second, staring at the orange tabby perched on the top edge of the door. The cat's long tail swooped back and forth, annoyance in every swath. "Rufus!"

Still sprawled on the floor, Clara began to giggle. She rolled to her side, covering her mouth with one hand, and her entire body shook.

"This is not funny!" Michael hissed. His erection ached at the sudden shift, pushing against his clothes, and he reached down to adjust himself, deflation already in process. "Clara!"

She sat up, continuing to giggle behind one hand as she straightened her gown and tucked away her exposed breast. Her cheeks seemed to glow a bright pink in the dim light, and her eyes gleamed with mirth. She caught a breath. "Yes, it is."

He glared at her but could not hold the anger at either her or the cat long. He reached out to stroke the cat, who snarled and hissed, setting off another spurt of giggles from Clara, who now pushed to her feet.

"I tell you, he just does not like men."

"The same men who feed—"

"Hello? Is anyone there?"

The young male voice echoed down the hall of the stable, and Clara's eyes widened as she clamped off her snickers. Michael held a finger to his lips as he nudged Rufus off the door, then eased out of the stall.

At the far end, one of the younger stable boys lifted a lantern higher. "Lord Michael?"

"I did not mean to disturb you. I hope I did not wake the others. I am just back from the ball and wanted to check on a few things."

The boy, who could not have been more than ten, gave a quick tilt of his head. "You didn't, my lord. We just wondered if it was that cat or if somebody had done snuck in."

We. Damn it. "Mostly the cat, I'm afraid. He likes Copper. Not me so much."

The boy's brow furrowed as he glanced at Copper, who stood placidly in the stall across the hall.

Across the hall. Michael smothered the vulgarity on his lips. "You can go back to bed, lad. I'll make sure everything is secure as I leave."

The boy hesitated, then gave another quick tilt of his head. "Yes, my lord."

Michael waited until the boy disappeared up the narrow steps leading to the sleeping quarters on the second floor, which housed not only the stable boys but the coachmen and grooms— who definitely would have known what was going on had they heard Clara's voice in the middle of the night. He looked around at Rufus, who had returned to his perch on Copper's door. "Behave yourself."

The cat hissed.

Michael slipped back into the stall to see Clara gathering a few last pins off the floor and dropping them into a pocket in her skirt.

"Won't those poke you?" he asked, his voice barely above a whisper.

She adjusted the gown again, and he could see that both side pockets bulged. "Not if I'm careful. Remember I am used to walking with a squirmy kitten tucked away."

He pulled the pelisse off the door and went to her. "Clara—"

She put a finger to his lips as she shook her head. "We were foolish to attempt anything in a stable with all sorts of staff above us." She paused, tilting her head, and she grinned. "At least it was not Lord Robert this time. Although I see you have as much difficulty talking to the servants as I do. I'm sure the duke would have simply ordered the boy back upstairs."

"As if *that* would raise no gossip among them."

The touch on his mouth lightened, and she pushed up on her toes, replacing her finger with her lips, a feathery touch that made him shiver and want more. He draped the pelisse around her shoulders, then pulled her into his arms. "I will find a way. I promise. I don't know how or where or when, but I will claim you as my own."

She leaned against him, the side of her face resting on his chest. "I believe you. And please remember this is the hope I need to get me through this."

Michael held her like that for a long time, just breathing in the scent of her, feeling her warmth seep through his clothes. Her hair felt like silk against his jaw, and he closed his eyes, his mind envisioning a time when he could hold her like this in his bed, her skin satiny against his as he caressed her. A time dependent on so many things changing for both of them. "Clara—"

Clara leaned back and gazed at him. The pure adoration in her eyes sank into his very soul, welding him to the spot. Whatever he had been going to say fled from his thoughts. He merely stared at her, taking her in.

After several moments, her smile widened. "I should return home."

"I will walk with you. It is not safe—"

"I have two pockets full of pins and combs. I could take on an entire army of thieves."

He shook his head and released her, stepping back. "I do believe you would try. I have seldom met a woman less likely to swoon in the face of trouble."

"Especially now that I can breathe again."

"But I'm still going to walk with you. At least as far as your back gate."

She secured her pelisse around her, then pulled her hair free from the collar and let it cascade down her back. "Then lead on, sirrah."

He grinned and peered over the door. The stable boy had gone, so Michael donned his top hat and pushed the door open. Their steps light, they exited the stable, dowsing the lanterns and securing the door. He held out his hand and she took it as he led her through the alleys round the edge of the square. Near the back entrance to the Beckcott Hall yard, he paused, squeezing her hand one more time. He kissed her temple, then whispered again, "I *will* find a way."

She nodded, touched his cheek, then disappeared through the gate. Michael watched the closed wooden slates for several minutes, listening for the latch on the servants' door.

Silence closed around him for a short moment, then he heard wheels—more carriages returning from the ball—the calls of coachmen and hackney drivers to their horses. The song of a nightingale. A faint whiff of baking bread reached him—a cook already preparing for the next day. This was the time of year when the servants barely rested as the nobility moved from one event to another, sleeping until noon before heading out again to soirees, calls, and musicales.

Michael strode back to his own home, entering through the front and heading for the stairs. Two steps up, however, the light sound of voices caught his attention, and he backed down, looking down the hall toward his father's study. A light shone from under the door, and Michael headed for it. His quick rap on the door stopped the voices, and the door opened.

Robert stood there and his eyebrows arched. "Talk of the devil." He moved backward and gestured for Michael to enter.

"I thought you were going to stay in Kent."

"I changed my mind."

"Why?"

Robert pointed into the room and Michael slowly stepped inside, an unexpected wariness building in his gut. The Kennet clan did not gather in the middle of the night for no reason. Philip

Ashton, the Duke of Kennett sat behind his desk, his face drawn with shadows but his eyes alert. His wife's illness had disturbed the heart of the family and exhausted the duke, but he seemed to be returning to his old self with gradual and graceful progress. Stacks of papers, folders, and ledgers, like orderly rows of soldiers, lined the edges of the desk. As the weather remained too warm for fires, even at night, the fireplace opposite Philip's desk sat cold and empty, and the two wingbacks that normally faced the flames had been turned toward the desk.

In one, Thomas Ashton, the oldest of the three brothers sat, reviewing a sheath of papers. Thomas had taken on the burden of running the estate in this first month following Emalyn's apoplexy, and he remained more partner than son to the duke. As Michael entered the room, Robert shut the door and dropped down into the other wingback, stretching his long legs out in front of him.

Michael focused on his father. "Why am I the devil?"

Philip took a deep breath. "Because we were discussing your ambition to go into competition with Tattersall's. Which, of course, you cannot."

Michael glanced at the three men again. "Whyever not?"

Thomas continued to study the papers as he spoke. "Because you do not have the resources or the backing. Or the history. Or the trust among the peers."

"I know it takes time but—"

"You only have two months." Robert shrugged one shoulder.

Michael glared at him. "What did you tell them?"

"Enough," said Thomas.

Philip held out his hand, palm toward Michael. "Just listen a few moments." He gestured toward a cabriolet armchair closer to the desk. "Sit."

Michael did, placing his top hat on the floor next to the chair.

Philip pointed to the papers in Thomas's hand. "Robert brought us your plan and your budget, and we've been reviewing it, waiting for your return. Booth had orders to send you to us, should you go to your bedchamber first."

Michael turned his ire on Robert again. "You said you would wait."

His older brother looked uncharacteristically subdued as he rested his hands on his thighs. "Please listen."

Thomas neatened the sheath, stood, and handed it to his father. "Actually, little brother, we were all a bit surprised. The plans are quite well put together. Ambitious and expensive but impressive." He sat down again.

"I am not a complete dolt."

Robert snorted but stilled when Thomas scowled at him. Thomas then studied Michael. "No one truly thought you were." He leaned back in the chair. "But you have had some difficult years."

Robert smirked. *"Difficult years?"*

Philip rested his forearms against the edge of his desk. "Robert."

Robert held his arms wide in mock innocence. "It is hardly a secret."

Michael tamped down his temper but focused on Robert. "Why would you do this?"

Robert's damaged face calmed. "Because Thomas and I have learned the hard way that this family is stronger together than when each of us goes his own way. We need each other."

Silence settled on the four men, leaving only the mantel clock's ticking to echo around the room. Michael looked from his brothers to his father, trying to ignore the annoyance that this discussion had started without him. "What do you have in mind?"

Philip spoke first. "Would you consider going parallel to Tattersall's instead of competing with them?"

Curiosity spiked in the back of Michael's brain. "What do you mean?"

Philip sat a little straighter. "Tattersall's is not just about horses. It's about politics and betting and making connections. The subscription rooms of the Jockey Club are a hive of rumors and political maneuvering. There is as much politicking going on in those covered galleries and stables as horse-trading. Tattersall's is a long-established business, entrenched in Society as an entity, not just a commercial operation. It is about visibility, which is what you need. A reputation."

Philip paused for a breath, then continued. "Coming alongside them, being parallel to them, would mean establishing a company that would facilitate some of those activities. Taking and placing bets as an entity instead of an individual, for instance. Building a stable of some of the finest thoroughly bred stallions in the realm that could be hired out for stud as well as traded and sold at Tattersall's. A horse shown and sold at Tattersall's for a high price could be raced with increased levels of bets. You will have a greater chance—and a faster chance—of succeeding if you allied with Richard Tattersall, not made him a competitor."

"And on that first part," Robert said, "I have both the resources and the established entity to do so."

Michael turned to him. "Campion's."

Robert gave a single nod.

"So you are not divesting yourself of it." Michael wondered what else he had missed.

Another long pause settled on the room, then Philip cleared his throat. "We do not think that is the best course of action at this time."

Apparently he had missed a great deal. "So we will continue to skirt the edge of scandal."

Thomas gave a low growl. "It appears that is what we do best. High risks—"

"But with great reward." Robert straightened and braced his hands on the arms of the chair. "Campion's has vetted the income of some of the most powerful men in the kingdom. Some of the women as well. Some of whom would never publicly bet their fortune—for any number of reasons—on a race or reveal what they could pay for a horse. As the facilitator for these people, you could be the reliable face of secured monies, even if the backers were anonymous."

"And you know such people."

"Oh, yes. Remember what a network of information Robbie Green—"

"And Rose," muttered Thomas.

"And Rose have linked together. Tonight alone, I have discovered that the three horses you plan to buy Monday, including the two geldings from Embleton, will have competitive bids. High bids, with the intention of derailing yours."

"I would expect no less. Those geldings are potentially two of the finest race—"

"From Wykeham."

Michael stared at Robert. "Wykeham."

His brother glanced at Thomas, then Philip.

Understanding settled on Michael. "That's why you told them."

"He aims to lay waste to your plans before you even get started."

"How could he have known—"

"Rumors," Philip said, his bass voice a low rumble, "are a two-edged sword. They helped spread the word about your recent purchases, which opened the door to Embleton—"

"But also to Wykeham," Thomas finished. "And we are not about to let him undermine our little brother without a thorough counterpoint in the offing."

"A flanking maneuver called double envelopment," Philip said. "You will be the face of a new company, with obvious and notable intentions. Robert and Thomas will engage the friendly forces on either side, and I will provide the entrenched defense."

Michael swallowed, studying his father's face. "You make it sound as if we are marching to war."

"Oh, we are, little brother," Thomas said. "And we are about to once again remind Society that the Ashtons are a force to be reckoned with."

CHAPTER THIRTEEN

Saturday, 20 August 1825
Beckcott Hall
Half past one in the afternoon

RADCLIFF BROUGHT WORD that luncheon would not be served in the dining room. Instead, by orders of the countess, everyone would have a tray brought out—Clara and Honora would eat in their bedchambers, the earl in his study. With only the three of them remaining in the house, this was not an uncommon occurrence, although it usually occurred by happenstance, not an edict from Honora, who, apparently, had a bit of a headache.

Clara received the news with gratitude. She had dozed only fitfully, her mind still churning over and over the events of the night before, and she certainly did not feel up to facing her mother over food. But she still found the simple fare Radcliff brought to her room hard to swallow, despite her hunger. Her restlessness made her pace, seeking some understanding of all that had happened. The encounter with Michael in the barn had left Clara both exhilarated and exhausted, mentally and physically. Clearly he had wanted her—the way he touched her left no doubts about that. And she definitely wanted him—he stirred in her a heat, a pure desire she had barely dreamed about. In his arms she found not only passion but comfort. A comfort and passion she had replayed several times during the night as her thoughts about Michael and the duke began to clarify.

But Michael's reluctance to continue with their affection plagued her. It felt as if it were about more than the interruption of Rufus and the stable boy, more than the risk of discovery.

It was about the duke. Wykeham. The despicable man had become a Sword of Damocles over every aspect of her life—her future, her family, and now Michael's plans. As she went over every minute detail of the past few days, her mind had determined one crystalline fact: she had to find a way out from under that sword.

She continued to pace back and forth, lips pursed, the image of the simpering noble prancing through her mind just as he had through the Scotch reel with her mother. The smug look on his face haunted her, telling her he had already won, already conquered her.

No. She would not have it. She might not ever have Michael in her bed, but she would be damned if the duke ever ended up there, lording his conquest over her the rest of her life. The prospect of those long winter evenings in the North were evolving from a nightmare into a vision of a torturous hell. Clara felt everyone else's plans swirling around ever tighter—her father's, Michael's, her mother's, the duke's—a strangling noose.

Clara stopped pacing, her chest tight, her breathing shallow. She grabbed the edge of her escritoire, forcing herself to take long, deep breaths. Calm, she needed to be calm. After a few of those inhalations, Clara picked up the tray from her escritoire and set it on the bench at the end of her bed. She returned and pulled out two pieces of foolscap as she settled in the chair. If she were to make her way through this, she needed to have a plan of her own.

She wrote out a note to Lady Newbury, Rose Ashton, asking if she could call on her later that afternoon. Clara expected her mother to command her presence for tea, but if she could see

Rose afterwards, perhaps she would have more information that could help her flesh out the kernel of a plan forming in the back of her head.

A dangerous plan. But no more so that the image of infinite winter nights enduring the presence of a man who would turn every good thing about her life into a wound to be picked raw for decades to come.

She would rather hang.

Clara sealed the note and rang for Radcliff to take it and the tray downstairs. As expected, her maid came with the request to join Honora for tea at half-past three. After delivering the tray and note, Radcliff returned to help make Clara ready for both meetings. For the first part of her plan was quite simple—she had to appear pristine and obedient. For the next few weeks, Lady Clara Durham would become the perfect daughter, the perfect mate for a duke.

Perfect for all of Society.

Damn them all.

At the appointed time, Clara paused outside Honora's boudoir and took several deep breaths. *I can do this. Pristine and obedient.* She straightened her shoulders, tapped lightly on the door and went in.

Honora sat stitching on one of her endless—and never completed—embroidery projects. Her mother had never been particularly skilled with a needle but felt ladies must appear properly busy with appropriate activities. More than one trunk in their attic was stuffed with the unfinished work of the countess, who was also loath to rid herself of anything she had toiled on so long and hard.

"Mother."

Honora did not look up. The tea service already sat on a low table in front of the settee where she stitched. "Would you be so kind as to prepare the tea?"

Clara perched, stiff with the proper posture, on the other end of the settee and reached to pour hot water into the teapot. She swirled the water about to warm the pot, then dumped it. She added a small bit of tea from the chest on the tray and added the hot water. She folded her hands in her lap, waiting for it to steep.

Honora poked the needle into the fabric and set the hoop aside. She pushed back on the cushions and smoothed her skirts. "Have you considered what you will wear tomorrow?"

"To meet the dowager duchess?"

"Yes."

"I thought perhaps the burgundy and blue day gown—"

Honora gave a dismissive wave. "Too dark and informal. What about crimson and cream you wore to the Devonshire soiree last year?"

Clara scowled. "That was two seasons ago. The sleeves are all wrong for this season."

"The emerald and gold."

"I look like a frog. What about the sapphire satin from last Christmas?"

Honora paused. "Is it not too wintry? I remember a white fur trim."

"Radcliff can strip that off. It will be simple but direct."

"Which is what the duke says about you. Simple and direct."

Clara fought a tinge of ire. "He thinks I am simple?"

Another dismissive wave. "Not in the way you are thinking. Just that you are"—her mother struggled for the word—"uncomplicated."

That tinge kindled into a small flair. She tamped it down and turned to the tea as a distraction. *Pristine and obedient.* She held a tiny strainer over each cup as she poured the tea, then handed one cup and saucer to her mother. A plate of pastries waited near the tea service, but Clara ignored them.

Her mother sipped the bitter brew as Clara added a touch of milk to hers. "The dowager will mostly ask you questions, but do you have any prepared to ask her, in case the need arises?"

Clara blinked. "It did not occur to me I would need such. The Wykeham habit is to direct the conversation."

Honora stilled, the cup halfway to her lips, and turned a sharp glance on Clara.

Clara focused on her teacup. "Is this a new blend? It seems smoother than Papa's previous purchases."

"Clara—"

She set the cup and saucer back on the table and folded her hands in her lap. "I will make a list, Mother, so I will not embarrass you. If the conversation wanes, which I doubt—"

"Clara—"

"I will have perfectly proper and acceptable questions to ask. I will share these with you before we leave tomorrow, so you can see if they pass your muster. Will that be sufficient?" She took another sip of tea and looked at her mother, to find Honora's narrowed eyes studying her closely.

"What are you plotting, Clara?"

Clara widened her eyes. "Why, nothing, Mother. I only want to be a good daughter and appropriate match for the Duke of Wykeham."

"I do not believe you. If you are devising some way to sabotage tomorrow's call—"

"I have not considered any such thing."

Honora set her cup down on the table and leaned closer to Clara. "I warn you, Clara—"

"I promise you, Mother. For the next two months I will behave properly. Pristine and obedient. I will win the duke's favor, and you can gladly rejoice when he ships me to the border."

"Hm."

Clara sipped the tea, which had gone cold. She set it down. "Mother, it is really quite simple. It is too hard to fight you and Papa and the duke and Society all at once. I do not understand why things have changed among us, but quarreling with you exhausts me. I surrender. I will do what I can to secure a position so that you do not have to concern yourself with me any longer. If marrying the Duke of Wykeham is what is required to get me out of your house, then that is what I will do."

Honora pursed her lips again. "You will have to prove this to me."

"Anything you ask."

"You will deliver the questions to me just after breakfast tomorrow."

The tea began to sour on Clara's stomach. "Of course. What time is our call on the duchess?"

"Three."

Clara stood, feeling a bit lightheaded. "If you will excuse me, I will get Radcliff started on the sapphire gown."

Honora hesitated, then reached for her cup again. "Very well. I will see you at supper."

Clara wanted to run. Instead, she pushed her shoulders back and strolled from the room. *Please, Rose, let me come* was her sole thought as she headed back up the stairs. *Please.*

Saturday, 20 August 1825
Hyde Park
Just before six in the afternoon

MICHAEL LEANED FORWARD, his weight on the stirrups as he gave Copper his head. The big bay's muscles bunched and rippled beneath Michael as Copper broke from a canter into a gallop. Michael could hear as well as feel the rhythmic thud of hooves as the air whipped around them, forcing Michael to squint, even as he bowed closer over the horse's neck. Copper's head nodded as his legs stretched and bent, consuming the ground beneath them. The long mane streamed back, the ends stinging Michael's cheeks. His eyes watered, and the world narrowed to the wind and the sensation of Copper's speed and power. Michael's shoulders felt motionless, even as the rest of his body moved within the same rhythm, shifting as the horse's weight moved from front to back, over and over. He felt as if he were part of

Copper, as if they were one creature. Weightless, breathless.

Free.

It did not last long. Even in a field as far away from Rotten Row as Michael could get, this was Hyde Park, not the rolling hills and expansive meadows of Ashton Park. Too soon, they headed for a copse of trees. Using his knees, he slowed Copper gradually through the gaits, settling again on the saddle. Back at a walk—both horse and man gasping for air—Michael could not help but laugh. Joy soared through him.

"We have to do this more often, Copper, my friend."

The big horse's ears twitched.

"I know, I know. I'll get you to back to the fields as soon as I can. Patience, I am afraid, is needed of both of us. It is turning into a most eventful summer."

Copper snorted.

Michael laughed again and tugged on the reins, turning Copper toward Ashton House. "Believe me, I know. I will try not to neglect you for so long. But you will have new friends come Monday. With luck, their arrival will be a new beginning for all of us."

As they headed home, they met few people on the streets. Most of the visitors to Hyde Park were still strolling the Row, while it was that time of day when others would be paying late afternoon calls. He passed a few gentlemen obviously headed to court some young lady or another, while carriages transported young girls and their mothers to teas or soirees. Maybe. With his time in Kent, and with Beth's departure to Yorkshire for an extended stay with Rose's Aunt Sophie, Michael had lost track of pending Society events, with the exception of a few upcoming balls.

But with the plans the Ashton men had laid out earlier this morning, Michael knew his life was in transition once again. Society, at least for a bit, would take a back seat to business.

Returning Copper to the stable, Michael stayed for a bit, helping one of the boys groom the horse. Then he headed inside, intending to stop by the duke's study, which he found empty. His father must have returned to his wife's side. Michael turned toward the stairs but heard soft voices from his mother's sitting room. Michael scowled. That room went empty most days. His sister had departed, and his mother was bedridden. Rose did not usually entertain callers except on household business, and she met them in Emalyn's office. *So who could be—?* Michael moved closer to the partially open door, his steps padded by the thick hall carpet.

"The duke has not been active in Society much since his wife died—not much even before his marriage, as I recall. I can make inquiries, but I'm not sure—"

Rose, obviously. With a friend. Michael turned to move on.

"Any information would be helpful."

Michael froze. *Clara?* He pivoted, leaning closer to the doorframe.

"Are you sure this is the direction you wish to pursue?"

Clara's voice sounded firm and clear. "I am. If I am to play their game until the last moment—"

"I do not think they are playing a game."

"No." Clara's voice grew somber. "No, they are not. They mean for me to marry him and will brook no objection from me. They have made it clear that my opinion is irrelevant."

"Clara, I'm sure—"

"I understand it, even if I do not know the reason behind it. They will not tell me. But if I continue to protest, they will always be on their guard. I must find ways to reassure them, all of them, including the duke and his mother, that all is well and I am the perfect and contented match for Wykeham. However it galls me, they must not suspect my true feelings."

Michael's teeth ground together. *Clara, darling, what are you up to? What are you plotting?*

"So what is it you wish me to find?"

"Something—anything—that will convince my father that the duke is not a good match for me."

"You do realize that the Duke of Wykeham is considered aboveboard."

"That's because they have not seen his gambling debts at Campion's."

The voice in Michael's ear was soft but startling, and Michael gave a low bark of surprise. He whirled to face his brother.

Robert's eyes were wide with innocence. "On whom are we eavesdropping?"

The door swung open, and Rose stood there, a fierce scowl creasing her face. "What, pray tell, are you two doing here?"

"Exactly my question." Robert's wounded face twisted into a grin, and he pushed pass Rose and Michael and into the room. Spotting Clara, he paused and executed a precise bow. "Lady Clara."

On one of the two settees in the room, Clara sat as stiff as a March wind, and her glare at Robert, then Michael, was just as chilly. "It is impolite to eavesdrop on a lady's conversation."

Robert nodded at Rose. "True, but I had only just arrived and was about to scold Michael on that point—"

"Robert!" Michael hissed.

"When I heard Wykeham's name and something about him being above reproach. Which is, of course, not true."

Rose and Clara looked at each other, and silence reigned a few moments as each woman came to her own conclusions.

Michael hung in the doorway. He had never liked this room, the smallest of the Ashton House receiving rooms. Its very size made him feel cramped, and the overly feminine décor—with its numerous fringes, artfully draped throws, and overstuffed cushions in bright pinks, yellows, and greens—suggested that men had no place here. The two settees and several chairs formed a three-quarters circle around the fireplace and a low table, a reminder that his mother often entertained in this room. Rose and Clara occupied the settees that faced each other. Radcliff, Clara's maid, stood near the fireplace, her expression as condemning as that of her mistress. Several pieces of foolscap were spread across the table, which was odd, but Michael did not have time to consider why they were there.

Rose motioned to two of the remaining chairs. "Gentlemen."

Robert dropped into the one nearest Clara. Michael hesitated, remaining in the doorway until Rose glowered at him. "Please come in and shut the door."

He did, perching on the edge of a chair near Rose as she turned to Robert. "Please explain your comment."

Instead of answering, his grinning brother nodded at Michael. "You tell them."

Michael stared at Robert, his stomach clenching. "I do not—"

"You do. These words you do have."

Michael looked down at the floor a moment, then cleared his throat. He spoke for a few moments, focused on the carpet, detailing the encounter with the duke at Campion's. "Jimmy, the dealer, told us later that it was the duke who was cheating, and he was mostly angry that it was not working. But Jimmy and another player had spotted it earlier. Instead of calling the duke out on it, which would be dangerous for both of them, they simply made sure his efforts did not work."

Rose looked from Michael to Robert. "How would they know—"

"Because he has done it before. They knew what to watch for." Robert rubbed his jaw for a moment, making the still-red wounds on his face wrinkle and bulge. "Wykeham has a temper. A bad one. He keeps it tamped down most of the time, but he does not like losing at cards or not getting his way. Father has said as much about his appearances in Parliament. Opposing Wykeham can result in an outburst or, more likely, a subtle threat meant to intimidate. His title gives him a lot of power, and he enjoys wielding it. He considers everyone at Campion's beneath him, and when anyone else wins, he schemes to overcome his losses, even if it means cheating."

"Which he is apparently not very good at," Clara murmured.

Michael finally met her gaze. "He currently owes the house

almost five-thousand pounds."

"I beg your pardon?" Clara asked. "Did you say five-*thousand* pounds?"

Michael nodded. "He lost three-hundred just that night. He's banned for three months."

"The thing to consider," Robert said softly, "is that Campion's is not the only hel—establishment at which he gambles."

"So there is no determining how massive his debt is," Rose said.

Robert shrugged. "I can try to find out."

Clara inched forward on the settee's cushion. "Please do so, if you can." She sat a little straighter. "How much could he owe before he bankrupts his family?"

Robert waved one hand. "Oh, he is quite far from that. I would never have let him run up such a debt—nor would any other house—if we did not think he could pay it. At least for now. But there are rumors he is beginning to let his estate go fallow, which means his earnings may change. The rumors note that his wife ran the estate, and he did not pick up the slack when she died. So the bucket is not bottomless—and my guess he is searching for a wife with a substantial dowry, one who can do more than warm his—"

"Robert." Rose's tone remained sharp.

Robert's grin faded as he paused, and Michael knew he struggled to phrase it in a more appropriate way.

Clara filled the silence. "Ah. That's why I'm only one of his eggs."

Michael's mind tripped over the words. "You are—he thinks—um . . . an *egg?*"

She smiled, a soft expression that made his heart as well as his mind stumble. "Yes," she said, her voice dropping. "He said I am one of many eggs in his basket. He is considering other women. I've been trying to find out who."

Rose sniffed. "I think I can help with that. You are not the first to inquire about the duke." She gestured to the sheets on the table. "I have missives from five others, asking if I know anything untoward about the Duke of Wykeham. All are from women who have been running estates—three of them are widows—or have helped run households for invalid or incapable mothers. I have heard through the servants that three have already dismissed him as a suitor, without making such information public. That leaves but three, including Lady Clara."

"Ah," Robert said, apparently finding the proper words. "So he is not looking for a wife to, um, provide more heirs but someone to replace his wife on the management side of his estate and add to his income."

"Which, unfortunately, would not be a detriment in my father's eyes." Clara clutched her skirt in her fists, wrinkling the silk.

Michael felt her desperation. "But there is still the issue that he cheats—and has that temper. He's participated in more than a few duels. He is known for being a good shot, but eventually he will come across someone better, who is not willing to aim at the clouds. You could marry him but wind up an impoverished widow. Something I think your father would consider."

Clara's face shifted abruptly, from a furrowed brow to alarm in her eyes. "Duels," she murmured. Oddly, Clara turned her attention to Radcliff. "Duels."

Michael watched as the maid gave a single nod, which sent a spike of worry up Michael's spine. "Clara—"

"Lady Clara," Rose whispered at him.

Michael cleared his throat. "Lady Clara—"

She turned those emerald eyes on him, and Michael's heart skipped a beat, his words drifting into vapor as he remembered the warmth of her last night, the glorious touch of those lips. He felt like a lovesick boy, and he forced himself to sit straighter, to focus on the moment. "Lady Clara, please do not indulge in any foolish—"

Wrong word.

He saw that in her eyes the moment it left his lips, in the

narrowed glare. He swallowed it. "There are many ways that Lord Robert and I—and Lady Newbury—can help you without—"

God help him.

Robert snorted, and Rose leaned over and grasped Michael's forearm. "Lord Michael is merely concerned—as we all are—that we move with caution regarding the duke."

And the glare lifted. Clara's eyes widened and her face softened. "Thank you, Lord Michael. I know words are not always your friends, and I do appreciate your concern and consideration."

Michael wanted to kiss her right then and there. He stood and stepped toward her, his hand out, relishing the look of adoration in her eyes as her gaze followed him upward.

"Michael!" Rose's hiss stopped him cold.

"Good heavens, boy," Robert said. "I am going to have to lock you in the stable."

"Definitely not a good idea," muttered Radcliff.

They all stared at the maid, who curtsied abruptly. "My lord."

Clara snickered, then covered her mouth.

Rose's sharp gaze moved from Radcliff to Clara. "Is there something else we should know?"

"Nothing." The word came from Clara and Michael at the same time.

Robert burst out laughing, then stood and offered his arm to his sister-in-law. "Perhaps we should see Lady Clara to the door."

The ladies stood, and Michael offered his arm to Clara. She took it, peering at him as they walked, stumbling only once as they neared the front door. His grip tightened, and she whispered her thanks as she found her balance again. Their goodbyes were polite and distant, perfectly proper, but he watched as she and Radcliff descended the front steps.

"One of us should have gone with them," he said to Robert, who watched him as closely as Michael watched the women.

"If any woman in this city could cross Berkeley Square without a male escort, it would be Lady Clara Durham. In fact, I suspect she has already made that trip more than a few times."

"Robert." Rose's voice held a dark warning. "Do not even hint at such a thing."

This time Robert's smile held an unexpected tenderness. "If you have not noticed, dear sister, Lord Michael intends to marry her."

Rose's sharp gaze shifted to Michael, who merely nodded as he finally shut the door. She looked both brothers up and down before taking a deep breath. "Well, I know the four men in this house have something nefarious in the works—"

Robert put a palm against his chest. "Nefarious?"

Rose did not pause. "But I suggest you leave it to the ladies for the next step with the duke and this detrimental betrothal."

"And that is because . . .?"

Rose's smile held a twist of mischievousness. "Because you know the business and the gambling. But we know what the servants have to say." She turned a slight glower on Michael. "And as we just saw, the servants know everything."

CHAPTER FOURTEEN

Saturday, 20 August 1825
Beckcott Hall
Half past ten in the evening

CLARA PUT THE final touches on three letters to go out the next day, sealed them, then spent a few minutes making a list of the questions her mother wanted to see as well as jotting down the benefits of a marriage to the Duke of Wykeham. She had the deficits already memorized—and that list grew by the day. She had known visiting Lady Newbury would be a risk—her father had forbidden her setting foot in Ashton House ever again—but Clara felt quite relieved she had made the call. As expected, the Ashtons knew where most of the secrets were buried.

But in order to make her parents believe she had changed her mind and had become enthusiastic about her upcoming nuptials, she had to be able to sing the man's praises. Fortunately, dinner this evening had been a quiet affair, with her mother more interested in informing the earl about their upcoming call on the dowager duchess and the next appointments with Madame Adrienne than letting Clara express an opinion. Tomorrow would be the perfect time to begin that plan, however.

She glanced down at the first question and winced. Awful

question but it might enliven the discussion if the conversation turned sallow.

What was the duke like as a child?

Clara honestly didn't care, but perhaps his mother would relish sharing details about her oldest son.

What were the most positive attributes of his wife?

Everyone, including the duke, seemed to have a positive view of that first marriage. Clara had a feeling the dowager's response would be the most honest.

What are his children like? Will they accept me as their new mother?

After considering those two, Clara struck them. For most of the nobility, children were a secondary consideration, except as heirs, and many parents paid them little attention. Such questions might embarrass the duchess.

May I come to you for advice?

Hm. That one would depend on how the conversation progressed. If it turned cold or hostile, the older woman might consider such a question to be sarcasm. Still . . . Clara left it on the list—and continued to stare at the page for almost five minutes. Nothing else came to mind. *What does one ask a dowager duchess anyway? Her plans for the future should probably be avoided.* Clara decided to ask her mother tomorrow. It might help her plan along to be more congenial with her own mother.

Clara pushed the list aside and rang for Radcliff. She sat down on the bench at the end of her bed and looked around, trying to comprehend that this would not be her home much longer, especially if she was forced to marry the duke. And not just this house but Beckcott Abbey as well. The thought of surrendering Maid Marian made Clara's heart ache. The duke might make provisions, but if what she had heard tonight was any indication, any aspect of his estate the duke did not like would not be accepted.

You could ask him.

True. And he would be here on Tuesday afternoon. Better to

know now than dread the knowledge later.

Clara let out a long sigh. "I hate this."

"Hate what, my lady?" Radcliff pushed open the door.

Clara waved her hand in a circle over her head. "All of it. London. This business of courting and trying to find a husband. It's all just so much nonsense."

Radcliff pointed to the dressing table, and Clara moved to the stool in front of it, settling as Radcliff began to take down and brush her riotous hair. She glanced at the maid in the mirror. "How do maids go about finding a husband?"

Radcliff coughed a laugh. "Mostly we do not, my lady." She focused on a nest of tangles near the end of Clara's strands. "But when we do, it's because we've met some, we hope, nice boy at the market or at a dance or at church. In the country, one of the neighboring farms or a pub."

"Do your parents get involved?"

"Sometimes, just like yours. If the man is a scapegrace, the folks would step up, stop it. But we don't get all fancy about it, like your people do. Bloodlines and all that. When we're ready, we just go to the vicar, and he puts it in the books."

"Sounds so simple."

"Aye, but it's because there's no money. When people have money, life gets a great deal more complicated."

Clara choked on a laugh. "There is no doubt about that."

Radcliff glanced at Clara's escritoire. "More letters to go out?"

Clara started to nod, then winced as Radcliff attacked another nest of tangles. "Yes. It seems the attention the duke paid to my mother has raised a lot of curiosity in my friends." She grimaced. "And increased the number of my invitations."

Radcliff paused in her brushing. "Is this not a good thing?"

After a shrug, Clara let out a sigh. "I suppose it is. If I were to become a duchess, I would have a much higher place among the elite. But I expect I will find it difficult to discuss the weather and the latest fashions with people who did not know I existed two weeks ago."

"You seemed quite comfortable with Lord Michael."

"Yes. Always." Closing her eyes, Clara could envision those dark eyes, the elegance of his appearance, even though he stumbled over his words every time she drew near him. The eagerness in his expression when he stood up and lunged toward her—and the chagrin on his face when Rose had stopped him. "I only wish we had a chance to talk more, without others hovering over us like Marian over her prey."

The brushing slowed. "Would you, my lady? Would you take a chance if you could meet him in a place you could talk more freely?"

Suspicion flared in Clara's gut, and her eyes met Radcliff's in the mirror. "Radcliff. What are you thinking?"

A shrug, and Radcliff focused on Clara's hair again. "Just a notion. A possibility."

Clara spun on the stool and grabbed Radcliff's arm. "Tell me. Tell me now."

Sunday, 21 August 1825
Ashton House
Half past one in the morning

IT WAS BEAUTIFUL, the brandy, amber and rich with an aroma that enticed, beckoning Michael to sip, just one small sip. He swirled it in the glass, watching it coat the sides, eking back to the bottom. He knew it would help calm him, bring a delicious peace to his clamoring mind, perhaps even the calm of slumber.

Michael could not sleep. That nameless restlessness had returned, gnawing at him, dragging at his mind, his gut, and it would not be silenced. It had taken hold after the visit from Clara, and what had begun as a nagging tug had, over the course of the evening, become a raging beast. He had tried to sleep, donning his nightshirt and burrowing beneath the covers of his bed, but his mind raced with that—something—just out of reach.

Finally, he had gotten out of bed, wrapped his banyan around his body, and paced—first, in his room, then the hall. Up and down the stairs. Several circuits around the ballroom and halls of the first two floors. Nothing helped. Surrendering, Michael had retreated to his father's study, where a good supply of the finest brandy awaited. He knew all too well the delirium, the dreamless and dark sleep that could be had in that glass.

It would be easy. One sip, then another. One glass, then another. One bottle, then another. He raised the glass, holding it between his face and the single lamp he had lit. In that glow, the color of it reminded him of a good, strong tea, although the results of consuming tea were far different, and to his mind came the memories of what happened after those dreamless and dark nights. The headaches. The loss of days. The debts, both financial and emotional. And the relief from that strangling restlessness, the heartbreak of losing Eleanor, and the need to be under the midnight sky had always been temporary, all of it flooding back in once the drink had worn off. The cycle of torment repeating itself, night after night.

I cannot go back there.

After a moment, Michael released a long exhale and slowly poured the brandy back into the decanter. His hands shook a bit, but he did not spill a drop. He set down the glass and replaced the stopper.

"Wise move." Philip Ashton's bass voice sank into the book-lined walls, softening the edge in the words.

Michael turned. "I did not think anyone else was awake."

Philip's eyebrows arched as he leaned against the doorframe. "With you stalking the halls like some maniacal ghost? Your mother and I were beginning to place bets about where you would go next."

Michael's cheeks grew warm. "I did not mean to disturb anyone."

Philip pointed to the wingbacks in front of the fireplace. "Sit.

If you can. Tell me what is driving you back toward my brandy." He eased down in the chair, wincing as he favored one knee. He rubbed the joint as he stretched the leg.

Michael scowled. "Are you hurt?"

Philip's face twisted into the crooked smile typical of all the Ashton men. "I am almost fifty, boy. A good many things ache that did not use to. You will get there. Now," he gestured at the opposing chair. "Sit. Talk."

Michael collapsed into the wingback as if all his muscles and bones had stopped functioning. He scrubbed his face with both hands. "I do not really know how to explain it." He stared for a moment at the cold and empty fireplace. "It is as if there is something just out of my grasp. But I do not know what it is."

Philip studied Michael a moment. "You always were our midnight child."

Michael's eyes narrowed as he looked at his father again. "What do you mean?"

Philip pressed back against the chair and stretched both legs out, crossing them at the ankle. "Even as a young boy you were restless, always wanting out. Do you really think we did not know how often you snuck out in the middle of the night to go riding? More so at Ashton Park than here, obviously. But even here you often would go to the stables after everyone else was in bed. The grooms found you more times than I remember, asleep in a stall. Even after you went to school, I would get letters from your instructors warning us that if you kept violating the rules about hours, you would be expelled."

Michael gave a quick smile. "I remember that conversation."

"Your mother thought perhaps you were like most young men, more interested in girls than books, but even that did not seem to be the case. Then Eleanor came along. Everything seemed to come into focus. You made plans. Do you remember asking me if you could take over the management of Ashton Park? You had so many ideas for improvements—and you not yet twenty."

Michael huffed. "Cheeky devil, was I not?"

Philip grinned. "Yes, but I admired your ambition, and I liked the way your request put a fire under Thomas. He had virtually no interest in our country estates until then. It appeared both of you were coming into your own with the responsibilities of the duchy."

"Then Eleanor blew that all to flinders. At least where I was concerned."

Philip fell silent. After a moment, Michael shifted. "Father?"

"Miss Carlson, I'm afraid, was a detriment to both of you."

Michael scowled. "How so? She took my money and left me in Gretna Green. I thought she would be my wife and by my side all our lives. And I never understood it. If she had wanted money, I would have given her anything."

"She did not want money. She wanted the title. She wanted to be a duchess."

Michael blinked as his chest tightened. "How do you mean? She knew I was not the heir."

"Yes. But she thought you were a path to the heir. The night before the two of you ran away, Thomas found her in his bedchamber. Unclothed. He summoned me, and we insisted she leave and never see you again. She planned to claim that Thomas had ruined her so he would be forced to marry her, and I promised I could produce at least two men who would swear that would not be possible. She left, threatening revenge. The next morning you were gone." Philip sat a bit straighter. "Truth be told, we lost both of you that night. You to a broken heart and Thomas to the realization that women would not just pursue his title—which he already knew—but would betray his family to get it. He blamed himself for not seeing it and for your downfall. Afterward, you wanted to drown, and he wanted to get as far away from the machinations of Society's women as he could get."

Michael jerked to his feet and turned away from Philip, his chest so constricted that he struggled to breathe. His eyes immediately went toward the brandy decanter, waiting so temptingly on a table beside his father's desk. "Why did you not tell me?"

"In those first days, you would not have listened. Later, we never saw you sober enough to hear us."

Two steps. Two steps and he could have the brandy in hand. Michael took the first one.

Philip fell silent.

Michael slowly closed his eyes. "She was the love of my life."

"No, she was not. You thought she was the answer to this hunger you have."

"Yes! She was!" The words were a whispered hiss.

"No."

Philip's soft voice held a familiar finality to it. Throughout Michael's childhood, his father always had the final word on any family discussion—whether it was a political discussion or a decision on which biscuits were tastiest. And usually delivered in just this kind of low, unyielding tone. Michael pivoted. "How can you be so sure? What would you know about it?"

"Because I thought the same thing about your mother."

Michael stilled, staring at Philip, who returned the same un-wavering expression. After a moment, Philip gestured at the chair again, and Michael sat, perched on the edge of it.

"I loved Emalyn with every ounce of strength I had. I still do. But I recognize your restlessness because I had felt the same thing. I was convinced if I married Emalyn, it would be fulfilled. But it was not. It lingered, making our first years more tumultu-ous than they should have been. I wanted her to be the answer to everything. And she was not."

"So what was the answer?"

Philip drew his legs in, straightened, and leaned forward. "I'm not sure there is one. Certainly no one person is. Or perhaps it differs from one person to another. Some find it in God. Others in travel. For me, part of the answer came from taking on more of my duties as marquess, then duke. To find a purpose and direction for each day. I know you have struggled since your return. You have spent almost four years transferring your hopes in Eleanor to strong drink. Without either, you have floundered. Now you are trying to shift it to Lady Clara—"

"Father—"

"But as she grows closer to the duke, as she seems to slip away, you are aimless again."

Michael froze, then his eyes narrowed as a realization set in. "This is why the three of you concocted the idea of a facilitating company."

Philip's smile spread slowly but broadly.

"I will be damned."

"As I said, we are stronger as a family than as individuals."

"You think this will give me purpose."

"That's yet to be seen. I do think between this company and helping Robert fill out his stables, you will find a distraction and a direction."

"I still mean to marry Lady Clara."

Philip gave a single nod. "I am sure you do. But your grandfather married a woman he barely knew instead of the one he loved in order to fulfill his family duties, thinking he could be happy in spite of it. I married the woman I loved thinking she was the answer to all my problems. Neither of us was entirely correct. Yet both of us had marriages that suited us. Life does not always turn out as you hope it will. But you can find a path of purpose and contentment, if you do not fight the inevitable too hard."

Michael realized the meaning in his father's words, and he fought his desire to reject them, to disallow the thought to even enter his mind. "You think she will marry the duke."

"I think a woman in her position has fewer choices than you believe she does. Lady Clara, from all I've heard, seems to be a reasonable if slightly rebellious young woman. If this is the duty required of her, I suspect she will choose family over love. It is what we in Society do."

"Another reason to despise it."

"There is always the church."

Michael almost laughed. "I suspect I would be a most inappropriate vicar."

"Of that I have no doubt." Philip pushed up out of the chair, groaning a bit. "Now, boy, go to bed so the rest of us can as well."

"Yes, sir."

"And stay away from my brandy."

Michael smiled. "I will, sir."

"Walk with me."

Michael did, but they said little as the climbed the stairs to the third floor. Michael noticed that his father was a little more winded than usual, remembering that his grandfather had died when he was Philip's age. As they paused outside his mother's bedchamber—where his father had been sleeping since her attack—Michael touched his father's elbow. "Father—"

Philip waved away the concern in Michael's voice. "I'm fifty and tired, not dead."

Michael had to chuckle. "Yes, sir."

But his father peered closely at him. "You have seen it, correct? The way we have gotten through the last few months?"

Michael nodded. The last six months had been chaotic for the entire family. "I have."

"Never underestimate us, Michael. Never underestimate the power of family."

"I will not."

Philip eased open the door to the bedchamber and stepped inside. "Why are *you* still awake?" were his final words before it shut again, and Michael grinned, knowing his mother would expect a full accounting of the conversation.

Family.

And for the first time since Eleanor Carlson had abandoned him in Scotland, Michael was grateful he was an Ashton, son of the Duke of Kennet.

Ten minutes later, he was asleep.

CHAPTER FIFTEEN

Sunday, 21 August 1825
Wykeham Place
Half past three in the afternoon

WHEN CLARA TURNED six, the cook at Beckcott Abbey had made her a special pudding of raspberries, clotted cream, and puffy pastry. It had been three layers and almost six inches tall, five inches across the base, and topped with the ripest, reddest raspberry Clara had ever seen. The entire concoction was drizzled with raspberry juice and honey, and it almost melted in Clara's mouth. She savored every bite so slowly that her mother had lost patience and left the table before Clara finished. It was a pudding meant to be remembered.

Although Clara doubted Cook would be flattered to know her pudding came to mind now, as Clara stared at the Dowager Duchess of Wykeham, whose rose, cream, and beige gown had settled around her ample hips on the settee, the rose and beige ribbons attached to her sleeves and décolletage drifting down around her like so much raspberry juice and honey. A silver-gray mound of fur lay next to her, and Clara idly wondered why the lady would have a wrap with her in the summer heat. Her grandmother had once told her that old people stayed cold, so perhaps that was the reason . . . for the dowager was, indeed, old.

The dowager's soft cheeks lay in overlapping creases, like a sandy bank eroded by the surf, and her wispy gray hair had been topped with a rose and beige turban. Tiny gold spectacles perched precariously on the tip of her nose. Through those small round lenses, the dowager studied Clara, from the befeathered coiffure Radcliff had arranged down to the sapphire satin and leather slippers on her feet. Radcliff had done an admirable job of transforming a once-worn Christmas frock into a more summery contraption by replacing white fur with sky-blue lace and slitting the upper sleeves and slipping sky-blue panels beneath them.

They had been announced and shown into the dowager's receiving room, where she had motioned for them to sit, although she had not spoken a word of greeting. No tea service graced the room, although one footman remained, stiff and proper, next to the door. After they settled, Clara forced herself to remain still under the examination, although her mother, in a straightforward emerald gown with white embroidery on the décolletage, fidgeted a bit on the settee next to Clara as the tense study went on for several excruciating minutes. Finally, Honora could stand it no more.

"Your Grace, we are honored—"

The dowager silenced Honora with a wave, her eyes never leaving Clara. "Owen said you were something of a bacon-faced chit. I do believe he was being kind."

Honora stiffened, a gasp choking off whatever she had been going to say. Clara, having dealt with the duke before, refused to respond to the cut. She lifted her chin. "His Grace is a gifted wordsmith. He often flatters me when we are together. I am not surprised that he would be kind toward me in your presence, Your Grace."

The brown eyes behind the spectacles gleamed. "Ha! He also said you were an intellectual match for him, which I did not believe until now."

"Lady Clara is quite—"

Another wave. Honora stilled.

"The duke is a gracious man. He honors me."

Those eyes, a clear and lustrous brown, did not waver. "My son is a pompous fool, especially in London, but I am sure you already know that."

Clara blinked. "I do not—"

"I can assure you he is quite different at home. The northern counties are a foreign country compared to London Society, far more open, less refined. Here he prances around as if he were a prince who had sat on a pinecone. There he is more somber. Relaxed. Less restricted by protocol. Less seduced by his own sense of power."

Before Clara could think of a response, the dowager shifted on her settee and addressed the footman. "Please send in the tea at four."

As the footman vanished, the dowager reached down to stroke the silver-gray fur next to her.

And it moved.

"Oh!" Clara reached out over the table between settees. "It's a dog!"

The dowager's eyes widened and her mouth tightened. "Of course it is a dog. Did you think I had a fur wrap at hand in this heat?"

"Truthfully, yes."

The older woman chuckled, stroked the animal again, and a sweet face appeared amidst the silky fur. "You are refreshing, my dear. This is my precious Clementina. She is a Skye Terrier. And as you know, no duchess should be without her Skye when she is promenading in the Park." She touched Clementina near the ears, her gaze at the dog fond and warm. "Although neither of us promenade much these days. Too hard on our old bones."

"How old is she?" Clara could not take her eyes off the silky coat.

"Almost ten and five, old for a girl such as she." The dowager's eyes glanced at Clara. "Would you like to—"

"Oh, yes!" Clara was off her settee and sitting on the other side of the dog before Honora could finish clearing her throat.

"Clara—"

The dowager gestured again at Honora. "Oh, leave the girl be." Her hand joined Clara's on the dog's back, her fingers entwining in Clementina's fur with a grasp of pure affection. "Animals are one of the few pleasures allowed women such as us."

Clara looked up at the dowager. "Us?"

"Duchesses. We have many duties, few pleasures, especially if we are not in love with our husbands."

Clara's hand stilled on Clementina's hip.

The dowager fell silent as well, watching Clara. Suddenly, Clementina shifted, poking her nose into Clara's thigh. The dog's eyes brightened as she snuffled up and down Clara's thigh, leaving moist nose prints in the silk.

"Clementina, what the devil are you doing?" The dowager tugged at the dog, who resisted mightily.

"Oh!" Clara almost laughed and cupped Clementina's face, pulling it up to look at hers. "You smell Pockets, don't you, my pretty girl."

"Oh dear God," muttered Honora.

"Pockets?"

Clara released Clementina, who pressed her nose against Clara's thigh and held it there. Clara sighed, focusing on the dowager again. "My kitten. All my dresses are made with either pockets or slits for pocket bags."

"What?" Honora said.

The dowager and Clara ignored her. Clara went on. "She is still quite small, so she spends a lot of time in my pockets. Which is how she got her name."

"So you are fond of animals?"

"Inordinately," Honora said.

The dowager kept her gaze on Clara but nodded toward Honora. "Does she do this all the time?"

"Almost always."

"Quite annoying."

Clara bit her lower lip. She dared not respond, especially as Honora gave a slight huff and leaned back in her chair.

"So do you have many animals besides Pockets?"

Stroking along Clementina's body, Clara finally began to relax. With one more snuffle at Clara's thigh, the dog shifted and put her head in Clara's lap. "More so at Beckcott Abbey."

"Your country home."

"Yes." Clara looked up from Clementine to find the dowager studying her closely. "My horse, Aethelred, and Moses, who is my favorite hound. And Maid Marian."

The dowager's eyebrows arched. "Maid Marian?"

"My peregrine."

The dowager leaned forward. "You have a falcon? Do you hunt with her?"

"I do." Clara nodded. "Although not as often as I would wish."

Tilting her head, the dowager studied Clara a bit closer. "A peregrine is a royal bird. How did you come by her?"

"Our gamekeeper's mother is a falconer. She works on a neighboring estate, and I used to follow her around the mews. Her work fascinated me, so she allowed me to train one of her fledging peregrines, later gifting it to me, when it became clear we had bonded irreparably." Clara paused. "What did you mean, peregrines are royal?"

The dowager sat a bit straighter and closed her eyes, reciting. "'An eagle for an emperor, a gyrfalcon for a king; a peregrine for a prince, a saker for a knight, a merlin for a lady; a goshawk for a yeoman, a sparrowhawk for a priest, a musket for a holy water clerk, a kestrel for a knave.'" She opened her eyes. "It's the falconer's hierarchy, from the book of St. Alban's. Dating back to 1486, if I remember. Quite ancient. Your falconer did not teach it to you?"

Clara shook her head.

"Neglectful. Have you bred her yet?" When Clara hesitated,

the dowager went on. "You should, of course, especially given the love for her I see in your face." The dowager paused and caressed her Skye again. "You will outlive her, and your heart will be broken. It is why we breed Skyes at our country home. You must establish her lineage." She glared at Honora. "She must."

"But, Your Grace—"

The dowager waved Honora silent again, focusing on Clara. "You must."

"Your Grace—"

A sharp knock on the door brought the conversation to a halt as two footmen and the butler entered with the tea service as a clock somewhere chimed four times. The table between the two settees creaked as the laden platters of pastries, jam, cream, and small sandwiches were clustered next to a wooden tray bearing the hot water, a teapot, cups, milk, sugar, and a small tea chest. The butler paused as the last elements were set fast and gave the dowager a sharp bow.

"Do you wish me to do the honors, Your Grace?"

The dowager surveyed the table. "Not at all. I will take care of it." She looked up at him. "But would you return at half-past? Clementina will need her walk, and I do think I am not up to it today."

Another bow, and all three men left. With the door closed, the dowager began making the tea. "I do not know why we fall silent when they are here. The servants know everything anyway."

Clara smiled, picked up a plate, and added two sandwiches and a pastry to it, and offered it to Honora. "Mother?"

Honora took the plate, then eased back on the settee. When the dowager glanced at her, eyebrows raised, she said, "Just tea. Thank you."

The dowager turned to Clara, who responded, "Milk, no sugar."

The tea and food served, the dowager leaned back against her pillows, inhaled deeply and let the air out slowly. She addressed

Honora. "Now that the pleasant chatter is out of the way, tell me the plans my son has for Lady Clara over the next few weeks. I know he has a regimen planned for her." She gave Clara a nod. "It is what he does."

Clara waited as Honora perked up, finally engaging in something she could speak about with authority. As her mother went through all the details of the planned visits to the modiste and the events the duke wished Clara to attend, she took small nibbles of the pastry. The dowager listened intently, although she occasionally offered small bits of food to Clementina. The dog found the food by touch and smell, and Clara resisted saying anything about what she had seen when she had cupped the dog's face. She gazed at Clementina again to confirm her observation. The poor creature's eyes were almost entirely covered with a bluish film, something Clara had seen before in the older animals at Beckcott Abbey. Clementina was blind.

"Clara!" Honora's hiss broke through Clara's idyll.

She looked up, confused. "I beg your pardon?"

"Her Grace asked you a question!"

"Ah." She looked at the dowager. "My apologies, Your Grace."

The older woman looked from Clara to the Skye, then back. Her smile held a gentle sweetness. "Do not fret over her, my dear. Clementina has had a good long life and knows her way around. Dogs and their noses, don't you know?"

"Yes, ma'am."

"I asked if you had agreed to all this folderol." She waved one hand in a circle. "All that my son has asked of you."

"Yes, ma'am."

"Hm." The dowager took a sip of tea.

"It is understandable. He wishes to be assured I am capable of being his duchess."

The cup hit the saucer with a clink. "Then he is an arse."

Clara stared at her. "Your Grace?"

"No one is capable of being a duchess until one actually has to deal with being one. Prancing about balls and entertaining boring chits and pinks have little in common with running the household of a duchy. And to be honest, nothing can prepare you for it. When it happens, your only choice is to dive in, find those who truly know what's going on—which is usually your top servants—and find your own way. One real basis for being a reasonably successful duchess, indeed, is not becoming too assured in your own capabilities. That is one path to finding yourself in scandal or humiliation. Or both."

Clara glanced at her mother, but Honora had apparently lost the ability to speak. Her cup and saucer hovered halfway up her chest, her eyes wider than the pastry in her lap.

The dowager went on. "But once one has been a duchess for some time, as I have, more than forty years now, one can begin to see qualities in other women, and one recognizes who and who would not make a good one. You do know my son is paying suit to two other women?"

Clara dug deep to find her voice. "I thought three."

"As I said, my son is a fool. One of those ladies has recently become betrothed to someone else. The other two . . . my teas with them did not go nearly so well as this one."

Honora finally set her cup down.

"Do you love my son?"

Clara blinked. "I beg your pardon?"

"Ah, so no, you do not. Not that it is vital in an arrangement like this. Do you love another?"

Clara couldn't catch her breath, Michael's face immediately in her mind. "Your Grace—"

"So yes. Is he nobility? A good man?"

Clara's shoulders sagged in surrender, her voice weak. "Yes."

"Clara!"

The dowager ignored Honora. "Neither of them deserve you, if you ask me."

Clara looked up as yet another surprise left her speechless.

"I think you would make a fine duchess. You are strong and

you know your own mind. You would be a good match for my son, who can be a pompous bully when he does not get his own way. He is an excellent duke, but something of an arse. Your first years with him will be pure misery, my girl, especially if you already love another. Do you think you are ready for that?"

Something about the dowager's fiery words sparked something in Clara, something she had been afraid to reveal. She straightened and met the dowager's eyes. "As you said, Your Grace, one does not know what one is capable of until one is confronted with a situation."

The older woman cackled. "I do believe my son has met his match." Her voice dropped to a whisper. "Do not let him bully you, my dear. If you dislike something he insists on, stand up to him. He will bray, like the arse he is, but if you do not stand your ground now, those first years will be even more miserable."

"And if he throws me over because of that?"

"Clara!"

The dowager paused, then slowly smiled. "If he does, you write to me immediately. I will take care of it. You will not be ruined just because he is a fool." The smile turned sly. "I may no longer be the duchess, but after forty years, I have learned a thing or two about how Society—and my son—works."

A knock on the door got their attention, and it opened to reveal the butler, who looked at the dowager expectantly.

"Ah." She pushed forward on the settee. "It is time for Clementina's walk. Please see the ladies out first."

Honora and Clara set aside their cups and plates and stood as the dowager did.

"I am afraid I must rest." With that she stood and waited as Clementina hopped to the floor. They both tottered toward the butler, who accepted the dog's lead from his mistress, then turned his gaze back on Honora and Clara as the dowager headed down the hall.

He held one arm wide. "My ladies."

They left the room, silent until they settled in the carriage waiting for them outside. As the door closed, Honora muttered, "How extraordinary."

Clara felt numb, overwhelmed. But as she pondered over the dowager's last words, which at first had seemed supportive, an underlying message suddenly rang clear.

She believes he will throw me over. She does not think he will marry me.

And Clara was not sure if she felt relieved . . . or devastated. She did know one thing for certain. She needed to see Michael Ashton.

Soon. If Radcliff's plan works . . . soon.

CHAPTER SIXTEEN

Monday, 22 August 1825
Tattersall's
Half past ten in the morning

THE CACOPHONY OF Tattersall's began long before they reached the actual facility. The roads heading to the auction house had been crammed with people and horses for some time, and Michael fought the urge to flee down a diverging road toward Old Smithfield Market, where other livestock was bought and sold, including horses of less worthy lines and ponies perfect for a boys' school. More than once, Robert, riding at his side in a kit of purple and lavender, had declared, somewhat unprompted, "Do not think of it!"

No explanation of the words was needed. Whether his brother meant strong drink, a solid retreat, or Lady Clara Durham, Michael knew Robert meant for him to stay focused on the task at hand. But the crowd of magnificent beasts and highly skilled riders on the increasingly crowded road only served to remind Michael that he was far out of his depth here, more so than even at the most elaborate of Society ballrooms.

The thought terrified him.

Not that this was his first trip to Tattersall's. Philip had brought his sons to Tattersall's even as children. And then, as now, Michael had ridden with his father and brothers, and he had to admit they made for an impressive entourage. Philip led the group on a gray stallion of Arabian descent, a gift from his father-in-law. Philip's large frame on a horse that stood almost eighteen hands tall presented a regal bearing, resplendent in an emerald-green topcoat and hat of brushed silk, gold cravat and cream waistcoat with gold embroidery. Thomas, in indigo and silver, rode at Philip's side on the ebony stalwart Maximilian, his preferred mount for many years. Whitby Little and the Ashton House groom, who would lead the three horses Michael planned to buy back to their own stables, followed them. The horses, the stable boys, and the grooms bore the green and gold livery of the Kennet duchy.

Michael straightened in the saddle, trying to find courage in the family around him.

On his previous trips, however, he had been an observer, a boy fascinated by the process and exhilarated by the presence of so many horses of fine quality and distinction. Never before had so much been at risk. Michael knew he had only one chance to make an impression, to reveal to nobility and gentry what he had to offer. If this did not go well, he could struggle for months to bring recognition and favor to the fledgling company. His two-month window to persuade the Earl of Beckcott to consider him for Lady Clara's hand would slam shut.

The raucous noise of the crush escalated as they closed in on Hyde Park Corner, and Michael had to focus hard to fight both his anxiety and his abrupt craving for drink. Copper, who had been placid so far, picked up on his nervousness and pranced suddenly to the left. It was exactly the rush of motion Michael needed to ground himself, and he used his knees and a soft pull on the reins to bring Copper back in line behind his father. With Copper settling, Michael stroked his neck.

"Excellent move, Ashton."

Michael looked left, and the Duke of Embleton moved up beside him. "Thank you. It has been some time since Copper has been in this large a gathering."

The duke nodded. "Stallions can be a bit unpredictable, even well-trained ones. But you sit him as if you were born to it."

Michael could not help but smile. "If you listen to my father, that is an absolute truth. According to him, the first time I was on a horse, they had to secure me with my leading strings."

Embleton chuckled and nodded to the rear. "So you have major plans with these three?"

Michael twisted in the saddle. The two geldings, one a white-gray and one a bay with a coat as rich as Copper's, trailed behind the duke's entourage, led by two grooms; the black stallion brought up the rear. The geldings walked easily alongside each other, but seemed nervous, their heads jerking occasionally. "Have you raced them?"

Embleton shook his head. "I had planned to, come spring. They are not quite two, and just now adjusting to walking beside other animals, albeit not entirely well. Running alongside another animal is still to come."

Michael glanced at the horses again. "They are doing quite well in this crowd."

"So far, I have been pleased. They have proven quite easy to train." Embleton smiled. "Which will be a point made during the long trot."

Michael thought about the "long trot," those moments when a horse would be led back and forth along a dirt path at the far side of Tattersall's courtyard, just before the bidding began. The goal was to allow buyers to view the horse in action, but owners would often be in the crowd, adding their comments to the auctioneer's about the quality of the horse. "I have heard rumors that I am not the only one who will be bidding on your steeds today."

Embleton sobered. "I have heard the same. I have also heard that the goal will be more about driving up the price than any real interest in the animals."

"Wykeham seems to feel the need to compete with me, but

that may be linked to his current, um, investment with my brother."

Embleton glanced at him, then Robert, who seemed to ignore the conversation. Michael continued. "He may see them as a path to resolve certain . . . discrepancies . . . in that investment. I understand he means to race them. Soon. In order to recoup the cost."

Embleton's eyes dulled. "In order to bet on the races."

"So I hear."

Riding in silence a few moments, Embleton looked several times at the horses, each time his eyes narrowing a bit more, a hard line forming between his eyebrows. "They really need more training. Should not be raced for at least six months."

Michael shrugged.

"And your plans for them?"

"I mean to build a good stable at Ashton Park and the new boys' school. That's my primary desire for the stallion. But the geldings would continue their training. And would be used to teach the boys about caring for fine animals. Racing, when they are ready, when they are known for their performance, for which we would be facilitating major bets."

"So the other rumor I have heard—"

"Is also true."

The duke gave a sly smile and a nod at Philip's back. "Kennet was never known for shirking from a scandal."

"Or two."

Embleton chuckled. "I will meet you in the courtyard."

Michael touched his forehead. "I look forward to it."

The duke, whose left arm hung limply at his side, shifted the grip on the reins in his right hand and pressed in with his knees. Smoothly, his horse eased up and fell back into line with his own group.

Philip checked over his shoulder, then edged his horse to the right. The others followed, pulling out of the crowd and halting short of the twin arched entrances to the auction house. He dismounted and waited as the others did the same. As they gathered around, Philip laid out the plans for the next few hours.

"The grooms will care for the horses. I have an appointment with Tattersall, during which I will register the new business with him and let him know our immediate plans."

Michael stared at his father. "You made an appointment—"

"One must not hesitate when an opportunity presents itself, Michael. Saturday morning, I spoke with our estate solicitor, then sent a message to Tattersall." He addressed the group again. "While I am in with Tattersall, Thomas will begin circulating through the right-side gallery and stalls, as well as the Jockey Club and subscription rooms. Robert will work on the left side. Michael, you and Little will focus on the courtyard and the auctions themselves. Your main purpose today is to purchase those horses. We expect other bids, so do not hesitate to raise the price. I want you to be as visible as possible."

Philip paused and pulled a small leather packet from his inner pocket. "I have had trade cards printed for today. If they bear results, I will have more created." He opened the packet and drew out a stack of small cards and handed several to Michael and his brothers. "Once you engage in a conversation with a gentleman, offer one of these."

Michael looked down at the cards in his hand. Larger than a calling card but not by much, the front of the trade card bore a script F in the upper left corner and a script K in the lower right. In the middle, block letters announced "FAIRSIDE FACILITATORS." Fairside was the name of his father's shipping and storage company, so it made sense to use it for additional business dealings. "A CAMPION'S AUXILIARY" ran in smaller letters beneath the name, and in the lower left corner, "LD. MICHAEL ASHTON, PROP."

Robert cleared his throat. "Not particularly subtle, Father."

Philip adjusted his top hat. "I do not believe subtlety is a Kennet bulwark, Robert."

"More like a direct assault," Thomas muttered.

Philip handed his reins to the Ashton House groom. "Gentlemen, let us begin."

Robert and Thomas also passed their reins to the groom and strode toward the arched entrance ways into Tattersall's. Michael tucked the cards into his inner coat pocket, hesitating a bit as he examined the flow of men around them. All ranks, from the lowliest stable boy to dukes in their finest kits strolled through those arches, heads held high. The scent of animals, pungent and exhilarating, clung to the air, a perfume of both power and money. Whitby Little waited a few feet away from Michael, eyebrows arched in question as Michael took a steadying breath.

"Never forget you are the son of a duke." Philip's bass voice rumbled just behind Michael's shoulder.

He turned to face his father. "A third son," he muttered. "The invisible one."

Philip scowled. "Michael Ashton, you are as worthy, as intelligent, and as capable as any man in that courtyard. The hard knocks you have taken have made you stronger than you were four years ago, and our family is stronger and more powerful with you in it. You are not invisible. Just as we know when you are pacing the halls and riding under the stars, everyone in the household, from the scullery maids on up, has seen how you have cared for your mother when I could not, for Thomas after he was shot, for the horses, even though they were already well-cared for. You may be the quiet one, but you are not the forgotten one. You are an Ashton."

Michael stared at his father, trying to mask his astonishment, without much success. Neither would words form. He swallowed. "Father—"

Philip had none of it. "Don't dawdle, boy. Embleton has already registered his horses and his groom has stabled them. Go."

Michael glanced down, fighting a smile. "Yes, sir." He pivoted and joined Little, who followed him into the courtyard.

The noise was almost deafening. The clatter of hooves on

stone competed with dogs yelping and barking from the kennels, the calls of men, each trying to outdo the next to get someone's attention, and the bellow of the auctioneer soaring over them all. It was chaos with an ebb and flow that began to take shape in Michael's eyes as he moved slowly toward the right side of the courtyard, his goal being the stable in the far corner of the gallery. But his gaze continued to roam the courtyard as he examined some of the horses being led to and fro, the ones already on the long trot, and the faces of the buyers and sellers.

He searched especially for the Duke of Wykeham. Michael knew it might be difficult to spot the shorter, slighter man in the crush of the crowd, and he and Little had almost reached the stalls where Embleton's groom had placed the geldings before he spotted Wykeham within one of the open stalls, running his hands over the bay gelding, as if he knew horseflesh.

Which, obviously, he did not.

Michael halted some distance away, watching as the gelding shied and moved away from Wykeham's touch. Embleton's groom fidgeted nearby, his hands twitching.

"Hmph." Little let out a low huff. "Out on the road that horse was calmer than a cow with her cud."

"Perhaps the duke's touch is less than gentle."

"He's gonna make it buck."

Even as Little spoke, the gelding stamped a foot, trying to move away from the duke.

Enough.

Michael moved closer. "Wykeham!"

The duke straightened, stepping away from the gelding. Immediately, Embleton's groom was at the horse's side, soothing the animal.

Wykeham smirked. "Ashton. I was not sure you would be brave enough to come after all. After your surrender."

Michael stepped into the stall. "That was Society. This is business." He reached out to stroke the bay's nose. Even with the groom's attention, the horse still felt skittish, and Michael stepped between it and the duke, emphasizing his height over the duke's.

His expression remained smug, but the duke stepped out into the aisle. "An intriguing bit of bluster on your part, since you have no experience with business. I fully expect you to be as inept here as in the ballroom."

Michael smiled. "So you think I have learned nothing from my father?" He paused, dropping his voice a bit. "Or my brother?"

Wykeham blinked and his smile froze, but he did not relent. "One does not learn business"—he gestured with his cane—"or horses by proxy."

The movement of the cane caused the gelding to balk, and a hot snort blasted Michael's back. Michael glanced at Little, who joined in the effort to calm the horse.

Michael took another step toward Wykeham. "Apparently not, since you have not seemed to learn how to behave around a fine animal such as this. Can you not see that it is you disturbing him?"

Wykeham glanced around at the gelding. "An animal so out of control would be worthless on the track."

"And thus worthless for your purposes."

Wykeham paused, his eyes narrowing. "And what would such as you know about my reasons for buying an animal today?"

Michael arched his eyebrows. "You are the one who pointed out this particular horse, as fine as he is, would be worthless 'on the track.' Yes?"

The duke tapped his cane twice on the stone floor of the aisle. "Do not presume you know me, Ashton, or my reasons for being here. You know nothing."

Michael straightened. "True. I only know what I see and hear."

"I am not to be trifled with."

"So I hear. Thus, my 'surrender.'"

The smirk returned. "That was merely an acknowledgment of the superior player in this game. You are not worthy of her."

"True. And you think you are."

Red flushed into Wykeham's face, and his words snapped. "I am a duke! You are nothing but a rake. A failure on all accounts!" With that, he pivoted and moved away, the cane tapping ominously as he walked.

"What a complete arse."

Michael jerked as Embleton stepped out of the next stall. The two grooms gave quick bows. Michael tipped his head. "Your Grace."

Embleton sniffed. "Odious fool." He stepped toward the gelding and slid his right hand along the horse's neck and withers. The young horse calmed even more under his touch and turned his head to brush against the duke. "You do what you can to purchase my horses, and I will do what I can to prevent him from doing so. Especially this one." He glanced at the groom, who nodded. "It is almost time, gentlemen."

Monday, 22 August 1825
Beckcott Hall
Half past eleven

CLARA STARED AT the direction in her hand, a barely legible scrawl. "I cannot—" She looked up at Radcliff, who hovered at the side of Clara's escritoire. "Where is this?"

"Bloomsbury, my lady. Quite respectable, I assure you."

"I—I am sure. But—Radcliff, I cannot read this."

The maid's face flushed. "Oh. Sorry, my lady." She snatched the small piece of paper from Clara's hand. "My brother—he is not—he's a farrier, my lady."

Clara forced herself to remain calm. "Of course. He would not have much occasion to write anything."

"No, my lady. He does know how to read and write—"

"I'm sure he does."

Radcliff backed toward the bedchamber door. "I will re-write—"

"What time?"

"Half past eight. Cook said the countess has called for supper at seven tonight so all can rest early."

Clara nodded. They had not gathered for a family meal in several days. She had not seen her father in almost a week. "Mother is going to bed earlier and earlier these days, as is my father."

Radcliff paused a long moment before giving a brief nod.

Suspicion reared in Clara's gut. "Radcliff? What do you know?"

The maid took a step away. "It is not my place." She turned toward the door.

"Hold!"

Radcliff stopped, her back stiff. Clara went to her, stepping around the maid to face her. "Radcliff. Do not deceive me. Tell me what you know."

The younger woman trembled. "My lady—" She stopped, chewing on the inside of her cheek. "Dr. Oakley—"

Clara caught her breath. Theophile Oakley had cared for her family—as he did many of the elite families in London—since she was a child. "Dr. Oakley has been here?"

Radcliff hesitated, then nodded.

"For my father?"

Another nod.

"When?"

"Yesterday."

Clara turned, flinging open the door of the bedchamber and rushing toward the stairs. Near the top, she gathered her skirts in a most unladylike bundle and fled down the steps, clinging to the banister for balance. On the first floor, she knocked once and entered her father's study.

Jerome Durham looked up from his paperwork, peering at her over his spectacles, his eyes wide. "Clara?"

Clara stopped, dropping her skirts, her hands flitting in front of her. "Papa! Dr. Oakley—" She stopped unable to say anything more.

Her father returned his quill to its mount, leaned back, and released a long breath that rattled in his chest. His face seemed grayer and more sunken than usual. He cleared his throat, but his voice still rasped. "So you have heard?"

"Not that—only that Dr. Oakley—oh, Papa!" Clara put a hand to her mouth.

Durham motioned for her to sit, and Clara dropped into a chair in front of his desk. He took off his spectacles and set them to one side. "Dr. Oakley is doing what he can to make sure I am comfortable and as healthy as I can be. But there is not much at his disposal. My lungs are . . . too weak."

Clara clenched her fists in her skirts, twisting the fabric. "This is what Mother did not want to tell me."

"At my request."

"Why? I could help—"

"Because I do not want you hovering over me, looking as if I just strangled that blasted kitten."

Clara stared at him, chewing on her lower lip, fighting the heat of tears in her eyes.

Durham rested his forearms on the desk. "This is why I wanted you settled this season." He straightened a bit but shivered in doing so. "Your mother tells me you have decided to try with the duke."

Clara most definitely did not want to talk about Wykeham. "I have acquiesced as it is the right thing to do. What does the doctor say?"

"That the scarring from repeated pneumonias is irreparable. That I will continue to develop infections that will weaken me further."

"So you are dying."

Durham gave her a slow smile. "Daughter, we are all dying. Some simply do it faster than others."

"Papa . . ."

"Do you remember sitting in my lap as a girl?"

She had to smile. "A much smaller girl than I am now."

His eyes developed a slight twinkle. "But your sisters did not. Even as small children they were too proper. They would hug me, then stand to one side and wait for their nurse's next instruction."

Clara remembered. "They wanted to be like Mother. Starched and prim."

"Whereas you would scamper to me and clamber up in my lap as if I were a mountain waiting to be climbed."

"You always smelled like mint and tobacco. I loved to sniff your coat."

Durham nodded. "My wildest child. Honora warned me you would be spoiled."

"It seems as if she were right."

"In her eyes. Not mine. But now your sisters are married, and you are not." He coughed, then reached for a handkerchief inside his coat. He wiped his mouth. "I know Wykeham may not make you happy, but I do believe he will be kind to you. And that you will not be too unhappy."

Clara felt the truth in his words. "I know." She swallowed. "I know you love me."

Durham coughed again, then pushed to his feet.

Clara stood as well. "Papa—"

He shook his head. "I merely need to rest."

"Then I will go with you."

Her father nodded but did not speak as she took his arm, walking with him as he left the study and slowly climbed the stairs, pausing several times to catch his breath.

"Perhaps we should move your study to the third floor or your bedchamber to the first."

He patted her arm. "I believe your mother already has plans for the latter underway." He paused on the second-floor landing. "Do try to be kind to her. She is not taking to this idea well."

"I cannot fault her for that. I am not particularly fond of it either."

Durham gave a low chuckle. "Your wit will serve you well, child, despite what your mother thinks. The duke is not quite the monster he pretends to be."

"Can we not talk about him right now?"

Durham coughed, reaching for the handkerchief again. As he replaced it, he murmured, "I will not mention him more than necessary."

"Thank you."

They continued, stopping only once they reached the earl's bedchamber door. He touched her cheek. "Send me notes. You may not see me much, but I want to know how you are doing."

"I will, Papa. I promise."

He nodded, then entered his bedchamber and closed the door. Inside, he began to cough again, furiously this time, a seemingly unending struggle to breathe.

Clara leaned against the door, grief swamping her. But she did not cry this time. Instead a slow anger began to build in her, a fury fed by her mother's refusal to talk, by the illness that drove her father to associate her with a man far more despicable than anyone wanted to accept, by the secrets and protocols that made Society turn its daughters into little more than brood mares.

His wild child.

Her father had called her his wild child. And as Clara pushed away from the door, she realized that she was not quite done with that title.

Not yet.

CHAPTER SEVENTEEN

Monday, 22 August 1825
Tattersall's
Half past noon

EMBLETON'S GROOM WALKED the white-gray gelding across the courtyard just after noon, and Michael immediately sensed a shift in conversations in every corner. It was the finest horse to be auctioned so far, a tall boy at almost seventeen hands, exquisite balance, and a luxurious coat. He showed just enough spirit under the groom's handling to demonstrate his readiness to run. As the groom led him up and down the long trot, Embleton mingled among several clusters of observers, and Michael watched him as much as the horse as the auctioneer began reading the details on the animal, from bloodline to the length of his tail.

Embleton would be a valuable ally. When Michael had shown him the trade cards, he had asked for several, tucking them neatly away in his coat pocket.

Then the bidding began.

At first, it moved fast and furious, one call right after the other. Michael waited, slipping closer to the auctioneer. Then as the bids slowed, he placed his first one. As the auctioneer acknowledged him as "Kennet," heads turned. Two bids later,

Michael heard Wykeham's nasal tenor raise the bid. Michael returned the favor.

The other bidders stopped. Wykeham bid higher. As did Michael. Wykeham stepped out of the crowd near the left gallery and raised his cane as he called out one more bid. Michael increased both the volume of his voice and the bid.

Wykeham scowled and lifted the cane, just as a young boy dashed the length of the gallery, plowing into Wykeham. The duke sprawled on the ground, vulgarities lacing the air as the boy scrambled away, disappearing into the crush of men around them.

"Sold! Kennet!"

Feeling a rush of elation, Michael collected the slip from the auctioneer and looked around, searching the crowd. He found his father near the end of the right gallery and grinned as Philip nodded once and touched the brim of his top hat.

Embleton stepped up beside him. "Congratulations."

"Thank you, my lord."

"Although that escapade will not work a second time."

Michael stared at him.

Embleton's smile was sly. "Do not worry. My grooms have the boy safely tucked away. Wykeham will not see him again unless he visits me at home. Which I doubt he will do."

Michael found his voice. "That was quite a risk."

Embleton kept his gaze on the cluster of men currently helping Wykeham off the ground. "Not entirely. Wykeham has a tendency to use that cane for emphasis, even though he needs it for balance. He is especially prone to do so in Parliament, but there are desks to hold on to. I knew if you made him angry enough, he would start waving it about."

"Balance."

Embleton straightened. "Broke his pelvis several years ago. No one is quite sure how. Healed well, but he is slightly off center. Not noticeable unless he stumbles."

"Or someone bumps into him."

"The cane helps him recover."

"Unless it's up in the air."

"There are two horses before the bay gelding. The stallion will be right behind. You should prepare." Embleton paused. "Do you still plan to—"

"Yes. This is a long game."

Embleton nodded. "Still a risk with a fine animal."

"But a calculated one."

"So your stable manager is still assured—"

"No qualms. He knows his horses."

Embleton looked Michael up and down. "As, it has become clear, do you."

"I am flattered."

Embleton grinned. "Not flattery if this works."

"It will."

The grin widened, then Embleton touched the brim of his top hat and sauntered off, calling a greeting to a group of nobles, one of whom held as much sway as Philip Ashton in Parliament.

Ally, indeed.

Michael watched a moment, then felt a large presence move in behind him.

"That was somewhat unexpected," Philip said.

"Indeed. Embleton seems to be on our side."

"Wykeham has made more than a few enemies over the years. Embleton's father never liked Wykeham's father either. If you will give me that slip, I'll settle up on this one."

Michael passed the sales slip to his father. "I could do them after all the bidding."

Philip said casually, "I want to be seen in the counting room. And after you buy the stallion, it will be your turn in the counting room. It's all about being visible."

"And I thought only women wanted to make a grand entrance."

His father chuckled. "No woman on the planet could match the preening pride of an entitled nobleman who wants to be noticed."

"Especially one who is a head taller than the rest of them."

"You will learn to use all your advantages, Michael. Especially the ones God conveyed on you." Philip turned and smoothly melded into the crowd. Eyes followed Philip, with most heads having to turn upward to see his face, which remained placid, with a slight smile tugging at his mouth.

As Michael looked back toward the auctioneer, he realized the group of nobles Embleton had addressed now stared at him. Two held trading cards, which held their attention a moment, then they glanced up at him. Michael nodded at them, then turned to search for Little.

"My lord?"

He looked down. One of their stable boys stood before him, holding out a folded piece of paper. "Yes, lad?"

"A farrier asked me to give this to you."

Michael's eyebrows arched. "A farrier?"

"Yes, my lord."

He thanked the boy, took the paper, and unfolded it carefully. The words brought a scowl of curiosity to his face as he read them twice.

Lord Michael,

A friend of yours, Lady Clara Durham, suggests you could advise me about a horse I wish to purchase for my business. Her maid, Agnes Radcliff, is my sister and assures me you have good knowledge of such. I would be glad to ~~compe~~ *pay you for your time. If possible, please meet me at nine this evening.*

A scribble signature underneath was illegible, no matter how hard Michael studied it, although the scrawled capital R must mean the last name to be Radcliff. The direction at the bottom was slightly more readable, and Michael knew the street mentioned, a business area in Bloomsbury.

Even Michael recognized the inappropriate nature of the missive, and his eyes narrowed as he tried to decipher the whys and wherefores of it. A farrier would have to be mad to contact a nobleman in such a manner.

It vanished from his hand.

"What do you have there?" Robert squinted at the note.

Michael watched as his brother read it. "To be truthful, I have no idea."

Robert's eyes widened, then he glanced from Michael to the note again. His face split into a grin, and he chuckled under his breath as he handed the note back to Michael.

"You dog."

Michael stared at him. "What?"

"It's an assignation."

"I beg your pardon?"

Robert laughed. "Read between the lines, brother. You have found a woman both clever and brazen, and I suggest you marry her as soon as you can."

Pointing at the note, Michael stumbled over his words. "You think that Lady Clara—"

"You think you are the only equine expert a farrier could call on in this city? Especially when you are not established as such?"

"I do not—I am not—"

"Farriers usually live next to their shops."

"Robert—"

His brother clapped him on the shoulder. "Do not question it. Just go. Either you will have to deal with a farrier who has lost his senses, or a delightful surprise awaits."

"I do not—"

"Your gelding is coming up."

Michael jerked to stare at the auctioneer. "What?"

"On the long trot."

Sure enough, one of the Embleton grooms led the bay gelding along the dirt path, and the auctioneer began to read the details.

Robert leaned closer. "Stay rattled. It will play into the drama."

The bidding began. As before, there were several fast and furious back-and-forths, but as the price went higher, most dropped off. Michael did not enter the fray, and Robert, his grin twisted and broad, stepped in to compete with Wykeham.

For Michael, however, being rattled was not an act. The thought that Clara would arrange—Robert had to be wrong. *She could not risk . . . would not risk . . . dear God in heaven, what did she think—*

"Are you going to bid or not?" Robert spoke into Michael's ear. "Do not put this on me."

Michael shook his head to clear it, to focus, as Wykeham called out another bid. Michael stepped in, shouting a higher number. With a wicked grin, Wykeham raised it.

Michael glanced at Philip, who stood near and behind Wykeham. Wykeham caught the exchange and said something to Philip, who held still. Michael increased the bid.

Wykeham mouthed something Michael could not make out, then shouted a raise.

Michael looked again at his father, who gave a quick smile, then sombered and made a visible and overly dramatic draw of his finger across his neck. Wykeham caught the move, as he was meant to, and pushed his shoulders back, a wicked grin of triumph on his face.

Michael gestured to the auctioneer that he was done.

"Sold! Wykeham!"

"Excellent performance," Robert whispered.

Michael fought a grin, keeping his expression one of solid disappointment. Wykeham virtually skipped to the auctioneer for the slip, smugness lighting his face.

The long game, Michael reassured himself, hoping that Wykeham's foolishness would not injure the gelding before the game played through. Then he turned his attention to the stallion being led toward the long trot, and he smiled.

Little had spotted the qualities of the black beauty when they had visited Embleton's stables here in London. Older by six months but smaller than the geldings at barely fifteen hands, he had Arabian bloodlines and superb balance and build. His lines were perfection and his gaits smooth. For a stallion, he remained remarkably calm in the presence of people and other horses, and when they had taken him for a run in Hyde Park, he had been steady, even confronted by a pack of children who had fled from the care of their nurses. His chest was slightly broader than usual, but nothing untoward, and Embleton had spoken of his stamina.

A horse to be prized, but one that others would take for granted.

And, indeed, despite his qualities, the bidding began slowly. Wykeham and Michael stayed out of it, the duke barely paying attention. He had wanted the big geldings to race. He had no interest in a stud horse.

Until Michael placed his first bid. He had waited until it looked as if another buyer would win the auction, then stepped in with his first call. Wykeham's head snapped around. Michael ignored him. There was another competing bid, which Michael raised.

Wykeham stamped his cane on the ground and shout a bid, significantly higher than Michael's. A murmur shot through the throng, and some of the clamor eased as men looked from the auctioneer, to Michael, to Wykeham.

"Now," whispered Robert.

Michael bid.

Wykeham raised.

Michael nodded at the auctioneer, whose calls signaled the increase.

Philip Ashton slipped closer to Wykeham, nodding and greeting men as he stepped by them. The crowd in the right gallery parted to allow passage.

Wykeham called out again, another significant increase, and the murmuring in the crowd spread.

Michael looked at his father, who gave a single nod. Michael raised the bid.

Noticing the glance, Wykeham twisted to glare up at Philip. The two exchanged words Michael could not hear—Wykeham heated and frantic, Philip calm and smooth-faced. Both ignored the auctioneer, until the call echoed over the courtyard.

"Sold! Kennet!"

Wykeham pushed away from Philip and strode straight for Michael, who merely watched as the duke crossed the courtyard. Wykeham paused as he passed, spitting out, "A lot of money for a rubbish horse that will amount to nothing. But that's what the Ashtons do. A great deal of effort to little effect. I will see you at Epsom."

Robert opened his mouth, but Michael clutched his arm. "We will take our victories, Your Grace," he said slowly, "when the time is right."

Wykeham stared at him, then continued his path across the courtyard.

"Well done, brother." Robert adjusted his top hat. "Father may have laid the challenge, but I do believe you just primed the pump."

Michael continued to watch as Wykeham worked his way through the crowd toward another line of stalls. "Let us hope so."

CHAPTER EIGHTEEN

Monday, 22 August 1825
Beckcott Hall
Eight in the evening

CLARA EXAMINED HERSELF in the dressing table mirror one last time. A dark green muslin day gown from two seasons ago had been stripped of all frills and ribbons, rendering it plain and dull looking in the low lamplight of the room. Sturdy but comfortable leather boots encased her feet, and her hair had been tied at the base of her neck with a single ribbon, although a few combs held the strands away from her face. At least for the next few moments. A black woolen cloak that had once been her brother's had been unearthed from a trunk in the attic, and the oversized hood almost blocked her vision as well as covering the bright red of her hair. Hot but necessary for the subterfuge. Clara hoped she would not faint from being overheated.

"My word, you look as if you are out for murder and mayhem," said Radcliff.

Clara giggled. "Do I not? All I need is a domino mask and I would be ready for a pleasure garden."

Radcliff scoffed. "As if this were not scandalous enough."

Clara sobered, staring at her image. "There will be no going back from this, will there?"

"No, my lady. Are you sure you want—"

"Yes." She turned to face the maid. "I am tired of nothing, ever, being my choice."

"You will be ruined."

"Only for a little while. Then it will resolve itself—or I will hang."

"Please, my lady, do not say—"

"I will not marry him, Radcliff."

"You could always provoke Hadleyton in sight of the duke."

Clara laughed, which eased some of her tension. "It would only result in making my mother apoplectic. Poor Richard. For a man who risks being called out so often, you would think he would learn to shoot."

"A nobleman who does not shoot?"

"I have known the man since we were children. He could not hit a ship sitting at dock. No, I am afraid I need to find another solution."

The maid paused, let out a long sigh. "Then let us go." She opened the door and peered into the hall. "A tweenie," she whispered over her shoulder, and they waited. After a few minutes, Radcliff motioned for Clara to follow her. They tiptoed down the servants' stairs to the kitchen and out the back gate, Clara trying to ignore that being wrapped in a cloak in the heat of summer made her feel very much like a roasted fowl. At the end of the alley, a hansom cab waited, the sight of it bringing Clara to a halt.

"How did you—"

"Shh! My lady. He has been paid. He knows the direction." Radcliff opened the door. "My brother will meet you."

Clara paused long enough to give the young maid a quick hug. "Thank you."

Radcliff flushed to her hairline. "'Tis nothing. Only I'll need a reference when your mother dismisses me."

"She would not dare."

At Radcliff's look of pure disbelief, Clara snickered. "I will write you the best ever." Then she pulled herself up into the cab, gathering the cloak around her as Radcliff shut the door. The horses jerked the hansom into motion, and Clara pressed back against the seat, trying hard to calm her jittery nerves as she extracted herself from the cloak.

This is madness! Pure, unadulterated madness!

Clara took a deep breath, the words seizing her. She reached up, ready to knock on the roof. The cab would halt, and she could grab her cloak and run, dashing back to the safety of Beckcott Hall before anyone saw her. The driver had been paid. He would not give chase.

One knock.

You would be worth it.

Michael's words to her at the Blackwell Ball. Soft, tender words in that deep baritone, the timber of it searing into her soul. Of all the men she had met, all the courtiers to cross her path, only one had said those words.

You would be worth it.

He thought her worthy.

But so was he. And against all wisdom, she knew she loved him. She was not entirely sure why, but he had come to occupy her every waking thought—and occasionally her sleeping ones as well. He made her heart soar.

Clara leaned against the seat once more, closed her eyes, and thought abruptly of Maid Marian, soaring high about the fields of Beckcott Abbey. Michael made her feel exactly like that. Free.

"We are worth it."

"WELL, AIN'T YOU a tall one."

Michael stared down at the woman holding the lamp as she peered quizzically at his face. She—and not the farrier—had opened the door of the smithy when he had knocked. Strands of blond hair had escaped the scarf on her head, and several days—at least—had passed since her last bath. But she stood straight, her shoulders back, eyes bright as she examined him head to toe. He had at least fifteen inches of height over her, but she was not intimidated. "You sure ain't one o' us."

Michael, unsure of the propriety of such a circumstance, cleared his throat. "I received a note—"

She gave a dismissive wave and turned her back. "Oh, I know all about it. Come inside, my lord. My husband has a room set up for this."

Michael tried to clear his head as he followed the farrier's wife around the outside of the smithy's main room, a dark, smoky and cavernous area filled with the drifting scents of smelted iron and burning coal, and pushed open a heavy wooden door. *Was Robert right about this? In this place?*

They passed through a small, rudimentary kitchen and down a short hallway lit only by the lantern the woman held in front of them. A few steps later, she turned and headed up.

Michael's boots thudded on the thick tread of a narrow staircase, and he tried to shake the feeling this was not so much an appointment than a set up for an assault and robbery. But this was a respectable business—he had taken the time to inquire about the farrier—so surely they would not—

"Madam—"

"Almost there."

At the top of the stairs, they turned left, and she stopped in front of a door almost halfway down a hallway so low and compact Michael had to stoop to keep from hitting his head on the ceiling. She opened the door and stepped aside. "In there."

He gave her a nod of thanks, then stepped inside. He stopped, frozen into silence by the realization that his brother had been right after all.

It was a bedchamber, obviously, although the bed all but disappeared into the darkness of an alcove on the far side of the room. The narrow and dimly lit room centered on a table, which held a tattered ledger, quill, inkpot, and a flickering lamp. Two rough wooden stools flanked the table, and a small, dark fireplace anchored one wall, but the rest of the room vanished into the shadows barely held at bay by the lamp.

Michael's eyes narrowed in confusion. "I do not think—" He turned toward the door, to see it close firmly, leaving him alone in the room. He took a step toward it, only to be stopped by a soft voice.

"She offered tea, but I told her we did not need it."

Michael pivoted, his throat tight. "Clara?" He blinked, his eyes finally becoming accustomed to the faint light.

She stepped from a shadow at the foot of the bed. Her hair— that luscious cascading mane—flowed loosely around her shoulders. She wore only a pale blue chemise, her bare feet peeking from beneath the hem. Even in the yellowish haze of the room, he could tell how the fabric clung to her curves, emphasizing the sweet mounds of her breasts, the fullness of her hips.

His mouth went dry, his mind numb. He swallowed, trying to find some moisture, but his voice still rasped and broke, as if he were a boy in the first throes of manhood. "Why would you do this? What are you doing here?"

"Waiting for you."

He shook his head, trying to free it of the fog clustering around his thoughts, and glanced back at the door. His feet felt embedded in the floor. "But the note—"

"A lure. A ruse. Radcliff arranged it. I'm sorry I deceived you, but I did not think you would come if you knew."

Michael's feelings spiraled between outrage, desire—and fear. *She had arranged this!* "If anyone knew, if anyone finds out, you'll be ruined! We both would be—Of course, I would not have—"

"They will not find out. And if you wish, you may walk away. I will not tell anyone."

"Walk away—" His voice broke again. He knew he should. To save them both. He glanced toward the door again, then back at the woman he craved, had desired almost from the moment he helped lift her out of a mud puddle.

And that was the emotion that swamped him now. He *craved* her, like an undying hunger.

"But I had to try." She looked down, and her fingers curled into the fabric of the chemise at her thighs, crushing it in her fists.

Her words stopped him. "Try . . ."

"To be with you. If you want me."

Michael tried to make his mind focus, but all his blood seemed to be rushing south, his loins tightening, the sudden image of her against him pushing away all other thoughts. "But you—you deserve better—"

Her voice turned harsh, and she looked up again, her gaze snapping sharply. "Do you not understand? I do not want 'better.' There is no 'better' than you. Only you. I do not want a lush bed, or a fine mansion, or a title, or an estate. I want you. I do not want *him*—and I certainly do not want to be with *him* the first time. Or anyone else. I want it to be with you. I am falling—no, I have fallen in love with you. I know a lady should not declare such things, but I am tired of propriety strangling me. If you wish to walk away, then we will both forget this ever happened, but I could not—" She stopped and took a deep breath, straightening her shoulders. "I wanted to find a way for us to have a few hours together. Just us. I had to try."

The words flowed over him, a warm river that seemed to loosen his tongue, if not his feet. "Then come here." He held out his hand, palm up.

She blinked. "What?"

He curled his fingers, his voice low and raspier and more demanding than he meant it to be. But there it was, the craving that overwhelmed him. "Come here."

Clara took a tentative step, then another two. A fourth put her close enough that he reached out and cupped her cheek with one hand. She closed her eyes, pressing against his palm.

"You stunned me, my beautiful darling," he whispered. "You have turned my brain to mush, as you always seem to do, and my feet to stone."

"I did not mean to—"

"Shh." He stroked her other cheek with one finger, then slid his fingers into her hair. Holding her face in a tender but firm grip, he lowered his mouth to hers, brushing her lips back and forth before settling into a deep exploration, pressing his tongue into her mouth.

With a long sigh, Clara melted against him, clutching his coat as if expecting him to flee. The press of her breasts, the warmth of her body slipped over him like a warm bath, and the heat that surged through him caused his breath to catch and his erection to harden even more. Michael slid his hands down her back. He tugged at the chemise as he eased from the lingering kiss.

"Let us take this off."

Clara stepped away from him, and Michael lifted the chemise and cast it across one of the stools. He let his gaze linger on her bare form, wonder filling him that this beautiful woman stood before him. He traced one finger along her neck and shoulder, and she shivered. "You are so lovely," he whispered. "A goddess."

Clara giggled and put a hand to her mouth, as she shook her head. "I am hardly a goddess."

He tugged her hand down. "Oh, yes, you are. And if you do not stop insulting my goddess, I will turn you over my lap for a sound spanking."

Her cheeks pinked. "You would spank me?"

"Until you begged for more."

Her eyes gleamed. "Promise?"

Michael pushed both hands into her hair and pulled her closer. "You little minx. What would you know about being spanked?"

The red flushed down her neck. "I hear the servants talking. I'm not a complete innocent."

He slowly shook his head. "Oh, but I know you are, my beauty."

"You can change that."

He watched her a moment—the lovely red blush of her skin,

the glistening in her eyes, the pout of those glorious lips—and whatever hesitation he had dissolved away, like a cool stream washing away the grime of a long, hot ride. He knew then he wanted to spend a lifetime removing her innocence, proving to her what a pleasure being in his bed could be. "I will."

Then he scooped her up, holding her tight against his chest. Clara squeaked as her eyes flew wide. She pushed against him. "Michael! I am too—"

"If you say heavy, you will regret it."

For she was not. She felt warm and comfortable in his arms, and she relented, resting her head on his shoulder. He walked the few steps to the bed and lay her gently down on the mattress, which was surprisingly soft and silent. The bed itself, low but with a sturdy if raw wooden frame, had a bare headboard, rare for a home of this status.

When Clara saw his look of surprise, she poked his shoulder. "Do not be a snob."

Michael straightened and removed his coat. "My father has warned us about the rise of the unifying merchant guilds. I did not realize it would involve mattresses."

Clara pushed up, bracing on her elbows. "Everyone deserves a little comfort."

"I suppose." As he untied his cravat and unbuttoned his waistcoat, she reached out and ran her hand down the flat of his stomach and the fall of his breeches. Michael growled and caught her hand. "Not yet, my darling. Patience."

"I am not a patient person."

He grinned. "Then that is one more thing I have to teach you."

Something in her seemed to change then, as her face grew solemn, and her body seemed to tense. Michael dropped his cravat, waistcoat, and shirt to the floor, watching her face. "Is something wrong?"

Clara chewed her lower lip for a moment, looking toward the lamp. She shook her head, an almost reluctant movement.

Michael sat on the bed next to her. "Do you wish me to stop?"

Another slow shake of the head. He waited. Whatever had stalled her ardor, he would wait for it. He watched her for any slight sign that her thoughts would emerge. Still focused on the lamp, her eyes narrowed, then gleamed with moisture, which she wiped away with one hand. She swallowed, then chewed her lip again. When she spoke there was a tone of disappointment in her words. "Must we always change to be happy? To find our place?"

Oh, my sweet innocent! "Not always. But most of what we go through in life changes us in some fashion. I am not the man I was four years ago. Or even six months ago."

She looked at him. "How so?"

He studied her face. "You know about my—"

"Yes."

Of course she did. A humiliation of that level did not escape the awareness of the *ton*. "I was innocent. Naïve. Arrogant, as well. I did not believe anyone could be so deceptive, especially someone I loved." He shrugged. "I am still arrogant at times—"

"You are an aristocrat—"

"But I am not that man anymore. Sometimes change means growth. Something better. Do you believe all aristocrats are arrogant?"

"In my experience, yes. It comes with the status, I think."

"Or because we know no different?"

Clara sat a bit straighter and tentatively touched his chest. Her fingers trembled at the contact, and he put his hand over hers, holding it against his skin. "My love . . ."

"You should probably remove your boots. I believe Madam Radcliff has given us her finest sheets."

He tugged off one boot. "Then I will try not to be too disrespectful to them."

A light finally returned to Clara's face as he removed the other boot and his breeches and small clothes. Standing naked beside the bed, Michael watched as Clara examined him head to toe. Despite her bravado, the look on her face told him for certain she had never seen a man without his clothes. That expression moved from astonishment to glee, as if she'd been presented with a new treasure.

She raised her hand again, reaching toward him. "Oh, my."

Michael fought a laugh, then put one knee on the edge of the bed and lowered himself to cover her, spreading her legs and settling against her. She sighed as he kissed her and wriggled beneath him. He groaned, breaking the kiss. "You will be the death of me if you keep that up."

She wriggled again, glee lighting her eyes as she stroked his back and rear.

Michael grabbed her hands and pinned them over her head. She opened her mouth to speak, eyes wide, but he smothered it with another lingering kiss. She tasted like mint and lemon, and he could not get enough of the soft and pliable warmth of her mouth. He shifted, trapping both her hands in one of his as he let the other trace down her temple and cheek. She sighed as he brushed the mound of her breast with the back of his hand, kissing his way down her neck, his tongue flicking against the hollow at the edge of her collarbone.

He cupped her breast, squeezing gently, and Clara gasped, her back arching as he pulled the taut bud of her nipple into his mouth, sucking greedily before pinching it between his teeth. She squirmed, her hips writhing, as she struggled to pull her hands from his grasp.

"Let me touch you!"

He raised his head. "Not yet, my love." He moved his attention to the other breast, pressing it between his palm and his chest, rolling the nipple between his fingers as he watched her face. "You like this?"

Her word was almost breathless. "Yes!"

He tightened the pinch and she whimpered. "You want more?"

A frantic nod.

"You will leave your hands where they are? Over your head?"

Her eyes peered at him, half-lidded, but she nodded again.

"Then close your eyes. I want you to feel just feel how beautiful you are. How lovely you are like this, ready for me."

A flash of uncertainly crossed her face. "Michael—"

"Shh. Close them."

She did.

Michael released her hands, and she did, indeed, leave them curled in place over her head. This—her trust, her surrender—thrilled him more than he could have imagined. His desire for her became a painful tightness in his chest, his cock hardening. He moved down, now seizing both breasts—one in his hand and one in his mouth—his fingers and tongue working both nipples. He pulled and pressed, pinched and nipped, relishing the feel of her, the scent of her as desire overwhelmed her. Clara opened and closed her fists repeatedly, her arms jerking as she struggled to keep them in place.

He slowed his kisses, letting his fingers trail down her stomach to the now wet curls between her legs. He followed the bare touches with his lips, and her eyes shot wide. "Michael! What are you doing?"

He raised his head, his lips coated with her moisture. "Treating you like the goddess you are. Now close your eyes."

She did, shuddering as he parted her lush curls, then the soft folds beneath, and set to enjoying himself.

CLARA SQUEEZED HER eyes shut against the fire that seemed to consume her, a heat, a pure joy like nothing she had ever felt. Even the barest touch of Michael's fingers seared her, creating a desire she did not know existed. She fought to keep her arms over her head. Her need to hold him, to pull him to her, to feel his skin under her palms overwhelmed her. Her nails dug into her palms as his mouth settled between her legs, and she bit her lips to keep from crying out. His tongue and teeth pressed into her, exploring her as the pleasure built inside, a growing, expanding tightness that arched her.

Then she felt another pressure, this one pushing inside, and she gasped his name again. He continued, his movements gentle but insistent, and pressure increased. His fingers, she realized, as he began to slip them in and out. Clara was not sure she could stand anymore, and her hips bucked, her feet sliding up and down on the sheets.

"A little longer, my darling," he whispered. Then his mouth was at her again, sucking hard at the top of her sex as the pressure and thrust of his fingers increased again.

The pleasure seemed to burst within her, an intense wave of release washing over her. She cried out, a half sob, half whimper, and tears slid from her eyes. Her body went limp, and she fought for her breath.

Michael was at her side immediately, curling around her, cradling her against his chest. "Did I hurt you?" His words came between multiple kisses on her hair, her temple, her lips.

Clara shook her head, unable to speak. She felt as if she had been immersed in a hot pool, the water engulfing her, barely letting her breathe. He pulled her arms down, folding them against his chest, kissing her hands. Then he put his arms and legs around her, holding her close.

She opened her eyes to gaze at him. "I—" Words still failed her, and she swallowed. "I do not—"

He waited, watching her face, his eyes alight with joy. He kissed her forehead.

"That was—" She took another deep breath. "That was un-expected."

He chuckled. "That, my dear, was merely the beginning."

He could not have stunned her more had he slapped her. "The beginning?" He nodded, and Clara licked her lips. "Perhaps we should have had tea after all."

Michael's laughter soothed her soul. He stroked her hair and her back, his gaze tender. He cuddled her even closer, kissing her just beneath her earlobe. His words caressed her as gently as his hands. "You are the most remarkable woman I have ever known."

She touched his chest. "Then you could not have known many."

He fell silent, his eyes dulling a bit. "More than I should have."

Clara hesitated. "Then the rumors are true?"

Michael looked away from her, staring at the wall. "I suppose it would depend on the rumor."

The distant look in his eyes made her pause, but she would not deceive him, not here, not now. "One said you had not slept in your own bed in four years."

The muscles in his arms tensed. "Almost true."

Clara fought the wave of doubt that showered her. *No wonder he was so skilled*—"Did you seduce the sister of a duke? Cuckolding her husband?"

This time his hesitation lingered. "I did not know—" He stopped, a low growl in the back of his throat. "We met at the theater. I thought she was an actress."

"Did you know a lot of actresses?"

He focused on her again, his voice terse. "You knew who I was. Please do not tell me—" He stopped, his entire body rigid. "Yes. There were a lot of actresses." He started to push up away from her.

Clara put her arms around his shoulders. "I do not care."

He stopped. "What?"

She tugged at him. "I do not care if there were others. Not if they taught you . . . *that*."

He remained quite still. "Clara—"

"You said our experiences change us. We learn. We grow. So some time in the past, you must have learned"—she glanced down between them—"that. Yes?"

His lips twitched. "Yes. A number of them taught me how to"—he grinned—"do that."

"Then I have reaped the benefit of your experience."

Michael folded her into his arms again. "Oh my love, your 'reaping' has barely begun."

CHAPTER NINETEEN

Monday, 22 August 1825
The farrier Radcliff's bedroom
Eleven in the evening

MICHAEL RELEASED HER, sat up, and rescued his cravat from the floor. He slid the silk across one palm, then tested both its length and strength between his hands.

Clara watched, curiosity in her eyes. "What are you doing?"

He snuggled his hip in next to her waist, resting one hand on her stomach. "You seemed to struggle to keep your hands up."

The flush that had filled her face and neck earlier returned. "I wanted to touch you." She ran her fingers down his thigh. "To please you."

He stroked her with his thumb. "You please me in more ways than you can imagine. What I want is for you to experience nothing but the pleasure of my touch. Not sight—"

"But I love looking at you."

He leaned over and kissed her. "And I you. But there will be more intensity—"

"*That* was rather intense."

This was unlike her. Something was wrong. He studied her. "Clara, are you afraid of me?"

Her gaze darted to the cravat, then back to his face. "A little."

She chewed her lower lip. "I've—I've never felt anything like—"

"I will never hurt you. I promise."

She fell silent.

"If anything I do hurts, all you have to do is tell me to stop."

She paused, then nodded.

"Do you believe me?"

Another—brief—nod.

"Why did you want your first experience with a man to be with me?"

Her voice was hushed. "Because I am in love with you."

"And you trust me?"

No sound, but her lips formed the word *yes*.

He trailed the silk cravat across her breasts, watching as she shivered. He curled it around his left hand and brushed it along her neck and down her stomach, letting the end linger between her legs. "Touch," he whispered, "is vital in letting yourself accept the pleasure two people can make each other feel. Sight can distract from that. And you wanting to please me can deprive you of your own enjoyment. Even a moment's distraction can dissolve your most intimate joy."

Clara stilled, as if mesmerized by his voice, her eyes focused on his face. He pulled the silk back up her body, swirling it around her breasts. Her nipples hardened again, and he brushed them through the silk with his fingers, his touch growing firmer as he moved from one tip to the other. Then he pulled her hands together over her stomach, whispering as he wrapped the cravat around her wrists, leaving a length of it trailing down her side. "You are my goddess. I want to give you pleasure such as you have never felt."

He tied a secure knot in the cravat, then slowly pushed her hands up over her head. He tied the trailing end of the silk to the headboard, then gazed down at her. "Is it too tight?"

She shook her head. "But why—"

He kissed her. "You will see. Close your eyes."

"I like watching you too."

Michael smiled. "And you will. Just not yet." He kissed her forehead. "Close."

She did.

He released a long breath, then kissed each eyelid before slipping down, kissing his way down her neck and shoulder, his lips cherishing her newly aroused nipples, relishing each whimper, each sigh as Clara moved beneath him.

Yet what he was about to do made every muscle tighten with both longing and fear. His desire—a raging, overwhelming heat—battled with the terror of hurting her.

She deserves better.

The words thrown at him since he had returned to Berkeley Square—*"You are nothing but a rake!"*—stalled him now, echoing in his mind. *"You are nothing! Who are you to take her?"* Michael paused, his lips pressed against the tender skin between her breasts.

"Michael?"

He swallowed. "I do not deserve you."

She stilled. "Do you remember telling me that I was worth it?"

"You are."

"So are you." She opened her eyes. "Look at me."

He did, and his breath caught at the adoration in her gaze.

"You must understand this. The doubts you are having right now are precisely why I wanted you to be my first. Your care. Your tenderness. Your desire that I be treated like a goddess. You are a good man. And the only one I want."

You are a good man. Words he had not heard in four years, and Michael's chest tightened until he could not breathe. He kissed her, his hands roaming over her, caressing her face, chest, sides, and stomach. Inhaling deeply, he braced on his forearms on either side of her body and settled his hips between her legs. The feel of her skin against his soothed him with a lingering comfort, even as it urged on his desire. He stroked her hair, whispering, "You are my redemption."

Her eyebrows arched. "Of course, I am. What else is a goddess good for?"

He laughed. "Shall I show you?"

"Please."

CLARA CLOSED HER eyes. Michael remained still, and she could feel his breath against her neck. Slowly, so lightly she barely felt it, his fingertips glided over her skin. Starting just behind her right ear, he traced down her shoulder and across the mounds of her breasts. The caresses almost tickled, and she shivered as he circled one breast, then the other, pausing only to lick each nipple, then to blow a stream of air over them.

Her breath hitched. The simple action sent a crazed wave of arousal through her and she squirmed as a deep need spread between her legs. She felt oddly empty, a feeling that intensified when Michael cupped one breast and sucked hard on the nipple, pulling it into his mouth and closing his teeth on the taut bud. She jerked, suddenly pulling on the cravat, desperate to touch him.

"No, love," he whispered. "Just feel."

She whimpered as he moved his attention to the other breast, a rhythm he continued, attending to one enflamed nipple, then the other, until her world shrank to the flaring arousal that consumed her. Heat seemed to build within her, a stoked fire, as he pinched or nipped harder until she moaned, writhing beneath him. He would then kiss and lick the nipple, an exchange of sting and solace that made her lightheaded.

"Michael!"

"Hm?" He kissed her stomach, his fingers stroking her hips.

The need in her was a haunting ache. "Please. I want more."

He brushed his mouth through the curls over her sex. "More? Like before?" He ran a finger up and down her slit, which felt as if it had been flooded.

"Yes!"

His fingers delved into the tender folds between her legs, and her arousal surged through her. "Here?"

"Please!"

He spread her with his hands, teasing her with his tongue, brushing it over the hard bud at the top. "You are glorious."

"Michael!"

With a low chuckle, he moved up over her, pressing his hips against hers as he kissed her again. She felt the hardness of his cock against her and raised her hips to meet him, sucking hard on his tongue. He broke off the kiss, stroking her hair again, his lips closer to her ear. His soft words barely registered on her.

"This will be different. More pressure. It may be a little painful. If it is too much, you will stop me."

She nodded even as she declared, "I will not."

He chuckled again, then shifted his weight slightly as he slid one hand under her thigh and lifted her knee. "Raise both your knees when I begin. It will be easier."

She licked her lips, the need for him like a living animal within her, needing to be fed. Clara waited, pushing her head back against the mattress as she felt the first pressure of his cock against her opening.

It was definitely *not* like his fingers.

As his cock entered her, the fullness, the passion was all-consuming. Her knees drew up, almost involuntarily as he settled between them. Michael had been right—without seeing him, without touching him, all sensation narrowed to the feelings of him steadily pushing within, pausing, withdrawing, only to push in farther. The scent of his body over her—pungent with sweat and his own arousal—and the way he braced on one elbow as his other hand guided his erection, helped to intensify her desire with tender strokes.

But there was no pain, only the pressure that filled her to the point of discomfort.

Michael pushed fully into her, his breath hard in her ear. "Are you all right?"

"Yes." The whispered word cracked, and Clara licked her lips. "There is more?"

He nodded and began to thrust then, slowly at first, then building up a rhythmic speed.

Clara felt as if she were floating, a heady lightness that lifted her, almost as if she were not a part of her body, a sensation that built until she could not breathe. Then, with a rush of unanticipated joy, she crashed, falling hard, her body jerking in an unrelenting wave of pleasure that spiked through her. She called out his name as every muscle spasmed, her legs kicking wildly on either side of his.

With a stark cry, Michael pulled away from her. Alarmed, Clara opened her eyes to see him at her side, his hips jolting as he gasped into the mattress.

"Michael?"

His back rocked as he fought for air, his body shuddering. Then, with a moan, he turned toward her, his eyes wild. He lunged up and yanked on the cravat, and her arms were suddenly free as he gathered her to his chest, enfolding her in his arms.

The release was pure bliss, and she wrapped her arms around his shoulders, her hands finding the silky curls at the back of his head. She buried her face against his neck, absorbing his warmth, inhaling the mesmerizing scent of him. She whispered his name again, unable to say anything more.

Michael held her, his hands firm against her skin, until his breathing eased. He lifted his head to look at her, and the pure adoration in his eyes stilled her. No one, ever, had looked at her like that. But . . .

"Why did you pull away?"

He smiled. "I did not want to leave you with a child. Not yet."

"Oh." Clara suddenly realized that no matter what she had heard from the servants over the years, she truly knew little about men. But . . . "Yet?"

He stroked her face. "Whatever happens, I will find a way. We will find a way."

Clara trailed her fingers through his hair and down his cheek, not trusting herself to speak. Instead, she simply focused on him, on loving this man in this moment.

Because she already knew a way. Had a plan. She only hoped it would bring them together instead of destroying them both.

CHAPTER TWENTY

Tuesday, 23 August 1825
Ashton House stables
Eleven in the morning

"I THOUGHT I WOULD find you here."

Michael watched the black stallion finish scooping bits of apple from his palm before looking around at Robert. "And where else would I be?"

"I checked your bedchamber first, fully expecting you to be unconscious, given how late you returned to the house last night. Or this morning, rather. What was it, sometime after dawn?" Michael held his tongue until a wide grin split his brother's damaged face. "Ah, so it was not a brain-addled farrier who sought your company last night."

Scowling, Michael growled. "And would you be so willing to share your exploits with Lady Eloise?"

Robert clapped Michael on the shoulder. "Of course not. Gentlemen do not brag—"

"You must not have met many gentlemen."

"When their lady's reputation is at stake."

"This new ethic of yours is making me doubt your sanity."

"Did you sleep at all? You look as if you have returned from a month at sea."

In truth, Michael had not so much as closed his eyes. After seeing Clara to the hansom cab the farrier's wife had fetched, he had walked the streets until after dawn, his mind trapped by memories of the evening, by her scent, the feel of her skin under his hands, the blush when she had reached her climax, the tender way she had touched and held him after. Even after he had returned to his bedchamber, he could not rid himself of thoughts of her. It took an epic garnering of willpower *not* to seek her out, even in this moment.

"No." Michael turned back to the horse, stroking his nose.

Robert chuckled. "You will, but not today. Have you named him yet?"

Michael shook his head. "Not yet. Embleton was calling him the Star of Midnight."

"Apt if a little too like the name of a bad novel."

"I was thinking of Kennet's Job."

His brother paused. "Like Job in the Bible?"

"Yes."

"Isn't that a story of unending suffering?"

"But also one of redemption. Job rose from the ashes."

"So did a phoenix."

The horse snorted and tamped his front leg. Robert stepped next to Michael and reached to run one hand down the stallion's neck. "He likes it. Are you sure about this one? Is he up to what you and Father have planned for Saturday? You know the consequences if he is not. It will be another Hambletonian vs. Diamond, only he will be Diamond."

Michael hesitated, taking to heart his brother's reminder of one of the more famous match races in English history—one at which almost three-hundred thousand pounds had changed hands. His gaze wandered over the sleek body of the black. The words Philip had exchanged with Wykeham during the sale of the stallion had been a challenge. A one-to-one match race, between the black and any horse of Wykeham's choosing, to take place Saturday afternoon at Epsom Downs in Surrey. The stakes would be high, winner take all. Philip put up the stallion and five-thousand pounds. Wykeham resisted at first, then Philip had added the debt to Campion's, which made it a wager the duke could not resist. As they had expected, Wykeham put up the bay gelding and three-thousand pounds. A lopsided bet, but one that would garner a great deal of attention. Especially from those who would love to see either of the dukes get a bit of a comeuppance. Philip was generally liked by the aristocracy, but the respect most certainly was not universal. One did not have a commanding voice in Parliament without making a few enemies.

"I am sure. I have seen him run, and I have ridden him."

"Do you have a jockey in mind?"

"Yes. A young chap named Logan."

"I know the name. Chatter in the Jockey Club rooms is that he's a strong rider."

Michael nodded. "I am meeting with him this afternoon. If he suits, we will head to Epsom on Thursday, stay at an inn near there."

"Word is spreading fast about the race. I came through the entry hall after breakfast. The salver there already held a stack of missives for Father. Two for me." Robert reached into his coat. "And one for you." He held it out but pulled it back before Michael could take it. "It is not, apparently, from a certain lady."

Michael tried to hide the disappointment he felt, which he knew to be all too unreasonable. "It would be improper for her to contact me like this."

"Not that it has stopped her before."

Michael glowered. "What do you—"

Robert held out the note again. "Remember. Unlike yours, my valet *likes* to gossip."

Michael lifted the note from Robert's hands. "Rotter." As his brother chuckled, Michael broke the seal on the foolscap and unfolded it. The note contained only three sentences, all of which made his eyebrows arch.

Lord Michael,

There is no need to borrow your brother's waistcoats. Come to my shop tomorrow morning at half past ten. I have ideas you should hear.

Madame Adrienne Chenevert

She had listed the direction for the shop at the bottom. Michael read it twice, then handed it to Robert, who read it with the same resulting expression.

"How very curious."

Michael shook his head. "I am not entirely sure which part of that note is the most intriguing—that she knew I had borrowed your waistcoat or that she wants me to come to a ladies' shop."

"Are you intrigued enough to go?"

"I am, in fact."

"Good. So am I."

"Robert—"

"But right now we need to meet with Father, which is why I came to find you." He glanced over his shoulder at Copper, who moved restlessly in the stall behind them. "Then I suggest you take that horse for a ride before he breaks something. He appears to be quite jealous."

"Only because he knows I still have his treat in my pocket." Michael crossed to the big bay, who bounced his head and snorted, stepping back and forth in the stall. Michael grinned. "I did not forget." He pulled two chunks of carrot out of his coat pocket and held them out in his palm. Copper settled a bit, but did not take them right away, staring at Michael, who smoothed the horse's forelock. "We will go for a run later. A long one. I think we both can use it. What do you say?" Copper hesitated, then poked his nose into Michael's palm, snatching up the carrots.

"I swear that horse knows everything you are saying."

Michael stroked Copper's neck. "Of course he does."

"Then tell him you need to go see Father, make sure we do not make fools of us all."

Michael moved to Robert's side, and they headed back toward the house. "It would not be the first time we have looked foolish."

"True. But I would rather not make a regular habit of it. We have ladies to woo and fathers to win."

Tuesday, 23 August 1825
Beckcott Hall
Half past noon

CLARA LOOKED FROM the note in her hand to Radcliff, then to the note again. She chewed her lower lip, read it again, then looked at Radcliff. "This came in today?"

"Yes, my lady. This morning."

"And my father read it?"

The maid shrugged a shoulder. "The seal was broken when he handed it to me."

"He probably wanted to make sure it was not from Lord Michael. Have you read it?"

Radcliff's cheeks pinked, and she glanced down. "Yes, my lady."

Clara dismissed the embarrassment with a wave. "Do you have any idea what it means?"

The maid frowned. "It says—"

"I know what it says." Clara still read the three lines again.

Lady Clara,

I need to check the fitting on the gown for Thursday's soiree once more before sending it over. Please come to my shop tomorrow at eleven. A tiny adjustment. No need for the countess's consultation.

Madame Adrienne

"But what does it mean?" Clara sat down at her escritoire and spread the note flat on the surface. "She told me that she did not need me for more fittings now that she had three of the frocks complete. Why would she change her mind?"

"Whatever the reason, she clearly does not want your mother there."

Clara grinned. "Obviously. It is probably a good thing Papa read the note. He will already know why I need the carriage tomorrow. Perhaps he will let me take the curricle."

Radcliff paled. "Surely he will want a coachman to go with us."

"I promise. No more wild races through the park."

Radcliff looked disbelieving but said nothing.

Clara tucked the note away. "Help me prepare for the duke's visit. It will help keep me from trying to find some nefarious meaning in Madame Adrienne's note."

She sat at the dressing table, and Radcliff began working on her hair, which had already worked loose from the morning chignon. Clara dusted a light powder over her cheeks in an effort to dim the redness that had started to bloom beneath her skin, especially when she became too warm. Although some of the summer heat had begun to wane, London remained an uncomfortable place, and Clara longed for the cooler countryside of Beckcott Abbey. *Soon,* she told herself. *Soon.*

Radcliff helped her into a neat but simple day gown of pale blue, tying a plain straw bonnet over the curls. Clara did not usually wear a cap in the house, but she was trying to be more formal in the duke's presence. She glanced again at the clock. She had almost twenty minutes.

"I'm going to take Pockets to the garden while you gather your sewing." Clara went to her pillow and scooped the tiny cat up. Although they no longer had to feed Pockets with milk in the finger of a glove, the kitten remained underweight and slept a lot, despite her occasional adventures in the garden or stables. Clara was, however, pleased with her progress and dreaded the day when the cat would no longer be content to curl up in her pocket for a walk.

They left the bedchamber, but as they turned toward the back stairs, Clara heard Jennings call for her. "My lady?"

She turned. "Yes?"

"The Duke of Wykeham has arrived."

Clara's eyes widened as she glanced at Radcliff. "Already?"

"Yes, my lady."

Clara scowled, biting her tongue. "Thank you, Jennings. Please tell His Grace I will be down shortly." Jennings bowed and left, and Clara turned on Radcliff, not hiding the snarl in her voice. "He's testing me, the bastard. Checking to see if I have other callers. Or if I'm lazing about the house in my night rail."

"My lady, he cannot know—"

Clara cut her off with a slice of her hand. "It is not that. If he knew about Lord Michael, he would have been in Father's study before breakfast. No, this is more nefarious, and he wants me unsettled. Hmph." She took a deep breath and straightened her shoulders. "I am presentable?"

"Yes, my lady."

"You will have to do without your sewing today. Let us go see if the duke can handle with what I am prepared to deal out."

Downstairs, Clara paused at the door of the receiving room, took a deep breath, then flung open the door and entered with a flourish that would have impressed Queen Charlotte herself. She gave an extravagant curtsy, feeling the weight of the kitten against her thigh. "Your Grace. Welcome once more to Beckcott Hall. I'm sure my father would have welcomed you himself had he known you would arrive so early."

The duke had stood upon her entrance but now froze, his eyes narrowing. "Are you scolding me for appearing before our appointed time?"

Clara strode to the settee as Radcliff scurried around her to her chair near the window. "Not at all, Your Grace. I would never be so forward or impolite." She settled on the settee, spreading her skirts and making sure that Pockets was tucked against her.

The duke sat once more, taking up his usual posture with his forearms draped over the arms of the chair, one hand dangling as the other fiddled with his cane. "I hear you had a most intriguing visit with my mother on Sunday afternoon. She seems to like you."

Pockets, it appeared, was not as content as usual. Tiny kitten claws made their presence known in Clara's thigh. She fought not to wince. "Indeed. The Dowager Duchess Wykeham is a charming and delightful woman."

The dangling hand circled. "She is an unpleasant old bat who makes life as difficult as possible for her family and those around her. She should retire to the dowager house on our estate and never return to London. That she seems to enjoy your company makes this situation even more . . . intriguing."

"Should a mother not enjoy the company of her son's wife?"

He made a rude noise in the back of his throat. "She certainly did not enjoy my first wife's presence. Did all she could to torment her."

Clara tried to conceive of the woman who she would always think of as a lovely raspberry pudding as a tormenter. "I am sure that it was a mere clash of—"

"Nonsense. She knew my wife—Arabella—did not like animals in the house, nor do I, but my mother insisted on bringing her blasted dogs everywhere."

Pockets stirred, and Clara bit her lower lip. "I believe she said the family bred and raised Skye—"

"*She* does. *We* do not. They are an affectation for aristocratic women who see them as accessories in the same way they see combs and reticules. Nasty creatures."

Pockets mewed. Clara kept her expression calm, slowly placing her hand on the kitten's body. The duke looked around, puzzled, but Clara did not give him time to think. "Your mother seemed quite fond of Clementina."

"Too affectionate. That dog is blind, sick, and inconti—" He bit off the word, apparently realizing its impropriety. He glanced at Radcliff, then back to Clara. "It should be put out of its misery—and ours."

"Then let us hope you will not become as such as you age."

Radcliff choked.

The duke stared at her. "I am not an animal."

I beg to differ. Clara cleared her throat. "I am looking forward to Thursday's soiree as well as Friday's ball. I will go tomorrow for one final fitting on the gown for the soiree. I think you will be pleased."

The duke shifted and a sly smile crossed his face. "I am sure I will be. Your modiste has done admirable work so far. But I am afraid there has been a change of plans. I will not be at Friday night's ball."

That was news. Clara squirmed a bit, trying to avoid tiny claws. "Has something come up to interfere? I thought you were quite determined to make all the events on your list."

The smile widened into a grin. "Oh yes. I have been challenged to a match race by the Duke of Kennet. It will take place at Epsom Downs on Saturday. I am sending the horse down on Thursday to give it time to rest. I will follow on Friday." The glee in his voice was almost evil, making Clara shiver. "I look forward to taking them for the entire purse and their horse."

Clara could not accept his words. "The Duke of Kennet . . . the *Duke—*"

"Oh, yes. Philip Ashton himself. Apparently his rakehell sons are trying to start a gambling business for horse racing so that the aristocracy will not have to be so public with their wagers. Facilitated through Campion's Emporium. When I win, it will destroy their efforts and clear my debts—" He tapped his cane on the floor, apparently annoyed he had let that part out of the bag.

Disgusted, Clara sniffed. "You need not be so discreet with me, Your Grace. I know all about your debts and your association with various gambling hells around the city."

Wykeham's eyes narrowed, half-lidded. "You do not."

"You are a member of the *ton*, Your Grace, which trades in gossip the way bankers trade in stocks. Do not be naïve. Perhaps there is some value in this business idea of theirs after all."

His words were almost a growl. "No one has ever referred to me as naïve."

"Then do not assume I am, just because I am younger and a woman."

"Michael Ashton told you these things. He lies."

"He did not. As you have said to me so pointedly, gentlemen conduct business at society events. Women talk, mostly about men and their affairs."

"Gossip. No one could know—"

A thin wail split the air. Clara shot to her feet, as did Radcliff and the duke. She fumbled at her side, drawing Pockets free of the cloth and cuddling the kitten against her stomach. The tiny animal looked wild-eyed, panting as her front paws curled around Clara's fingers.

"What the devil is that?"

"My kitten. Pockets."

"She was in your dress!"

"Yes. I was taking her to the garden, but you had turned up far too early, and I had no choice."

"But she was *in* your dress!"

"That's because she stays there a lot. I have pockets. I carry kittens and rocks and flowers and other things I find in the garden or the fields. Unlike some people, I do not spend my days sitting by the fire poking a needle into things. I hunt and I ride, and I will love having Skye Terriers around my feet all winter long."

The duke's hands trembled. "Butler!" he screamed.

Jennings appeared in the doorway, looking as calm as ever. "Yes, Your Grace."

Wykeham pointed a shaking hand at Clara. "Take that blasted creature out of here!"

Jennings looked puzzled. "Lady Clara?"

The duke's face reddened. "No, you fool! That cat!"

Jennings hesitated, then took a step toward Clara.

Anger flushed through Clara like a hot wave. She held up a hand toward Jennings. "Stop!" As the butler did so, Clara turned on the duke. "You, sirrah, are a guest in this house. You will not order my servants about as if they were your own. You will not tell me how to live in my own home or whether I may keep my beloved kitten in my skirt. I am not yet your wife, and you will not yet treat me as if I am." She turned and motioned to Radcliff, who scrambled forward. She passed the kitten gently to her maid, whispering, "She's terrified. Take her to the garden and be kind to her until she calms down."

"Yes, my lady." Radcliff curled the kitten against her body and fled.

Clara looked at Jennings. "Thank you, Jennings. You may wait in the hall. I'm quite sure the duke will be leaving shortly."

Jennings backed away, and Clara was sure she saw a gleam in his eyes, even though Jennings would never be so bold in front of guests.

Clara turned back to Wykeham, who still quivered with rage. "You are beyond the pale—"

She pushed her shoulders back. "You forget yourself, sir. And apparently you are already assuming qualities about me I do not possess. I have acquiesced to be your wife, in part because of my father's wishes and health, and because you said you valued my feistiness, my ability to stand up to you in conversation. You will need to also understand that feistiness has two sides to it. If you think I will yield to everything you command just because the law says I must, then you have sorely underestimated my will. Your mother may have made your life unpleasant, but know now I have the capacity to make it a living hell, in the same way you can mine. The road to hell, apparently, has two lanes."

The Duke of Wykeham glowered, but his shaking had stopped. One hand clutched his cane so tightly his knuckles whitened. The two of them stared at each other for quite a while, neither moving. Finally, the duke tapped his cane twice on the floor. When he spoke, his tenor voice held a low growl. "In truth, Lady Clara, you are exactly who I thought you were. I did not expect this side of you to put in an appearance before the wedding, but I was quite convinced it was there. I wanted a woman unlike the rest of the ladies of the *ton,* and you repeatedly demonstrate you are such a woman."

Clara relented, well aware the scene she had just provoked could have—should have—ended the courtship. "An interesting assessment, Your Grace."

"But apt, as I usually am."

Good God, she despised this man. "Of course."

He stepped away from the chair. "And you are also correct. I should take my leave. I have a busy evening ahead, as I am sure you do." He stepped toward the door, pausing as Jennings once again appeared in the doorway, this time holding the duke's top hat. The duke faced her, bowed, then snagged the hat from Jennings and strode into the hallway.

Clara sank down on the settee, leaning back and closing her eyes. Once the anger had lifted, she was left only with an overwhelming sense of exhaustion.

"That was an interesting display of tempers."

Clara opened her eyes, peering at her father, who stepped into the room and closed the door. "I thought sure you had fouled it for all of us."

"So did I."

Jerome Durham eased down on the settee next to her, stretching out his leg. Clara felt a shot of agony at how gray his face was. "I hope I did not cause you too much distress."

Durham shook his head. "As I listened, I think you trapped him with a bit of information he did not realize you had. Information that could become a weapon were he to set you aside."

Clara straightened. "What do you mean?"

"Tell me about his debts."

CHAPTER TWENTY-ONE

Wednesday, 24 August 1825
Madame Adrienne Chenevert's modiste shop
Half-past ten in the morning

"P ECULIAR."

"How so?" Michael shut the door to the modiste's shop, which appeared oddly abandoned.

Robert peered through a curtained door at the back. "No one in there either."

Michael pulled the note from his coat pocket. "It does say half-past ten. We're a bit late."

His brother looked around at the empty salon that fronted the shop. "But not by that much. And the nobility in this city is not exactly known for its punctuality."

A thud sounded over their heads and both looked up, as the noise was followed by the sound of footsteps that traveled across the ceiling toward the back of the shop.

"Apparently," Robert muttered, "our friendly seamstress lives upstairs."

The footsteps continued, the sound changing to an apparent staircase and the sound of a closing door. Abruptly, Madame Adrienne appeared between the curtains of the doorway—and just as abruptly stopped, staring at Robert. "Why are you here?"

Robert tipped his hat. "Good morning to you as well, Madame Adrienne."

She fluffed the skirts of her burgundy silk day gown and nodded at Michael. "I only asked to see you."

"Which piqued the curiosity of us both," Robert said.

She sniffed. "Once again proving that men are far nosier than women."

Michael had to smile. "You must admit, it was an unusual request. I do have my own tailor."

Madame Adrienne relented with a smile and a wagged finger. "But he does not have the information that I do."

"Which is?" Robert asked.

She motioned for them to follow her into the back room. "The palette of every outfit the Duke of Wykeham plans to wear for the rest of this season. A palette he has asked Lady Clara to mimic in all her gowns." She stopped and turned, focusing on Michael. "A palette you should reflect in your waistcoats, so that you look even more matched with her than he does." She gestured at two dress forms near the rear of the room—male dress forms currently outfitted with shirts, cravats, and waistcoats.

Robert coughed a laugh. "Those colors are bloody awful."

"Robert!"

His brother could not stop laughing. "But they are!" He touched the brim of his top hat, dipping his head at the modiste. "My apologies, Madame Adrienne."

The modiste shrugged. "I am not offended, Lord Robert. You are quite correct. And they are much more agreeable than what the duke will wear."

"You are cozening us!"

"I am not. I have modified these to make them more palatable, as I did with Lady Clara's gowns."

Michael crossed to the forms and fingered the material. The waistcoats were quite well made. "How did you know my measurements?"

Madame Adrienne joined him and began to unbutton one of the waistcoats. "Ah. Those I did get from your tailor, after I heard that you had worn one of his"—she nodded at Robert—"to a visit a lady. Shameful. You are not the same size at all." She eyed both men. "Nor the same shape. You are broader across the shoulders and chest but slimmer in the hips. Your waist is slightly larger, but all that is expected from a gentleman who spends more time in the stables than the gambling dens."

"I think I am offended," muttered Robert.

"I am quite certain you should be," Michael responded. "You should also spend more time outside."

Madame Adrienne scoffed and tapped Michael on the shoulder. "Take off your coat. Let us see if these fit."

Both men stared at her. "Um, Madame—"

This time when she spoke, her French accent had vanished. In its place where the gruff words of a no-nonsense Englishwoman. "I am a modiste, sir. I have seen more naked men than you can possibly imagine. Modesty in this place will be a detriment to the next few hours. Now. Off with it."

Michael felt uncertain whether to laugh or be shocked. He decided laughter would be the best choice. He slipped out of his coat and handed it to her. "In all fairness, I have probably seen more naked women than you might imagine."

She hung his coat on a hook. "Oh, I doubt that. In London, Lord Michael, gossip is currency. The servants trade in it, the merchants rely on it, and the gambling hells"—she winked at Robert—"depend on it. I believe you were still wearing that lavender waistcoat the night you confronted a certain duke who has become an unexpected nemesis for the Kennet household."

Robert found a chair and dropped onto it. "You have spies in my establishment?"

"I prefer the word informant. I believe you, Lord Robert, and your sister-in-law have some of the same contacts. It would be foolish of you to think of them as exclusive."

Robert dropped his top hat to the floor. "Foolish indeed."

Michael slipped off his waistcoat and traded it for the one Madame Adrienne handed him. As he put it on, the difference in the way it felt—from the weight of the fabric to the precise nature of the fit—astonished him. It was exquisite . . . and he said so.

Madame Adrienne grinned. "Of course." Her French accent returned. "I am one of the best modistes in the city."

"But the color—" Robert muttered. "It looks like fresh goose shit."

Madame Adrienne chuckled. "It is yellow ochre. A more mellow version. His looks like goose shit left too long in the sun. The other is puce. Again, a more mellow version of the reddish-purple he will strut about in."

Robert shuddered.

Michael had to agree with Robert's assessment. "Lady Clara will look awful in this color. In both of these colors."

Madame Adrienne circled Michael, tugging on seams and running her hands over his back. "But she will benefit from elaborate trims. I have tempered hers with a dark gold collar and cuffs, and piping on the shoulders and back so this monstrous color will not be next to her skin or hair."

The front door of the shop opened and closed, and Michael felt a spike of alarm, looking in that direction.

Madame Adrienne patted his arm. "Relax, gentlemen." She disappeared into the front room, pulling the curtains closed behind her.

"It does look good on you, color notwithstanding."

"It is one of the most comfortable I've ever worn," Michael admitted. He stroked the front of the second waistcoat, running his hand along the details of the silver embroidery set into a puce silk-satin.

"That man has atrocious taste," Robert said.

"And once again," Madame Adrienne announced as she flounced through the curtains, "people I invited show up with people I did not."

Michael turned and froze, staring at Lady Clara Durham, who

stood in the doorway. Her maid Radcliff peered over one shoulder, mouth agape.

Robert was on his feet in a second, his face lit with absolute glee. "Oh ho! The plot is revealed as the curtain goes up!"

Madame Adrienne shook her finger at him. "You are a wicked, wicked man."

"So I have been told."

"What is going on?" Clara asked, her voice barely above a whisper.

"Well, it would have been much simpler if you"—she pointed at Robert and Radcliff—"and you had not come along for the adventure." She tugged Clara's arm, leading her into the room. "Now it appears Lord Robert and I will be taking"—she lifted an eyebrow at the maid, who said her name—"Radcliff for tea and treats at Gunter's." She glanced from Michael to Clara, then pointed at a second curtain door near the back of the fitting area. "Go through there, to a door in the rear wall. Up the stairs. Everything will become clear. We will be back in about an hour. You will hear us." She turned back to Robert. "You have money."

Robert nodded solemnly and put his palm flat against his chest. "I do, Madame."

Madame Adrienne took Radcliff's arm and turned her back toward the front door. "Then let us go."

Radcliff began to sputter a protest, when Lord Robert took her other arm and pulled her along. Over her head, he asked the modiste, "Have you heard from Lady Eloise?"

"I have not, and it is most concerning—" Her words vanished as the front door closed, and Michael heard the key turn in the lock.

Michael stared at Clara, who looked glorious in a deep blue silk day gown trimmed with piping the exact color of her hair. His mind felt numb, but he rallied in his thrill to see her again. "My lady—"

She looked around the fitting area of the shop as if lost. "Did you—did you arrange this?"

He took a step closer. "I did not. I got a note—" He looked around frantically for his coat, as if he had forgotten it hung on a hook less than two feet away.

"So did I!" She pulled a wrinkled piece of foolscap from her reticule. "She said she needed to check a fitting—" Clara looked around again. "Which I suppose was a lie."

"She wanted to present me with these waistcoats." He pointed to the one he wore and the one on the frame. "Because I had borrowed one of Robert's."

"How would she know—" Clara's eyes narrowed as she looked closer at the waistcoats. "Those look like . . ."

"She said they would be like the ones the Duke of Wykeham will wear."

Clara's hand went to her mouth, and her eyes glistened. At first Michael thought that Clara had begun to cry, but after two steps toward her, he realized she was fighting laughter.

"Clara?"

The laughter came through in full force then, with gulps as she fought for breath. "You—you look—"

Michael put a hand on his chest and tried to look all innocence. "Are you saying you do not think I am appealing in a waistcoat the color of goose shit?"

Clara lost all sense of control, doubling over and laughing so hard she began to snort, which made her laugh even harder. Her cheeks turned bright red, and tears streamed down both cheeks. She wavered, and Michael grabbed the chair Robert had occupied and helped her sit, dropping to one knee beside her. As her laughter eased, she wiped her eyes, then plucked at his shoulder. "Please take this off."

He grinned and slipped it off, draping it over the back of the chair. Her hair had come loose from whatever styling it had before, and he lifted one of the strands, tugging lightly on it.

"I must look a mess."

"You look like—"

"Do not say it."

"A goddess."

"Liar."

"I adore watching you laugh."

"If you do, then you should be there the night the Duke of Wykeham shows up in"—she gestured at the waistcoat behind her—"that."

"I will wear mine and stand as close as possible to him."

Her eyes gleamed and she put a hand on his cheek. "I shall shatter from laughter that night."

He covered her hand with his. "Do you wish to see what Madame Adrienne left for us upstairs?"

"I still wonder how she knew."

"She said something about gossip being the currency of the *ton*. I suspect in this case, her knowledge comes via Campion's. Robert said that some of the women who work there also work for her as seamstresses. And that place is the absolute crossroads of London gossip." He stood and held out his hand. "My lady."

Clara took his hand and stood. They found the door in the workroom and ascended a narrow set of stairs into an open and airy set of rooms filled with the scents of cinnamon, cardamom, roses, and soap. Sunlight streamed in through polished and partially opened windows draped with lace curtains, which stirred slightly in a soft breeze. To the left of the staircase was a sitting room and kitchen, but a scattering of rose petals led to the right, where a small bedroom beckoned. The four-poster bed in the center of the far wall had been painted white, and the covers were neat and tidy but had been peeled back. The trail of petals led to the edge of it, and a single rose lay on one of the pillows.

"It appears she was expecting us," Clara muttered.

"I also suspect this may not be the first time she has done this. She achieved it all too easily." Michael turned her to face him. "And I know this may be too soon—"

She shook her head and slid her arms around him, pressing her cheek to his chest, a warm touch of affection that made his heart soar. "It is not. This feels like a grand gift from the universe." She looked up at him. "I suppose that sounds pretentious—"

"No. It does not. I do not know why she is doing this for us, but in this moment I do not care. I will grasp any chance to be with you. We do not know the future, and if something happens and we cannot be together, I will count myself blessed to have the moments I can."

"We will be together. We must."

Michael shook his head. "Clara, a lot of things would have to happen, and I am not convinced they will. This society, it may not allow me to regain—"

"I know about the match race."

He brushed a strand of hair away from her cheek. "How?"

"The duke told me. He is convinced he will win. That the Duke of Kennet and his family—especially you—will be humiliated. He is planning on winning."

Michael nodded. "I know. The current word among the members of the Jockey Club is that he is organizing a rather substantial celebration afterward."

"Cocky son-of-a-bitch."

Laughing, he pulled her tighter against his body. "That's because he has convinced himself that he is an excellent judge of horseflesh. Which he is not."

"I do not see how he could believe that, given he doesn't particularly like animals."

"What do you mean?" As Clara described the previous day's encounter with the duke and Pockets, Michael watched her face, concern building within about what life with the Duke of Wykeham would be like for her. "You think he would be cruel?"

"If not cruel, then . . . indifferent. Neglectful."

Michael had seen at Robert's new estate the detailed results of indifference and neglect. There were many layers of cruelty available to the human existence. And a new understanding settled over him—all the more bothersome than anything else he knew about the Duke of Wykeham. He urged Clara to sit on the bed. "That explains some of the other rumblings I have heard through the Jockey Club."

Her face lit with amusement. "Do you mean to tell me that men gossip? Horrors!"

He grinned. "We make women look like amateurs, my dear." He slid his hand into her hair, dislodging the last combs and pins from the style. As they dropped to the bed, he plucked them up, one at a time, and placed them on a table near the bed. "The word is that the duke is determined to win you because he sees you as his saving grace."

"I beg your pardon?"

Michael paused, grasped her hands, and brought them to his lips. He kissed each finger, then pulled the index finger of her left hand into his mouth, sucking gently as he focused on her eyes. A sweet, light blush spread over her cheeks and neck, and her lips parted. "Like me," he whispered, "he sees a woman worth far more than Society has ever acknowledged, with more potential than they have allowed you to have. Unlike me, he does not recognize your beauty"—he kissed the tender skin on the inside of her wrist—"nor has he fallen so completely in love with you."

He cupped her face with his hands, brushing her temples with his thumbs, as he kissed her. She whimpered and clutched his shoulders, the heat of her hands through his shirt sending a spear of desire through him. His cock swelled, pushing against his clothes. Her mouth opened, and his tongue explored with fervor and a growing passion. He eased her back on the bed, and their kiss broke as he lay beside her.

"My dress—" she gasped.

"There is no time. But let me show you—" He kissed her again, tugging at her lower lip as he cupped one breast through the stays and cloth of her gown. Michael let his kisses drift downward, over her neck and across the bare mounds above her décolletage. As her breaths became deeper, heavier with her arousal, he paused briefly to admire the perfect shape of that luscious flesh. He ran the tip of his tongue along the edge of her neckline, and she whispered his name as her back arched. "Do you want more?"

"Yes!"

Michael shifted to kneel beside her, tucked his hands beneath her shoulders, and slid her upward on the bed. He fanned her hair out over one pillow, running his hands through the riotous curls. Then he stood and slipped out of the rest of his clothes, his cock standing almost fully erect.

Clara gazed at him, a wicked grin on her face. "I definitely want more."

He laughed. "Minx."

"Without a doubt."

Grinning, he pulled one of the pillows from the stack near the head of the bed and knelt next to Clara's hips.

She pushed up on her elbows. "What are you doing?"

Michael could not keep the glee from his voice. "You will see. Now lie back."

She did, and he lifted her arse with one hand, sliding the pillow underneath her. With her pelvis now tilted upward, he slid even lower in the bed, his face near her knees. Reaching down, he pushed the slippers from her feet, pulled up her skirt and chemise, spread her legs, and rolled to lie between them.

Clara giggled, pushing up. "Michael, what—"

"Shh. I'm exploring. Now lie back, before I tie you to the headboard again."

"That is *not* a threat."

God, he loved this woman. "I will keep that in mind."

He lifted one leg and began at the ankle, his fingers tracing up and down her calf, kisses and light nips of his teeth following them. Her stockings were silk, tied with a blue garter, and his tongue made small circles on the bare skin above it. With a sigh, Clara sank back against the pillow, her fingers curling into the sheets near her side. As he moved up her thigh, the nips became a bit harder, and the scent of her arousal bloomed around him. He found the slit in her drawers, not at all surprised that her curls and the silk were damp, the lips of her sex swollen and a lovely rosy pink.

Michael spread the slit wider, annoyed somewhat when it ripped at the top and bottom seam. *I used to be better than this.* But the extra room only set his senses alight as he found her entrance with two fingers and pressed in. She was abundantly wet, the fluid coating his hand and fingers. Clara gasped, arching, as he made several hard thrusts with his hand, the heel of it grinding on the swollen bud at the top. He watched her as he did, thrilled to see the blush on her chest deepen and spread. She bucked against him, riding his hand as her climax neared.

He withdrew his hand, shifted, and placed the tip of his cock against her. She whimpered. "More?" he asked, drawing it up and down, spreading her moisture over both of them. Clara nodded frantically, and he pushed into her, one hard thrust that put him all the way in.

CLARA COULD NOT breathe.

She tried, but between her stays, Michael's weight, and the ecstasy that seemed to freeze her in place, no air moved. Waves of intense pleasure had swamped her, carrying her to the brink, again and again, but never quite over. Now, with his cock deep inside, she soared closer again, her hips seeming to respond of their own accord. More.

Michael began to thrust slowly, which pushed her closer but not quite over. A tinge of frustration bit at her, especially as he watched her with that stupid, irritating grin, as if he knew she was close.

"Please," she begged.

His eyes gleamed and he shifted his hips, increasing his speed. "Like this?"

The resulting euphoria filled her mind, her breasts, her cunt, as if she had lifted from the bed, floating in the sky. The air she had sought rushed back into her lungs. "Yes!"

"Close your eyes. Just feel it."

She did, and his breathing became rapid pants as he drove his cock into her harder and with more speed. Pleasure became pain became pleasure as she writhed under him, desperately seeking that release.

"Now, my love," he gasped, and shifted again, and a new pressure on her most tender flesh sent her cascading over the edge. She cried out, her legs kicking, her entire body bowing under him.

Michael slid an arm under her back, pushing her hard against him. "Hold on to me."

Clara threw her arms around his back, clutching him, feeling her nails dig into his back as her peak passed. He continued to thrust a bit longer, then with a stark cry, he withdrew and rolled next to her, his hips rocking as he spent into the sheets.

Clara watched him as her own breathing slowed, her gaze lingering on the taut muscles of his back and arms, the true strength of his body that had been hidden beneath his clothes. The statues in the museums were not as well sculpted. Only the statues did not have red half-moon cuts in them.

She pulled the pillow from beneath her butt, then sat up and ran her hand along that beautiful back. "I'm sorry if I hurt you."

He turned around, instantly gathering her in his arms. and laying her back against the pillows. "You did not hurt me." He stroked her cheek, and she could smell the scent of both of them on his fingers. "When a woman does that, it feels as if my cock gets even harder." He flinched. "It's hard to explain."

She smiled at him. "Then do not. I am pretty mindless myself right now. I only want to hold you."

"Then that is what we will do." He settled deeper into the pillows, wrapping all limbs around her.

Clara nuzzled against his side, relishing this moment of peace, trying to ignore the fear of the consequences if all their plans went awry. "What happens if you lose on Saturday?"

Michael remained silent several minutes. Finally, he released a long breath. "I would prefer to focus on what will happen when we win."

She had to smile. "So what will happen when you win?"

He stroked her hair, picking up one strand and kissing the tip. "If we win, I will acquire the gelding he will race and three-thousand pounds. But it's more than the wager. All the aristocracy will be watching, to see how the new company handles the betting, what part Campion's will play. Winning will demonstrate that I do, in fact, know the quality of a horse. It will raise visibility for Robert's school. I will invest the three-thousand into the new company, which will provide for a sound backing. It will put my name back in the good graces of much of the *ton*. Perhaps even your father. And Wykeham will be so deep in debt to Campion's that we would have to ban him."

She entwined her fingers in the spray of hair on his chest, not wanting to meet his eyes. "And if you lose?"

"My reputation as a facilitator will be damaged, and I will lose any chance of regaining it this season—and possibly the foreseeable future. It will take longer to establish the stables at the school, and there is a good chance I will have to abandon that for a different direction for my life." He took a deep breath. "And I will lose my last chance to win your father's approval. I will have to watch as you head north with the duke as your husband." He tilted her head up to look into her eyes. "I am not sure I'll survive that."

Clara stretched up to kiss him. "Then obviously you must win."

Michael smiled. "Obviously."

The front door of the shop slammed with force that resounded into the apartment, followed by laughter.

Michael sat up. "I believe that is our signal to get dressed." He looked around the room. "Unfortunately, most of my clothes are downstairs."

Clara swung her legs off the bed. "Do you want me to—"

"No. I'll go. And I'll send up Radcliff to tidy you back into propriety." Michael crawled past her and stood, gathering his small clothes and breeches. "And do whatever it is she does with your hair."

Clara tried to straighten her stays and push an errant breast back into place. "Some days I wish I could cut it all off. It is such a nuisance."

Michael froze, his lips parted. "What did you say?"

"I hate my hair."

"Your hair is glorious. All I can think about sometimes is touching it."

"Yes, but you don't have to fight it and sit for hours while someone wrestles it into submission or to have hairstyles that hurt. Or have people make fun because it is an unfashionable color or has too many curls. It comes loose when I ride, and I've gotten it tangled in the reins or in a tree."

He finished tucking his shirt into his breeches and buttoning the fall. Then he sat down next to her and pulled on his boots. "You do seem to wear an extraordinary number of pins and combs."

"All of which poke and prod and stab my scalp." She sagged on the bed.

He twirled a lock between two fingers.

Clara looked up at him, caught by the studious gaze he gave her hair. Not a look of desire as much as one of cogitation, of trying to solve a problem. And her heart swelled a bit more with love for this man. "Michael."

"Hm?"

"We must go."

He seemed to snap back to the present. He dropped the lock, kissed her quickly, and headed for the stairwell. "I will see you in mere moments."

The sound of his boots on the treads reminded Clara of the precarious nature of their situation, but it also sparked her imagination with thoughts of what it might be like to be with this man every day, to hear his boots in the hall, to see him at breakfast as he prepared for the day, to lay next to him every night.

The alternative simply was no longer acceptable.

"This has to work," she whispered to whatever gods or fates might be listening. "All of our plans have to work."

CHAPTER TWENTY-TWO

Saturday, 27 August 1825
Epsom Downs, Surrey
Half-past noon

MICHAEL WATCHED THE crowd of people who had gathered near the Epsom Downs home stretch, deciding that the majority of the *ton* was either bored beyond reason or his father's place in Parliament carried more weight than he had realized. He stood near the largest of the Kennet carriages—a massive vehicle that could seat eight, plus the coachman and two footmen— which his father had brought up from the Ashton Park estate just for this event. They seldom used it in the city because of its size and what his mother referred to as its "royal gaudiness." It had a shiny black finish but was trimmed in the Kennet house colors, as well as having the gold blazon of the Kennet duchy on the doors. All the Kennet servants wore the house livery today, including the grooms.

Michael did admit it all made an impression.

But the Duke of Wykeham presented a similar one, and the two ducal carriages sat next to each other, both beside the Prince's Stand, the only permanent structure at the Downs. Both dukes were resplendent in full kits in their respective house colors, and Michael could not help comparing them to birds—

Philip, the big, proud peacock, who did not strut as much as saunter around the grounds—and Wykeham, who cocked around the grounds like a small but self-important rooster. All crow but few chicks.

Michael had come down early with the carriage, grooms, horses, and the jockey, Logan, to find that most of the nearby inns were already overrun, as were several of the local country estates. He had secured a place but tried to keep a lower profile at what the scandal sheets had called "The Dukes' Match." But the stack of trade cards his father had printed had disappeared into the hands of potential betters and investors, and he had received his fair share of curious looks over the past two days. Many of the cards had been handed out by Jimmy, the lead dealer at Campion's, whom they had brought along to manage the wagering. He had set up in one of the local pubs, and business had been brisk. As of the previous evening, almost one-hundred thousand pounds was in play.

The *ton*, it seemed, would bet on anything.

"My lord? You sent for me?"

Michael turned to Whitby Little, who stood slightly behind him. Little gave a quick bow and Michael nodded. "How is he?"

Little glanced around, as if searching for listeners, although no one nearby paid them any attention. The crush of people milling about seemed more interested in socializing and drinking. "He's steady, my lord. Calm as a summer morning."

"You think putting him on the course helped?" Michael and Logan had walked Phoenix the entire length of the course twice yesterday, and Logan had ridden it once, putting the horse through all his gaits.

"I do."

"Wykeham—"

"His gelding has not set foot on it."

"The man is a fool. This course can foul up even the most experienced flat racer."

Little held his tongue, and Michael almost laughed. Speaking out against members of the aristocracy was a privilege confined to other members of the aristocracy. Little dare not speak out in a crowd. Michael took a deep, steadying breath. "No matter. This day will be monumental for all of us, including the horses."

Little nodded and left to return to the makeshift shelter for the horses, and Michael began to pace. That unnamable restlessness had returned in full flare last night, and he felt as if his heart were racing without pause. He wanted to know how the betting was going this morning, but he did not want to risk a visit to Jimmy at the pub—the call of strong drink remained a raging hunger, especially today.

"You are going to wear yourself out before the horses even reach the track." Robert fell in beside Michael. Dressed in the signature green suit he had adopted when he had disguised himself as Robbie Green, Robert was there to represent Campion's. Still theoretically disinherited from the Kennets, Robert avoided both the carriages and the dukes.

"Have you been to the pub this morning?"

Robert nodded. "It's up over one-fifty."

Michael stopped. "What are the odds?"

His brother paused. "Not in your favor."

"This could ruin a few lives."

"And make some quite rich."

"Did you bet?"

Robert grinned. "Of course I did."

"I thought the house never bet on its own."

"Who said I bet on you?" At Michael's expression, Robert laughed. "The house only bets on a sure thing. And that man is never a sure thing."

"The gelding is strong. And fast."

Robert looked away for a moment, turning uncharacteristically somber. "I asked you to help me with the school's stables for more reasons than helping my brother. I trust you to know horses. This has been your passion since you were four and begging Father for rides in the middle of winter. You saw something in that stallion that few others do."

"His heart. His heart for running."

"And believe it or not, I think you have the same heart. It just needs focus."

"This is quite unlike you, brother."

Robert turned back to him, gesturing to the scars on his face. "If you listen to Lady Eloise, it is not."

"Do you think Father felt this way when he fell in love with Mother?"

"Without a doubt. And if she were not already up and about more than she was a month ago, he would not be here. Would not be doing this. Would you be as obsessed if not for Lady Clara?"

"Most likely not."

Robert clapped him on the shoulder. "Then let us hope this race is one for the history books."

CLARA HAD NOT wanted to go to Epsom Downs, but Wykeham left her little choice. Although ladies often went to the races, especially the Derby and Ascot, Clara despised them. Too often, horses and riders both were injured or killed, and she could not bear the thought of any animal suffering. The Tattenham Corner at Epsom had been a frequent site of pileups as too many riders had urged their mounts into the turn too fast and too close to the other animals. The tumbles were notoriously disastrous. She did not want to see any of it, even if it meant seeing Michael.

Her father understood. Her mother and the duke did not, and he simply announced he would pick up Clara and Honora the day of the race so they would ride with him to the course. The earl's health would not allow such a trip.

Thus, Honora had appeared in Clara's bedchamber at seven that morning, pushing Radcliff in front of her. Fortunately, Clara was already awake and had eaten breakfast. By eight they had joined Wykeham in his carriage and his entourage was well on its way to Surrey, with the duke's horses moving at a swift clip. He regaled them almost the entire trip with the beauty and speed of his racehorse, as well as sharing minute details of the wagons and supplies he had sent to the racecourse the day before. By ten, they had arrived, and his servants scurried to set up a booth, tables, and chairs.

Clara felt completely at odds with everything around her. The crush of people and horses ebbed and flowed around her, and she did not know where to look or who to talk to. Her mother immediately found a group of women to gossip with, and the duke disappeared to parts unknown. Once the footmen finished setting out lunch in the duke's booth, she took up residence in a corner between the booth and the carriage, a spot too narrow for servants with trays or passersby to wander through.

The Kennet carriage sat between the Wykeham setup and the Prince's Stand, and Philip Ashton seemed to be holding court, a handsome and formidable presence with height and bearing. She did not see Michael but knew he had to be around. Searching the crowd yielded nothing until after noon, when she spotted him and Robert pacing back and forth near the ropes that separated the crowd from racecourse. He looked handsome but nervous, and Robert seemed to do most of the talking.

She desperately wanted to go to him, to reassure him, but she knew it was impossible, and would probably distract him when he least needed it. She hoped she would be able to tell him later that she had witnessed his victory on this day.

The noise of the crowd washed over her, and Clara struggled to make sense of any tidbits of conversation. Not even a crowded ballroom with a full orchestra could compare with the sounds of horses, rumbling carriages, calls, and shouts of a soaring crowd. The smells were almost as overwhelming, as family groups began serving luncheons of extravagant foods and drinks. One of the footmen brought her a plate of salted fish, fruits, and cheeses, and she nibbled at a few pieces but had no real appetite.

She wanted to be anywhere else but here.

At half-past one, Wykeham reappeared, red-faced and enthused. He found her and pulled her toward the front of his carriage. "They are almost ready. The horses will be going to the starting point shortly."

Clara could smell wine and some other kind of spirit on his breath. He did not eat but ordered another glass of wine as he sat in a throne-like chair near the front of his booth and motioned for her to sit in a smaller one nearby.

"Kennet will be thrashed," he announced. "This will be the end of whatever pretensions the Ashton brothers have of returning to Society."

Clara glanced at the Kennet carriage, where Philip seemed to be holding an equivalent court. "They look equally as confident."

Wykeham made a rude noise. "Philip Ashton is a petty martinet who has too much faith in his sons. He will be humiliated today, as will they all. And they deserve it."

"I just hope neither of the horses is injured."

Wykeham stared at her. "That gelding can fall down dead at the end, for all I care, as long as it wins."

Clara fell silent. She would not argue with a man who was a drunken despot in his own right.

A change in the mood of the crowd told her the horses to be raced had emerged and were heading for the track. Cheers and catcalls rose up, and there was a surge toward the ropes. She and the duke stood and stepped out of the booth. Philip Ashton also moved closer, a cluster of well-wishers around him. On the track, Michael walked alongside a liveried groom as they led a black stallion toward the starting point, the jockey sitting lightly on the horse's back.

The duke's groom led the bay gelding alone, as the lithe jockey settled in the saddle.

Clara stared, fear for Michael surging into her throat. *What was he thinking?* The stallion was smaller both in height and breadth. He had clean, well-balanced lines, but the power in the muscles of the larger gelding were obvious.

"You see now?" Wykeham snarled. "Lord Michael Ashton is an absolute fool, and I am about to prove it for all the *ton* to witness."

Clara's stomach roiled. *Why would he risk so much on that horse?*

Michael separated from the groom with a pat on the man's back, then trotted toward his father's carriage. Clara stepped backwards, putting a tall footman between herself and the Kennets, but she need not have bothered. Michael, with an unexpected agility, climbed nimbly onto the top of the carriage and stood with his feet spread, his arms akimbo. Clearly he saw nothing but the horses.

She turned back to the track, fear gripping her as the horses took their places, and the grooms moved away.

And the race began.

$$\sim$$

CHAPTER TWENTY-THREE

Saturday, 27 August 1825
Epsom Downs, Surrey
Two in the afternoon

A S MICHAEL WATCHED, the bay gelding leaped forward, first off the mark. Within seconds, Wykeham's horse had a commanding lead of two lengths, as Phoenix settled into a sleek, steady gallop. Michael knew half the *ton* would be watching him—which is why he climbed to the top of the carriage—and half would watch the race. He tried not to smile—hard, because he knew with certainty what was about to happen.

Epsom Downs, unlike many flat racecourses, was not, in fact, entirely flat. Or straight. From the starting point, it rose, ascending to the top of a hill, a hard pull for an inexperienced horse. The course then went into a broad turn to the left—the Tattenham Corner—which had been the site of many an accident. The half-mile straight that then headed to the finish line was primarily downhill, allowing the horses to pick up speed. The last one hundred yards, however, had a sharp ascent that challenged the endurance of most mounts, even those with good stamina and power.

All of which went into place as the horses dashed across the turf. The bay gelding increased his lead as the hill rose, and as they headed into the left-hand turn, his jockey maneuvered him to the left. The move seemed to puzzle the horse, and his speed dropped suddenly.

Phoenix closed the gap, pulling within one length. He wavered not one iota in the turn, his speed constant and sure. As they pulled out of the turn, the bay found his stride again, maintaining his lead for the next quarter mile.

Michael waited, placid, carefully controlling his expression. Just before the start of the race, Robert had told him exactly how many people had wagered against him and the black stallion. He had not been surprised. Over the last four years, he had done a lot to destroy the faith others, even his closest friends, had in him. But today would be different, and he had spotted the one horse at Embleton's that could make it happen.

The horses headed into the last one hundred yards of the course and that sudden, steep ascent. The bay's speed dropped abruptly, his strength spent. Phoenix sailed on, competent, steady, and sound, surging ahead in the final moments.

A gasp echoed through the crowd, almost a split second of silence, as Phoenix crossed the finish line, a half-length in front of the bay. The sound that followed would be one Michael knew he would remember the rest of his days. The shock gave way to a combination of raucous cheers and bellows of outrage. The crowd surged forward, breaking through the ropes, rushing for the horses. Startled, the bay began to balk, rearing in fear. Phoenix stepped smoothly aside, tossing his head, as if celebrating his victory. Little moved in, taking the stallion's reins and leading him toward the Kennet carriage, as Wykeham's grooms swarmed around the bay, trying to calm him and move the crowd away.

People clustered around Philip, and several men began to rock the big carriage, throwing Michael off balance. He clambered down to clamps of hands on his back and arms. Curses and congratulations blended merrily. A bottle of champagne appeared, and a glass of it was pushed into Michael's hand—then quickly plucked away by Philip, who poured the liquid on the ground and handed the glass to a footman. He grabbed Michael's hand, shaking it wildly.

Michael relished the pure joy on his father's face. There had not been a great deal of joy in the Kennet household the past few weeks, and Michael felt a jolt of pleasure that he had been able to bring such an expression back to Philip. And he realized for the first time that this had never been truly about his reputation or the horses or Robert's estate—or even Clara.

It had been about family.

"How did you cheat?"

The demand came from behind Michael, and he turned. Wykeham stood there, his eyes bulging and red, his cheeks mottled and blotchy.

Michael recognized the look all too well. Wykeham was drunk—and he repeated the question.

A well of silence circled the two men as those around them went quiet. The roar of the crowd seemed distant, and Michael knew the next few minutes would be vital to both their futures. This was a precarious situation—one did not accuse another man of cheating at a horse match without consequences.

"A man does not have to cheat when he has the better horse," Michael said softly. "The stallion merely outran the bay."

"Nonsense!" Wykeham made no effort to keep his voice low. "The bay was clearly the stronger horse!"

A crowd of men began to gather near his father, but Michael ignored them, focusing on Wykeham. "Stronger, yes, but without the stamina or the experience of the black. The bay is still unsure of himself on the track. The stallion was born to run."

"How did you know?" came a call from the crowd.

Michael did not look away from Wykeham as he answered. "Because I examined them both at Embleton's stables and at Tattersall's. I have ridden them both. And I walked the track with the stallion before today's race. When you plan to race a horse, you need to know the horse. And the course."

"What weak-minded rubbish!" Wykeham spat, taking a step

closer to Michael. "I want to know how you cheated!"

The silence around them spread, except for a hissed, "Wykeham, have you lost your mind? Are you accusing—"

"I am. How did you cheat?"

"I did not. I merely chose the best horse to run."

Wykeham glared but did not respond for several minutes. The bleariness in his eyes deepened, and Michael wondered for a moment if the man were about to pass out. Then Wykeham blinked and straightened. "I will find out."

"There is nothing to discover."

Around them, the crowd began to disperse, and Philip shifted, encouraging them to do so. Clearly, Wykeham had lost the will to continue. The man swayed, then braced himself with his cane. But he gathered a last surge of determination, straightening. "Well, I know one race you are destined to lose." He looked around, to his left, then his right, squinting toward the back of the booth.

Confusion clouded Michael's thoughts for a moment, then horror set in as Wykeham shouted through the crowd behind him, "Girl! Come here!"

Michael saw the flaming red of her hair first, and his stomach clenched. Whatever style her hair had been wrestled into had come free, and tendrils of curls had escaped from a bonnet made of straw and silk. Her dress matched Wykeham's livery, and as she was pushed forward by others around her, she stumbled, falling against one of the footman, who steadied her.

Wykeham pointed at the ground beside him. "Here, you clumsy chit."

Michael took a step forward, only to be stopped by his father's hand. He waited, fighting the rage building within, as Wykeham grabbed Clara's arm and yanked her forward. He looked up at Michael with a wicked glee. "This race I will win. This pony I will ride first."

A gasp behind Wykeham drew everyone's attention to Honora Durham, who had gone stark white. "Your Grace!"

Michael shuddered with rage, and he knew he would kill the man if someone did not stop him.

Then someone did, as a small, sweet voice spoke quietly. "Actually, Your Grace, you have already lost that race as well."

CLARA HAD NOT meant to speak. The pure humiliation of the moment had pinned her to the ground, the heat of embarrassment roasting her inside and out. To be compared to a horse. To be thrown at Michael as if she were the next wager at Campion's. She had been startled to see that even her mother had been horrified by the duke's words.

But the rage in Michael's eyes brought her out of her stupor. His hands clinched at his side, dark fury in his cheeks. His body shook as if he were a spring about to release all his anger and power at Wykeham. She feared for both men in that moment.

And the words were out before her mind could hold them in.

Her mother swooned, dropping to the ground in a lump, her skirts settling over her.

Wykeham snapped around at her, staggering again. "What did you say, girl?"

Clara raised her eyes to face him, digging deep for the courage. "Those words were for you only, Your Grace, and I believe you heard them plainly. You may drop your suit, for I am already ruined."

His eyes narrowed, and he took one weaving step away from her and raised his cane, swinging it toward her head.

A woman shrieked and several male voices bellowed his name. But the cane stopped short of her face, blocked by a dark hand, which snagged the cane and jerked it from Wykeham's grasp. That same hand raised it over Wykeham's head, and Clara screamed, "No!"

The cane halted, and Clara shoved between Michael and

Wykeham, facing Michael. "You cannot kill him!"

Michael's eyes found hers, his breathing still heavy. "Yes. I could."

Philip Ashton reached over them both and pulled the cane out of Michael's grasp. "But you will not."

Wykeham staggered backwards, stumbling over Honora Durham, who finally stirred. Two of his footmen grabbed to right him, and he found his footing and jerked away from them, barking orders. "Pack everything up! Prepare for departure! Now!" He stepped over Honora again, making her flinch.

He grabbed Clara by the arm and forced her away from Michael, his grip on her bicep like hot iron. She opened her mouth to speak, but he shouted at her. "You will be silent!"

Clara snarled but kept silent as Wykeham turned on Michael. "You, sir. I call you out. Here and now, in front of these witnesses."

Clara blinked. *Did he really mean . . .*

Philip stiffened. "Wykeham, do not be ridic—"

"For cheating and cuckolding."

Clara screeched. "What? No!"

Philip stepped forward. "Nonsense, Wykeham. No one duels anymore. The authorities will—and you are not—"

"Hyde Park. Monday. At ten. You will have my challenge this afternoon. Name your second. And all the *ton* will know you for a coward if you do not show. I will destroy you in every way I can."

Philip began to speak again, but Michael held up his hand. "I will be there."

Clara could not believe what was happening. "Michael, do not do this! He can put me aside! I am not worth it!"

He looked at her, eyes solemn and sad, and she could almost hear his words. *You* are *worth it.*

She shook her head. *No, I am not.*

Wykeham stepped back, almost losing his balance again. Philip held out the cane. Wykeham snatched it away, an action that forced him to use the cane for balance again.

One of the onlookers had helped Honora to her feet, but she remained so pale, Clara feared another swoon. She moved toward her mother, but Wykeham stopped her. "Both of you. In the carriage. This is not over."

"What do you mean?" Honora asked.

"I will see the earl when we get back. I want the first of the banns to be read tomorrow."

Clara could not breathe. "No. You said two months. But you should put me aside."

"Apparently, we have all changed our minds about something." He loomed over her. "You are mine, girl. No matter what."

CHAPTER TWENTY-FOUR

Monday, 29 August 1825
Hyde Park
Dawn

"Y OU DO NOT have to do this. No one will think ill of you. Everyone in the *ton* knows you won that race in a fair match. Dozens saw his lack of sportsmanship. You have seen the inquiries we have received. It will not be you who suffers. Do not do this."

Michael glanced at his father but remained silent as Copper moved restlessly beneath him. Michael calmed the bay with strokes on the horse's neck and a gentle pressure with his knees. When they had come to Hyde Park this early in the past, it had been to run, to dive into a wild gallop, not to stand between two other mounts at the edge of a remote meadow near a small copse of trees. A low, thick fog hung in the air, leaving the grass damp and the copse to appear an impenetrable miasma. A chill in the air reminded him that autumn lay not far away.

Copper wanted to run. So did Michael. Even knowing this was probably his last day on earth.

He heard in Philip's words the desperation of a father who was about to lose a son. Words he had heard since Wykeham had laid out the challenge. The words of a man who had spent an entire day trying to comfort his wife after she heard about the duel.

But it was Clara's words that had haunted Michael since the race. Sentences that tumbled over in his head in endless circles. Words that had generated a nagging suspicion that he did not want to believe but that he could not release. A suspicion that had torn a raw, burning wound in his gut at first, but now left him feeling remote and numb.

You have already lost that race as well.

You may drop your suit for I am already ruined.

He can put me aside. I am not worth it.

Since the day they met, Clara had insisted that she would find a way to make the duke end his suit . . . and she had. A suit that had begun before Michael had met her. A suit that had intensified after Michael had shown interest in her, interest he had believed—desperately wanted to believe—she returned, to the point of setting up their night at the farrier's.

But she also knew that Wykeham had a propensity to take part in duels. Michael had told her that fact himself, and now the look she had exchanged with her maid that day at Ashton House entwined itself with his other suspicions.

Suspicions that told him that Lady Clara Durham was not, in truth, different from other women. Not an innocent. That like Eleanor Carlson, she had used him for her own goal—to divest herself from the Duke of Wykeham. Everything that she had done led to this moment.

So be it. It would end here. All of it. The pain. The restlessness. The betrayal.

"Are you sure the challenge said dawn?" Robert shifted on his horse. "At Epsom he said ten."

"After Father brought up the authorities, Wykeham decided dawn would be better. Less risk of arrest for murder."

"No duke has ever been convicted of murder after a duel." Robert adjusted the balance of the wooden box holding the dueling pistols across the pommel of his saddle. "No one takes these things seriously anymore. You can end this. Focus on the success of Saturday."

Michael fell silent again. He had tried. Since the race, they had received so many inquiries and responses to the new business—and Michael's obvious knowledge of horses—that their butler had replaced the silver salver in their entrance hall with a wooden box. He knew he should be celebrating.

But the image of Clara defiantly throwing what they had done at Wykeham—*I am already ruined*—overthrew all other sensations. She had wanted him to ruin her, not to show her affection but to make herself undesirable to the duke, after all other efforts had failed. And if that did not work . . . a duel. A duel intended to end the life of a duke. But this effort would fail as well. Michael would not shoot. Wykeham would kill Michael and still claim her.

So be it.

"Ashton!"

Michael looked to his left. Wykeham approached, his horse in a canter, along with two other men, only one of whom Michael recognized—the doctor who treated so many members of the *ton*. They slowed their horses as they grew close to the Ashton men, stopping a few yards away.

"Who is your second?"

"My brother, Robert."

Wykeham gestured to the two men with him. "Lord Alexander Pym, my second. I believe you know Dr. Oakley. He is here in case I only wound you by mistake."

"Very thoughtful." Michael ignored the sharp look his father gave him.

"Shall we do this?"

Michael nodded, and the six men dismounted. Robert pulled Pym aside to confer with him as Wykeham and Michael merely examined each other.

"You know she contrived this." Wykeham shifted his weight to give favor to one side. "She used both of us."

The numbness had settled over Michael, a consuming blanket with an expanding sense of apathy. He was about to die, and part of him simply no longer cared.

"I will have her anyway. You know that. I am not about to let that little chit ruin my plans."

"Even if she makes your life miserable?" Philip asked. "You have never struck me as a man who would court misery."

Wykeham smirked. "It will be she who is miserable. I will ensconce her in my country estate along with my mother and return to London. I have mistresses who await my company."

Philip shifted his eyes to Michael, eyebrows arched, probably expecting Michael's temper to flare. But the numbness held sway.

"You have nothing to say?"

"Aim straight. Do not make the doctor work hard this early in the morning."

Wykeham froze, then some of his bravado seemed to slough away. He took a step closer. "Ashton—"

"Here are the rules," Robert announced. The seconds returned, each carrying the wooden boxes holding the dueling pistols. "Twelve paces apart. When you both nod that you are ready, Pym will call out, 'Ready, aim, fire.' Upon 'aim,' you will both do so. Upon 'fire,' you will pull the trigger. I have examined Wykeham's pistols and find them satisfactory. Pym has examined ours to the same effect." Robert opened the box of Ashton pistols and handed one to Michael. Pym did likewise, presenting a pistol to Wykeham. Robert continued. "A misfire counts as a shot. If you both miss, you have the option of a second shot, or you both may retire, honor satisfied. Is that understood?"

Michael and Wykeham nodded, although Wykeham's examination of Michael held more curiosity than Michael believed possible. But it no longer mattered.

Pym walked off the twelve-pace distance, and the two men took their positions. The seconds moved to a safe distance. Oakley moved to stand next to Philip, who had gone stark white, his fists clenched at his side.

"Ready."

Michael spread his feet, bracing himself. Both men bent their elbows, pointing their pistols at the sky.

"Aim."

Michael's pistol remained pointed toward the clouds. Wykeham aimed directly at Michael's chest, but behind the trigger, his eyes narrowed, his gaze shifting from Michael's pistol to his face.

A gunshot sounded, a report that seared through the morning air. All six men jerked, and for a moment, Michael thought the shot had come from Wykeham. But the duke stood, pistol suddenly turned upward, his eyes locked on the thick copse of trees behind them. Michael lowered his gun and turned.

Emerging from the fog-laced trees, Lady Clara Durham strode toward the group of men, a smoking pistol in one hand and the soaked skirts of her rust-colored day gown dragging and slapping around her ankles. Radcliff stumbled along beside her, struggling not to drop a wooden box as Clara thrust the now empty gun at her. Clara halted nearly twenty yards from the men, her face a red mask of fury, her gravelly words strangled with rage.

"I did not truly believe you jackasses would go through with this! Have you all gone absolutely mad?"

Robert made a choking sound, but the rest of them simply stared at her.

"Did you honestly think this would resolve anything?" Her words turned derisive, taunting. "'Oh, we must answer this challenge to our honor. Nothing is more important than that.' How about life? Would that not be worth anything to you? There is an entire world beyond the *ton*, but you think nothing of destroying each other over a bloody race! A debt you could resolve with one season's harvest! Are you fucking insane?"

Wykeham lowered his pistol, stepping toward her. "This is none of your affair, woman. You are not a man, and you will never understand this. You and that simpleton maid, leave now! Let us get on with this." He gestured at Radcliff with the barrel of his pistol.

The maid stiffened. "Simpleton?"

Clara snapped her fingers. For a moment, the meadow remained silent, then Radcliff, juggling wildly, opened the box in her arms and replaced the spent pistol. Then she removed the second one and handed it to Clara, who took three steps forward and aimed the pistol at Wykeham.

"Dear God in heaven," Philip said.

Wykeham, however, laughed. "What? You mean to kill me."

"Yes."

Wykeham stilled. "Why?"

"Did you not intend to kill him? Were you not aiming at him while he pointed his gun at the sky?"

Wykeham glanced at Michael. "Yes. He is the one to answer for the insults to my honor."

"Even though he did nothing to insult you?"

From the corner of his vision, Michael realized that Oakley and Pym were exchanging looks of puzzlement, slowly moving closer to each other.

"He cheated—"

"He did not and you know it. All this bluster and bravado because you cannot stand to lose, cannot stand the thought that you are not the best, that you do not know better than everyone else. Because you do not. All the *ton* knows it, just as they know this duel is because you do not have the fortitude and grace to lose even as much as a simple card game."

"And that is worth shooting me? You would hang!"

Clara's aim did not waver, even though Michael knew the weight of the gun had to be pulling down on every muscle. "If you kill him, I will kill you. I would rather hang than spend a single day as your wife."

The words hung in the air. Michael watched as Wykeham's face jerked through a half dozen expressions, from astonishment to disbelief. The duke gestured at Michael with his pistol. "He ruined you!"

"At my request."

"Bloody hell," muttered Pym.

Wykeham lowered the pistol to his side, his face turning sallow. "Your request."

"Yes."

"To get rid of me."

"Despite your belief, the world does not circle around you, Your Grace. Not even the *ton*. Your title is a construct of the aristocracy, not a designation of your merit."

Wykeham's shoulders sagged and he shook his head. "Dear God, woman, we would have had the grandest conversations ever possible."

"But conversations do not a marriage make."

"You would be wealthy. Secure."

"Miserable. And lonely. Do you not think I heard the plans you stated earlier?"

Pink tinged Wykeham's cheeks and he straightened. He looked at Michael. "Ashton."

Michael understood. He pointed his pistol at the sky and pulled the trigger. The shot resounded across the meadow, somewhat muffled by the fog, and dissipated quickly. He had listened to the exchange, growing ever more hollow and numb.

She had admitted it. *At my request.* All her doing. Her manipulation.

Her betrayal.

With a bare glance at his opponent, Wykeham turned his gun to the sky and fired. As the sound died away, Robert stepped forward and pulled both pistols from their hands, announcing. "Honor is satisfied. This duel is concluded in a satisfactory manner to all parties." He handed Wykeham's pistol to Pym and returned the Ashton one to its box, which he handed to Philip.

Wykeham pursed his lips and nodded. "I will contact your father this afternoon. The suit is ended." He headed back to his horse, his limp suddenly more pronounced than ever, and Michael realized the entire event must have cost Wykeham dearly, in far more than honor. The man might be despicable, but he was not inhuman.

The three men mounted and turned their horses back across the meadow.

Michael watched them, then looked at Clara, but his inability to feel anything had consumed him. "I thought you were different, but you are not. You got what you wanted."

Her eyes widened. "What?" She handed the gun to Radcliff and moved toward him.

He held up his hands. "Just stop."

She did, her eyes beginning to glisten. "Michael—"

"No. You are just like the rest of them. Games. Manipulations." He stepped backwards, toward Copper, his voice rising. "Anything in pursuit of your own goals. No matter who you use. Or destroy."

Her mouth gaped. "Michael! I love—"

"No! You do not!" He swung nimbly upon Copper's back, gathering the reins. "You love no one. It was all a game to get rid of him. You used me to get rid of him. A bloody pawn. I never want to see you again."

Michael jerked the bay's head around, rage and pain finally searing through the frozen wasteland of his emotions. Copper jerked wildly, then responded, bursting into a gallop as they headed across the meadow. Near the far edge, he turned Copper, urging him toward a hedge, knowing what lay behind it—an open field recently added to the park by the king.

The big bay soared, clearing the hedge easily, his strength solid and pulsing under Michael. He bent over the horse's neck and gave Copper his head, the mane flaring in the wind, stinging Michael's face. The run pushed another sensation from deep within, an exhilaration long buried.

Michael screamed, a bellow that made his chest ache, a sound of rage and pain exploding from within. They reached the edge of the field and bounded over another hedge. A quarter mile later, they hit the streets of London, mostly empty at this time of day, except for a few workers and delivery men, lamplighters snuffing out gas wicks. They barreled through the thoroughfares, Copper's hooves pounding a thunderous rhythm, until exhaustion claimed them both.

Slowing the bay to a walk, Michael headed back to Berkeley Square, the numbness settling again, unsure of what he would do next. The past few months, he had realized part of his descent following Eleanor's betrayal had come because he could not forgive her, could not forget what she had done. But these past few weeks had given him hope that his world could be better, brighter.

Clara's betrayal had destroyed part of that hope, turning it to vapor, like the fog of the morning. But Michael refused to go back. He might not be able to forgive her, but he would forget her. Her and all her kind.

Other aspects of his new life loomed, although at the moment, his thoughts remained jumbled. But he would find a new path.

Damn Lady Clara Durham. Damn her to hell.

Chapter Twenty-Five

Monday, 29 August 1825
Hyde Park
Just after dawn

"MY LADY." RADCLIFF shook Clara's shoulder. "My lady, please. Please get up."

Clara had watched Michael jerk Copper around, breaking into the wild gallop. She had heard his bellow of rage and pain, and her knees had given way. The tension, the fear, the fury of the morning vanished as his words hit her heart, and Clara had dropped to the ground as if all will had disappeared from her bones, her muscles, her mind. She covered her face with her hands and sobbed.

Radcliff tried again, but Clara could not move.

"How did you get here?" Robert's voice was low, gentle.

"Our horses are in the trees," Radcliff answered.

"She made you ride?" This time Robert's voice held a hint of amusement.

"Yes, my lord. She always makes me ride."

Never again, Clara thought. *I will never make you do this again. I swear it.*

"Fetch them."

"Yes, my lord." Radcliff's footsteps padded away.

Robert's hand rested on her arm. "Clara, you must get up. It will be vital that you be home before the duke's dismissal arrives. Tell me you brought a cloak to cover your gown and hair."

Clara finally moved, giving a single nod. "On my horse. Not that it matters after Saturday," she murmured into the grass.

"It matters, damn it. Now get your arse off the ground."

Robert's curt words penetrated her mind, and Clara pushed up. He tucked his hands under her arms and lifted, almost forcing her upright. She found her footing and stared at him. His eyes narrowed, the muscles in his face hard. "I should leave you here in a lump for what you have done—"

"What I—"

"But I know my brother, and if anything is to be salvaged from this, you have to go into this with your head high and proud. We Ashtons know about scandal, and if you act defeated, the *ton* will eat you alive. Stand straight and stare them in the face. Withdraw for a period, if that's what you want, but never ever cower."

Clara thought abruptly about Beth. "Like your sister."

"Precisely." Philip spoke from atop his horse, his hands holding the reins of Robert's. "Time will not cease all gossip, but if you do not feed it, it will lessen as the weeks pass. They will find another target."

"I will have to leave the house. My mother will insist." She grimaced. "Has already insisted." She shuddered, thinking about the storm that had rampaged through Beckcott Hall in the last twenty-four hours. "The end of the duke's suit will not exactly be a surprise. I just do not know where I will go."

Philip nodded. "I will call on Durham. Discuss options."

She peered up at him. "Truly?"

Robert coughed. "We are not exactly innocent parties in all this, despite Michael's outrage."

"He hates me."

"Only because he loves you."

Clara jerked, staring up at Philip, who gave her a slight smile.

"It's a two-edged sword."

"And you have no idea the damage Eleanor Carlson caused," Robert said.

"I have opened old wounds." Clara sighed. "I promise you I did not intend—"

"We know. He does not." Robert gripped her arm as Radcliff neared with their horses. He pulled the cloak she had left draped over her horse and stopped. "There's no saddle."

"Bareback was faster."

He looked back at her. "You ride bareback."

"Now is not the time," Philip muttered.

Robert shook his head and swung the cloak around her shoulders. He helped her mount, then almost scooped up Radcliff as if she were a child and set her on the pony, which did have a saddle, one the maid clung to as if it were a lifeline. Clara had to smile at Radcliff's squeaking protests, but she felt little amusement.

"Go. Get away from the city. And hold your head up."

Clara did, urging her mount, a strange one borrowed from their stables before the grooms awoke, out of the park. They walked, more for Radcliff's comfort than her own, because she knew they would be back to Beckcott Hall well before anyone but the servants was awake. They returned the horses to the stable, leaving instructions with one very sleepy stable boy that they should be groomed that morning.

Inside Beckcott Hall, Clara sent Radcliff to the kitchens for a tea tray, to check for a response to the message she had sent to Madame Adrienne Sunday afternoon, and to ask Jennings to let Clara know when the duke arrived. Then she sat at her escritoire to examine the notes that had arrived over the course of the last two days. As expected, they primarily were rescinded invitations to various Society events. Most were stiff but polite, although more than a few were blunt "Please do not plan to attend" notices. Clara knew she should be offended, even horrified, but all she felt was a deep sense of relief.

Radcliff did return with a note as well as the tray. Madame Adrienne expressed her condolences and agreed to cancel the remaining orders. She also agreed to take back the previous gowns. The ones not yet worn would be sold, and the ones worn but not soiled would be reworked for customers on more restricted budgets.

After tea, they began going through every piece of apparel in Clara's dressing room. The day before, two of the hall boys had brought down a trunk and two portmanteaus from the attic. Although the first banns had been read that Sunday morning, everyone knew Clara's appearances in Society had ended. The immediate plan, worked out in an hours-long battle with her parents Sunday afternoon, was for Clara and Honora to withdraw to Beckcott Abbey to await the last readings. Whatever happened after that would be up to the duke.

Now that Clara knew the duke would be ending his suit, she expected her stay at the Abbey to be extended. But she had a wardrobe there, and only planned to take the basics with her.

"Place all the gowns to be returned to Madame Adrienne in that one." Clara pointed to the portmanteau on the foot of her bed. "That one for drawers, stays, and night rails, as well as items from the dressing table and wash basin. Save the trunk for everything else."

"They will not hold much."

"I am not taking much." She gestured at the escritoire. "It is rather apparent I will not be venturing out much. Stained gowns can be burned. Out of season frocks can be offered to any of the servants who want them. Focus on the sturdiest day gowns and boots. My days of satin slippers are over."

Radcliff paused, studying a day gown clutched in her hands. "My lady . . ."

"Do not worry. You will go with me to Beckcott Abbey. After that, depending on where they send me, you may or may not be able to go. If not, I will make sure you get a good reference. I'll ask Lady Newbury to help as well. She will care less about scandal than finding you a proper place."

Radcliff let out a long breath. "Thank you, my lady."

They continued to work until a light tap on the door got their attention. Clara glanced at the clock. Just after ten. The duke was prompt but considerate of aristocratic sleeping habits. Few arose before ten. Radcliff tidied her hair, and Clara headed downstairs.

She heard the shouts before she reached her father's study—not shouts of anger but of alarm. Clara had barely entered the hallway before the door flew back and Wykeham stood there, pale and shaking. He saw her but turned to Jennings, crying out, "Send for the doctor! Now!"

Stunned, Clara pushed by him into the study. Jerome Durham stood by the desk, leaning over it, coughing to the point that he could not breathe. Blood spewed from his mouth as he pounded the desk with one fist, the other clawing at his chest. Outside the door, the shouts spread, a clamor echoing through-out the house.

"Papa!" Clara flew to his side. Pulling at his arm, she pointed at a chair. "Please sit! Papa!"

Behind her, Wykeham grabbed a wingback chair from near the fireplace, spinning it closer to Durham. Tears flooded her eyes as she begged him to sit. But he shook his head, his face growing dark red as his lips faded to blue. With one last blood-laden cough, Durham's knees gave way and he dropped to the floor.

"Keep him on his side," Wykeham ordered, struggling with Clara to turn the earl. "So he does not choke."

But Clara watched as her father clawed at the carpet beneath him, a harsh, gurgling rattle deep in his throat. He tried twice more to gasp for air, then the red in his face became mottled . . . then gray. His eyes became glazed and fixed.

"No!" Tears flooded Clara's face until she could not see. "No! Papa!" Wykeham attempted to pull her away, but she shrugged him off, shaking her father. "Papa!"

Behind her, a wail arose from the doorway, as two footmen tried to steady Honora on her feet, to no avail. The wail became a keening cry, which ended abruptly as Honora slumped in her helpers' arms. One picked her up to place her on nearby settee, as Wykeham again gripped Clara by the arms.

"Come away, Clara. He is gone."

This time she let him guide her back from her father's body, although she continued to stare at him. "I do not know what—"

"Send for her brother."

Clara was not sure who Wykeham had issued the order to, but she nodded.

"The doctor is on his way, Your Grace." Jennings' voice.

Clara finally found hers. "Thank you."

Wykeham's words were low and near her ear. "No one else knows but the Ashtons. I will wait until after the funeral. If you change your mind, send me a message."

She nodded but could think of little right now but the unfathomable sorrow that began to flood over her. She pulled away and again knelt by her father, stroking his back. "Papa." But in the back of her mind, the guilt clung, as did Wykeham's last words.

You should have married the duke . . .

. . . and you still can.

⚜

CHAPTER TWENTY-SIX

Monday, 7 November 1825
Ashton Park, near the River Kennet
Two in the afternoon

"RELEASE HIM."

The gamekeeper next to Michael gave the command, and the dog, currently on point, rushed into the line of brush that crossed the field in front of them. With a thunder of wings, grouse burst from the verdure, a flock of at least fifteen birds. Michael swung his shotgun toward them and aimed at one in front.

It vanished.

He jerked the gun away from his face, blinking. The damned thing had just disappeared in thin air. He turned to the game-keeper who smirked and pointed. Michael squinted, following the man's line of sight, yet it still took a few moments for him to register what he was seeing.

There, on a slight rise in the field, a falcon set atop his grouse, now dead from a broken neck. Both birds were almost invisible in the brown and golden grass of the field. If not for the falcon's dark head and its sudden shift on its prey, he might not have seen them at all.

"It's a peregrine, my lord, although he must be far afield.

They prefer cliffs for nesting."

A peregrine.

Michael's chest tightened. *It could not possibly be . . .* "Or mews," he said. He handed his shotgun to the gamekeeper.

"Mews? But the closest mews would be—"

"Beckcott Abbey." He pointed. "Just over that rise."

Michael made a low clicking noise with his tongue. The falcon's head turned. "Maid Marian." The bird changed position, shifting to face him. "Stay here," he said to the gamekeeper. Then he moved slowly, approaching the bird carefully, speaking quietly. "Maid Marian. You are a pretty thing. Are you lost? That's a plump grouse you have there. We did not even see you coming."

The falcon cocked her head, peering at him, then fluffed her feathers and let out a stark cry. But she did not fly.

As Michael shortened the distance between them, he could see the jesses on her feet, but they looked odd. "You are beautiful, but you are a long way from home." Clearly, she was going to let him approach, and he kept his tone smooth and even. He pulled out a second set of gloves and tugged them on slowly. "Were you hunting for your mistress or on your own? Why are you way over here?"

He squatted and held out one hand. Almost as if expecting it, the peregrine beat her wings and leaped to perch on his fist. He stood slowly, picking up the grouse as he did.

They studied each other, the peregrine twisting her head, examining him this way and that. He did the same, realizing that the reason her jesses looked odd is that they had been cut short, the ends jagged and torn. They were too short to wrap around his hand, but long enough for him to tuck them into the grip of his fist.

"Do not hurt her!" The shout rolled over the field. "Please!"

Michael looked up, and his breath caught. At the top of the rise, Lady Clara Durham sat astride one of the most splendid chestnut thoroughbreds he had ever seen. She rode bareback, and her dress and cloak fanned out over the horse's rump—an indication that he was a well-trained lady's mount. Her gown was a bright blue, the cloak black. Her hair was loose, but it had been cut, now stopping above her shoulders instead of flowing down her back. On her right hand was a thick leather glove.

She looked magnificent.

He moved the peregrine slowly away from his body. "Call her!"

Clara hesitated, then raised the glove, her call echoing over the field. "Har! Har!"

The peregrine jerked, head pivoting. Michael released his grip and gave a push upward. Maid Marian took flight, streaking low over the grass, ascending abruptly as she closed on Clara, landing on the upheld fist and settling with a soft beat of wings. Clara stroked the bird with the back of her other hand, then slipped a hood over the falcon's head. The bird calmed.

Clara looked up at Michael and nodded, then she turned the horse with her knees and headed back toward Beckcott Abbey.

"Clara!" He took three running steps but stopped as she urged the chestnut into a canter. Within seconds, she was gone from sight.

Michael felt an unexpected urge to go after her. He did not want to—her unexpected appearance had caused a sharp pain to re-emerge, one he had thought buried these past three months— yet he did. The sight of her, looking so much like a—yes, a Celtic goddess—on that hill reminded him how much he had cherished her. And how much her betrayal had stung.

Still stung.

He had tried to put it all aside, walking away from her and into an autumn filled with more activity than he could possibly have foreseen. The race and the following drama had caused his new business to explode. Dozens of noblemen, most not wanting their family names involved, had come to him for facilitating their wagers with the different gambling organizations. It meant expanding Campion's involvement beyond games of chance and into the broader gambling culture of the *ton*, members of which would bet on anything from horse races to how much a gentleman could belch after too much ale. It was an obsession, and it was making Robert and Michael a great deal of money. The coffers overflowed, which meant more money for horses. The stables at Robert's Maidstone estate—now officially the Surrey-Ashton School for Boys—had been completely renovated and stocked. The first students would arrive in January for the spring term, mostly recruited from the staff at Campion's. They would attend without charge, with an eye toward apprenticeships in the future.

They had hired several additional managers, and as September moved into October, Michael gradually moved out of the role of facilitator to focus on the horses. He had come to Ashton Park with his mother in an effort to replenish the number of horses here, and he had brought Phoenix up as a stud. After the race, requests for that service had piled in as well.

"Do you know that woman?" The gamekeeper asked, pulling Michael from his reverie.

Michael nodded. "Lady Clara Durham." He pointed back toward their horses, which grazed placidly a hundred yards away. "We should return. I'm sure Mother will want me for tea."

The gamekeeper looked surprised. "The old earl's daughter?"

"Yes, why?"

The gamekeeper hesitated, and Michael stopped. "What is it?"

"I should not say—"

"Oh, bloody hell, man. We are out in a field with our Wellies covered in grass and mud. Speak."

"She did not look much like a lady in mourning."

Michael stopped. "What? What are you talking about?"

The man's eyes narrowed. "You did not know? The old earl died. Back in August. Rumor has it that the daughter and dowager countess are only here until the new earl settles the estate."

That urge to go after her strengthened. "This is the gossip among the servants?"

"Yes, my lord. My sister is one of their scullery maids. There is a dowager house on the property, but they say the daughter will be sent north. No one knows where. Perhaps to marry."

Marry?

Surely she would not . . .

But he had not heard anything about the suit being canceled.

Not that you have bothered to look up for the past three months.

He had to find out. He resumed his trudge back toward the horses. "We have to get back. I need to speak with my mother."

Monday, 7 November 1825
Beckcott Abbey
Half-past two in the afternoon

CLARA COULD NOT stop shaking. Her fingers trembled as she removed the torn jesses from Maid Marian's legs and replaced them with the ones she had made two days ago. The peregrine had been gone for three days, since Honora had trashed the mews and cut the bird free, forcing the falcon to flee into the wild, with just enough of her jesses remaining to be a danger to her safety. Clara had searched every day, roaming the fields and tree lines on Aethelred, returning only when it was too dark to see and both woman and horse were exhausted. She had not spoken to her mother since.

But she understood Honora's rage, more than she wanted to admit. They had not been allowed to attend her father's funeral— aristocratic women seldom did—and her brother had insisted they leave the townhouse before they even pulled their mourning clothes out of storage. He blamed them both for the scandal that had descended on the family as well as the earl's death. And he had inherited Honora's strict sense of protocol and propriety as well as the entire estate. He allowed them to retreat to Beckcott Abbey but reminded them it was a temporary arrangement. He had declared that only if he deemed it feasible and proper, Honora could move into the dowager house.

Clara, on the other hand, would have to make other arrangements by the end of the year.

It made her look twice at Wykeham's final offer, but in the end, Clara had decided she simply could not, even in pure desperation. And in a moment of weakness, she suggested to Honora over tea that perhaps Sutland's mother could find her a position as a falconer.

Her mother's reaction had been . . . unfortunate.

"Do you need help, my lady?" Sutland's voice was kind.

All the servants had been extraordinarily kind to her since their arrival. All of them, it seemed, understood great loss. A common but unfortunate bond across the classes.

Clara had managed to secure one of the jesses, but Maid Marian continued to respond to Clara's state with her own brand of nervousness. Clara lowered her hands to her sides in frustration, the remaining jess dangling from her fingers. "I cannot—I cannot seem to—"

He stepped in beside her. "Let me, my lady." He gently tugged the jess from her hand and wrapped it around the falcon's foot in barely a moment.

Clara chewed her lower lip. "Thank you."

"I am glad you found her."

She nodded, swallowing hard.

"Did something happen while you were out?"

"I saw—" She broke off.

"What, my lady?"

She blurted the words. "I saw Michael Ashton." She pointed over her shoulder. "In the southwest. Near the boundary with Ashton Park."

"Lord Michael. He is the gentleman who . . ."

Clara nodded.

"Ah."

"It was so unexpected."

"So you have had a shock."

Another nod. "He never wanted to see me again, so I suspect it was a shock to him as well." She twisted her fingers in her skirt, trying to halt the quivering.

"Perhaps, when the shock wears off—"

"No!" She shook her head. "I do not believe anything will happen beyond this." She backed away. "I should—I should go. Thank you for your help." Clara stumbled rushing out of the mews but caught herself and slowed her steps. She passed by the stables and entered the grand house by the kitchen, pausing to nod as a few of the maids curtsied at her passing. The increased kindness and deference to her during this stay only agonized Clara further, reminding her that she was not their friend—as she had believed in childhood—nor their mistress.

Clara was now a stranger, one merely passing through to her next destination.

Tears blinded her as she tripped up the backstairs and made for her bedchamber, where she found Radcliff waiting outside the door.

"Your mother wishes to speak with you, my lady."

Clara wiped her eyes. "Will you help me change?"

"Of course, my lady."

In a fresh gown, Clara settled before the dressing table, allowing Radcliff to pin up what hair remained on her head, tucking the rest into a simple cloth cap. She had taken the scissors to it in a fit of pique not long after they arrived, when Honora had once again berated her for her unkempt appearance. She now let it loose when riding, but the shorter length made it easier to keep covered in the house.

One of the few decisions in the last three months she had not regretted.

Honora waited on a settee in one of the smaller sitting rooms, a cozy abode warmed by a fire in the grate. A tea tray sat on a low table in front of her. She laid aside her book and gestured for Clara to sit opposite. She began to make the tea, barely glancing at Clara.

The weeks had not been kind to Honora. She had lost weight, and her skin sagged under her chin. Her complexion was sallow and gray, and her eyes were perpetually swollen. Clara knew she had resorted to laudanum again in order to sleep. The whole household had become aware of her nightmares, and her voice retained a hoarseness Clara had never heard before.

But she dared not ask about Honora's health.

"You wanted to see me."

Honora nodded and added milk to one cup, which she handed to Clara. "I have made inquiries."

Clara paused before sipping. "Oh?"

Honora leaned back, wrapping both hands around her cup, as if clinging to its warmth. "I have a cousin. In Glasgow. He owns several businesses. I have not seen him or his wife in years, but they seem quite respectable."

"I see."

"I wrote to ask if he could find you a position."

"In Scotland."

"It is somewhat better than Newgate Prison."

"Indeed. And?"

"He has replied yes. He owns a bookshop that is in need of a new clerk. There are rooms over the shop that have been used for storage, but he could make them available to you for living quarters. Your brother has agreed to give you one hundred pounds in order to travel and get everything set up."

"Very generous."

Honora slammed the cup down on the tray so hard the saucer shattered. Tea splashed over the tray as she screamed, "It is generous, you ungrateful cow!"

Clara stared at her mother, horrified. "I know it is! I was serious!"

Honora pressed both hands over her face. "I know. I know!"

She twisted, shoving her face against the back of the settee as sobs racked her shoulders. Her wail was heartbreaking. "I have lost Jerome. I have lost you! My own son hates me! I do not know how we got here!"

Clara set down her cup and went to her mother, in a way she never had. She pulled Honora to her, just as Michael had done for her when she wept. She pressed Honora's head against her shoulder and held her, rocking gently. "I miss Papa, too," she whispered. "Every day. He was our anchor. Our captain."

Honora nodded, and Clara held her until the sobs eased. As Honora slipped from her arms, Clara pulled a serviette off the tea tray and handed it to her mother. Honora looked at it, then at Clara. "This is not a handkerchief."

Clara shrugged. "Any port in a storm."

Honora looked at the serviette again, then snagged it, wiped her eyes, and blew her nose, as quiet and polite a sound Clara had ever heard.

"You sound ladylike even blowing your nose."

Honora straightened her shoulders. "There is never a need to be impolite." Then she giggled.

Clara's eyes shot wide. "I have never in my life heard you giggle."

"You have never hugged me either. Not like that."

Clara reached for her tea. "Perhaps I should do so more often."

"Perhaps. Will you go to Glasgow?"

Clara nodded. "First, let us get you moved into the dowager house. Then I will go to Glasgow."

"But your brother—"

"Can hardly evict you once you have settled in. Removing his own mother from the property would be more of a scandal than his weak-livered constitution could handle."

Honora's lips twisted. "He has turned out to be quite the twit, has he not?"

"And you were always the most formidable of us all. He will

not cross you."

"You truly think so? I thought it was your father?"

Clara shook her head. "Papa anchored us, but you were the one who faced the world. Or the *ton*. Which was the tougher stance, I'm sure."

"You have no idea."

Clara returned her cup to the tray. "Let us go to your office. We have plans to make."

CHAPTER TWENTY-SEVEN

Monday, 7 November 1825
Ashton Park, near the River Kennet
Half-past three in the afternoon

MICHAEL STOOD IN the doorway and watched his mother use a cane and the help of a footman to settle into a wingback chair near the fire in the main receiving room of Ashton Park. She motioned for the footman to bring a small stool closer, so that her legs did not dangle, which made Michael smile. His mother's lack of height had long been a subject of teasing in a household where all the men were taller than six feet. Even Beth had a full head of height over their mother. But Emalyn took the humor in style, and footstools and short ladders littered both houses—Emalyn let few obstacles stand in her way for long.

Michael had to admire her fortitude. On July 17, she had a hemorrhagic apoplexy, and the doctors had given her little hope of a full recovery—or even much use of her left side.

But they did not know his mother. As a girl, Emalyn Benjumeda, the daughter of an Andalusian wine merchant, had fallen in love with a young marquess—not a recipe for success in England. But the two of them had been so determined to be together that they had changed the history of both families. Her stubbornness was the fodder for legends. Within a month after her attack, she had been able to feed herself again with her right hand and move around her bedchamber with a cane and the help of her husband.

Now, just over three months later, she could maneuver mostly on her own, and her husband no longer had to carry her about the house, although he still did much of the time. Much of her speech had returned, except for a lingering lisp—all her soft S's had acquired an H—and the occasional dropped letter. She had come to Ashton Park to organize preparations for the Ashton Park Christmas celebration. Multiple parties and gatherings would lead up to the pinnacle event, the Christmas Eve Ball, and a great deal had to be done before the first guests arrived exactly a month from today.

Michael planned to spend much of his time in the stables.

The Ashton Park butler arrived with a tea service, which he laid out on a table near the duchess's chair. He made the tea and handed Emalyn her cup, which she grasped carefully in her right hand. Her left hand remained in her lap. She peered at Michael over the rim, then glanced at the chair next to her. "Come. Shit."

The butler flinched and Michael pressed his lips together to keep from laughing. He crossed the room but declined the offer of tea with a wave. He eased into the chair, which was soft, and warm from its proximity to the fire. Comforting, like the rest of the plush and feminine décor in the room. The primary colors of yellow and blue reflected the winter sun streaming through the tall windows. "Mother?"

"Yesh?"

"I sincerely advise you to avoid using the word 'sit' in polite company for the near future. Especially as a command."

She cackled, almost jostling tea from her cup. "Prude. How was your hunt?"

He straightened. "I saw Lady Clara Durham."

Emalyn stilled. "Where?"

"The northeast fields. Near the boundary with Beckcott. Her falcon had strayed over our property. She came looking for it."

"Did you shpeak to her?"

He shook his head. "No. We were too distant. She looked . . . wild."

Emalyn took another sip, watching him closely. "How sho?"

"Her hair was loose. And short. She rode astride. And bare-back." He closed his eyes against the vision—the wild goddess who had once owned his heart. And apparently still did. "Like nothing I had ever seen."

"Clara always went her own way."

"The servants say she's going to be sent away. Possibly up north." He rubbed the back of his neck. "Possibly to marry. Do you think she would still marry Wykeham?"

She paused halfway through a sip, then finished and set her cup down. "You think I would know? I have not exactly been out and about."

"But Rose has."

Emalyn grinned and wagged a finger at him. "It should be our shecret why I know so much about the undershide of the *ton*. Did you know that Clara and Rose were good friends?"

He shifted in the chair. "I knew they were acquainted—"

"Closhe friends. It was Rose who . . . orchesh . . . contrived your afternoon at the modi—dressh shop."

Michael leaned forward, intrigued. "Why would she do that?"

"Because we all thought Clara was what you needed to finally heal."

"Heal. From alcohol."

"From Eleanor."

Michael sank back against the chair. "Eleanor."

"She poisoned you."

"Is Clara any different?"

"Do not be a fool." Emalyn hesitated and adjusted her left hand with her right. "How did it feel, sheeing her like that? Truth."

"Like Copper had kicked me in the gut."

"Do you shtill think she intentionally betrayed you?"

Michael scowled. "Why do you say 'intentionally'?"

Emalyn lowered a stern look at him. "Because you have been paching this housh like a madman. I have heard you leave at midnight. Know you have been pushing Copper hard. I thought maybe you had realized that Clara ish not and was never Eleanor. That not all women are like Eleanor. Clara was deshparate, not cruel. And you were a fool to think sho."

Michael jerked back as if he had been slapped. And perhaps he had been. "Mother—"

She waved a hand at him. "Do not. For once in your life, listen to reason. You loved her. You shtill do, or it would have meant nothing to you to shee her on that horsh."

Michael crossed his arms, pressing back against his chair. "I told her I never wanted to see her again."

"Grovel."

He blinked. "What?"

She gave another impatient wave with her right hand. "Do not be daft. She loved you. Probably shtill does. But you crushed her."

"I did not—"

Another wave. "Shtop defending being a fool. If you want her, you will have to beg forgivenessh. Grovel."

"I doubt she will see me."

"Then I will invite her and the dowager to tea."

"I doubt they will come. Especially if she is about to marry the duke."

Emalyn shook her head. "There are times when I realize that Philip and I coddled you children too much. Did not teach you enough about protocol."

His eyes narrowed. "What are you talking about?"

"Honora ish a dowager countessh. I am a duchessh. She will have no choice but to come."

"Oh."

"And it ish not the duke."

Wednesday, 9 November 1825
Ashton Park, near the River Kennet
Half-past three in the afternoon

CLARA STARED AT the unexpectedly simple entrance of Ashton Park, her entire body quivering. While the front door was deceptively plain, with a few concrete steps and a narrow cover against the elements, the approach to the home of the dukes of Kennet had sparked every nerve. The manicured U-shaped drive had been lined with towering oaks, and between the legs of the U, a reflecting pool mirrored the massive five-story red brick country house. Ashton Park might be understated on the outside, but its size and grounds represented the wealth of a bygone age, a reminder that despite scandal, the Duke of Kennet remained one of the most powerful and wealthy men in the realm, a confidante to the king, and a broad voice in Parliament.

And Clara was about to have tea with his wife.

She did not want to do this. Seeing the Duchess of Kennet would be hard enough, but the thought that Michael could be in the house . . .

"Stand up straight, girl. Stop slouching."

Clara shook her head. "I do not know if I can do this."

"You can and will. An invitation from the Duchess of Kennet is not to be ignored. Given the circumstances, it is a gift."

"Mother—"

"And you do not want me to have to tell your brother that you refused to meet with the one person who could ease the sting of this scandal, who could re-open all the doors now slammed in our face."

"Mother—"

"If this goes well, perhaps she will invite us to the Christmas festivities."

Clara stared at her. In the twenty-four hours since receiving the duchess's invitation, the dowager racked by grief had found her footing again.

The front door opened, and the Ashton Park butler looked them up and down, as if making sure they were appropriately attired. Still in full mourning, they were both in black, cap to slipper, although Honora's gown bore a great deal more lace. Honora offered him the invitation. "We are here to see the duchess."

He accepted the invitation, then stepped back, ushering them into the hall. "This way, your ladyship." Then he led them down a hall that branched off to the right and to a door that stood open. The duchess waited inside, seated in a wingback chair near the fire, her feet propped on a low footstool. The butler announced them, then retreated from the room.

They entered and curtsied. "Thank you, Your Grace," Honora said, "for your kind invitation."

The duchess gestured to a settee that was placed at a right angle to the wingback. "Please, sh—make yourshelves comfortable."

Clara did, trying not to focus on the duchess's limp left hand. So the rumors about her lingering impairment were true. She swallowed and spoke her much-rehearsed first comment. "We are pleased that you have returned to Ashton Park, Your Grace."

The duchess looked from one woman to the other, then sighed. "Thank you. But I do not, I'm afraid, have the energy or wherewithal for Shochi—polite chatter."

"Your Grace—" Honora began.

The duchess cut her off with a wave. "We are both houses wrapped in schandal. If we are to weather thish, we must present a united front. May I call you Honora?"

Clara's mother stuttered. "Of—of—of course, Your Grace."

"Then I am Emalyn. As you can shee, I have not yet fully recovered. I have an exshellent shtaff, but I need another lady to aid me with the upcoming Chrishmash events. Would you be willing to work with me? I will need someone to help with vendors, welcome guestsh, overshee gatherings I cannot."

Honora looked as stunned as Clara felt, but Clara found her tongue first. "What about Lady Elizabeth?"

"In Yorkshire. Will only arrive for the ball."

"Rose?"

The duchess grinned. "She ish with child. Will only arrive for the ball."

Clara was stunned. "What? I thought she could not—"

"Clara!"

The duchess cackled. "So did we all. God had other plans. Which ish why I need assh—damn it!—help."

Clara looked down, biting her lip, unsure whether to laugh or cry. The duchess's frustration with her infirmity was both sad and charming, but spoke clearly of her determination.

Honora let out a sigh. "Your Grace—"

"Emalyn."

"Em—Em—alyn." Honora stumbled over the word, clearly uncertain about referring to a duchess by her Christian name. "Our situation is somewhat precarious."

"No more sho than my two youngesh shons. Your preshench will bear no ill on our housh. And if that folly of a shon of yoursh objects, I will shend the duke to shpeak with him."

The image of her cowardly brother facing off with the massive presence of the Duke of Kennet made Clara snort a laugh, and she covered her mouth with her hand as Honora glared at her.

The duchess chuckled. "It does create a vision, no?"

Clara nodded.

"Mother?"

Clara's heart stopped as her dreaded fear materialized. She closed her eyes.

"Come in, Lord Michael."

Clara's hands clutched her skirts.

The duchess continued calmly, as if one of her guests was not sitting there wrapped in a blanket of horror. "These are my guesh. The Dowager Countessh of Beckcott, Lady Durham, and her daughter, Lady Clara Durham."

She heard his heels click. "My ladies. It is my pleasure."

"Likewise, my lord," Honora said.

Clara kept her eyes closed. *I cannot do this!*

"Clara!"

Honora's voice was sharp, but the one that followed was seductively mellow, the baritone that had once awakened her soul—and scorched her heart.

"Please forgive her, my lady. The last time I was in Lady Clara's company, I was an unforgivable arse. It is understandable she would be reluctant to see me again."

Clara's eyes snapped open, and she glowered at him. "How dare you—"

Michael dropped to one knee in front of her. Mortified, Clara jerked back against the settee, drawing her hands up to her neck as he reached for them. "What are you doing?"

"Begging."

Clara's throat tightened, her voice squeaking. "What?"

Beside her, Honora had gone stark white.

"I have been a fool. I know you did not mean—I should not have thought that you—" He broke off, muttering at the floor. "Damn it!"

Like mother, like son.

Emalyn spoke softly. "Shlow. Breathe."

Clara turned her glare on the duchess. "You arranged this?"

The older woman nodded. "When one's child ish an arsh-hole, one tries to make amends."

Honora began to pant.

"Michael, get up! You are giving my mother the vapors!"

Instead, he went down on both knees. "You know I am not good with words. But when I saw you on that hill . . . you were magnificent. You were a—"

"Do not say it. Do not!"

"A goddess."

Honora found her voice. "A goddess? Are you mad?"

Clara turned on her. "Should someone not think I'm a goddess?"

Michael persisted. "I was wrong. I thought you betrayed me, that you were like—"

"Eleanor Carlson." Clara thought she would choke on the name. No wonder he had turned away from her.

"But I have realized you are not. Were not. But when I thought about the look you gave Radcliff when you knew the duke was prone to dueling. It felt as if it had been your goal all along."

Clara swallowed the lump in her throat. "Hadleyton."

Michael froze. "What?"

Honora's eyes narrowed. "That despicable man who tormented you for so long?"

Clara nodded, and Michael leaned back on his heels. "What about him?" The wariness in his voice almost amused her.

"That look I gave Radcliff was about Hadleyton. I despise the man and hope he spends a great deal of time being humiliated, but I did not think he deserved to die because he kept dousing me with lemonade. The more the duke put a claim on me, the more Hadleyton risked getting shot. You said the duke is a good marksman, an experienced dueler. I have known Hadleyton since we were children. He does not even hunt. He could not hit a stag from fifteen feet with a shotgun. You lifted him off the ground by his cravat. Wykeham would have put him in his grave."

"So the duel—"

"How could I have known your father would challenge the man to a horse match? That you would try to win me by starting a new business to prove your worth? To build your reputation with horses by creating such a scene at Tattersall's that it will be talked about for years?"

"He what?" Honora sat straight, looking from Clara to Michael. "He did what?"

Clara rubbed three fingers across her forehead, which had

begun to ache. "Mother, all you saw was Wykeham's title."

"We wanted you settled! You rejected every other suitor."

"Except Michael Ashton! You would not believe I would be happy as the wife of a vicar."

"How about the manager of Ashton Park?" Emalyn said, a voice of calm in the storm.

Clara looked at her. "What did you say?"

Emalyn's grin was sly. "Philip agreed to make Michael the manager of Ashton Park. Thish eshtate will become hish reshpo—hish charge, and he will live here with hish family, ash long ash he lives."

Honora frowned. "But Lord Thomas—"

"Hash agreed," Emalyn said. "He will manage everything elsh. Philip has grown Kennet beyond the management of one man."

Michael reached for Clara's hand, and this time she let him take it. "Please forgive me. I was a fool, but one no longer."

"Yet to be seen," Clara muttered.

Emalyn cackled. "He ish a man, my child."

Michael sent a sour look toward his mother, then rose up on one knee again. "When I saw you on that hill—"

"Say that word again and I swear I will slap you."

He grinned. "I knew how wrong I had been. I want you. In my life and in my bed."

"Dear God," muttered Honora. "We are all going to hell."

Michael folded both hands over hers. "Marry me."

Clara looked at her mother, who gave a long sigh. Then a nod. "I will deal with your brother."

Looking down at Michael, Clara realized all the tension had left her body. She felt light. And free. And loved.

"Yes."

"Exshellent!" Emalyn almost crowed. "Now we will have tea and talk about Chrishmash. Get up, Michael, before you put a dent in the carpet."

EPILOGUE

Tuesday, 3 January 1826
Ashton Park, near the River Kennet
Half-past nine in the morning

LADY CLARA ASHTON stirred, the pungent aroma of coffee piercing the fog of sleep. Her shoulder felt icy, so she pulled the covers higher and snuggled deeper into the bed. But the covers lifted to a rush of cold air, and she shivered. "Please," she whimpered.

A far superior warmth pressed against her back. "Please what?" Michael whispered in her ear. He kissed her temple and ran a hand along her thigh.

"I do not want to get up yet."

"I brought coffee."

She wriggled against him. "I'm cold."

His hand moved up and circled her waist. "You feel quite warm to me."

"Because you are hotter than Copper after a run." She rolled to face him. "Why are you so warm?"

He brushed a kiss across her lips. "Because I have been in the kitchen. Getting you coffee."

"Why did you leave me?" Clara stroked his cheeks, her fingertips lingering on the two-day stubble on his jaw.

"Because you were wiggling in your dreams, and it made me want to take you again. And I did not think either of us was up for that."

She kissed his chin. "Are you sore?"

"Are you not? The last two days have been . . . active."

She grinned and put her arms round him, tucking her head beneath his chin. "Regrets?"

"None."

Clara sighed. They had married New Year's Day, as most of the revelers at Ashton Park had slept in. Eschewing a large celebration, they had wed at the local vicar's, with Thomas and Rose Ashton as witnesses. Emalyn had set aside a guest room in one of the far wings for them, until Michael's bedchamber and two of its neighboring rooms could be renovated into adjoining suites for the newlyweds.

They had barely left the room since, only venturing out to gather the food trays left outside the door.

"They must have been surprised to see you."

He chuckled. "It was me, one cook, and a scullery maid. They had not even known I was missing."

Clara looked up at him again, almost mesmerized by the adoration she saw in those deep brown eyes. "I would have thought the whole county would have something to say about our absence. About your . . . proficiency."

Michael entwined his fingers in her curls, tugging her head back against the pillows. "There is only one person alive who needs to be pleased with my . . . proficiency." He moved over her.

Clara spread her legs to welcome him. Sore or not, she wanted this man, and she knew that feeling would never end. "And that would be?"

"My goddess."

The End

About Abigail Bridges

Abigail Bridges wrote her first historical romance, titled *The Belle of the Ball*, when she was thirteen. It was, of course, horrid. But it firmly established her love of all things Regency, a mild obsession with Georgette Heyer, and a determination to become a writer. After a master's degree in English and years of being paid to write and edit other types of material, she has returned to her first love. She is busily binge-reading all her favorite authors, resuming her study of the history and culture of the Regency era, and plotting like a madwoman. She does all this in a small cottage near Birmingham, Alabama.

Twitter: @AbbyBridgesAuth
Instagram: @abigailbridgesauthor

www.ingramcontent.com/pod-product-compliance
Lightning Source LLC
Chambersburg PA
CBHW052026220726
48293CB00015B/349